Mrs Queen Takes the Train

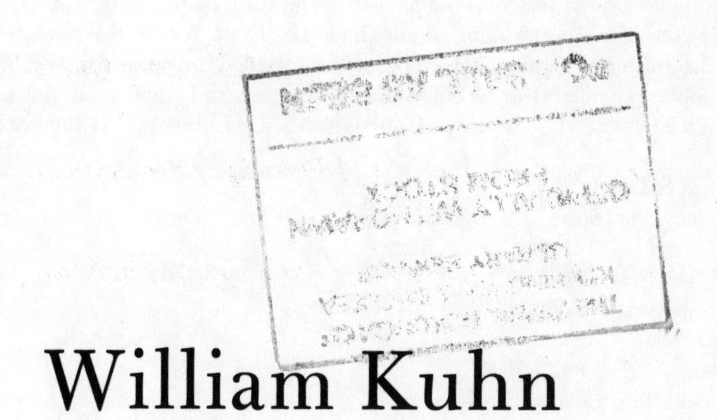

William Kuhn

ALLEN&UNWIN
SYDNEY • MELBOURNE • AUCKLAND • LONDON

First published in Australia and New Zealand by Allen & Unwin in 2012
First published in the United States in 2012 by Harper,
a division of HarperCollins Publishers.

Allen & Unwin
Sydney, Melbourne, Auckland, London

83 Alexander Street
Crows Nest NSW 2065
Australia
Phone: (61 2) 8425 0100
Email: info@allenandunwin.com
Web: www.allenandunwin.com

Cataloguing-in-Publication details are available
from the National Library of Australia
www.trove.nla.gov.au

ISBN 978 1 74331 287 2

Internal design by Michael Correy
Printed and bound in Australia by Griffin Press

10 9 8 7 6 5 4 3 2 1

The paper in this book is FSC® certified.
FSC® promotes environmentally responsible,
socially beneficial and economically viable
management of the world's forests.

For Fritz Kuhn

Part I

Warrior Two

Several years ago, on a dark afternoon in December, Her Majesty Elizabeth the Second, by the Grace of God, of the United Kingdom, Northern Ireland, and Her Other Realms and Territories Queen, Head of the Commonwealth of Nations, Defender of the Faith, Duchess of Edinburgh, Countess of Merioneth, Baroness Greenwich, Duke of Lancaster, Lord of Mann, Duke of Normandy sat at her desk, frowning at a computer screen. The desk had once belonged to Queen Victoria. Its surface was polished but uneven, like many other pieces of furniture in Windsor Castle, so the computer keyboard wobbled when The Queen pressed on it. She folded a piece of paper into a tiny square and slipped it underneath a corner.

The keyboard was one thing, but the computer itself was another. She expected it to work, but in her experience it was just as bad as the keyboard, though the reasons were more mystifying. It was always locking up just when she found something she thought she might like to see. She had been instructed to look for the cursor when this happened. Even though the young woman who handled information technology for the Privy Purse had helped her increase the magnification of the screen, her diminished eyesight made it difficult to find the tiny flashing bar, which she understood she was meant to move around with the mouse, which wasn't a mouse at all, of course. Why was it called that? She pressed what she took to be an appropriate key and the screen changed color. She tried another and the document she'd been working on (a memoir of her favorite horse, Aureole, who'd nearly won the Derby in 1953) disappeared. She punched a third and the computer emitted a startled *beep*. She sat back against her chair and sighed with frustration.

She had already called the IT woman three times. She couldn't call her again. The Queen knew she needed help, but she hated to appear helpless. Everyone around her seemed to know what they were doing on the computer. She was the only one who didn't. When computers had first begun to be commonplace she thought she could leave them to the experts. Pen and ink and paper would see her out. She wouldn't need to learn. But she was wrong. Now it wasn't only the young who consulted the computers that were apparently inside their mobile telephones, it was also the butler who entered her choices for luncheon on a computer in the cupboard, the private secretary who communicated with Number 10 via what was called instant messaging, and even the Mews posted online films of mares foaling. It had dawned on her that she was going to have to learn the language if she didn't want to be left behind. She had had what she thought of as endless lessons. And still, learning how to manage the machine was more difficult for her than learning Chinese. She'd learned a few words of that with no trouble for the Chinese state visit a few years ago.

She stood up from her desk and looked out the window, up the Long Walk in the Home Park toward the statue of King George III. An old Boeing 747 which had just departed from Heathrow lumbered into the air above the Castle, rattling the windowpanes. The sound was briefly deafening. The Queen had grown so used to this that she seldom noticed. She supposed that if one's back door opened onto the railway into Waterloo, one also became accustomed to the noise of the trains. When the wind was in the northeast, the air traffic controllers always sent the planes taking off over Windsor. She didn't mind the noise. It was like a mini weather report. When she did notice the aeroplanes, three minutes apart, she thought to herself, "Ah, wind from the northeast." No, the noise didn't bother her, but something about being thwarted by the computer, and the impossibility of asking for more help, did bother her. She felt tired. She sat down dispiritedly in one of the chairs next to the unlighted fire. "Oh, Little Bit," she said to herself, "what now?"

People had been writing about her from the very day she was born in April 1926. The newspapers had reported her learning to talk. "Lilibet," they wrote, was one of her first words, a small child's pronunciation of her own name, Elizabeth. That was entirely wrong, as reports about her often *were* wrong. Actually, it came from a cake that she had been served one teatime in the nursery. It had pink, raspberry-flavored icing. Her eyes lit up when she saw it. Nanny told her she might only have "a little bit" of the cake if she were a good girl. "Lilibet! Lilibet!" she'd cried and Nanny had reported this to her mother. "Lilibet" had nothing to do with Elizabeth, but it was a name that had stuck, and she'd grown up with it as the diminutive people in her family persisted in calling her. It was a tease really, a pinch, a reminder that it was undignified for a princess to be greedy for cake, not the sweet nickname people thought it was. Nevertheless, she even used it with herself from time to time, especially when she blamed herself for doing something wrong. She forgave Nanny for telling her mother about the cake as she connected the one with treats and the other with teases. She could recall Nanny taking her on the train to Sandringham all by herself one Christmas. What a treat that was!

Sometimes it amused her to pick up a recent biography and to annotate it. The librarian had once shown her some nineteenth-century biographies in the archives that her great-great-grandmother had annotated. Queen Victoria had written in the margins, in her distinctive sloping hand, "I never did," or "Not true," alongside the passages to which she objected. Inspired by the example of her predecessor, The Queen would correct errors in the margins herself. Lately, however, she hadn't the energy. Did it matter to get things right anymore?

She knew that sitting alone in her chair, thinking gloomy thoughts, and staring blankly off into space made things worse, but she couldn't help it, no more than she could have stopped eating the pink cake if Nanny hadn't been there to prevent her when she was a little girl. Only her internal nanny told her that sitting alone in her chair doing nothing was bad for her. Still, the part of her that felt rather sad was stronger than her internal nanny, more than a match for her, really.

No one had warned her that she might lose confidence as she grew older, and it was true that many of the things she'd known how to do formerly without a second thought, such as asking for help, she couldn't bring herself to do now. She also worried more than she used to. A sheet of paper delivered the evening before to her sitting room with the coming day's list of engagements sometimes made her lose sleep. She wondered what would happen if a Lady Mayoress chatted too much at the unveiling of a plaque and made her late for the luncheon at the factory she was scheduled to visit next. Would they lose patience with her, as she nowadays sometimes lost patience with herself?

Enough of this. Nanny suddenly got the upper hand. She shook herself out of her fit of anxiety and heaved herself out of the chair. She stalked toward the computer on the other side of the room as if it were game and she meant to shoot it. A sudden burst of creative energy gave her an idea. She reached over and turned the damned thing off. Then, a moment later, she turned it on again. She suddenly recalled the woman from IT doing this. "Yes," she said under her breath, "turn it *off*. Then on again." The machine whirred into action, flashing several screens which she could not in the least comprehend. After several moments, however, a screen appeared that did look familiar. It had several vertical rows of symbols on it. She recognized the symbol for the Web browser: she knew if you clicked on that you could what was called "surf the net." The IT woman had a bit of Italian and had told her the Italians said "*navigare in rete*," which The Queen liked better, as she silently amended it to an Italo-English pidgin phrase, "navigate in rot." That's what she liked to think of the so-called wonders that were available online, a lot of rot.

It was Prince Edward who'd begun to indicate a few things on the computer that were not rot. First he'd shown her the website of the Household Cavalry. Splendid young men. Scarlet tunics. Groomed mounts. Brave boys. Then he'd shown her a page for the Royal Mews, where a mare was giving birth to a foal. He'd shown her a little place on the right-hand side of the screen where you could move the cursor, press it, and then a short video of the foaling would play. Superb animals. Remarkable little film. He'd also shown her (he knew his mama's bad habits) a website where she could place a small bet on the races. The site itself was too complex for her to understand entirely, but she kept coming back to it, studying the race meetings, the odds, and the names of the runners, promising herself that one day she might place a small bet, no more than five pounds.

Prince Edward had also shown her how to save websites, under a heading at the top of the screen labeled "Bookmarks." He'd shown her how to save places there for Google and Twitter, which she silently called "Mr Google" and "Miss Twitter," as their names seemed to have been invented for a nursery story. He'd also called up different screens for Yahoo and Facebook. She didn't see the point of what she called to herself "Yah-Hoo." How was it different from Mr Google? She didn't like to interrupt him, as Prince Edward was so evidently proud of what he was showing her. Facebook he showed her at the same time as he attempted to demonstrate what she thought he described as "cutting and pasting," though there were no scissors. She didn't understand that at all, confused it with Facebook, and started thinking of the two as somehow related, "Pastebook." It made her think of being a little girl and sticking pictures into a large scrapbook with a big pot of paste.

Prince Edward had created an account for her with Miss Twitter. He asked her what she would like as a username. She looked at him blankly. "What do you want to be called on Twitter, Mummy?" he said with some exasperation. "Little Bit," she said, and he'd entered that as her Twitter name and then come up with the idea of using the Buckingham Palace postcode as her username, @SW1A1AA. In fact there hadn't been time for her to do much exploring, but she'd made a few notes on the back of a used envelope she reclaimed from the wastepaper basket as he'd talked. She gathered that she had to "follow" other people with Miss Twitter if she were to learn what everyone was talking about. She also understood that to follow people, to read what they had to say, she had to click on a little colored square at the top labeled "Who to follow." She sat down again cautiously, grasped the mouse as if it might shock her, and then, when it didn't, selected Twitter from among her bookmarks. She began entering the names of people it might be interesting to follow. Typing with her two index fingers, she put in "Boris Johnson," and @MayorofLondon came up with a photo of a handsome blond, now past his prime and a little stout. "Bit of a belly he has now, Mr Johnson, didn't used to," The Queen thought to herself. "An amusing fellow." She looked at the text that had been entered, and it was all PR bumpf from the mayor's office.

Next she put in "Duchess of Cornwall" and up came a photo

of Camilla next to @DuchessCornwall. Here the text was more interesting, absurd, rather funny actually. Camilla had described herself as "Future Queen of England. One does like to chat with the public . . . but from a safe distance. Lover of Horses and Gin." All that was true enough, thought The Queen to herself, except the "Future Queen of England" bit. There were still some legal niceties to be sorted out there. She didn't think it was very wise of Camilla to write about the gin, however. She made a mental note to have a word with her. As a Twitter novice, The Queen was so far unaware that many people posted Tweets pretending to be people they weren't.

The Queen then entered her own name and @Queen_UK appeared. The text here, however, made her indignant. Every day, for the past several weeks it appeared, at six p.m. @Queen_UK had tweeted "It's gin o'clock!" She wondered whether Camilla was already daring to tweet as Queen of England. The gin did seem to be a telltale motif. She'd have to ask Sir Robin to take a look at this. What annoyed her still more was that The Queen did rather like gin herself. She didn't think she'd ever abused the green bottle of Gordon's, however, just long ago got in the habit of having a cocktail before supper. Usually the same one. Only one. Couldn't hurt. In fact she found it helped a great deal.

The gold clock on the chimneypiece struck a bell indicating the half hour. Late afternoon in Windsor. Monday after breakfast she'd have to go back to London. Business. The office. She had a full week of engagements ahead, she reflected with a Sunday-afternoon sigh. Before that, however, her yoga instructor was coming for her weekly lesson. Prince Edward had also introduced her to yoga. He'd also told her how much he enjoyed what he described as a combination of meditation and exercise, how Sophie Wessex had got him started, how good it felt to have one's muscles stretched, how even an octogenarian like his mother might feel the benefit. She'd cautiously agreed to a trial. With anyone else she would have laughed and said, instantly, "No," but she had a soft spot for her two younger sons, whom she'd managed to protect from some of the public attention she'd lived with all her life. An instructor had turned up and now The Queen had been doing her yoga practice for several months. She found it did calm her down. She always walked more slowly and deliberately afterwards. But some of the poses were more difficult than others. And the instructor expected her to remember them from week to week. There were only a few she had memorized. She decided to try out a few of them before the instructor arrived, to warm up a little.

The Queen stepped out of her patent-leather shoes. She then walked across the Turkish carpet in her nylons and stood in front of a long mirror at one side of the room. The Queen had no vanity whatsoever, so her appearance didn't interest her in the least, but she did feel she needed the mirror to check the shape of her body while she was practicing the poses. She recalled one of her favorites, where she stood with her back foot at a right angle to her body, facing forward, front knee

bent, arms outstretched before her and behind. She thought she might get into this pose and hold it, breathing steadily, to the count of sixty. She hitched up her skirt slightly and, as she assumed the pose, she heard in her mind's ear the instructor proclaiming: "Warrior Two!"

Shirley MacDonald was a practical woman who was nearing sixty. She lived in part of a small grace-and-favour cottage in the Home Park at Windsor. This was a flat she occupied for free by the "grace and favour" of The Queen, so long as she was employed in the Royal Household. She would be turned out when she retired. Windsor suited her, really, and she thought that when she did retire she might try to buy a large enough house so she could do bed-and-breakfast for day visitors who didn't feel like going back into London after a day of seeing the parts of the Castle that were open to tourists. She also had a room she could use overnight in Buckingham Palace when she needed it for work. She hadn't enough money saved to buy a place in London, and she'd miss that, as she loved everything about London, but she was philosophical and resigned to spending her retirement somewhere not too far removed from the Castle walls.

Shirley was the most senior of The Queen's dressers. She was a ladies' maid who served, technically, under the Mistress of the Robes; an aristocratic woman who had that title turned up only for ceremonial occasions. She was, in Shirley's view, useless. Shirley had no time for this particular palace archaism, but she'd learned to put up with it. Shirley herself had plenty of work to do. She drew The Queen's bath in the morning, and sometimes in the evening too. She cared for the whole of The Queen's wardrobe, from the heavy mantle she wore for the Garter service in June to the country clothes she wore on weekends. She cleaned, catalogued, and repaired everything The Queen wore. On a daily basis she laid out her shoes and underthings, her dresses, jackets, and jewels. Usually The Queen emerged from the bath in her dressing gown about half past eight. Shirley would appear from behind a screen. "Good morning, Your Majesty."

"Good morning, Shirley," not unfriendly, a little perfunctory. Then they'd have a little conversation about the weather, and Shirley would give as an excuse the growing coolness of the autumn for a heavier wool skirt she'd laid out. The Queen seldom wanted something different from what Shirley had chosen for her to wear. Whatever she wore The Queen regarded as not unlike a uniform. She put on pearl earrings in the same spirit that a policeman did up his silver buttons. They were part of the job. They indicated who she was. They were not pretty things for her ears. They were her name badge. "I'm Mrs Queen."

Shirley respected The Queen, but she was not in awe of her. Shirley's grandmother had been a laundress at Balmoral, and she remembered her forever mending the edges of frayed sheets, even on weekends, even at home. Shirley's mother had come south to work in the kitchen for the royal family. Shirley had seen the insides and outsides of all the royal residences since she was a girl, and that was precisely why she'd been offered a job close to The Queen. She was familiar. She wouldn't bolt. She wouldn't sell her story to the *Daily Mirror.*

If The Queen took no particular joy in her clothes, Shirley did. She adored the weights placed in the hems of her skirts so they'd hang properly and protect her from embarrassment on a windy day. She loved the lining of the coats, usually chosen in a contrasting but complementary color. A plum-colored jacket made of raw silk had a green-apple lining that no one ever saw but the dressmaker (who was proud of her craft), The Queen (who seldom noticed), and Shirley (who liked to hold the jacket's tart interior up to the light).

Shirley was friendly with one of the senior butlers, William de Morgan, who would sometimes stop by her room as she was at the ironing board, steaming out a few creases. His method was to come in her ironing room smiling ear to ear, surprised, and happy to see her. Then he would point to something of interest outside the window. "That's a thunder cloud if I'm not mistaken!" When she turned to look, he whipped the purple jacket off the ironing board and before she could even turn around to protest, he'd put it on and stood proudly before the mirror, imitating some of The Queen's well-worn sayings. "Have you come far today?" "Good morning, Shirley." "That will be all, William."

"Give it here, William," Shirley said, noticing how much more proudly William wore it than The Queen did. It made him taller, more erect. He glowed in it. The Queen always put on her jacket with something of a repressed sigh, an elderly knight putting on his armor. But for William the jacket was a shaft of sunlit magnificence.

Unlike Shirley, William could not point to generations of royal service in his family. He'd grown up in a postindustrial town with no particular prospects or talents except a love of opulence and the daring to add a "de" to his name when he was in his twenties. He'd seen an exhibition of Victorian tiles by an artist of the same name. It sounded much more impressive than "Bill Morgan," which he'd been called since he was a boy, so he went to the registry office and took it for his own. It was, after all, only a small change. He also worked hard. He'd worked for two other members of the royal family before he was taken on by The Queen. Before that he'd spent a decade working for a duke, then for a sheik, after having been a waiter at Brooks's and sommelier at Wilton's. He knew wine and food. He knew how to sense what someone might want in the instant before they knew it themselves. For him there was nothing humiliating or degrading about service. It was his religion. It was what he knew how to do well. He was proud of it. He left all these places with warmly satisfied employers who were sorry to see him go.

Working for the Royal Household didn't pay as well as these other positions, but it had a prestige the other places hadn't, and William was a connoisseur of prestige. He knew the difference between the daughter of a baron and the daughter of an earl. He knew how to address the envelope of a letter to each, a distinction that confused most people in modern Britain, when it didn't actively annoy them. He could distinguish between a supermarket game bird and a pheasant that had been properly aged and hung. He could see at a glance whether a man's suit was off the peg in a shop or made by a tailor.

The monarchy spurred his imagination in a way that used to be widespread in the late Middle Ages, but had now faded to a loyal few. The Queen coming into a room gave him an electric shock which he had to work hard to conceal. A photograph of Prince Harry changing his shirt in Afghanistan made his mouth dry. A view of the Royal Standard whipping in the wind above Windsor Castle caused his heart to race.

Much of this he did not share with Shirley. They both voted Labour. They were both devoted to their work, but if for William the monarchy was poetry, for Shirley it was prose. She put in long hours and was getting to the age where she noticed being on her feet more than she used to. If The Queen had a formal event in the evening that would require a change of clothes, Shirley found her chattier than in the mornings. Shirley would brush out her hair before The Queen dressed in an evening gown. She remembered very well when The Queen had first explained to her that she would be meeting a few people she didn't know well in the evening and would Shirley mind reading out their *Who's Who* entries so The Queen could ask in an informed way about their children or wives or parents. It was something Queen Victoria used to do, and The Queen liked to do it too.

If she were tired in the evenings, Shirley tried not to show it, as The Queen was more than twenty years older than she was, and she continued to keep up a brisk pace, or had until recently. In the last months or so, The Queen had seemed to slow down perceptibly, to be feeling not quite herself, to be a little more somber than was usual. Shirley noticed this, but it was one of the rules of her job that she would never bring it up unless The Queen brought it up herself. Shirley was quite certain that she never would, so she was surprised one evening as the autumn darkness extended that The Queen did bring it up. It was a Sunday in Windsor. Shirley would return with The Queen to Buckingham Palace on Monday after breakfast and stay in a room there, as The Queen had a busy week ahead starting on Tuesday and the other dressers were on holiday. The Queen sat in silence as Shirley brushed vigorously through her hair. After a few moments, The Queen asked Shirley whether she remembered "Miss Julie Andrews. *Dame* Julie Andrews, as she now is," added The Queen.

"Yes, Ma'am."

"I made her DBE a few years ago."

"A good thing too. You don't always give honors to those that deserve them." Shirley sometimes used a little exaggeratedly rough talk with The Queen because she liked it, just as she liked rough strokes of the brush. They'd worked together long enough for Shirley to feel confident about speaking her mind on some subjects.

"Well, it's the Government, of course. I don't choose most of them myself."

"The Order of the British Empire for David Beckham. What did that young man do to deserve it?"

"He's a very good footballer, Shirley."

"He may be, but I don't think he deserves the OBE for kicking a ball about."

The Queen changed the subject. "Julie Andrews, now. Do you remember that song of hers? From a film? I believe she played an excellent nanny." The Queen's voice grew warmer on the word "nanny."

"*Mary Poppins*, Ma'am?"

"Not that one. The other one."

"*The Sound of Music*?"

"That's it! It was a song about her favorite things." The Queen could still command a surprising soprano, and she sang out tentatively, "When the dog bites . . ."

Shirley replied in a voice that was closer to a throaty baritone, "When the bee stings."

"When I'm feeling sad," sang The Queen, her voice cracking slightly on "sad."

"I simply remember my favorite things," answered Shirley.

"And then I don't feel so bad," the two women ended in unison. They made eye contact and giggled lightly.

"And what are your favorite things, Mrs MacDonald?" continued The Queen after a pause.

Shirley was wary of replying to this. She was unmarried, having given her whole life to royal service, but the palace preserved the antique custom whereby the most senior members of the female staff were all called "Mrs." It was an old-fashioned way of showing respect, even though it was very much out of step with the age of women's liberation. The palace pretended not to know that the title "Ms" had even been invented. When The Queen called Shirley "Mrs MacDonald," it was a kind of diminutive. It was affectionate. But she almost never asked for personal information, and to ask Shirley to name her favorite things was very unusual indeed. Shirley guessed that The

Queen was looking for some way of speaking about what was bothering her. She also could list with confidence some of The Queen's favorite things, so she decided to answer with something that might plausibly be on her list of favorite things, but which was certainly on The Queen's list too.

"Well, Ma'am, I did enjoy working on *Britannia*."

"Oh yes," answered The Queen, as if an invisible bell had just been rung. "Have you been to visit her?"

"No, Ma'am, I haven't."

"Moored at Leith, I believe."

"Yes, Ma'am."

"A pity."

Shirley thought it best not to reply to this. She'd seen the

pictures of all the royal family on the verge of tears at the yacht's decommissioning in 1997.

"Not a tear for Diana," one of the tabloid newspapers had put in a rude caption beneath the photo, "but we all blubbed buckets for *Britannia*." "To blub" was a verb Shirley had heard The

Queen use before. It was one of those unusual words, not unlike her monogrammed drawers, that had an Old World feel to them.

"How do you suppose one gets there?"

This took Shirley by surprise. The Queen never in her recollection asked for directions. "Edinburgh, Ma'am?" said Shirley incredulously.

"No, no. Not Edinburgh. I know how to get *there*. I mean to Leith."

"Well, there must be a bus, or a local train from the railway station, Edinburgh Waverley."

"A bus. What number?" The Queen replied instantly. She was said to be a very rich woman, but The Queen, in Shirley's experience, hated spending money. She always wanted her clothing repaired, or cut up for other uses, before she'd give in to the proposal that something new should be bought. She particularly hated spending money on new clothes. She insisted on wearing certain Norman Hartnell and Hardy Amies outfits she'd worn since the 1970s, though they were several times repaired and beginning to show signs of their age. Shirley had successfully managed to confine The Queen's wearing them to the days she wouldn't be in the public eye.

Shirley replied, "I don't know what number. Shall I inquire?"

"No, don't do that," said The Queen with some energy and shifted the subject to the weather. In three minutes, however, she returned to it. "And what is the fare nowadays on an Edinburgh bus?"

Shirley was so surprised that she hadn't time to reply "I have no idea," before The Queen rushed forward with "You see, some men from the Edinburgh Council are coming to the investiture on Thursday. I'll need something to speak to them about." And with that The Queen signaled an end to their chat by taking a dog biscuit out of her pocket and holding it in the air until it caused a small riot among the sleeping dogs, who all woke up and began yapping.

Several months earlier, at the very beginning of that autumn, The Queen had still been in Scotland, delaying her return to London as long as possible. A late Scottish September next to the river Dee can be unusually sunny and warm. The Queen liked to order a "picnic" luncheon at one of the outlying cottages on the Balmoral estate. These were often damp, uninhabited little places with long views of barren hillsides. Though uncomfortable, they had a kind of stark glamour. Some members of the Household regarded lunching there as a dubious treat. An equerry would go out early, taking bottles of spirits and wine. He would build a fire in order to warm the place up. If it were an unusually sunny day, he would move a table outdoors for luncheon. A butler would follow to lay the table and bring along wicker baskets of cold poached salmon and grouse pie. Ultimately, The Queen herself would turn up around one or half past one in the afternoon, with a lady-in-waiting, whatever private secretary was on duty, whoever happened to be staying in the Castle, and the occasional invited neighbor. They had a drink standing up in groups and then sat down at the table, six, or eight, or sometimes even ten.

"Oh, Anne, I've left behind my headscarf. Now it's sure to start pouring down."

Lady Anne Bevil was in the backseat of a black Range Rover with The Queen, bouncing along over a rutted road twenty minutes from Balmoral. The security man was sitting in front and the deputy private secretary was at the wheel. They were driving to a remote cottage. Anne was fuming. The Queen's remark was no passing observation, but a command that when they got there Anne should get in the car and drive back to the house to fetch the missing headscarf.

"Ma'am, I'll go get it. I have left behind my pills, and I must have them with me."

"Oh, Anne, such trouble. But I'd be very grateful. Not a good time for either of us to be getting wet," said The Queen, making a little joke about their age.

Lady Anne came from one of the country's richest and most aristocratic families. Her ancestors on her father's side had been made earls in the eighteenth century. They agreed to vote with Sir Robert Walpole in the House of Commons. Walpole had rewarded their loyalty not only with a peerage but several commissions to sell the army cotton breeches for soldiers. This quickly built their minor fortune into one of epic proportions. Under Queen Victoria the Bevils had been promoted in the peerage and become marquesses of Thyonville. The money on her mother's side was newer but greater. A Canadian newspaper tycoon had acquired shares in several tabloid newspapers during the early twentieth century. Soon members of every government, of whatever political shade, accepted the tycoon's invitations to dinner, and his daughter married a Bevil, eventually becoming Marchioness of Thyonville. Anne was born in 1936, the youngest child of the union between the Canadians and the Bevils. She was ten years younger than The Queen. Her eldest brother, who was due to inherit the family title, had once been talked of as a potential husband for The Queen. Instead, Lord Mountbatten had produced Philip of Greece for The Queen to marry before the Bevils and the rest of the aristocracy quite realized what was happening. So Philip married the woman who would one day be queen and, as it turned out, Anne's elder brother had died young. The title had gone to his son, Anne's nephew.

Anne herself had married a man who took her not inconsiderable dowry from the Thyonville estate and lost it in the City. Mortified by what he'd done with his wife's money, he then died of a stroke. Anne found herself a widow in her forties. She had a son, with whom she was not on speaking terms, and a small pension left to her by her husband. She had a large flat in Chelsea on Tite Street, but that was hardly enough to keep her fed and clothed in her old age. She clung to the shreds of her former glory by giving up her married name and returning to her Bevil maiden name for both herself and her son. She also retained her courtesy title, "Lady Anne," as the daughter of a marquess. She insisted on its being used more often than was common among other British women in her position in the first years of the second millennium.

She struggled on with the pension and some small investments left to her by the death of maiden aunts. The Queen sometimes chose for her ladies-in-waiting women from good families who were financially down on their luck. They usually welcomed the small stipend from the Royal Household and had manners suitable for making royal social life run smoothly. The job was really about being a companion to The Queen in her formal duties outside the palace: collecting bouquets from children, replying to letters on behalf of The Queen, making conversation with politicians in the twenty minutes before The Queen was ready for their audience with her.

It didn't mean that Anne was particularly happy with routine chores, no matter how light. She drove back to the Castle and then returned to the cottage to find that drinks were already over. The party was about to sit down to some soggy fish as a first course for luncheon. Hardly the thing one wanted when one had been driving down poor roads and steering around large chunks of granite in—The Queen had been right about the weather—heavy rain.

Anne put The Queen's headscarf quietly next to her handbag and made her way to the table, noting from a sheet of paper with the *placement* on a sideboard that she was sitting next to the young Guardsman who had just come on duty as equerry, Major Thomason.

To her surprise, she heard The Queen say, "Darling, thank you." Anne and The Queen had known each other for years, and The Queen always thanked for the smallest of services, but this was the first time The Queen had ever uttered anything remotely affectionate to her. She began to murmur with embarrassment that it was nothing when she noticed that The Queen had actually been speaking to a black Labrador that had put a bone into her hand. Anne saved herself from speaking just in time by turning "Think nothing of it, Ma'am" to "What a loyal dog, Ma'am."

Anne made her way to her place at the table. She smiled at the deputy private secretary on her left, and then turned to introduce herself to the young man in a tweed coat on her right. "I don't think we've met. Anne Bevil." The equerry turned to her and first mouthed silently, "Darling, thank you." She shut her eyes and permitted herself a little laughing shake of the shoulders. When she opened her eyes, he was smiling broadly at her and saying, "Luke Thomason."

"You're a very young man to be in such august surroundings," said Lady Anne, glancing up at the damp spot streaming down the cottage wall and expertly flicking away a few bones from her salmon. How she wished for the boneless fillets you could have from Sainsbury's rather than these skeletal fish gutted in haste by ghillies next to a peat fire.

Luke caught Lady Anne's ironic feint in his direction and answered in kind. "Well, I was in Iraq, love, I expect that's it." Anne laughed delightedly. A young man who didn't mind flirting with a woman his mother's age—how rarely one ran across that.

"Iraq, now? That took some courage if I'm not mistaken." She paused for a moment to allow him to see that she was partly making fun of him, but not entirely. "I don't expect you'll tell me about it. Your friends, perhaps, but not some strange woman at a sumptuous luncheon."

He pretended not to have heard her properly. "Strange women at scrumptious lunches are okay by me," he said, flashing a corner of a smile. He always expected to like people that were a bit older than him, something about the way he was put together, and he liked this lady-in-waiting. He'd heard of her, but as he was still newish, and she'd just arrived in Scotland to replace one of the other ladies, this was the first they'd met. He'd found the Household could be a chilly place. It was good to have friends, as the others on duty didn't, in his experience, warm up very quickly. Prior to becoming The Queen's equerry, Luke had been at a public school and trained for his commission at Sandhurst. As his father and grandfather had both been in the Grenadier Guards, the army as a career came naturally to him. He'd especially liked Germany. The officers' barracks were nondescript 1960s bunkers, but the feeling was a good deal more matey than Sandhurst. There were fewer full-dress occasions. The men under his command were happy to have light work and regular pay, and for many of them it was a change just to have a reliable roof over their heads. They regarded it as somewhat better than jail.

Among the other junior officers, few had wives or local girlfriends, so they were more or less available for constant horseplay, drinking, and messing about. Near bedtime someone would often kick a ball into the corridor. One by one they'd emerge from their rooms, some as spectators, some as players, and a rough game of football would be played. Often they would end up in rugger scrums unknown to the playing of football on a pitch. It was nice to be wrestling with several mates. The feel of their flesh and muscle was reassuring. You could see the work they were doing at the gym. You also felt you could count on a man in a foxhole whom you'd once tackled, laughing and protesting and swearing and genuinely enjoying it all underneath a veneer of simulated anger.

Working for The Queen, and seeing her on a daily basis, was a tremendous honor. He knew it was a high point of his army career, but he was still learning how to do the job and suffered from the impatient corrections of senior members of the Household. He recalled absentmindedly writing "the queen" in a memorandum about some arrangements he was making for her transport on a day when she was to be away from the palace. The private secretary had crossed it out with his fountain pen and written "The Queen," with bold initial capitals, and Luke felt not only foolish, but wondered at the departure from practice everywhere else in the world, where he could think of few other people described in that many caps. Nor was there anything like the camaraderie of Germany in the palace. Luke had a small flat in London while he was on secondment to the Royal Household from the army, but he sometimes stayed the night in the palace if they had early travel the following day. The door to his room shut noiselessly and no one came out into the corridor, even for a chat, after eleven at night.

If there were no official dinner or other evening engagement, Luke usually stopped by The Queen's sitting room before leaving for the evening. He would ask her if there were anything more she'd like. Most of the time her answer was a not unfriendly negative as she looked up from the news on television or a racing paper she'd spread out on the sofa next to her. If she were in an expansive mood, which was rarely, she might say, "I suppose you're in too much of a hurry to have a drink with a granny," her eye twinkling—it was the side of The Queen that still surprised him the most. Of course, she was not to be refused. He tried to rise to her tease with something in the same spirit. "Well, if Ma'am will take a drink from the hands of this establishment's most junior barman, he'd be delighted." A smile was The Queen's assent. He didn't have to ask her what she'd like. A potent combination of gin and Dubonnet was her usual, and, like the senior officers at whose tables he'd sometimes dined, she never acted as if she'd sipped anything stronger than lemonade.

Luke's duties at the palace were mainly social. He often managed the local transport for what were called "awaydays," the palace lingo, recalling an old British Rail ticket promotion, for when The Queen travelled to do duty outside London. It was harder work keeping a clear head through long luncheons with many courses and different wines. He could usually handle the light conversation if he concentrated on what he was doing, but with this lady-in-waiting it was a bit trickier, as she instantly set off over more difficult terrain and he had to follow. After a pause, Anne had begun, "My father was in both wars, First and Second. He'd never talk to anyone about them. Even in his cups. Even to me. I was his favorite."

"Well, it's not polite, is it? I expect he didn't want you to know that they sat around a great deal. Were bored. Wasted time. Played with their walking sticks and neck scarves. No one wants the family to know that."

"Ah yes. But men did fail to come back. There were horrors. We knew more than they thought we did."

A chill went up Luke's spine. He was not sure he could maintain his insouciance in the face of her well-aimed darts of sympathy. In Iraq there had been horrors. He had told no one about what happened to Andy.

⁂

At Paxton & Whitfield on Jermyn Street the air smelled of cow-pats and straw. The shop sold the most expensive cheeses in London. It was always cool and damp there. The sales clerks were nearly all under the age of thirty. They wore wooly jumpers under their long aprons. Rajiv Laroia was an unpublished poet who worked there slicing and weighing cheese. A host of rich eccentrics who didn't care about ingesting milk fat or cholesterol or paying London's highest prices for cheese came into the shop. He secretly observed them, making notes about them in his journal the next morning. Sometimes odd phrases appeared in his dreams:

Ne t'inquiètes pas
Ne me quittes pas

Don't worry, dear
Don't leave me, dear

He wrote these down in his journal and hoped they'd later turn into poems.

His rich grandparents had come from India to live in England after the Second World War. Their money insulated them from some of the local prejudice, and many Englishmen were anyway in the habit of regarding Indian princes and high-caste Hindus as somehow related to their own homegrown nobility. Rajiv had no trouble fitting in at Eton. Outside of the metropolitan orbit, however, the Laroia family discovered that being brown could still be something of a liability. Rajiv as a boy had found out that even London wasn't entirely safe. When he was twelve, on an afternoon he was returning home from having bought a plastic airplane kit at a hobby shop in Holborn, he'd taken a shortcut through an alley. Three boys about his age had started smashing bottles they picked up from a recycling bin uncomfortably near where he was walking. When he took off in the opposite direction, they ran after him, knocked him down, and took one of his shoes. They threw it under a delivery van just arriving at the other end of the alley. They laughed hysterically when the van stopped just on top of his shoe, called him a "Paki bastard," and disappeared around the corner.

This incident convinced Rajiv's parents and grandparents to send him back to India for a season. They were happy in England, but they would not have him being ashamed of his heritage. He should hold his head high. To that end, he attended an

Indian boarding school, where his fellow students didn't know what to think of him. He found Indian boys more conscious of the gradations of skin color than they were even in England. In England he was made fun of for being dark. In India they regarded him as so light-skinned that he was almost white. As his manners and accent were also more English than anyone else's, a drama teacher at the school asked him to play Lord Mountbatten, the last English viceroy, in a school play about India's winning independence from England in 1947.

Rajiv returned to England at the end of the year feeling as if he didn't belong on either continent. He had been more seriously piqued by the English boys calling him a Paki bastard than by the vague humiliation of being asked to play Lord Mountbatten in the Indian school play. It was to the deeper insult that he felt drawn to return, as the well-meaning drama master hadn't really made the same impression on him. His parents grew anxious that he should start seeing some Indian girls from good families who were near his age. He found himself more and more attracted to the sisters of his friends at Eton, whose vanilla cheeks grew strawberry when he talked to them. He couldn't help thinking up metaphors for skin color because a girl's skin was always the first thing he noticed about her.

He wasn't afraid of people, so he could talk to anyone, whether it was persuading the man in the corner shop to sell him and his underaged friends a bottle of vodka, or discussing literature with the Provost's wife at a tea party. He hadn't studied hard, but his interest had been stirred by an English master's asking him to read Shakespeare's sonnets. He'd written some verse of his own that was considered good enough to get him a month's fellowship at the Wordsworth Trust in the Lake District. While his friends were going off to gap years in places like Tanzania and Peru before university, Rajiv decided he'd spend his gap year in London, working at a cheese shop and trying to write poems.

He took several weeks' unpaid leave from Paxton & Whitfield in London to take up the fellowship that autumn and enjoyed fell walking in the rain, as well as the company of other poets around smoky fires. The local landowner leased some of his cottages to the Wordsworth Trust at a peppercorn rent as one of his philanthropies. The Queen happened to be staying privately with the landowner and turned up by surprise one day outside the cottage where Rajiv was staying while on a walk with the landowner. He had a new camera given to him by an indulgent aunt and picked this up to snap a picture of the sovereign. He didn't feel as if he were doing her any harm. Her grandchildren, William and Harry, had been at Eton near enough to the same time as him, so it was just as if he were taking a snapshot of a mate's grandmother on a school sports day. As he'd played Lord Mountbatten in the school play, he even had a feeling that he was vaguely related to her. She smiled and he snapped.

He'd shown the photo to someone at the shop who knew an editor at one of the tabloid newspapers. As something between a joke and a dare, they decided to offer it as bait and see whether the editor would bite on it. The other shop assistant acted as his agent, and to their surprise, the newspaper wanted it. The sale of the picture—The Queen standing in the rain, ankle deep in a puddle—had led to Rajiv receiving a check that was more than a month's salary. He didn't exactly need the money, but as the grandson of someone who'd struggled to pile up a fortune, the sum itself impressed him.

One afternoon a young woman in a scoop-necked dress came into the shop. She was wearing two strings of onyx beads. It was the first of the chillier October weather and the skin on her upper breasts was covered in goose bumps. He found this both touching and erotic. She asked if he knew Rajiv Laroia. "The one, the only, at your service," said Rajiv, giving her at the same time a mock deferential wiggle of his head and neck. The woman rattled her onyx beads appreciatively, and as there was no one there but the two of them, opened her handbag. She handed him her card. She was from the tabloid newspaper that had bought his photo. They wondered whether they might pay him for more. "Of course," said Rajiv. He wanted to be accommodating. "Trouble is, I don't run into her that often."

The newspaper had thought of that. They'd bribed one of the officers at Scotland Yard in the Royal Protection unit, an officer who'd seen the royal family living in luxury and editors of the tabloid press living in greater luxury still. He didn't see why he shouldn't take part. It was his job to vet the temporary staff employed for big events at the palace when extra help was needed. The newspaper paid him to pass Rajiv's application to be hired as temporary kitchen staff. There was no question of any danger to the royal family or to their guests. It was Scotland Yard in cahoots with the press to provide the occasional scoop or surprise photograph. The paper wanted Rajiv to join the catering staff for an upcoming state banquet. Queen Beatrix of the Netherlands was making an official visit and the newspaper asked him to slip away from the kitchen to take more pictures of The Queen. In the immediate post-Diana generation they'd had success appealing to antimonarchical resentment in Britain, and what they required were more compromising photos. The young woman suggested one of The Queen drinking wine, or yawning, or in some other ungainly pose.

Rajiv had no particular love of the monarchy. Nor did he despise the royal family as some of the quality newspapers did. He had heard some catering gossip that the new chef at the palace was commissioning marvelous work. Working at Paxton & Whitfield had given Rajiv a new interest in cheese. The palace bought some of Paxton & Whitfield's best cheeses: washed-rind Epoisses, Livarot, and Pont L'Evêque that expanded at room temperature and, when cut, allowed a lush wave of white to run across the cheese board. Although he had no views about the politics of the heir to the throne, he did think it was important for children to grow up knowing Shakespeare's verse, one of Prince Charles's public causes. The shop also sold some of the Duchy of Cornwall's cheddar, which was the same color as an Elizabethan brick. He loved it. So perhaps going undercover in the royal kitchens would not be a bad thing. He might see what they were doing. If there was anything interesting, he'd photograph it.

The day arrived and Rajiv turned up at the side entrance of Buckingham Palace, wearing some checked trousers and a chef's jacket he'd found in the window of a kitchen supply shop in Soho. He was met by an under chef, also smuggled in by the rogue Royal Protection officer, with a muttered message that he should try to make himself look busy as there really wasn't a job for him to do. Having grown up in a household where suppers prepared by others appeared unceremoniously on the table, Rajiv had never taken much notice of food before. Working at the shop had given him a new behind-the-scenes look into the preparation of rare foodstuffs, so he now approached cooking as if he were an enthusiastic explorer on a new continent. Finding food well prepared and presented gave him the same pleasure as finding a poem that spoke to him. Both of them had a surprisingly evanescent magic. He circulated among the palace cooks and waiters, frankly admiring their work. He was amazed at what they'd accomplished. There were several cheese boards ready for passing that had hard and soft cheeses already breathing their uddery aroma into the late afternoon. As both a tribute and a tease to the Dutch cheese industry, someone had carved a huge round of English cheddar to look like the roofscape of the Dutch village of Gouda. Another expert carver had made a pair of Dutch wooden shoes out of a block of Stilton. These were to sit as centerpieces on tables in an anteroom where cocktails would be served before dinner. In the dining room itself, the long table was covered with a wintry scene of crystal and silver. The spectacle of it all astonished him. Seventeenth-century William and Mary vases from the Victoria and Albert Museum (so a curator told him as she rushed by with insurance forms) filled with orange autumn leaves, orange chrysanthemums, and orange roses, to mark the visiting head of the House of Orange, marched down the center of a long table. He couldn't stop himself from snapping pictures of all this, though he knew it wasn't his brief. Everyone assumed that if he'd got past security he was permitted to be taking pictures as official records for the Lord Steward.

His only chance at fulfilling the newspaper's commission was when The Queen came downstairs at five in the afternoon to review the tables. She brought the Dutch Queen with her, and the two elderly ladies exclaimed and laughed delightedly at the townscape of Gouda. He photographed The Queen leaning over the cheese village, her skirt riding up over her legs to show well-shaped calves ending in leather pumps with blocky heels cut on the diagonal. "Not bad for eightysomething," Rajiv thought to himself. The only photo he could get that was in the least compromising was a tiny chat between the two Queens on the terrace overlooking the garden. The Dutch Queen was smoking a cigarette with gusto and The Queen waved away the smoke with a grimace. After he got that, the other undercover chef, afraid that Rajiv's picture-taking was becoming too obvious, shooed him out of the room.

Rajiv's photos created a quandary for the staff at the tabloid newspaper. None of the pictures was in the least embarrassing. The editor with onyx beads who'd commissioned the photos had gone away on maternity leave. Her deputy knew how much they'd paid for Rajiv's work, so he thought it would be best to run them anyway. He tried to cover for the low smear quality of the pictures by writing some sneering captions. "All this cheese for me?" he put under The Queen leaning over to admire the townscape of Gouda, and "No smoking please, we're British" under the two Queens chatting on the terrace.

The effect was the reverse of what the newspaper intended. Instead of the post-Diana resentment of the royal family that the paper had hoped to exploit, the paper's blogosphere lit up with questions about how to reproduce the William and Mary flower arrangements. Everyone hated smokers, and The Queen wrinkling her nose at Beatrix's secondary smoke was a hit. Moreover, everyone was ecstatic over The Queen's shapely calves and her beautifully made heels. A grandmother's shoes, flexing forward on tiptoe, with the patent leather gleaming in the light, made them proud to be British. Even an American website, Thesartorialist.com, had picked up the photo, sparking a fashion furor for orthopedic footwear.

Luncheon at the remote cottage on the Balmoral estate was over. The Queen and the rest of the party had taken the dogs for a walk down by the Muick. Luke and Lady Anne remained behind, giving as their excuse that they would straighten up the table, but in fact because they wished for some minutes alone. The equerry was responsible for gathering up the bottles—those that still had anything in them—and taking them back to the big house. Lady Anne had no real responsibilities, but she was conscious that the staff had enough to do when The Queen was in residence without driving to outlying cottages to do the washing up. So she cleared the table and, with Luke's help, got an ancient boiler in the kitchen roaring so there would be enough hot water to fill the sink. They found some Fairy Liquid and rubber gloves as well as several ironed dishtowels in one of the cupboards. Anne washed. Luke dried.

It was precisely because they had some work to do, and had no need to look at one another, that their conversation could, once again, turn confidential. Her cashmere cardigan pushed up over her elbows, her hands in the steaming water, Anne began: "How long were you in Basra?"

"Two tours. About two years in all," said Luke.

"The newspapers made it seem as if Basra was quite quiet and the Americans had all the fire."

The way she had put it chilled him, as if she knew his history before he'd told her. He was determined to gloss over the complexities of what he knew of the British and American armies in the Iraqi desert. "Yeah. Well, there was plenty of time for messing about. It wasn't all house-to-house reconnaissance with daggers drawn."

Luke looked for a new, less serious direction to the conversation. He chuckled to himself, remembering an incident during what seemed interminable afternoons of doing nothing. "Someone took a picture, I think it was a Yank with the camera, actually. It was the lads wearing carnations and fooling about with long cigarettes. Rather foppish I'm afraid. It got into one of the papers."

"And what were you playing at?"

"Oh, I don't know. I think we were pretending to be mad

dogs and Englishmen in the noonday sun. Something like that. Showing the Americans how tough we were."

"And apart from imitating Noël Coward, you also went in drag for theatricals on Saturday nights to entertain the men, I imagine?"

There had been some of that, but Luke didn't know Anne well enough to confess to it. There was a sort of military code that prevented him speaking to her too intimately about what had gone on in Iraq. "Well, now, we did have theatricals."

"Of course you did. It's a trademark of Englishmen serving abroad."

"Is it?"

"Oh yes. Make a tour of our embassies, and no matter where you stop, Cairo, Dubai, the Philippines, it doesn't matter. There will always be some sort of amateur version of a West End play being performed."

"Well, ours weren't West End plays, exactly."

"Oh. What were they?"

"Um, music videos, *karaoke*. Boy George, a bit of Madonna, sometimes a Stones medley."

"What fun. And I suppose you had cameras to film it all?"

There were cameras, and Luke wasn't proud of everything he'd performed that the camera had captured. But she did seem to know who Madonna was, and that was a start. "Some of it filmed, yes, but in the Guards archive with a fifty-year seal on it, I'm afraid, Lady Anne."

She laughed appreciatively. "I suppose you made some good friends out there."

"Well, it was good times with some of them, yes. I did have mates out there. But they went away to different units. They're all over the country now. And here I am on secondment to the Royal Household, doing Her Majesty's washing up."

"A very great privilege it is too, young man," said Anne severely, but then, twinkling, she caught his eye and added, "for both of us."

"No doubt, your ladyship." He stretched out the last word and gave it a comic pronunciation, "lee-adie-ship."

"And do you see some of your chums sometimes?" Anne continued.

"Not as often as I'd like. They sometimes ring up of a Friday night when they're feeling drunken and rowdy. We have a laugh. But it's not the same."

"And no one in the Household appeals, do they?"

This was cutting near the bone. What did she mean by asking about his friends? How had she perceived his loneliness so distinctly?

"Well, blokes are more solitary than birds, I expect."

She knew he meant this to be a batting away of the ball she'd tossed him, but she could also intuit his suffering about something she couldn't quite put her finger on.

"Quite a few come back changed by the war, I believe. Post-traumatic stress disorder. Lots of divorce. Lots of depression. Lots of drinking. The three D's. I do some hours on an army helpline when I'm not up here or somewhere else with the Household. Gives me something to do. Lots of my family were in the army too. In fact, I think all of them come back changed in some way by the fighting, and not always for the better."

Luke felt the gravitational force of her compassion, the magnetic attraction of someone who understood army ways, and knew a little about Iraq without his having to tell her. "Well, when you've changed, if you've changed, you can't always say how or why yourself. Others outside see it, but you just feel like you're carrying on the same as ever. Still you." He thought for a moment, and then admitted, "Maybe a lonelier you, or an angrier you, but you yourself, well, you're not the best judge."

"I see that. Yes."

"As for post traumatic whatsit, I don't think there were too many what you'd call traumas out there."

"Yes, well, I don't believe you."

Luke wasn't used to receiving such flat negatives from the Household. They usually went out of their way to make a charming apology before they said, in their silkiest manner, "No."

In the midst of his surprised silence, Anne said, "You see,

it's just that the helpline is busy all night long with men who can't get over what happened to them. And sometimes the worst thing that happened to them was that they had to leave their lives for a year and spend it in the desert in an air-conditioned tent, with a group of other men whom they didn't know and didn't choose to be with. I believe that's trauma enough for most people."

"It's a volunteer armed force. They didn't have to go. It's what they signed up for."

"They didn't know what they signed up for. How could they know till they got there? And no one signs up to die. Death was close enough out there for plenty of them to see what it looked like. And that's traumatic too."

Luke felt as if he'd been driven into a corner, and not by some insurgent with a gun, but by an old woman from the army helpline. He wasn't sure which was the way out to keep this talk on a polite plane. He would, after all, have to work with her again. He struggled and then admitted his failure to find a conversational exit. "Give."

"What?"

"I give in. What do you want to know?"

"You lost someone out there, didn't you?"

"I did."

"Tell me."

"An American. On loan to our unit. Meant to be helping us liaise with some of their units. Only with us for a few months. Didn't understand all the regimental horseshit. I mean, excuse me. I mean . . ."

"Go on."

"Only that most of the American units don't have quite the same traditions, or history, or dress, or funny ways of doing things that we do in the Guards. They're not used to it. As if having been recruited in the seventeenth century to fight for bloody Charles the Second is going to keep you alive in Iraq. And Andrew, well Andy he was, Andy didn't understand any of it, but living with us he saw it, and the others ragged him for not getting it right. And I guess I was the first one to tell him to pay no attention and, well, we got along." This was not the full story, but it was a true part of it.

"You gave him a hand, did you? Taught him what he needed to know to get along with these Trobriand Islanders?"

"That's what it was. He didn't understand the first thing about the lingo or which fork to use or how to have his gear pressed."

"All of the first importance among the Trobriand Islanders."

"Well, yes, as you know."

"I do know."

"It might have been easier for me to be friends with him, to get close to him, because he wasn't one of us. You sometimes kind of, well, let your hair down with foreigners, don't you? Anyway, he went out one day on a patrol. They were in a convoy of Humvees. They drove by an explosive device on the roadside. It went off. His vehicle rolled over. He'd been up top and it rolled over on top of him. Died right there. I wasn't even with him. They brought him back to the base. He was already in a body bag when I found out. I went over. I could have taken a look. I had the right. It would have been okay for me to unzip the bag."

"You wanted to remember him as he was."

"Maybe that was it. He was a happy young man. Short hair. In his twenties. Already going bald, but handsome. Always making jokes. They teased him about not knowing Guards' rules and regs, but they loved him because he was always life of the party. Kept everyone laughing."

"And you loved him too."

"I did." Luke turned away with the dishtowel in his hand. He couldn't face her, this little woman with blue veins in her forehead, no-nonsense manner, and flashing eyes. He could not now suppress half of a sob, which he tried to make resemble a clearing of the throat.

"I know you did," and then she did something quite as shocking as having led him into this emotional thicket to begin with. She reached out with her yellow rubber gloves and pulled him toward her, turning him around, clasping him in her arms. Her head with its white hair only came two-thirds of the way up his chest, and the water and suds from her gloves rolled down the back of his tweed jacket.

A moment later the distant bark of a dog let them know that The Queen was nearby, and hearing that, he moved hastily away from her. He picked up a wineglass, which he began drying and judging against the light. "What will Her Majesty think of us, eh? I don't think we're meant to be liaising during our downtime, are we?"

"Well, she might be quite jealous, if she knew," said Anne, going back to the sink with a smile.

The popularity of Rajiv's photographs of the Dutch state banquet had mystified the editors at the tabloid newspaper. The tide of royal popularity seemed to be shifting back in a positive direction without their having anticipated it and they wanted to wait for more definitive indications of popular mood before publishing anything further. Rajiv was under the impression that he'd produced good work and was anxious to do more. He was in the shop a month later, in mid-November, wondering why the editors had stopped replying to his e-mails, when another young woman came in the door. He couldn't believe the flame color of her hair or the clotted creaminess of her skin. She had on riding boots as well as a hoodie with skull and crossbones on the back. As she looked at rounds of Camembert, he thought of ways of taking her picture without her noticing. Might he just hold up his phone as if he were trying to improve the angle of light on the screen and snap her photo with the sound of the shutter clicking turned off? But then he surprised himself. "May I help you?" he said and then added in a hurry, "What amazing hair you have."

He could see in an instant that it was the wrong thing to say. She gave him a practiced half smile. Clearly she got that compliment once every two days. What he'd said was unoriginal, too obvious, almost an irritant. "I mean we have some cheese rinds that color. Smelly ones." He'd meant "smelly" as a desirable characteristic in a cheese, but she bridled, thinking he was referring to her smell. But then she saw his broad grin and immediately gave him a more natural smile, as if allowing an insult from a friend.

"Look, I need an unusual cheddar. Elizabeth likes it."

"Who's Elizabeth, then? Your girlfriend?" This was very

bold indeed. Rajiv was aware that he wasn't very good at talking to girls his own age, much as he wanted to please them. With boys his age, the way to their hearts was to insult them, mildly, but deliberately. Maybe this would work with a girl too.

The young woman with flame-colored hair was annoyed. She did not have a girlfriend, but she had nothing against women loving women. On top of that, his question was far too personal. "Elizabeth is a horse, actually," she said, her face darkening and her voice cooling. "Likes cheese. Especially cheddar."

"Never heard of a hoss like cheese before," Rajiv said, using what he took to be a John Wayne pronunciation of "horse." He'd seen that the girlfriend remark hadn't worked. This was his desperate attempt to regain her favor. "But cheddar goes with apples, and I know hosses like apples."

His struggling with a false Texas accent and all those "s" sounds made her smile again. "Well, this horse does. Likes cheese, I mean. Is a bit spoiled. Gets whatever she wants."

"Like you?" he said, sending her a smiling glance under his eyebrows. Then, without allowing her time to react to that, he began showing her all the shop's dizzying array of cheddars. She was in difficulties because she'd come away from the stables without adequate information. All she knew was that one afternoon a while ago The Queen had swept up some leftover cheddar from her lunch and brought it over to the Mews. She'd discovered that Elizabeth loved this cheddar and asked Rebecca to make sure the Mews bought some more to give to the horse as a treat. All Rebecca could find out from the palace kitchens was that the cheddar on The Queen's cheese board had come from Paxton &

Whitfield. So she'd walked over with instructions to buy more cheddar from Paxton & Whitfield without realizing that there would be sixteen different varieties available.

"You wouldn't happen to know what sorts of cheddar have been sent over to the palace lately, would you?"

"Oh, my dear! You want the same cheddar that The Queen has, do you?" Rajiv saw this as rich teasing material. He put his hands on his hips and smiled at her as winningly as he knew how.

Rebecca knew very well that she could hardly disclose the nature of her errand or the eventual destination of the cheese. She was a nervous young woman, more at ease with animals than people. Talking to people, even people in shops, required an effort from her. She had never been much interested in boys before, mainly as a defensive posture because in school they had never been interested in her. Flirting with boys was certainly beyond her ability. She began to retreat. "Well, I might have to look around a bit. Thanks, anyway." She turned to go.

"Hang on a minute. I've got just the thing for you. They carved up a big round of cheddar for the Dutch state visit a little while ago. Smashing pictures in the papers. I expect that's the one you want. It's right here. One of our best. I might slice you just a little wedge of that? Bring it back if Elizabeth doesn't like it."

He spoke so quickly and seemed to care so much about regaining her favor, that she couldn't help but smile and nod her head "yes" to give her assent. When he was giving her change from her £20 note, he added, "I'm actually an amateur photographer. And I don't suppose you'd allow me to photograph you giving Elizabeth her cheddar?"

She couldn't tell him where she worked, or that The Queen preferred to give Elizabeth the cheese herself. On the other hand, his bad cowboy accent had made her laugh and he had her attention.

"No, I don't think so," she said.

"What about I photograph just you, then?"

"No," she said again.

"What about we never see each other again as long as we live?"

She smiled, though she hadn't intended to.

"I'm Rajiv. What about you tell me your name?"

She couldn't say no again. "Rebecca," and she held out her hand to shake his.

"What about we meet for a totally harmless, no-photos-allowed cup of coffee one afternoon?" he said to her.

She gave him one of her e-mail addresses, but then turned on her heel and left quickly, as if she'd already regretted what she'd done.

Having celebrated his forty-fifth birthday, William de Morgan decided that romantic love was pretty much out of the question for him now. He'd had his share of sex, and even love once or twice, but as he looked at himself in the mirror, he could see plainly that the passage of time was having its effect. His sagging neck began to look as if it would be better covered up with a very high Katharine Hepburn style collar.

He didn't want to complain about his fate. He'd had more than enough fun in his twenties and thirties. The number of sexual partners he could recall easily topped those of his married friends, and he believed some of these early-married husbands, straight as they were, envied him some of the sexual variety he'd experienced. Unlike them, he'd also been free to come and go, move on and move up, as he pleased. His career had prospered.

But he envied his married friends for having someone to share the events of the day with while cooking supper together. He would have given up some of his sexual variety for their mutually sustaining coupledom. He wondered whether, perhaps, something in him didn't prevent him from settling down.

He poured more than tea into The Queen's teacup. He poured everything he had, all of himself, and that meant there was little enough time or energy or interest at the end of the day to put into finding and keeping a lover. He knew how the cloth should look on the silver salver. He knew how to hold the cup up to the window so that the light caught its eggshell fragility. He knew how to disappear so noiselessly that The Queen hardly knew he was gone. He had no idea where to look for a man. It had been that way for many years now, and he didn't expect it to change now that he was middle-aged.

There were attractive men in the palace, and having grown up in the provinces in a dull town, he liked upper-class men. Plenty of good-looking men fit that description where he worked, mostly army officers on loan. They came and went, often serving no more than two years or three. Of course he noticed them, from the corner of his eye, but it was his job not to let them know he was looking at them; on the whole, they were blind to people they thought of as "servants." And these young officers in their twenties and thirties generally knew better than to call such as William that. Sometimes they got wine poured on their crotches by mistake as a way of teaching them not to use that word. "Oh dear, I *am* sorry, sir!" William never disciplined ill-mannered young men in that way, but some of his colleagues did. If a young captain didn't know already, he quickly learned that William, or anyone else who waited at table, was "a member of staff." After they got that right, they no more gave it a second thought than they did about having their wineglass silently refilled. They were thinking about what to say next to the person on their right and were worried about not missing the moment when the table would turn, and they must shift to the person on the left. It was a complex, choreographed performance. They were onstage. As far as they were concerned, William merely set the scenery and kept the lights on.

William had noticed Luke when he arrived, a young man in a worn but form-fitting wool suit, remarkable for his lack of confidence. He was polished enough with The Queen and her guests at luncheon, but there was something rather silent, even catatonic, about him in the moments when he thought he wasn't being watched. He sometimes seemed to hold back, or to be slightly confused at a moment when one of the other equerries would have leapt forward, like a horse over a hedge, with a bit of whimsy, or some self-deprecating candor to put people at ease.

William discovered Luke by accident one day when he came

in to lay the table for a solo luncheon The Queen was going to have that December Monday in her sitting room. Luke was on his hands and knees under her desk, wool worsted stretched across his rump, as he struggled with the computer cords and a power strip. He thumped his head as he was scooting out from under the lower drawer. "Christ!" As he came up on his knees, rubbing his head, he noticed William by the door, appraising him.

"Like the view from up there, then, William?" he said, still pained by the blow to his head.

This was a double surprise to William. He hadn't thought this equerry even knew his name. Nor had he ever been caught out in recent history looking so unguardedly at young Guardsmen. "Well, sir, have a care for those trousers. They weren't cut for going on maneuvers."

"So kind of you to be looking out for my kit," said Luke drily as he stamped one foot on the floor, and then the other, bringing himself upright. There was a pause while he looked rather fiercely at William, as if he might hit him.

Then, awkwardly, he stuck out his hand. "Name's Luke, by the way."

This was a minor breach of palace protocol. The Queen's upper servants, the private secretaries and equerries and ladies-in-waiting, might call the staff by their Christian names, but they were seldom anything other than "sir" or "ma'am" in return. They might all be quietly on a first-name basis after long years of service together, but not so quickly as this, and there was seldom shaking of hands. Upper-class Englishmen had a horror of shaking hands. They abhorred it. It was one of those arcane rules with them. They only relaxed the rule for dealing with foreigners. It was completely arbitrary.

"My very great pleasure," said William, swallowing ironically where the "sir" should have gone. "Is information technology now part of the equerry's job description?" he asked nodding at The Queen's computer.

"If butlers are also tailors, I don't see why a soldier shouldn't know how to make a flipping computer work."

"Hmm, yes. But does she use it?"

"Well, she had it on this morning. It lost the Wi-Fi and locked up when I was showing her how to do MapQuest. I was down there powering it off to try to get it to connect again. I thought she might like a little online music during her lunch."

"Music? During her luncheon?" said William laughing. "You must be joking."

"Well, she might like a little Tony Bennett, now, mightn't she? Or, let's see, Noël Coward?"

William looked at Luke skeptically.

"Or Dusty Springfield? Eartha Kitt, now?"

William rolled his eyes to the ceiling.

Luke pushed the joke a little further: "Uh, Bronski Beat, then?"

William replied a little archly, "You seem to know all about that music."

"Well, we had a bloke in Germany. A gay DJ. He did 1980s nights."

"And all you big brutes danced together, did you?"

"Stood up against the bar drinking, mainly."

"Well, it was the bonding, I expect." There was a pause while both of them looked out the window.

"I do miss them occasionally." It was the first serious thing either of them had said, and William's antennae picked up the shift in tone. He'd just been told something relatively private by this young man and he thought it was as well to leave a respectful silence to acknowledge it.

"I mean," said Luke falteringly, half wincing at what he'd said, and half impelled forward by something he couldn't quite spell out, "not so many chums around here."

In the midst of this, the door lock clicked. A page in red brocade, wearing eighteenth-century court shoes, put his head through the doorway, "Look sharp! Herself will be through in three minutes." Having thoroughly interrupted their moment, he shut the door and disappeared.

William approached a small round table with a starched white cloth. He began singing just under his breath, but audibly, a Bronski Beat anthem from the 1980s that had a lyric about Jonah in the belly of a whale, as he spread out the silver and plates he took from a sideboard.

Shooting a glance at William as he left the room, Luke started humming in a falsetto another hit from the same band about a boy from a small town. His voice could still be heard outside the door as he disappeared down the corridor.

Just then The Queen walked in the door on the opposite side of the room.

"Your Majesty," said William, quietly bowing from the neck as he caught The Queen's eye.

"Hello, William. What's that?" she said, referring with a motion of her head to Luke singing "Tell me *why*," which could still be heard faintly disappearing on the other side of the opposite doorway.

"1980s disco music, Ma'am. I believe they played it on special nights in the Rhine Garrison for the Grenadier Guards."

"I see," said The Queen, sitting down in front of her computer, and with an arthritic hand on the mouse she selected The-racehorse.com from her bookmarks.

Later that same Monday afternoon Luke advanced down the corridor, still wearing the suit made for his grandfather at Huntsman. If The Queen noticed it was a bit threadbare at the cuffs, rather shiny in the seat, he could tell her it had been made for his grandfather, and she'd smile. He knew she would. She generally liked holding on to things that had worked well for previous generations. His own appointment as an equerry to Her Majesty belonged to the same category. He was only in his early thirties and had served, so far, in Britain, Germany, and Iraq, where he had been decorated for bravery in joint action with the Americans. Most of the ladies and gentlemen attached to the Royal Household were closer to The Queen's age than to his. Queen Elizabeth, however—she was known as "The Queen Mother" outside the palace, but inside she was "Queen Elizabeth" to distinguish her from "The Queen"—had liked good-looking young men. So she always had a young equerry attached to her Household among the senior ladies and gentlemen.

The Queen did not share all her mother's tastes. She was less partial to champagne, the theatre, and bachelors than her mother had been. Nevertheless, The Queen liked keeping up traditions started by her mother, so she too would have a younger equerry appointed to her Household, usually for two or three years at a time. The equerry's duties involved being an extra man at luncheon or the dinner table, entertaining her guests, as well as arranging some of the transport on The Queen's days away from the palace. He also steered unschooled visitors through the ritual minefield of bows and curtseys necessary for first meetings with The Queen. It was not hard work. It was an acknowledgment of hard work elsewhere. Few people knew how much The Queen's court was still a military court, and how many of the male duties in the Household were undertaken by officers whose more ordinary experience was of unglamorous, uncomfortable postings in remote corners where they had often served with distinction.

Luke approached The Queen's sitting room. It was a smallish room at the rear of the building with a view on to Buckingham Palace Gardens. The palace had miles of state rooms with painted ceilings and gilded furniture, but when she was on her own, The Queen preferred sitting in this ordinary room at the back, furnished only with a television, a comfy chair, a worn sofa, and a desk. There was also a computer, in which she took only an intermittent interest. The room was no more than a biggish-sized closet, really. Discovering The Queen's pleasure in sitting alone in such an unqueenly setting was the first of Luke's surprises when he'd started working at the palace. Now he was used to it, and he expected her to be equally unconcerned about the request he was about to make of her. Usually, on days when he didn't travel with The Queen, or when there were no engagements in the evening, he was in the palace from about ten in the morning until six at night, but this afternoon, he'd received a pressing letter from Andy's mother. He wanted a few hours at home in his flat to reply to it properly. As The Queen had just returned that Monday morning from her weekend in Windsor, and there was nothing official on her program until Tuesday, he didn't expect her to object to his leaving a few hours early. She was easy about things like that.

The door to her sitting room was closed. It always was. Doors were seldom left open in the palace, another of his early discoveries. He stopped in the corridor, listened briefly at the door to see whether he could hear her talking to anyone on the telephone. He wouldn't interrupt if she were, but there was nothing, not even the sound of the television. He fully expected to find her reading briefing papers at the desk while the dogs slept on the carpet. He tapped gently with his knuckle and waited for her reply.

Instead of The Queen's voice what he heard was a strange noise from the dogs. It was not unusual for his knock to make the dogs bark, but then he would hear her shushing them. Now they did not bark. They whined. He knocked again, which prompted somewhat louder whining from the dogs, and an isolated howl. He opened the door a crack to see the door to the garden terrace ajar, a December shower wetting the rug and blowing the curtains into the room. He walked in and shut the door into the garden. She'd clearly been here and was gone. Stepped outside for a moment? Gone for a walk in this weather? If she had, she would have taken the dogs with her. Instead, they waddled back and forth between the door and the center of the room, as if they were children shocked at their abandonment.

Luke went to the telephone, dialed the number of palace security and asked where The Queen had gone. "In her sitting room," came the reply down the line. Luke was impatient with the palace's old-fashioned communication system. The man clearly could not see that he was already telephoning from The Queen's sitting room. "No, I'm in her sitting room, and she's not here," said Luke with grim determination.

"Oh, probably out walking the dogs," came the careless reply from security.

"No," said Luke, "the dogs are here."

"Wouldn't worry. She won't have gone far." The man rang off.

Luke was fairly familiar with The Queen's routine, and her aversion to deviating from it in the smallest way. She wouldn't be anywhere else in the palace at this hour. The open outer door left only one possibility: she must have stepped outside. His current job was a desk job, but he could still summon up some strength from years of doing very little in his spare time but working out in an army gym. He went back and reopened the door. Buckingham Palace Gardens was itself the size of a small London park, but he thought he could jog around the perimeter quickly enough to satisfy himself that if The Queen had gone out, and for some reason not come back in, she was all right and needed no assistance. He sprinted down the stairs on to the wet gravel and jogged first around the edge of the gardens, and then down several of the central paths in twenty minutes, sleet mixed with rain stinging his face. With a rising sense of panic, he found nothing.

He came back inside, winded, wet, and breathing hard. He knew rationally that now was the time to raise the alarm, but he did not trust palace security. It was not only that they were often lazy and inattentive, that they'd ignored The Queen herself when she'd sounded a buzzer to summon help some years ago after a lunatic broke into her bedroom before breakfast. It was Luke himself. Since he'd been back from Iraq, he trusted people less, and men in uniform not at all. He also imagined that somehow the newspapers would find out if he told security, and when it was discovered that The Queen was out somewhere on the London streets by herself, unattended, Lear in a winter's storm, the papers would say she'd lost her mind. Or, she'd be approached by strangers in some unspeakable way. And he was responsible. He went miserably to The Queen's desk chair. He sat down and put his elbows on the desk. He had no idea what to do next.

At that moment Luke heard the latch of an interior door and leapt from the chair, assuming that now, at last, The Queen was returning from God knows where. He felt relief, mingled with terror lest she catch him sitting in her chair. Instead, it was William, who sailed through the doorway, saying, "All right, young fellow, what have you done with her? Very odd for her not to be here at this hour."

"Gone."

"The Queen does not just get up and walk away. Tell me where she is. And don't you look as if you're in a state? Do you realize that's an Aubusson carpet you're dripping all over?"

Luke just looked at him, terrified, wordless.

The dogs looked back and forth at the two men, first at the one, then the other.

Part II

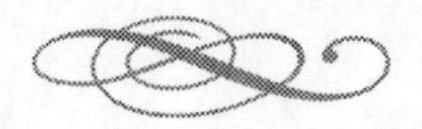

Swami Vivekananda

When she'd turned eighty in 2006 The Queen had reluctantly decided to give up riding on horseback. The royal physician, whom she persisted in calling "the apothecary," as if he were someone who merely dispensed pills from green vials, had begun hinting some years earlier that it was dangerous exercise "for we old-age pensioners, Ma'am." He was quite as old as she was. Because he was familiar, she hated switching to some newer younger man. That didn't mean she liked his advice. Riding on horseback was about the only exercise she took, and, besides walking the dogs, the only exercise she enjoyed. She hadn't fallen off in recent history, she was proud to say, but she did feel a disabling stiffness in her hips that made walking difficult after an afternoon's gentle amble on one of the horses at Windsor or Sandringham. This did leave rather a hole in her weekend afternoons, and she'd consulted Queen Victoria's diaries to see what the alternatives might be. It turned out that in old age The Queen had a two-seat pony cart which she used for outings on the estates at Osborne and Balmoral. She asked the

private secretary to see whether he couldn't find out what had happened to it. By some miracle the wooden cart was found disassembled into fourteen pieces in an outbuilding next to the Glassalt Shiel, a small house the old Queen had built on Loch Muick in 1868.

The Queen remembered first reading about the Glassalt Shiel with a wry smile. It was considered something of a joke in royal history. Queen Victoria had built the house up on the loch, a few miles from the Castle at Balmoral, as a sort of "getaway," but as the Scottish Castle itself had been built as a holiday escape from London, the Glassalt was actually a getaway from a getaway. One of the old Queen's minor self-indulgences, it was felt. The Queen didn't look at it that way anymore. She understood precisely what Queen Victoria had been feeling because she felt more and more that she wanted to get away herself. Although she was happier in Scotland than anywhere else, even there the Prime Minister made an annual visit, and he often brought unwelcome news or tendered disagreeable advice.

She'd been looking forward to the new man coming to visit as he was the first one in a long time who actually behaved like a Scotsman, and she anticipated getting along better with him than with his recent predecessors. Of course, she already knew him from his previous posts in other departments, but as he was now in Number 10, she'd be seeing more of him. There was something dour, humorless, and unhappy about him that suited her present mood. He'd arrived at Balmoral with his wife for a weekend stay in early September. She'd detailed Lady Anne to take care of the wife. "Go and have a look around the cutting garden, perhaps." The Prime Minister she'd take care of herself. She thought he might like to see her new, reassembled pony cart, and go for a trot up to the distillery. The distillery didn't belong to her, but always welcomed a royal visit and didn't mind shutting down to the public during a little informal call from her. She loved looking at the enormous brass vats and all the Victorian plumbing. The whiskey she cared about less. Wasn't her drink really, but she'd accept a small tumbler to keep off the damp, and then off they could go back to the Castle. Shouldn't take more than an hour there and back.

She came down the tartan-covered steps to the portico to find the Prime Minister hanging about awkwardly in a tweed coat that looked as if he'd bought it especially for the occasion. A ghillie held the reins of the pony that was harnessed to the cart. A footman stood by with cushions and two rugs to put over their knees once they got in. The footman put in one cushion for her, and arranged the rug over her knees as the ghillie handed her the reins. The footman was about to put in the second cushion for the Prime Minister when he said, "No thank you. I won't need that."

"I advise you to take it, Prime Minister. Roads can be a bit rough up here. Wouldn't want you jostled."

The Prime Minister was already getting in and waving the footman away. "Oh no, Your Majesty, you see I have so much natural padding in that area that I won't need it. My wife is always saying I must exercise more."

"Well, don't say I didn't warn you." The Queen clicked her tongue, and called to the pony, "Come on, Smoky!" The cart pulled away from the portico with an unusually hard jolt to the back of the Prime Minister's neck. He hadn't been expecting anything to happen so quickly.

They rode down the long drive to the main gate surrounded by gloomy pines still dripping from that morning's rain shower. The police had blocked off the road to the distillery so they'd meet no traffic, and The Queen turned the cart up that way, keeping the pony at a trot as the animal pulled uphill, but allowing him to walk at the top. As the cart went more slowly, the Prime Minister was suddenly more aware of the silence and birdsong, and having nothing in particular in the way of small talk to share with the cart's driver, he decided to go straight to business. "Ma'am, there are one or two matters which I have to discuss with you."

"Oh yes?" said The Queen. She was mildly surprised. Usually the business part of a Prime Minister's visit took place around the drinks hour before supper on the Saturday night. Then they could both sit down comfortably in front of the coal fire and discuss whatever matters he'd brought along in the dispatch boxes. However, this one was new and didn't know the form yet. She was prepared to talk now, however, and she bid him continue with a nod of her head.

"Well, Ma'am, it's the royal train. The upkeep is considerable. I'm afraid we're going to have to consider decommissioning it."

With a sudden unexpected surge of anger, The Queen remembered the private secretary had warned her that the Prime

Minister might bring this up. It was part of her recent forgetfulness that this had taken her by surprise. She was grumpy with herself, and furious with him at this new attack on her dignity.

"What do you mean?" she said angrily.

"Ma'am, the Government can no longer advise your continuing to use such an expensive, and, may I say, unusually luxurious, form of transport."

"But the Privy Purse already pays for part of it. The Government only subsidizes those journeys on which I go on public business. Most of those journeys are advised and approved by you! If you want me to run up to Doncaster at nine in the morning to open a new hospital, no picnic, may I add, how am I to get there?"

"Other forms of transport will have to be found, Ma'am. It's too expensive for a modern monarchy."

"The monarchy does not exist to be modern, Prime Minister," said The Queen acidly. She directed the pony along a gravel shortcut which had the Prime Minister bouncing up and down on his wooden seat. She could see with satisfaction that he had gripped the side of the cart to hang on.

She thought it was best to control herself, and the cart, before things got out of hand. She'd found that yoga helped her contain her emotions and modulate her anger. Her yoga instructor had even given her a pamphlet which, unusually, she'd read from cover to cover, on Swami Vivekananda. He had been responsible for the spread of yoga as a philosophical ideal as well as a physical practice in the nineteenth century. The Queen had been surprised to read that Vivekananda believed

that all religions were true and that by serving man one could also serve God. She was aware that modern Britain was peopled with believers in many more different religions than it used to be. Vivekananda's teachings appealed to her mostly inarticulate Church of England sense of how it was right to behave, and thus offered a possible way forward with other religions too. So she at once began to take her yoga practice more seriously. But she'd have to learn a lot more patience from Swami Vivekananda if she were to deal calmly with prime ministers, like this one, who seemed always to want to chip away at the foundations of the monarchy.

"Popular opinion is against excessive spending on the monarchy," the Prime Minister continued, raising his voice above the rattle of the wheels on the rough road, and looking worriedly at the ruts up ahead. "As you know, the approval ratings of the entire royal family dropped dramatically during the days of the troubles in the Wales marriage, and of course at the Princess of Wales's death. Although the numbers have begun to recover somewhat, certainly since the Jubilee of '02, the Government cannot advise your continuing to travel by private train in the light of adverse public opinion."

"Public opinion is fickle, Prime Minister. It changes weekly, monthly, annually. Why, in three years it will have altered altogether. Beyond recognition. The public will demand a new train to be built, and at vast new expense. It will be impossible then. Unaffordable. And I'll be stuck on my way to Doncaster in a pony cart." Then, taking aim at what she took to be his most vulnerable side, she added, "You'll be out by then."

Surrounded as all recently arrived prime ministers are by public relations advisers with the ability to say yes in the most charming way, it was the first time anyone had dared suggest to him that he might be out of office in so little a time as three years. He turned to look at The Queen in shock.

Only months after he'd arrived in Basra to serve with British forces in the Iraq War, Luke Thomason's commanding officer had asked him to coordinate the visit of an American unit from Karbala. The high commands of the two armies had thought it a good idea that there should be some small-scale exchanges between the two forces to learn some of the differences in one another's methods for dealing with the insurgency. Luke came out to meet the arriving Americans, who turned up in two Humvees, with twelve men, a staff sergeant, and one very junior commanding officer, Captain Andrew Brainard. Andy had joined the army in a kind of blind fury after 9/11. It was his senior year in college in St Cloud, Minnesota. He had no idea what he was going to do with an English degree, so 9/11 hit him as if it were his destiny. He'd joined the army, gone quickly through an officer-training program, ended up in Iraq as a newly minted second lieutenant, and been promoted quickly to captain for having—more through reckless enthusiasm than through skill—routed a cell of insurgents responsible for having killed several Americans. He was still in his twenties, but already his unit had lost a significant number of Minnesotan farm kids, and he regarded this diplomatic visit to the Brits as a distraction from the real war. He was shocked by the slackness of Luke's salute when he came out to greet them, as well as by the British officer's drawling "Hello, Yanks!" which came nevertheless with a warm smile.

In the Grenadier Guards, teasing nicknames and slack salutes were all signs of friendliness and good form, so Luke was a bit put out by the American officer's humorless rigidity. They were allies, after all, weren't they? After the initial introductions were made, Luke had suggested, ironically, that perhaps Captain Brainard would like a tour of the British camp, as it was midday and very temperate, he'd just go and call his mad dog so they could be off.

Andy didn't realize that this was a self-deprecating reference to a 1930s cabaret tune. He'd never heard of Noël Coward. He said to Luke incredulously, "How about waiting until sundown, Captain? It's over a hundred degrees Fahrenheit. I'd like to get the men under canvas first, please."

Luke saw immediately that the American officer hadn't caught his musical reference and was inclined to think he was being too clever anyway. The Americans had a reputation in the British forces for being tough, straight-shooting, and also a little slow. Luke was miffed, however, by Andy's implication that he wasn't interested in the welfare of the men.

"Oh, in that case, perhaps you'd like to move your vehicles off our parade ground first, Captain," said Luke. This was another slight joke, as the parade ground was in fact a rocky patch of desert inside the encampment, with earthen walls bulldozed up around the perimeter.

Once again Andy did not understand. "Parade ground? What do you think this war is, Captain, a Fourth of July parade?" Since he was getting hot, and had not received the respectful and formal welcome he was expecting, he decided on some sarcasm with his opposite number. "Are you Brits going to put crepe paper in between the spokes of your Sting-Rays and give us a show?"

Luke had no idea what was entailed in an American Fourth of July parade, but he had heard what he guessed was a slight sneer at "Brits," and a definite slur at "Sting-Rays," whatever those were. Bicycles? Sunglasses? His response was to become icy and more cutting. "No doubt the traditions of the Grenadier Guards, which go back some years before the settling of the American colonies, are somewhat confusing to strangers. What people do in America during July is entirely up to them. We take no notice."

"Oh, sorry, I guess you don't celebrate the Fourth of July. Wasn't a big win for your side, was it?" countered Andy. He did not like being called a "stranger."

"Well, if what we hear from Baghdad is correct, I don't think the current American approach to the insurgency will produce a very big win for your side here. You behave like cowboys with the locals. Round 'em up and shoot 'em up. *Yee haw.*" Luke tried saying this with his notion of how cowboys might sound at a cattle roundup. To Andy's ears it sounded like "*Ye whore.*" "They won't thank you for it in the long run," Luke finished, laughing at this because he quite intended Andy to understand the insult.

Andy did understand the insult. Because he'd already witnessed the bloodshed firsthand, lost men in his unit, and had to write letters home to grieving parents, he was not for a second going to accept this from some Brit with a bad salute who appeared to him to be dishonoring the dead. He looked Luke in the eye a second and said in a whisper, "You fucking take that back."

Luke was surprised that the American had so quickly lost his temper during their verbal sparring. In his regiment, coolness was all. "Goodness me, calm down, my dear."

"My dear" in the Grenadier Guards counted as the silliest of *Monty Python* style insults. It was, if anything, faintly self-mocking and wasn't an attack on Andy's manhood, which was, however, precisely how Andy understood it. He thought Luke was saying that he was gay. It was enough of a trigger for him, who no longer had the words to deal with this superior-sounding Englishman, to tackle Luke at the knees. Luke fell with a hard thump and a cloud of dust in the sand. Luke was so surprised to be physically assaulted that at first he didn't know what was happening as Andy started pummeling him in the ribs. He managed to roll over and bring his arms up to protect his head. Unlike the play fights he'd had in the barrack hallways in Germany, this fight was real. Andy rolled with him and kept searching for a way of giving him painful blows to the body. He didn't intend to harm the head.

As the two men rolled on the ground and kicked up dust, Andy's men came pouring out of the Humvees and gathering round, though at a safe distance, as they knew there might be hell to pay for witnessing a fight between two officers. "Fight! Fight!" they yelled delightedly. "Kick his ass." "Get him, Brainard!" The American sergeant began corraling the men, inwardly amazed that the junior officer could have been so stupid as to make such a display in front of the men, which was about the worst thing possible for keeping them in line.

After several minutes of tussling, Luke's commanding officer came up to the two men struggling on the ground. "Captain Thomason!" he said, loud enough to be heard over the noise of the fight. It was enough to make Luke stop resisting and to accept Andy's final blow, before Andy realized what had happened and stopped fighting. He looked up to find a British major saluting him with the kind of formal, angular gesture of his hand and elbow he'd been expecting all along. He was briefly torn between helping Luke back to his feet and jumping up to return the salute. He stood up, leaned over to give Luke his hand, pulled him up, and then turned smartly to salute the British major.

After that, Luke and Andy became friends. They planned maneuvers together. They listened to lectures together. They deciphered maps together. They tried to figure out computer software for the weapons systems that often malfunctioned together. Outside of duty hours, they spotted one another lifting weights in the gym. They got on the cardio equipment and ran in place until their T-shirts were soaked with sweat. They exchanged playlists of their favorite music to listen to on their iPods. Their favorite thing to do was to play video games. They had each taught the other the rules of their national sport: “Football,” Luke said. “Soccer,” said Andy, refusing to retreat. “Better than American football,” said Luke. “No, it’s just ‘football,’ not ‘American football,’ ” said Andy, standing his ground. They saved their best jabs for when the video games grew heated. “You fucking take that back,” Luke would say in an accent that was part Arnold Schwarzenegger and part Bruce Willis. Andy replied in a voice drawn from somewhere between Austin Powers and Harry Potter, “Goodness me, calm down, my dear.”

Lady Anne Bevil was amazed by the multiplication of coffee shops all over London in a short period of time. The clever, won’t-take-no-for-an-answer Americans had been first with what she called “the Starbucks,” because she thought it had something to do with a species of deer in the Pacific Northwest. She thought they must be different from the variety she saw often in Aberdeenshire. After the Starbucks got their foothold, Costa Coffee, Caffé Nero, and Prêt à Manger had rapidly followed. Now these coffee shops, and half a dozen more just like them, could be found all up and down the King’s Road, not far from her flat in Tite Street. She had first stopped in one of them out of idle curiosity, and found the shop populated by the young, tapping away on their laptop computers, listening to music on earphones, and reading from a stack of used, but current, newspapers kept in a central bin. No waitresses. She walked in prepared to command attention, as she had been taught by her parents to enter all retail establishments. She approached a scruffy young man behind the counter. "I'd like a cup of coffee, please." She looked around doubtfully and wondered whether she'd be allowed to stay if she hadn't brought her computer. "How does it work?" she asked him, a little more fiercely than was necessary.

The young man examined his customer with a glance, and quickly saw that this white-haired woman with the imperious manner didn't want questions about soy or skinny or grande or latté. "Is it a filter coffee you want, then?"

"Yes," said Anne, feeling that there was no other kind, but aware that in this foreign territory there probably were many other kinds. "With a little warm milk on the side, please."

"Won't be two secs," said the young man.

Anne was surprised that he was not only friendly but prompt. It was a vast change from London coffee bars of, say, not more than twenty years ago, when the service had usually been sullen, unwilling, and female. She paid for the coffee, took a used newspaper out of the bin, and sat in a comfortable leather armchair. She was shocked to see that people didn't move on after twenty minutes. Apparently, the price of one cup of coffee brought you the rental of an armchair and a free newspaper for as long as you liked, the whole morning if you wished.

She got in the habit of coming in at mid-morning when she wasn't "in waiting" at the palace and staying for two hours at a time. She stopped taking in the morning newspaper, as she could read one without paying for it at the coffee shop. She was always looking for economies, and discontinuing *The Times* was a pleasure, as it read more and more like one of the tabloid newspapers anyway. She liked being surrounded by the young, who were usually transfixed by what was taking place on their computer screens. One or two of the regulars began to recognize the old lady who came in wearing an indestructible tweed skirt and sturdy shoes. They'd smile at her in a glazed way, and she'd smile back, happy enough to be in their company without any conversation.

She'd not only married late, but also had a child late, a single son, whom she brought up when she was already in her late thirties and early forties. His name was Dickon, an old-fashioned shortening of Richard, sometimes found in the Middle Ages in references to King Richard III. As her marriage hadn't been wonderful, the boy Dickon was in many ways the best thing that had ever happened to her. Born to a life of historic country houses and ample flats in London, she'd never known any ambition to improve her physical surroundings or her social set. With the birth of her boy came ambition for the first time. She wanted this little boy to be happy, successful in the world, and admired by all eyes. She adored him.

Dickon had first prospered in the glow of all this maternal attention, and then gradually come to find it suffocating. She supervised playtimes with his friends from school more than other mothers, and was quick to censure interests or pastimes that didn't fit with her ideas of what a boy from one of the country's first families should do with his life. Every male on her father's side of the family had had some sort of military career before going on either to farming or local government. On her mother's side, they were journalists and businessmen before entering national politics. She thought a brief spell in the army was what was best for Dickon after he finished school and began steering him in that direction well before he was twelve. Dickon at first didn't mind dressing up in uniforms, marching in step, and visiting museums which showed the vermin at the bottom of the trenches during the First World War. He also liked the outdoors, and was quite happy building forts in the woods when they visited country relations, collecting caterpillars and taking samples of odd varieties of tree bark. "Botanizing," was what his mother called this, and he could hear the faintly amused contempt somewhere in the back of her voice. It was the first of the really difficult, warring times between them. He began to be interested in environmental politics, which she associated with unshaven anarchists. There were terrible arguments as he entered his teens and fought for his independence.

Anne fought back with the only weapon she'd ever acquired for warfare within her family, the slashing tease that she'd experienced herself growing up in an aristocratic household. She recalled vividly when she'd been allowed to come down from the nursery for the first time to dine with the adults. She had on a long sparkling dress which she was proud of and had spent days admiring in front of the mirror. She walked into the dining room to a chorus of murmured approval from her parents' guests, only to hear the woman to her father's right say, "She *is* a beauty, but that dress is a bit Hollywood, don't you think?" The table had chortled mildly, but Anne rouged to her eardrums. Now she directed the same thing at Dickon, with a mixture of love and cruelty. He'd bought a pair of American denim overalls to attend his first rock concert outdoors during a weekend at Glastonbury. "Are you planning on baling hay, darling, or listening to the music?" Anne had asked with an air of unconcern as he presented himself to his mother for her approval before going off with his friends.

Soon Dickon was going absent without leave from his public school to join demonstrations in London against genetically modified corn, and in favor of sustainable, small-scale agriculture. She read him the riot act and told him he must finish school. This decided him against it, and he disappeared from the school to join a group of activists who were living in makeshift tree houses to block the construction of a highway bypass. The headmaster got wind of where Dickon had gone, but the school soon lost touch with him altogether, and so did Anne. He didn't respond to the phone calls she made to the mothers of his friends. He had no mailing address. He no longer came home. He had the income from a small trust fund that had become his at age eighteen. He was gone.

Anne did her best to conceal this grief from everyone she knew, keeping her answers vague when people asked about Dickon. It was about this same time that the doctors had diagnosed her rheumatoid arthritis, and she was convinced that the emotional and the physical malaises were connected. The coffee shop soothed her because the scruffy young man at the counter reminded her of Dickon the last time she'd seen him. The other young people seemed to tolerate and accept and even to acknowledge her presence in a way that her son had increasingly refused to do in their last years together. She liked that too.

Then one morning as she was nursing her lukewarm coffee and reading the paper she came across an article about Greenpeace. Activists in pontoon boats had been harassing Japanese whaling vessels to protest their killing endangered species of whales. A photograph showed a daring pass by one of these pontoon boats, which was dashing just in front of the prow of the much larger whaling ship. The larger vessel would have cut the pontoon boat in two had they collided. The caption to this photo read: "Dickon Bevil commanded the Greenpeace protest against the Japanese whaling ships Wednesday."

She was seized by a moment of terror that slowly became a moment of pride. What he'd done reminded her of the feats of courage that had often been spoken of when she was growing up. Charging machine guns, parachuting behind enemy lines, escaping from the German prison at Colditz: these were all daring acts that had been performed by family members in the last century in the two World Wars, and they were part of Bevil family lore. Here was Dickon taking his place in that story. She took out a used envelope from her handbag and began drafting a letter to him. "My darling Dickon," she wrote, using the same legible hand she used in The Queen's correspondence. No, that wasn't right. It ignored too much of the ill feeling that had grown up between them. "Dear Dickon," she started again, but that was too heartbreakingly common for the beginning of a letter to an only son. How could she be friendlier? She'd once had a cleaner who'd sometimes left her cheerful notes that began "Hi Lady Anne!" so she tried that, "Hi Dickon," but, no, it was hopeless. Didn't sound like her at all. She crumpled up the envelope, gathered her things together, and walked unseeingly out of the shop and onto the street.

Eton had the unusual distinction at the turn of the twenty-first century of being one of Britain's most famous public schools, not because it was public, because it wasn't; nor for sending more of its boys on to Oxford and Cambridge than any other school, which it didn't. It was still costly to send a boy there for the usual five years between the ages of thirteen and eighteen, but there were many more boys there on scholarship than ever before in its history. It was also more diverse than at any other time in its history, but that wasn't the reason most parents tried to get their boys in. It was because more future prime ministers had gone there than to any other school in Britain. It was because the Duke of Wellington once offhandedly remarked, nearly two hundred years ago, that the Battle of Waterloo had been won on the playing fields of Eton. It was because many were under the impression that the boys still wore top hats.

The school was laid out along an eighteenth-century high street down the hill and across the river from Windsor Castle.

Tourists poured out of buses and trains twelve months a year to go through the public rooms of the Castle, but they almost never took notice of the school not more than a few hundred yards away. Eton had a gothic chapel that was the equal of St George's Chapel within the Castle walls. It had boys walking up and down in white tie, tail coats, and square-toed motorcycle boots, which they were allowed to wear under their striped trousers. It had playing fields laid out along the towpath bordering the river. Although there were no rules to prevent outsiders coming to see it, outsiders almost never did. The boys themselves sloped around Windsor in semi-disguise after hours, wearing the same low-hanging jeans, trainers, and baseball caps akimbo that other boys their age also wore. After four in the afternoon, when the dress rules were relaxed, an Eton boy who happened to be in Windsor trying to buy a sticky bun or a forbidden can of lager was as hard to pick out as a leopard in the jungle with his spots.

It was to this school and this society that Rajiv's parents and grandparents were thrilled to learn that he had been admitted. This was Britain's *ne plus ultra*. Now the family had indisputably arrived. When he got there, Rajiv found otherwise. First, all his new acquaintances started calling him "Paki bastard." It was affectionate, he knew that. Their method was to use the most appalling invective they could imagine as a way of being friends with him, but it revived memories every time they did it of the bad incident when he was younger in a Holborn alley. He told no one about that. It would have been against the boys' unspoken code to bring up any real racial grievance.

Second, when he was included in a group of boys invited up the hill to visit the Castle and dine in the private apartments of one of The Queen's senior courtiers (his grandson was the same year and in the same house as Rajiv), he found that Eton didn't protect him from the ignorance or the narrow nationalism of the older generation. The courtier had begun by assuming that Rajiv would know the geography of postcolonial Simla, where the courtier had spent many happy summers while working with the Indian army. "Haven't been there, sir," said Rajiv politely.

"Not been there?" said the courtier. "Why, it's the most beautiful mountaintop spot in all the world."

"Ah yes, sir, no doubt. But, you see, I was born here." All the boys addressed men older than themselves, their teachers of course, but all others too, as "sir."

"Mother came to Blighty to find a decent hospital and have you, I bet."

"No, sir. She was born here too."

"What?"

"Both of my parents were, sir. We're British."

"But you're Indian, surely?" he said, looking confusedly over Rajiv's head.

"Well, my passport is British. My grandparents on both sides came here from India after the Second World War, but my parents were born here."

The courtier said to himself, "But you're still foreign," at the same time as he said genially to Rajiv, "Have some more of this Côtes du Rhône, boy. It's delicious."

Rajiv could read both the spoken and the unspoken messages

on the man's face. He also knew the Côtes du Rhône was not the best wine in the courtier's cellar. He'd been pawning his second-rate stuff off on the visiting boys. Rajiv knew a thing or two about throwing parties, as he was one of the most popular boys of his year. He kept a constant supply of Diet Coke, beef jerky, Mars bars, and fizzy water in fruity flavors in his bedroom. It made his small room, with its narrow bed and wooden desk, the place of first resort for most of the boys in his house, who preferred to be crowded there in a warm fug, laced with constant ribaldry and laughter, than in the unheated and lonely quarters assigned to them. Rajiv did not forget what the courtier had said to him, and repeated it in an elaborately posh accent to his friends, complete with exaggerated facial expressions. It became one of the boys' favorite stories. It sometimes rankled, nonetheless, and he did not dare tell his parents or his grandparents, because it would have upset them.

Rajiv was completely immune to the passions and romances that went on among the adolescent boys. They teased him about being from the "Sotadic Zone," as India lay in a geographic region, so they'd been taught in a course on global history, where homosexuality was relatively tolerated, especially as compared to the Christian West. But in fact he didn't find the boys at school remotely appealing. Their sisters were different. He was wild for them, and though he knew exactly what jokes and insults to use in speaking to their brothers, he constantly said the wrong thing when he was introduced to girls his own age. "You're *so* sexy!" he said to one demure sister, and her brother cringed at how badly Rajiv had put his foot wrong. He'd been made fun of by the boys, and told not to do it again, but his next outing was just as bad. On the Fourth of June, an annual school festival that celebrated the birthday of the school's most famous patron, King George III, a whole commuter train full of sisters and female cousins and girl friends of friends took the line down from London Waterloo to the Windsor & Eton Riverside railway station. The girls were all dressed in the slatternly fashion of the times and vied to show as much breast and thigh as was possible within the bounds of decency, which shocked most of the adults present as entirely indecent. Here Rajiv would have been well within the bounds of reason and frank assessment if he'd said to any number of girls, "You look *so* sexy!" Instead, he tried "You're so beautiful," and "You look incredible." Neither of these worked any better. The male verbal style the girls were willing to reply to was ironic, yawning, and laconic. Dozy was the thing. Although the girls had tried hard to put their clothes together, it was not done for the boys to comment on what they looked like. At Rajiv's overly serious compliments they just giggled and turned away. He hadn't understood, and he couldn't imitate the correct form. He was too keen.

William de Morgan had entered the Royal Household by working first for The Queen's sister and then for her mother before arriving at the pinnacle of royal service, working for the sovereign herself. It was the palace version of trying out a show in Boston or Philadelphia before putting it on Broadway. To have survived working some years for Princess Margaret or Queen Elizabeth, demanding engagements in their own right, established pretty clearly a member of staff's discretion, talent, and staying power in the face of many provocations.

Among her friends, Princess Margaret was legendary for being an impossible houseguest. If she didn't have a whiskey and water in her hand by half past six of an afternoon, there might be several ugly incidents at the supper that followed. She had to have a canopied bed, and she had to have guest lists well in advance, from which she often crossed off people whom she didn't like. She'd never had proper work to do. She'd been happier among the stylish and the hedonistic than among the dutiful and the self-sacrificing set that surrounded her sister. She was her sister's exact opposite. She was covertly jealous of her elder sister's position, while pretending all the time that she was assisting in keeping it up.

Princess Margaret had detected right away in William's interview with her a prissy earnestness that she might have fun playing with, as a cat plays with a vole before killing it. Of course he came well recommended from all the best places. His excellence as a butler was not in question. Her own ability to live with him in her private rooms was what she wanted to know about, because, frankly, the servants knew everything. Hiring a man to be in and out of all the rooms in your house at all hours of the day was a little like sleeping with him. She first met him at the cocktail hour in her sitting room in Kensington Palace. She sat and didn't ask him to join her, so he stood, not exactly at attention, but at a respectful distance from her. "And what was it like working for the sheik?" she said, fishing for some gossip she might retail at a dinner party later on.

"Well . . ." William replied, aware that what he said would be repeated, and not wishing to compromise his former employer in any serious way, " . . . they had quite a lot of gold leaf on the ceiling."

"Have you seen the new state rooms at Windsor? The ones done up since the fire? Acres and acres of gold leaf. If you walk in on a sunny day you've got to wear your dark glasses. It might be Miami Beach."

William gave this a small quarter smile. To laugh at it too openly would only have been all right if he had been sitting down and he were an HRH at the least.

Princess Margaret allowed a pause to fall. She swirled the ice cubes around down at the bottom of her glass, ruminating.

Giving her a warmer, and slightly more conspiratorial, smile than he'd given her before, William said, "I daresay Your Royal Highness could use a top-up as this important decision is considered."

At this she smiled more naturally, and held out her glass. He took it from her and went to the bar at the side of the room to fill it up. As he was making her drink, she called out to his back, "Nothing to decide. You're engaged." Then she paused to consider. She did like to drink, it was true, but she wasn't entirely happy with the fact that William had worked this out so quickly. "Oh, and by the way, don't let me catch you in the closet trying on my shoes."

William was glad he had his back to her when she said this, because it took him by surprise, and he needed a moment to clear the stricken look from his face. As a boy, he had adored sneaking into his mother's closet to put on her high-heeled shoes and to pose in front of the long mirror wearing them. They made him feel taller, more elegant, more desirable in his own eyes. No one had ever caught him at it, nor had he gone in for dressing up in ladies' clothes much beyond his boyhood. For most of his career he'd been working, and he hadn't had the time.

He turned to bring her the drink with his face a mask of clear unconcern. "No, Ma'am."

"Nor my frocks," she said, still hoping with patient malice to get a rise from him.

"No, indeed."

"There are one or two furs of course."

"Are there, Ma'am?"

"You mustn't try them on either."

"No."

"Nor the *parfum*." She thought she might get him with the odd surprise word in French.

"I promise."

"I see," she said with a reluctant sigh. "That will be all."

William withdrew to the double doors, and just as he was about to reverse through them, closing them with a small bow, he came back into the room as if he'd forgotten something. "What size did you say you were, Ma'am?" Then he closed the doors and she let out a delighted whoop, slapping the velvet pillow at her side.

When, several years later, one of Queen Elizabeth's butlers died, William was recruited to fill the spot. She had a reputation for being sweet as a sugar plum, but in fact the old Queen was tough and didn't mind stealing away the best staff from her younger daughter, if need be. Princess Margaret had grown used to this kind of behavior from her mother, so when William came in to make his farewell, she said simply, "Rat," and dismissed him with a wave of her hand that might have been either angry or affectionate.

The Queen Mother's parties were often as gay as her younger daughter's had been. Among the regular guests were bachelor biographers, gossip columnists for the highbrow newspapers, and disgraced curators from the Victoria and Albert Museum. The staff was gayer still. William enjoyed working in Clarence House for Queen Elizabeth, but it hadn't been an easy posting. She liked anything that was an extreme statement of style, so large luncheons on warm days were often moved impromptu to underneath a large spreading shade tree in the garden. Beautiful to look at from the terrace windows, but it was a lot of work at the last minute to get the table on a level out there on the uneven turf. She was a demanding but also a charming boss, referring to "this intolerable honour" if anyone happened to refer to her position. Usually only the unschooled did this, as her staff knew the topics to avoid. Working with a cadre of high-strung and extremely touchy gay men had been one of the biggest challenges of his career. Even though he was gay himself, it was hard to know what stray comment would set his colleagues off. They tended to be harsher and more judgmental about gay staff than about the occasional straight waiter who was brought in as a temporary for a big occasion. All of these colleagues were talented, and some were good-looking, but William wasn't in the least attracted to them. Something about their love of drama entirely put him off them as romantic partners.

When Queen Elizabeth died, in 2002, The Queen cherry-picked the youngest of her mother's staff to come over to Buckingham Palace. The older ones were pensioned off. When William arrived in the big house, he looked about him with a sense of pride. He'd now reached the top of his profession. With any luck, he'd be allowed to stay, and possibly to reach retiring age himself working for The Queen. There was no question that the work would be a challenge, but he was also confident he could do it. What he now hoped to do was to look about himself and to find some real friends at work, to fill some of the emotional need he'd sometimes repressed when working at his other posts. Almost immediately he met Shirley MacDonald, and although she was fifteen years older than him, she was just like him in having given her life to the job and her caring every day about doing it well. Most afternoons he made an excuse to stop by the room where she was pressing clothes with a steam iron. They'd have a little gossip about what was going on. Who on the staff was in trouble, who was in favor, and who was out? This progressed to their having a regular Saturday evening on their calendar whenever they were both in London. They'd go to an Indian restaurant off Victoria Street for a curry early in the evening and then often afterwards see a film. The films they enjoyed most had something to do with their jobs, so they'd loved seeing Judi Dench playing Queen Victoria in *Mrs Brown*, and Cate Blanchett playing the first Queen Elizabeth. They'd also seen a kind of pseudo-documentary about life in a Russian palace called *The Russian Ark*, which confused and stimulated them at the same time. Their all-time favorite was the film where a butler and a housekeeper of an aristocratic house before the war fell in love, but didn't ultimately get together, *The Remains of the Day*. They liked it not because they thought it referred to their relationship with one another, although they pretended as if it did, but because it captured the dedication and self-denial that both of them felt in their work together at the palace. Their interpretation was exactly the reverse of the disapproval the filmmakers had intended.

Their being entirely of one mind about most of the films they saw together was what brought William up short one day when he proposed their seeing another together one Saturday. It was called *The Adventures of Priscilla, Queen of the Desert*. It was about three drag queens in the Australian outback, and the elaborate rituals of makeup and dressing-up that went into their performances. William never talked about being gay with Shirley. He assumed she knew. Nor did he discuss his dressing up as a boy in front of his mother's mirror. He'd had reason to believe she wouldn't be shocked. That's why he was surprised that when he proposed it, Shirley had said abruptly, "No."

"But why not? It sounds fun."

"No, definitely not. Horrid. Disgusting. I'm not seeing it," said Shirley in a voice that brooked no further discussion.

It was as if his closest friend had just slapped him in the face.

Rebecca Rinaldi grew up in the country and went to a comprehensive school that had no claim to distinction whatsoever. Few of its students went on to university, and Rebecca herself knew from an early age that her own talents lay elsewhere than in reading books or studying for research degrees. She brought up bantams that lived under the iron roof of a dilapidated shed on her parents' farm. There were no fences, and the whole property was easily accessible to foxes, which quite regularly made off with one of the birds. Suffering this loss, even though it happened often, was like losing a member of her family for the first twenty-four hours, but then she was fascinated to see how the loss of one hen or cock led to a rearrangement of the pecking order of the entire roost. She also looked after a flock of geese, a group of nearly feral cats, a pony, and a thoroughbred horse that had been retired and put out in the Rinaldis' pasture for a small rental fee by their much richer racing neighbors. Each one of these animals inspired greater respect and affection in Rebecca than any human being she'd ever met outside her mother and father.

Even her parents were a trial sometimes. They were vegetable farmers who considered themselves above the law. They discovered early on the value of fresh manure in increasing the yield of their small holdings of carrots, onions, turnips, and beets. So they took their rusting van to the stables at the racecourse, to the neighboring pig farm, and even to the man who provided port-a-loos to the outdoor concerts at Glastonbury, collected the fragrant soil in plastic tubs and stacked the tubs in the back of their van. This was completely against the health and safety regulations which governed the fertilization of foods raised for human consumption, but Rebecca's parents gloried in their flouting of the law and in their embrace of what they saw as the most natural, sustainable, and organic way possible of raising root vegetables.

One by-product of this carting of so much manure was that the family van, in which Rebecca was also driven to school, smelled pungently of dung and, downwind, could be scented coming a hundred yards away. This led to merciless teasing of Rebecca by her schoolmates, who, with adolescent lack of imagination and infant fascination with feces, called her "Poo." In school she was as untouchable as the member of a leper colony. Even the kindest of her fellow students hesitated to reach out to her. If they had, her fierce pride would have made her issue a rebuff.

When she finished school, she had no idea what she would do next. Because her parents were active proponents of organic farming, they'd happened to meet the Prince of Wales who, like them, cared about sustainable agriculture. They mentioned Rebecca's love of riding and her excellence at taking care of the retired thoroughbred, whose owners the Prince also knew. There happened to be a vacancy at the Royal Mews and Rebecca was appointed via the influence of the heir to the throne. She got on well there. There was a tiny studio flat, what used to be called a bedsitter, with a sink, a small fridge in the corner, and a shared shower down the hall that went with the job. No one in the Mews cared or remarked upon her smell, as the care and disposal of horse manure was a pretty constant part of the job. She didn't have friends in the Mews, nor did she keep everyone there at such angry arm's length as she had in school. It was one of the contrasts of her young life, too young for her to remark on it even, that although no one had addressed more than three or four friendly words to her at school, she now occasionally had casual conversations with The Queen. Her only threatened humiliation was that her parents were convinced that manure from the royal stables was likely to be even richer than what they currently collected, and they were always devising schemes, which Rebecca had to thwart, of taking it away with them when they visited her.

Although she had lost many of her bantams to foxes, she was not a friend to foxhunting, which she thought of as giving license to privileged people to engage in cruelty to animals. Three years before she began working at the Mews, while she was still in school, she had attended an antihunting demonstration in Trafalgar Square, where she happened to meet one of the speakers. He denounced the methods used by those who facilitated foxhunting by killing badgers. The badgers themselves sometimes killed fox cubs, so they were considered enemies by friends of the hunt. He was a passionate speaker. He had a young badger which got the crowd's attention, and Rebecca met him when he came off the platform after his speech. Or, rather, she got over her fear of him and slight attraction to his passionate way of denouncing the slaughter of badgers, by wanting to meet the badger he had in his arms. The young man with the badger thought Rebecca was beautiful. Her red hair and shyness and unconcealed delight at holding the animal made it difficult for him to ignore her.

Rebecca knew how to hold the badger, but she had no idea how to handle the young man. He was ten years older than her, and he was the first man who'd ever paid her any attention. Some kind of instinct, which she thought it was better to obey, made her curious about why he found her so fascinating. She was more than a little wary of him, but she could answer the questions he put to her by dwelling on the animal in her arms. He had an alert way of looking at her that she half suspected, from watching the mating behavior of cocks and hens, would lead to his trying to mount her. They'd gone to his flat. He'd served her wine with supper. She saw by the way he started touching her, more than was strictly necessary, that he wanted to have sex. A better-socialized young woman might have resisted more. Rebecca gave in easily because she was unsure of the rules that governed human romantic interaction. She'd been told by her mother that her extensive experience on horseback would make her first sexual experience easy, but the encounter was physically painful, made more unpleasant because she hadn't expected it. He could see she was in distress and was gentle with her, but the damage was done, and she drew away from him to the edge of the bed. This was something he would not allow. He murmured apologies and encouragement into her ear, wrapped her in a white sheet and put his arm around her middle, spooning her protectively from behind, until he could hear her breathing become less frightened and more regular. She awoke a few hours later and briefly forgot his brutality at this first feeling she'd ever had of human intimacy with a man who was not of her own family. It was nearly like being returned to the warmth and security of the cradle. It was marvelous.

Then she recollected where she was and what had happened. She felt like a trapped mink that must gnaw off its paw to escape from an iron trap. She couldn't even conceive of wanting to do ever again what they'd done a few hours before. She disengaged herself from the man as stealthily as was possible. Once free, she slipped back into her discarded clothes. She collected her backpack and crept out of the door, still under the cover of night. She walked all the way from the Elephant to Waterloo, where she still had time to catch the last train to a village near enough to her parents' farm that she could walk there when she arrived. She was sure she would never hear from him again. She was relieved to be escaping without a trace. She forgot she'd signed his petition to ban foxhunting and written down her mobile phone number on the form for submission to Parliament.

To be The Queen's senior dresser was, along with the senior butler, housekeeper, and cook, to be among the four most elevated positions anyone could reach on the royal staff. Shirley MacDonald's grandmother and mother were proud of her, but it sometimes embarrassed her. Her granny had been a maid of all work, a kind of dogsbody, who toward the end of her career looked after linens. Her mother had worked in the royal kitchens, and though she too had served long, she never rose high in the outmoded Victorian hierarchy of servants, which still held sway at the palace. They were now all called "members of staff," but their history of being servants was still very much just under the surface of their daily lives.

Shirley's mother had died relatively young, overcome by smoking, long hours, and a series of husbands and boyfriends who had disappointed her. Shirley had no other siblings and her relationship to her granny was the last remaining tie she had to her family. She would occasionally go for holidays at the cottage on the Balmoral estate that her grandmother had been given as part of her retiring benefit. Although she was well into her seventies, her grandmother insisted on doing extra duty at the Castle. Shirley was aware, from staying with her granny, that she was neither as sharp nor as able as she'd once been. All the kitchen surfaces were sticky. The plastic flowers had a permanent layer of dust on them. The cotton bathroom mats in cheerful colors smelled faintly of pee. Shirley would do what she could to clean up when she went to visit, but she had to do it discreetly, because if she were discovered doing spot cleaning, her grandmother would take offense.

Shirley would also accompany her granny to the Castle to do a few hours of work, because she knew that she could not do the work she once could. Shirley had also heard via the palace grapevine that the serving full-time staff sometimes had to redo her grandmother's work and were annoyed by it. So one summer day, in the run-up to The Queen's arrival in mid-August, with the Castle gearing up for the longest formal residence of the year, Shirley and her grandmother drove up the South Deeside Road, parked in the staff car park, and went upstairs to complete an inventory of the bedsheets, pillow slips, and towels. Shirley was on a stepladder counting the sets of sheets that were folded into crisp, symmetrical squares on one of the top shelves in the linen cupboard. Her grandmother was standing below, making small checks on a folded piece of paper. The first Shirley knew that something was wrong was when she heard her grandmother say, "Oof," and saw her lean back heavily on the doorjamb.

"What's the matter, Granny?"

"Nothing's the matter. Carry on. Where are we? Six top sheets. All Queen Victoria? Or some King George V?" The sheets had embroidered monograms in the corners and had been folded in such a way as to make the monogram easy to locate. These monograms identified the reign in which the sheets had been acquired. The staff had been trained always to preface the sovereign's name with "King" or "Queen," even though many of these figures were long dead. It was an instinctive sign of respect mixed with a practice that was as antique and old-fashioned as the sheets themselves.

"Look at your forehead, Granny. You're all wet. And it's not even hot in here."

"Never you mind, Shirley. It's the work. Want to get this right."

"Let's have a small break, shall we, Granny?"

"Break? Break! We have to get on. The Queen's coming in two days."

"This can wait, Granny."

Shirley's grandmother now began panting slightly, put down the paper and pencil that had been in her hand, and reached around to rub her shoulder. "Must have put out this joint reaching up to the third shelf just now. Ow."

Men and women of her grandmother's generation never admitted pain or ill health unless they had no time consciously to suppress involuntary groans. If possible, this was even truer of the women than the men, and of Scottish old ladies more than the English. So Shirley knew her grandmother was seriously unwell. "Come, now," she said to her grandmother in a stern voice that allowed no argument, "let's rest a moment here on this bench." She had to be severe with her grandmother because when The Queen was in residence this was a corridor off which the upper members of the Household and guests would be staying, and the bench, strictly speaking, was for them. Ordinarily, if her grandmother had been feeling entirely well, she would have refused to sit there.

The bench had worn tartan cushions supported by deer antlers which served as arms and legs. If you didn't sit carefully, the bench looked as if it might gore you. Shirley and her grandmother sat on the bench, with the old lady still holding her shoulder and unable to get her breath. Shirley massaged her other shoulder, feeling that the bones underneath the blouse and skin were more like those of a bird than of a human skeleton.

Suddenly, to their surprise, a lady-in-waiting appeared, coming down the corridor, wearing a brown corduroy jacket and matching skirt with unflattering cut. "Ah, taking a break, I see.

Things always a bit slack here before Her Majesty arrives." She said this as if she were trying to make pleasant conversation, but it sounded like a rebuke, with a swallowed "Tsk, tsk," at the end of it, just barely audible. The lady-in-waiting had arrived two days early, before her waiting actually started, to go and see some friends in the neighborhood and to make use of the free accommodation she could claim from the imminent start of her duty.

"My grandmother's not feeling well," said Shirley, looking up from the bench with a combination of explanation and appeal.

"Ah, do you know, in *my* grandmother's time you never saw the serv—I mean staff in the corridors. They got up and did the work so early in the morning that it was all done by the time you appeared. My God they were good." She then turned to look at Shirley and said with a slight narrowing of her eyes, "That's all changed now, of course."

"Perhaps when you go downstairs, Mrs d'Arlancourt, you could send us up some help, please," said Shirley. "I don't think I should leave her."

Her grandmother just looked up at the lady-in-waiting with frightened eyes, knowing that something was badly wrong, but unable to say exactly what.

"Oh, yes. Of course, I will. I'll send someone up right away." Then the lady-in-waiting leaned menacingly over Shirley's grandmother and said, "Had a nip too many with your coffee this morning, did you, dear? Don't you worry. Help's on the way!" With that she went on down the staircase at a leisurely pace. The lady-in-waiting had the old English suspicion that most Scots were drunks and thieves, a prejudice that went back as far as Shakespeare, but which, in the circumstances, made Shirley's heart thump with rage.

Help arrived and Shirley's grandmother was taken by ambulance to a hospital in Aberdeen, where she died the next day. A young doctor came and told Shirley, "It was a myocardial infarction. She had hypertension. Her cholesterol was very high," as if that explained the loss of the last living family member whom she had ever loved. Some weeks later, there was a memorial service for Shirley's grandmother at the little Victorian church over the river from the Castle and up a slight rise. The Queen came to this service and sat in the front pew. Letitia d'Arlancourt, whose waiting had begun, sat next to The Queen. Shirley, who sat across the aisle from them as the principal mourner, did not know whether to give in to her anger, or to acknowledge the considerable honor The Queen was bestowing on her. High-colored and angry gratitude was the emotion she managed to convey when The Queen and Letitia d'Arlancourt spoke a few words to her at the door on their way to one of the black Range Rovers drawn up in front of the church.

That was the only moment, fifteen years ago, in which Shirley had ever considered leaving the Royal Household. She was furious with The Queen for tolerating someone like Letitia d'Arlancourt. She blamed not only this particular lady-in-waiting for her bad behavior, but also began to see all the upper levels of the Household as being in league with such as Letitia d'Arlancourt. Rather than take her fury and use it to find a new position, Shirley used it to redouble her efforts on behalf of The Queen. Although she would have been eminently employable elsewhere, Shirley felt a kind of inertia when it came to looking for other work. What came to her more naturally was to take her constant, seldom-abating wrath and to put it into pressing and packing The Queen's clothes, attending her mistress early and late, in a defiant spirit illegible to The Queen herself but which would have read: "I'll be damned if you'll have anything but the best of me even though one of your ladies once did me wrong and I will never forget."

Part III

Child's Pose

A single lamb chop with a thimble full of mint jelly. Three Brussels sprouts. A steamed carrot. A glass of burgundy. That had been The Queen's solitary Monday lunch. The afternoon now stretched ahead of her, unusually free of engagements, but with plenty to attend to on her desk. She stood at the window, looking out on to Buckingham Palace Gardens with the light fast diminishing into the west of the wet December afternoon. She had briefing papers to read for Tuesday, but in the midst of her unusual melancholy, she couldn't bring herself to look at them. It had occurred to her to ask the apothecary whether he might not prescribe some antidepressants. She recalled with shame how little she'd taken it seriously when Diana Wales was suffering from depression. None of them had. In her generation depression was really only something that soldiers returning from battle suffered, "shell shock," yes, but everyone felt dejected every now and again. You didn't take medicine for it. You pulled up your socks. You went for a walk. The whole Diana business had taught her that depression was an illness and that there were drugs that would help if it didn't lift after a month or two of feeling unhappy. Still, she couldn't bring herself to ask the attending physician for these pills. It would have been too humiliating, much worse than asking for more help on the computer. So she fell back on her usual tricks to try and feel better.

It was usually as simple as that old Julie Andrews song. What were her favorite things? There was a mare in the Mews born on her birthday in April. Elizabeth. The horse's name was a bit of a joke really. But The Queen was delighted to discover that Elizabeth would eat cheddar. Not only would she take it from The Queen's hand, but she would snort and stamp and neigh afterwards. Elizabeth adored it.

Now, what else, The Queen asked herself. Well, Scotland of course. People left her alone more there. She went on a Scottish holiday at the end of the summer, and sometimes in May as well. She'd spent some of her honeymoon there too. And the Scots, so bluff, no-nonsense, straightforward, none of the capering about and insincerity she often met with in the South. She loved the Scots, so, yes, Scotland was one of her favorite things too.

What else? *Britannia*, of course. The yacht was now permanently beside a quay in Leith, outside Edinburgh. Tourist attraction. Such a pity, really. She had loved that ship. She'd fly out to the Caribbean, meet some governors, tour the hospital wards, look at the new sewers, and then they could all retire to *Britannia* for a few days, having justified the expense of sailing her out by holding some official dinners on board. How lovely she looked, white and buff and blue, rising up out of the haze on a hot afternoon. And when she became too old, too expensive to run, well the Government absolutely refused to build another yacht. It was that word "yacht," wasn't it? The Queen couldn't appear to waste public money on personal pleasure. She understood that, but she wondered if the newspapers actually knew how many boring Commonwealth suppers she'd had to sit through. If anybody had earned a bit of a treat, she had, what with the endless small talk she'd engaged in on national business. She imagined that about three-quarters of her life had been used up in idle chitchat. Had it ever done any good? And now the yacht was something she couldn't use, or even see, anymore. Tied up for day-trippers to visit at, what, ten pounds a time? Yes, *Britannia* was a favorite thing, but she was far away.

These had been her reflections as she wondered what to do after luncheon. She glanced back at the table, which William had not yet been in to clear away. There was an apple, and yes, a small portion of the cheddar. Walk over to the Mews and take Elizabeth these leftovers. It might help. She wouldn't take the dogs. They might worry the horses. Aside from these careful thoughts about the animals, she wasn't quite thinking as sharply as she usually did. She took the precaution of putting on a headscarf, but she didn't put on a coat, even though it was a wet and windy afternoon. Nor, though she pulled the terrace door to, did she pull it entirely shut so that it would stay latched. She noticed her handbag sitting on the sideboard. Yes, she would take that, and stepped briefly back into the room to hook that over her arm before stepping out again onto the terrace.

The Royal Mews were exhaust-stained buildings behind the palace, with tourist buses rushing by every five minutes, heedless of the romance behind their grey façade. There was a little-visited museum with harnesses and carriages and the big gold wedding cake on wheels that had been used in 1953 at the coronation. The real attraction was the horses, who stood in ample stalls walled with glazed tiles, their names hanging above them on wooden boards: Mossy, Puller, Buster, Elizabeth, and Lucia. These horses' biographies were as familiar to The Queen as those of members of her own family.

The Queen had put the apple and cheddar into her pocket, and when she turned up at the door, wearing only some muddied pumps, from having taken a shortcut through a hedge, and a headscarf, Rebecca, who was hosing down the floor, was a little worried. Not to see The Queen. She often turned up at unexpected times to give the horses treats and to stroke their velvet noses. But it was cold for early December, and other than the scarf over her head, The Queen was not dressed for the weather. That was unusual.

Rebecca coiled the hose and pretended as if the woman who'd just wandered in among Elizabeth's straw and was feeding her cheese was of no particular importance. She briefly considered asking The Queen whether she'd like some of the mud hosed off her shoes, but then thought better of it. As she wound up the hose she heard The Queen remark, "Elizabeth's very well, I see."

"Yes, Ma'am." She did not go in for the "Your Majesty" first, as she'd been taught, nor did curtseying seem necessary in a stable, so she kept her response to a simple affirmative. The Mews were a good deal more informal than the palace, and Rebecca was herself awkward when it came to dealing with beings on two legs instead of four. She did not and could not make an exception for The Queen.

"Are horses ever sad, do you think?" asked The Queen.

Rebecca considered this a strange, but not an uninteresting, question. "Well, Ma'am, they're sometimes out of sorts. Sometimes they won't feed. Or they're not friendly to the brush."

"But they always pull, don't they? They always pull when they're in harness?"

"The young ones don't always, no. But, yes, the older ones don't usually shirk. Something about the bit and the harness wakes them up. It's as if they've a job to do and they're tired of standing about."

"Yes, I know," said The Queen.

Rebecca wasn't sure whether The Queen meant that she'd seen older horses take the bit and harness that way, or that she felt like an old horse in harness herself sometimes. She suspected the latter.

The Queen gave an involuntary shudder, as if she'd just noticed the cold. Elizabeth gave a sympathetic snort. Rebecca suggested, "I've got a hoodie over there. Hanging on that peg. You could wear it back and then have it sent over to me here. You'll need it," she said as a blast of sleet peppered the windows.

The Queen accepted the hooded jacket without protest, instinctively sticking out her hands to have it slipped on her from behind. Rebecca hadn't offered to put the jacket on. She expected The Queen could manage that herself, but when she saw the older woman with her hands outstretched, Rebecca picked up the hoodie and helped The Queen into the sleeves. It had a zippered front with two pockets. She slipped up the hood over her headscarf without The Queen's protesting. Then The

Queen turned around as if she were an obedient child, and Rebecca saw that she was meant to zip it up as well.

Instantly The Queen felt as if returned to some darkened cotton womb. Protected. Anonymous. Warm. She murmured, “Thank you,” giving it two percussive syllables, and wandered off, noticing that the pockets contained a pack of cigarettes, a folded £20 note, and a Swiss army knife.

Rebecca watched The Queen walk off toward the open courtyard in her still muddy shoes, carrying her handbag over the crook of her arm, and wearing her hoodie, which, until now, she'd forgotten had that skull stenciled on the navy material at the back.

Earlier that same afternoon, Rajiv and Rebecca had planned on meeting for coffee. She replied only to one out of every two e-mails he sent her, and still he persisted. Why wouldn't she meet him some afternoon for just twenty minutes? That was the sense of his latest, and she didn't see the point of continuing to ignore so much energy and certainty. Men were so urgent, so unremitting when you gave them the least encouragement. She didn't understand why. She wasn't built that way herself.

She agreed to twenty minutes on a weekday afternoon. He was working at Paxton & Whitfield that Monday. As he couldn't go far, he suggested a coffee place across the street that operated out of an annex of a church, St James's, Piccadilly. He said he'd meet her there. She got there a bit early and looked around the churchyard outside, the wet slate underfoot feeling slippery. She wondered if there were tombs underneath the lettered paving stones. Were people actually buried there or were they just memorials? There were rusting outdoor tables stacked in the corner, waiting for summer. Would people in July have their lattés sitting on someone's grave? Then she looked up to inspect the soot-stained wall of the church. There was a plaque.

The church had been built in 1684. It had been damaged by what was called "enemy action"—funny phrase—in 1940. She guessed a German plane had dropped a bomb. They rebuilt it and a bishop came to reconsecrate the church in 1954.

It was strange to think of London in the 1940s as a battlefield, the bombs raining down night after night, people sleeping in the Tube, then climbing upstairs in the morning to go about their ordinary lives. Here she was, walking in a churchyard, looking up on a dark afternoon to imagine the roof of a church in flames during the Second World War. London was occasionally a battlefield now too. She had tried to go down into the Piccadilly Line at King's Cross on July 7th of 2007 just after a suicide bomber had let off his explosive in one of the trains, killing many people. The police were just arriving to string yellow tape over the entrances and to send people away. She recalled the ambulances pulling in at odd angles to block off the traffic in front of the station.

Rebecca wasn't afraid of terrorists, even though the Metropolitan Police was forever warning people to be on the alert against bombers of all sorts. In the days after the 7/7/07 bombs, Ken Livingstone, the mayor then, had run an advertisement in the Tube stations about how international the victims had been: Australians, Americans, Africans, New Zealanders, people from Europe, in fact a typical cross section of London. It made her proud to be one of them. She sometimes saw that same "spirit of the war" feeling in really old people who recollected what the 1940s were like in London. The outdoor churchyard, the plaque on the wall, the paving stones with nearly illegible lettering that might once have covered coffins in the clay, all this made the spot feel holy.

Just then Rajiv appeared at the glass door of the café in the annex. His amused brown eyes and evident tail-wagging pleasure to see her all wrung a warmer smile for him than she'd quite meant to give him. She thought better of it, and immediately resumed her more neutral expression, looking away from him.

"Don't panic," he said, opening the door for her. "It's only coffee. Come inside."

She smiled again. He had a way of intuiting what she was thinking. She found it disconcerting. "I imagine you're busy at work and will have to get back before too long."

"Hang on a minute, I just got here," said Rajiv as he scraped a chair back along the floor.

"Yes, well, don't get too comfortable."

Rajiv had been a much-loved child. Both his father and mother had shown him unreserved and uncomplicated affection. It was what he had come to expect from the world, so this beautiful young woman's coolness did not deter him. "My God, those boots," he said, for the first time noticing her leather riding boots that came all the way to her knee.

She hadn't thought about dressing to attract him. It was just what she happened to be wearing. Perhaps he thought she'd worn the boots to encourage him, which was the reverse of what she'd intended. She was just there really to see whether there was anything in this young man's persistence. She wasn't attracted to him. She wasn't attracted to anyone much. But she thought that someone who was as interested in her as he was ought to be investigated. "They're not for you," she said defensively. "I've got to take Elizabeth for some exercise after this."

"You're going to ride Elizabeth, then," he said with an arched eyebrow.

She caught the slyness of his remark, looked the other way, and said nothing. She thought it probably wasn't the sort of thing a boy was supposed to say to a girl when they first met, but she wasn't sure.

"Elizabeth for whom you bought the cheddar?" asked Rajiv in his most cheerful voice.

"Mmmm," she assented.

"What is it about young misses and riding?"

She didn't like the direction he was taking and, picking up a paper coffee cup he'd brought to the table for her, said, "If you think I came here to listen to smut, you're wrong."

"Hang on, hang on. I'm sorry for the suggestion. But, you know, it is an interesting question. A young woman breaks her hymen while horseback riding. She never loves men quite as well as she loved her first horse. Is that right? Why is it?"

Something about his use of the word "hymen" indicated to her that he wasn't entirely interested in the erotic dimension of this. As she'd had a hard time being sexually interested in human beings herself, she did stop and reconsider and sit back in her chair. "Well, it has something to do with this enormous animal that will let you climb on her back. And take you all sorts of places. And go at a trot. This big strong thing, twice as tall as you are, which will eat an apple or a sugar cube out of your hand without biting you. Could even kill you with a kick. To be with an animal like that. Well, there's some awe in it, isn't there? And when you see a horse jumping over a fence, all that thousand pounds of grace and point and muscle, well, that's close to some kind of miracle. Afterwards she'll let you come near, sometimes, and put your hand on her neck."

Rebecca surprised him. She didn't speak much. She didn't reply to most of his e-mail messages. Within the first three minutes of his showing up, he had to persuade her to stay. Now, she'd just given him an essay on love and horses. He sensed an opening in her saying "she'll let you." That was the nub of some incipient feeling, which he knew was not shown to everyone. "And people, boys and girls, won't let you do that to them? Stroke their necks?"

Rebecca set her jaw against Rajiv. This was twice he'd wrongfooted her. She'd said much more than she wanted to straightaway. It came from being around animals too much and around people her own age too little. She didn't know how to talk to them. Hitting out at Rajiv with the kind of fear and rage she usually kept veiled, she said, "Look. I'm not for you, all right? I shouldn't have come. I already have a boyfriend." Both her anger and her confession were out of proportion with what he'd just said. Nor was the confession strictly true.

The color rose hot into her cheeks and Rajiv thought she was the most beautiful thing he'd ever seen, like the models for CoverGirl makeup in magazines. He'd once swooned over them as an adolescent boy. He'd even tried kissing one of these beautiful women on the slippery paper in order to practice for the real thing. Her declaration, intended to shove him roughly away, didn't dismay him in the least. "Come on, it's okay," he spoke to her as if she were a frightened pet. He tried to calm her with the sound of his most comforting words. "It's fine. Really it is. Boys and girls can talk without stroking necks. It's all good." He beamed benevolence and good will in her direction.

She gave a brief glance at the wattage emanating from his eyes, and decided she couldn't look there for long. It was too bright.

"Well, I'm not telling you any more about that."

"Don't have to. We can talk about anything you like."

"You talk, then."

"Well, let's see. How did Elizabeth like the cheddar I sent over with you?"

Just then, Rebecca's mobile phone vibrated. She tugged it out of her pocket to see that it was a phone call from the man she'd met three years ago at the animal rights demonstration. "Could you excuse me, please?" she said to Rajiv, a little more harshly than was necessary, but he could see that was her way.

"Don't worry, I'm just going to put some more sugar in my coffee," he said as he stepped away from the table.

Rebecca went back to the phone. She hadn't seen him often. She didn't know him well. When he first called her back, she was shocked that he even had her number. He pointed out with a laugh that she'd put it down on his petition against foxhunting. She thought that was unfair. She hadn't given him her number because she wanted to be his girlfriend. They met again a few weeks later to go to another demo, this one in the country. The disaster that had resulted from that was what really made her uninterested in seeing him again. He'd been in touch occasionally over the years. She'd sometimes agreed to talk to him, but never to see him again. It was not that she couldn't recall some of the promise of sleeping with him in white sheets. It was just that ever since her two jarring experiences with him, she'd distrusted men with easy words. The time with him had also undermined her satisfaction with her life up to now, based as it was on solitary self-sufficiency.

She was worried about how she felt and doubted herself. She looked at the name and number vibrating on her phone and then pressed a button to send the call to her answerphone.

Rajiv came back to the table.

"I'm afraid I've got to go," she said.

"Now? We only just got here."

"Something unusual's come up." She knew she was being irrational, but she couldn't stop herself.

Rajiv could see from her face that she was rattled.

"Want some help?"

"No, thank you."

"Why not?"

"Well, I've got to get back to work."

"Okay," said Rajiv evenly, trying to hit upon some formula that might calm her down. "Maybe I could come watch you ride sometime? I bet you're amazing on horseback."

"I don't think so."

"Oh, come on. Really I'm harmless."

"Strict security around where I work."

"What, a stable?"

"I've told you more than enough already."

"Well, I guess you'll e-mail me soonest and tell me what's up." He flashed her an ironic appeal.

"We'll see."

His "Goodbye" had to be addressed to her back, because she was already running out toward the iron gate onto Piccadilly, taking long strides in her knee-high boots. He took out his phone and sent her an e-mail saying, "Whatever it is, I can help."

Then he shoved the phone back into his pocket and turned with a sigh to go back to work.

Once she'd seen Elizabeth, fed her the cheese, and chatted briefly with Rebecca, The Queen turned to go back to the palace. Wearing Rebecca's hoodie, she approached the door she'd come in by which would take her back via a gravel path through the gardens. In between the time of her arrival, and her turning to go, however, two workmen had come in to paint the door. "Sorry, love, not out this way. Not while it's wet," one of them said to her when she approached the door from the Mews. "You'll have to go out into the road over there and get back inside through The Queen's Gallery."

The Queen found it odd that the man had called her "love." No one called her that. It set her back on her heels for a moment. Then she put her hands into the pockets of the hoodie, felt the cigarettes, penknife, and banknote that were there, and suddenly recalled that this was not her coat. It was Rebecca's. Her hood was up, so the workmen hadn't recognized her. That's why they were so familiar. "Not rudeness, Little Bit. They call all old women 'love,' don't they? Don't jump to conclusions," she murmured to herself.

So she turned and did as she was told. She walked out via the main entrance to the Mews into Buckingham Palace Road. There two red tourist buses roared by her, splashing oily water onto the pavement, unaware of the major tourist attraction right in front of them. The Queen felt a brief moment of elation. She was so rarely on the street by herself, unrecognized. Here was all the busy world rushing by. Everyone seemed to have a place to go in a hurry: taxis, pedestrians bent double against the wind, and lorries. No one gave her so much as a second glance. It was marvelous. Why shouldn't she have a place to go too? It suddenly occurred to her. Rebecca had mentioned that the Mews didn't have a reliable supply of the cheese. Theirs was nearly all gone. It came from Paxton & Whitfield in Jermyn Street. Why shouldn't she go and get some? She didn't think it was far. And, come to think of it, why not Scotland itself? Earlier, she'd idly checked the railway timetable on the computer in her sitting room, telling herself it was time she learned how the public railway worked. Trains seemed to go rather frequently in the early evening. Why not *Britannia*?

She had been used to following the rules since she was a little girl. She always did as she was told. She'd been taught that it was her job as a constitutional monarch always to stick to the program, to follow the Government's advice, to adhere to the timetable, to act according to precedent. For most of her life she'd done that, and been rewarded for it. The monarchy had been reasonably popular. Playing by these rules, however, had not saved her from the disasters that had befallen the monarchy at the time of the breakup of the Prince and Princess of Wales. What's more, she'd been blamed for much of what happened. "Her Majesty a Wicked Mother-in-Law," "No Hugs for Diana from Queen," "Cold Palace Shuts Out People's Darling." That's what the papers had said. As far as she knew, republican and openly antimonarchical feeling was relatively rare in modern British history. There had been a little in the 1870s, when people wanted to see Queen Victoria out-of-doors more often. There was a lot more expected if Britain had lost the First World War, which didn't happen, thankfully. So the anger and hatred that hit her square in the face after Diana died was something entirely new to her. She'd carried on as usual, of course, but things were not the same. She knew that part of what she was feeling now, whatever it was, maybe just something all old ladies suffered from, was also a kind of delayed reaction to the *annus horribilis*—all her children's marriages breaking up at once, Windsor burning, a bungled announcement about payment of tax—and all that had followed from it. She'd internalized the shock, stored it up, and now she was suffering. The combination of the sadness, and the sense that doing as she'd always done hadn't helped anyone when the crisis came, least of all her, made her ready all of a sudden to do something she'd never done before: to walk away from the palace on her own.

The Queen set off in the direction of Green Park. She knew where Jermyn Street was. She and Margaret had been allowed by Nanny to walk up and down there when they were little, looking at the shop windows. It had been a long time since she'd been there, but she did know the way. So The Queen passed by The Queen's Gallery, turned left in front of the palace, and walked by the big memorial to Queen Victoria on the other side of the road. She came to a crossing that would let her into the park opposite and looked curiously at a yellow button on a pole. What did that do? She pressed it. Miraculously the light changed and the traffic slowed to a halt so she could cross the road. What a surprise. That was handy, wasn't it? She walked across, giving the drivers who'd stopped for her a little wave. She then went up the gravel path at the end of Green Park toward a gate she knew to be just behind St James's Palace. If she found that gate, if she remembered the streets aright, she could find her way into Jermyn Street.

The Queen felt the swell of excitement from doing something unusual. She had been on her own in front of the palace on only a handful of occasions. On VE day in 1945, she and Margaret had gone outside the iron railings with some other officers and stood with the crowds chanting "We want the King!" At first she'd pulled down her peaked cap over her forehead so no one would recognize her, but one of the boys with them, a fussy Grenadier, had refused to be seen with her if she weren't wearing her uniform in the regulation way. So she had to put the cap on properly. Still, no one had known who she was. They had shouted and shouted until Papa and Mummy had come outside on the balcony to wave. How funny it was to see the whole performance from the stalls instead of from the stage. They'd gone out again on VJ day in August and got away with it several times more that summer, princesses pretending to be just girls in the crowd.

Then, in 1986, when Andrew had married Sarah Ferguson, at the end of the wedding breakfast, as the newlyweds were driving away in their carriage, a great crowd of grandchildren had run after them from the inner quadrangle into the palace forecourt. If she hadn't run after them to grab their hands, all those grandchildren would have run out into the street. There she'd been, sixty years old, running along in her heels with her jacket flapping, but she had to admit, that was ripping as well.

Now with her hood up, the rain mixed with sleet, and the wind moving the big wet branches of the plane trees, she felt in a holiday mood. She loved wet weather, and a storm always cheered her up. She could recall being in a California rainstorm with the Reagans one afternoon when they were driving her up a hillside to their ranch in Santa Barbara. The President wanted to show her his horses. She liked him. He might not have been all that bright, but certainly he was the most charming of all the American presidents she'd met. The rain came down in buckets and the mud flowed down the gravel road. Mrs Reagan twisted her handkerchief and wailed about the luncheon being ruined. "Nonsense!" The Queen remembered telling her. "It's an adventure!" She meant it. A good storm was always exciting. It was also The Queen's instinct as a farmer, the owner of many thousands of arable acres, that wet weather more often than not was a good thing. So she bustled up the gravel path with the wet boughs tossing overhead and scanned the opposite wall for the gate she was sure was there somewhere.

Attempting to allay the misery that was clearly in the younger man's eyes, William said airily to Luke, "I imagine Madam's just gone to find a few biscuits for the doggies. They like them with their tea. Little thugs that they are."

"No, really gone. At least half an hour now."

"Gone where? I thought she had an evening in?"

"She was meant to. But I stopped by around half past three to see whether she needed anything before I buggered off for the afternoon, and she wasn't here. Door to terrace open. Dogs wandering about. No one knows where she is. I telephoned security and they think she's in here. I ran around the garden just now to try and find her. Not there. Telephoned St James's and Windsor, even Sandringham. Not there either."

"The Duke of Edinburgh?"

"In Brazil. To promote the World Wildlife Fund. Left this morning. Not back for two weeks."

William looked at him gravely and after a moment asked, "Well, we call the police, don't we?"

"No, we certainly do not. Do you want the Metropolitan Police to know that The Queen of England is wandering around unattended in the rain? What will that say to them about her? About us? And when the newspapers find out? Alzheimer's will be the mildest of their headlines, I can tell you. Are you daft? We cannot tell the police."

"I expect she's gone walkabout."

"Don't speak to me in riddles at a moment like this."

William caught Luke's weariness and frustration, but he didn't particularly like being talked to as if he were just playing about. He saw in a moment the seriousness of the situation.

"Well, if you did a little reading as well as playing polo and lying in sunbeds, you might know that old aborigines go walkabout when they're getting ready to die. It's in Bruce Chatwin's book."

This was too much for Luke: the suggestion that not only was she gone, and gone on his watch, but that The Queen might have gone somewhere to die upset him more than he'd been upset when William came walking in the room. He folded his arms on the desk, put down his head, and sobbed. He couldn't stop himself. He knew he cried more often since coming back from the war, but knowing that didn't help him to prevent it.

"Oh God! The big strong ones are always like this. Weak as kittens in a crisis." William's instinct was to fill up the space in the room in order to cover the young man's embarrassment. But Luke himself seemed to be without shame. One of the dogs came over to lick a bit of exposed skin between the top of his sock and the bottom of his trouser leg. "Come now, *sir*, we're going to go and find her, aren't we?" William put his hands lightly on Luke's shoulders. "We're going to have a look-see. We'll have her back here in a pair of pumps and tiara, ready to receive, in twenty-four hours, won't we?"

It was the first time Luke had been touched by a man in a very long time. He lifted up his head. "How?" he asked as if he were a petulant child speaking to a parent.

"Well, I'm sure that we can piece something together, can't we? She didn't say she wanted to go somewhere, did she?"

"No, she didn't tell me anything. You?"

"Nor me."

"I found this railway timetable on her computer," Luke said, blowing his nose on a crusty handkerchief he extracted with difficulty from his trouser pocket. He hit a button and brought the London King's Cross timetable back up on the screen.

"Trains to Edinburgh Waverley," said William, reading the

screen. "Go to Scotland and die. Yes, it would kill me if I had to live up there."

"I fancy she rather likes it. Would stay up there longer if she could."

"Oh yes, they all love it up there. Wear their kilts all the time. They take it a bit far, if you ask me."

"Well, I think we've got to go after her."

"After her where? To Edinburgh? It's four and a half hours by train! And what do we do when we get there?"

"I don't know, but it's my job to look after her and I'm going," Luke said, standing up from the desk and looking for some assent from the man who'd just touched his shoulders.

William hesitated. This was definitely outside the line of duty. He liked Luke, but he'd intended to keep their relationship on a basis of distant flirtation. He was thrown off balance by the proposition that they should go to Scotland together.

"Yours too," said Luke.

"Mine too what?"

"Your job to look after her too."

William signified a qualified assent with a ragged sigh. "But I'm not going anywhere, especially with you, without my dark glasses. And let's not rush off half-cocked. The Queen sometimes walks over to the Mews of an afternoon. Have you tried over there? What about Shirley MacDonald? Not much escapes her. Have you interviewed her?

"No, neither one," said Luke, his posture slumping with the admission that these might be two critical sources of information if they were going out to look for Her Majesty.

"Is that what they teach you at Sandhurst? Prepare to attack with no reconnaissance first? Look splendid in your gear, don't you, but I must say the intelligence gathering on this operation is distinctly slipshod."

Luke marveled at William's ability to tease him in the midst of a crisis. How did he manage to keep his wits about him? "I believe Mrs MacDonald and Lady Anne Bevil are both stopping in the palace tonight, ready for The Queen's early start tomorrow. We might go and speak to them."

"Oh no. Shirley MacDonald is not telling what she knows to some toffee-nosed boy. I'll go and speak to them, young fellow me lad. You deal with the Mews. Look smart. Meet up back here in twenty minutes."

Without so much as goodbye, or a further kind word, William was out the door.

Although Rebecca was on fairly easy terms with The Queen, The Queen's private office was another story. The Mews seldom dealt with the private secretaries except on arrangements for ceremonial occasions, and then they were certainly terrifying. The equerries were chosen by The Queen's private office even though their name, "equerry," pronounced "eh-KWHER-ry" went back to horses. It derived from the French *écurie*, for stable. Sometime in distant history the equerries were officers in charge of the stables. Nowadays they sometimes arranged for transportation in cars, on trains, and by airplane, almost never on horseback, so Rebecca in the Mews knew of them, but she had little to do with them. Their proximity to The Queen made them rather arrogant when she did have to deal with them, so the phone call from Luke calling her over to the palace made her nervous.

Luke had worked out that William had served her lunch in her study after one and that was the last anyone inside the palace had seen of her. He telephoned the Mews to see whether she had gone over there after lunch. Rebecca had picked up Luke's call and confirmed that The Queen had been there earlier in the afternoon. He asked her whether she'd walk over to have a word with him in The Queen's sitting room. He gave her instructions on how to find it. She'd never been in it before. She appeared after having run over from the Mews. She was out of breath. Her riding boots were splattered with mud.

"I don't think we've met," said Luke, standing up from The Queen's desk. "How do you do?" He nodded her in the direction of the comfortable chair. He did not reach out to shake her hand. If Rebecca were breathing heavily from her run, he was thoroughly distracted by the enormity of what was before him. "Look," he began right away without trying to smooth things over, as the upper levels of the Household usually did by asking her about what she was doing. It was their cover for being about to ask her to do some significant and time-consuming job. Luke, however, went straight to the point. "Her Majesty has disappeared. Before the police and the secret services are alerted, I'd like to try to find her quickly myself. The papers will make a fuss if they know she's walked off *hors de routine*, as it were. It might injure her. I'd like to keep it quiet as long as we can. But that means we have to find her before anyone else does. So there's not much time. She came to the Mews this afternoon, did she?"

"Yes," she said and gave him an angry look.

"And?"

"And nothing. She often comes over. She had some cheddar for Elizabeth. She likes it."

"Cheddar cheese?"

"Yes, Elizabeth likes it."

After a split second of confusion, Luke gathered Rebecca was referring to a horse, rather than the sovereign. He would have been rather taken aback if she'd addressed The Queen by her Christian name. He also gathered that this young woman was as upset about something as he was, possibly the disappearance of The Queen, possibly something else. "Her Majesty make any peculiar remarks?"

"Well, she wasn't dressed for the weather. Only a headscarf on. It was pelting down outside. I gave her my hoodie."

"Your hoodie?"

"She had no coat. She needed something."

Luke waved this away. "She say anything?"

"She asked if I thought horses were ever sad."

"Oh Lord," Luke groaned.

Rebecca put in defensively, "Well, they're sometimes not as contented as they might be. And she likes talking about that. Is all."

"Yes, I see. But don't you think she might have been talking about herself too?"

Rebecca's focus with The Queen was always on what they both cared about, the horses, not on each other. Whatever it was that had made Her Majesty turn up earlier that afternoon was far too personal to be sharing with this man in a grey suit. She just pursed her lips and made no response.

"Look, I don't like asking these sorts of questions any more than you like answering them. Why is it so hard to get people in this bloody place to pull together? If you and I don't make common cause and find out where she has gone to, they'll be very rough with her. Don't you see?" He paused to see if she would volunteer any more useful news.

She did not. She looked over his shoulder out the darkened window.

"William thinks she's not herself. Has gone . . ." he couldn't say "walkabout" to this unresponsive girl with high color and muddy boots, "to get ready to, um, die." He'd blurted out the word before he'd had a chance to think.

"*Die?*" she said, momentarily shocked out of her determination not to share anything with him. "Die. She wasn't dying. She was fine."

"Yes, but perhaps was having some gloomy thoughts, and asked you whether horses had gloomy thoughts too?"

Now that he put it that way, it didn't seem so odd. She had seemed somehow a little different than usual. "Well, she wasn't what I would have called cheerful."

"Said nothing to you about where she might be going after she left you?"

"No, just was going out into the weather, so she let me put my hoodie onto her."

"Hoodie," said Luke with a combination of incredulity and distaste. "Isn't that what the boys wear on the street when they're about to knife you? And you put one over Her Majesty's head, did you?"

"Look, *I* wear one, and I don't carry a knife." This wasn't strictly true. Rebecca did have a scout knife she kept in her pocket for small tasks. She didn't carry it as a weapon. "Thank you. Is there anything else?"

God, she was difficult, Luke thought to himself. He left a pause to see whether it might allow her indignation to disperse a little. "And where might such a woman go, who was curious about whether horses were ever depressed, on a December afternoon?"

Rebecca saw that he would not allow her to go until she provided something more. She wished she knew what else she could tell him. The only thing she could really think of was that The Queen still found it funny that Elizabeth liked the cheddar. She'd told The Queen it came from Paxton & Whitfield, and that they'd run out of their supply at the Mews. Now, why wouldn't she send someone out to get more if she wanted it? Or why not send Rebecca herself if it came to that, as she had done before? But if she were behaving oddly, which Rebecca could see for herself she was, mightn't The Queen go to Jermyn Street to get the cheese herself? She was surprisingly unrecognizable in that hoodie. This thought flashed through her mind and she as quickly determined she wouldn't tell the equerry. As a man, and as a member of the upper level of the Household, she simply didn't trust him.

"I have no idea," she said, separating the words so he could see she had determined to tell him nothing more.

"All right, then," said Luke, defeated. "But here's my mobile number in case you find out something. I am thinking of going to Scotland tonight. William too, possibly. Found a railway timetable on her computer screen." He stopped a moment and caught her eye. "Please do let me know," he said separating his words, imitating what she had just done, "will you, if you find out anything."

"I will," she said. It was the least brusque thing she'd said in the twenty minutes they were together. Something about the use of a Christian name in his sentence made her soften a little. She had no idea who "William" was, but he had now mentioned him twice. The equerry in his own way was as defiant as she'd been meeting his questions, and his breaking the usual spoken order of things had got her attention. Perhaps he wasn't just a grey suit after all.

The Queen had an early engagement on Tuesday and those who would be attending her needed to be up early. Lady Anne, instead of spending the Monday night in Tite Street, was spending the night in the palace. She was across the corridor from a bedroom occupied by Shirley, who was up from Windsor to dress The Queen and do her hair before the day's activities began. William had knocked on Shirley's door and they'd had a quick but voluble conversation in the hall about what had happened. He reported that the equerry had discovered, and confirmed, that The Queen had left the palace sometime after luncheon and was now officially missing. He also told her about the Scottish railway timetable they'd found on The Queen's computer, which made them guess that was where she was headed. William had asked whether Shirley knew anything about this. He'd received a blustery negative. She verbally boxed his ears for frightening her, and threatened him with physical punishment if this were a joke. "Dead serious, Shirley," said William with all the light and play gone out of his eyes. In the midst of this, Lady Anne, hearing the commotion, had come out into the corridor and heard the story of The Queen's disappearance repeated. As she knew nothing either, William told them that he and the equerry were trying to find out if anything could be learned from the Mews, but that they thought of going to Scotland themselves, maybe together, as soon as they were able. He'd then disappeared down the corridor, leaving the two women looking at one another in confusion.

Shirley and Anne had both served The Queen for a very long time, though in different capacities. Shirley stood behind her in the morning and brushed out her hair. Anne stood behind her in the afternoon and made small talk with the wives of factory owners during official visits. Shirley's mother and grandmother had both been pensioned off by the Royal Household and retired to cottages near the Dee in Scotland. Anne's brother had nearly married The Queen but had died young, and the present Marquess, Anne's nephew, was unknown at the palace. He was never invited to anything. Shirley and Anne were accustomed to seeing one another in the corridors and on the backstairs, and though they were as polite and distantly friendly as palace manners required, they were frankly suspicious of one another. Shirley regarded Anne as just another version of Letitia d'Arlancourt, and as such, her bitter enemy. She thought there was little enough difference between the ladies-in-waiting.

For her part, Anne was rather jealous of The Queen's evident affection for Shirley and the way she relied upon her for everything. The two of them would be in the backseat of the big palace Bentley, known as "the Beast," going off to an afternoon event. The Queen would introduce many of her opinions with Shirley's point of view. "Shirley says, and I agree, it will be hot when we go to Kentucky." What does Shirley know about the weather in Kentucky, thought Anne. Or, "Shirley has found the most marvelous things for your lips. Peppermint with a tingle." "Has she, Ma'am?" replied Anne flatly. Even, "Shirley thinks Labour will be out before long." Anne thought she might just mention this to the Prime Minister the next time she was entertaining him with a drink, softening him up, as it were, in the ten minutes before The Queen was ready to give him his audience on a weekday evening. She imagined with satisfaction the surprise on his face. The Queen's most trusted source of political information her Scottish dresser. How that would make him pale.

The two women were unprepared for much intimacy when they stood facing one another in the blue-carpeted hallway lined with white wainscoting. Both of them had planned on early nights, tea on a tray, some television, and lights out well before nine in the evening. They'd both got out of their street clothes and into their dressing gowns, though for different reasons. Anne had been having arthritic pains in her lower back and shoulders. She hadn't the money to pay for a private nurse, and she couldn't face leaving her flat to go live in sheltered housing paid for by the National Health Service. She wasn't sure but she thought her condition might be degenerative and she would have to face something like that before too long. To bed early with a couple of pain pills and a hot water bottle was her remedy. Shirley, for her part, missed the all-female bedtime chitchats she'd had in her girlhood with her mother and grandmother. With no men about, and one or two women friends who were staying, everyone in flannel nightdresses or cotton pajamas, it was her fondest memory of belonging and being looked after. Getting early into her nightclothes was Shirley's way of remembering those far-off days of sisterhood. Nevertheless, both Shirley and Anne were embarrassed to be seen in *déshabille*, especially by one another, when it was still early.

"This is very unlike Her Majesty, Mrs MacDonald," said Anne, raising her chin and pretending as if she always met Shirley MacDonald while only dressed in bathrobe and slippers.

"It is, Lady Anne," said Shirley, more abruptly, rather short-tempered with herself for not knowing more about what her mistress could be doing outside the palace walls.

"I hate to think what might happen to her, um, outside," said Anne.

Both women knew that she was not talking about the weather. They both paused a moment to let the more horrible possibilities pass through their minds. An elderly woman falling off a curb she didn't notice into the path of an oncoming taxi was the least of the horrible things they imagined.

Recovering herself, and shuddering slightly, Shirley offered, in a feeling of desperation, "She mentioned something about Leith."

"Leith! What would she want in Leith?"

"*Britannia*, Lady Anne."

"*Britannia*, Mrs MacDonald? Surely not. On her own? At this time of day? They all said goodbye to her years ago." Anne was thinking as she said this of how they'd all blubbed in the most undignified way. Blubbing about a boat, indeed. Sometimes she wondered why she worked for this family. But then she recalled there had been some merry times, especially when they were in turquoise seas, away from the cold waters of this miserable little island. She knew too how The Queen was usually at her best on board ship, most natural, least shy, unbuttoned. Why shouldn't she want a visit to her happy place, as she believed it was called now? Ministers had been unwilling to pay for a new vessel when *Britannia* was decommissioned. It was a slap in the face. There had been a royal yacht ever since Queen Victoria's day, and The Queen set store by doing everything as Queen Victoria had once done it. Anne decided it wasn't impossible that The Queen should want to revisit the old yacht. "What did she say about Leith, exactly?" She used a tone to convey that they were in this together, the two of them, almost as if to apologize, without actually saying so, for the tone of voice she'd used a moment earlier when she'd poured scorn on the idea of The Queen going by herself to Leith.

"I mean only that now that you mention it, Mrs MacDonald, it doesn't seem all that preposterous. She mentioned Leith, did she?"

"Yes, Lady Anne." Shirley was not about to allow herself to be cross-examined by a bad-tempered lady-in-waiting at this sort of crisis. She'd noticed The Queen not entirely herself in the last several weeks, more absentminded, abstracted. She was afraid it might be that thing President Reagan had had. The prospect of it was too unappealing to consider at length, but it wasn't something Shirley wanted people finding out about. She had an intense protective instinct and she was willing to put herself forward as the human barrier against an outside world that would regard The Queen's slight absence of mind as an illness. She knew that Lady Anne was an old palace fixture, but she didn't intend to confide in her either. She was silently determining how she might get up to Leith at this hour to look for The Queen, and where she would stay, and how she might pay for this if she were travelling on her own limited pocketbook.

"Now, look here," said Anne in her bossiest regimental tone. "I have the use of a flat in Edinburgh. Charlotte Square. My nephew's. Used to belong to me, but it doesn't anymore. Still, he'll let me use it. What if the two of us were to go up and look for her? We could stay in Charlotte Square. My nephew has a small plane. He'll pay to fly us up there. It's the least that young man can do for us."

"No, thank you, Lady Anne," said Shirley stiffly. She operated on the principle of no excess information to the upper servants that they didn't need to know, and she wouldn't rely on Lady Anne any more than she would on the private secretaries or the Mistress of the Robes, or even the Prime Minister, as of course he was, technically speaking, an upper servant too.

Anne detected her error in addressing Shirley MacDonald as if she were a private soldier. "What I meant, Mrs MacDonald," she said changing to a friendlier tone of voice, "is that we won't serve her well if we're at cross-purposes. You have a sense of where she might have gone. Leith. I can get us there with the minimum of fuss. Shan't we join forces?"

"Shan't," said Shirley to herself, inwardly harrumphing at the words. Shall not. Sounded biblical. Still, what Lady Anne had said was sensible. She had no idea how to get to Leith at this hour, and a place to stay in Edinburgh would be useful. The Queen might not be at Leith, after all. There might have to be some hunting and searching.

"Very well, let's go together." There was then an awkward pause. She drew herself up to her greatest height and tightened the belt on her housecoat. "On one condition. I'm Shirley."

"Very pleased to meet you, Shirley," said Anne, her eye twinkling. She didn't put out her hand. "I'm Anne, as you know." A pause while the two women sized one another up for the first time as women rather than as coworkers in an unusual and antique hierarchical order. "Shall we meet out here in fifteen minutes? Pair of jeans and a headscarf?"

Shirley rolled her eyes. "*No headscarf.* You might as well wear a name badge saying, 'I'm Her Majesty's Lady-in-Waiting.' We don't want people to *know* she's gone. We're winging up there on the q.t. Got it?"

"Got it," said Anne meekly, newly aware of a gruff habit of command that she'd never noticed in Shirley MacDonald before. "But it *is* raining. What are we to wear?"

"I've a baseball cap. Pulls down right over the eyes. Have one for you too."

"A *baseball* cap? Really."

"Do you want your picture on the front page of *The Scotsman*? 'Her Majesty's Lady-in-Waiting Found Trawling Around Leith After Midnight'"?

"No, of course not. You're right. We must keep this hush-hush."

Shirley sighed with exasperation. "Now, go and dress yourself. Meet me back here in a quarter of an hour."

Rajiv had returned to the cheese shop feeling a little disconsolate after his coffee with Rebecca. He found that his colleagues now wanted their breaks. So he was left alone on the darkened afternoon with no customers and no one beside him behind the counter. When the tiny woman with a blue hoodie and a headscarf came through the door, he could see immediately who she was. He'd photographed her before. Her coming through the doorway now, alone, told him that something unusual was up, so grabbing his phone to take her picture didn't occur to him. There was something that touched him about her vulnerability, an old woman out by herself on a wet afternoon three weeks before Christmas.

He also saw instinctively that, if she weren't exactly wishing to appear *incognita*, that she wasn't at Paxton & Whitfield on an official visit either. He was a polite young man and he thought at the very least a bow was probably necessary, but he wasn't sure how, or whether it came before speaking to her or afterwards. What was he meant to call her? Instead, he just addressed her as he would any other customer. "A very wet afternoon, Ma'am."

The Queen had forgotten the weather as she'd tried to remember how to find Jermyn Street. She didn't mind actually. It was quite fun looking for places on your own rather than being driven straight to the door by someone who knew precisely where he was going. "Yes," she said, turning around to look back out at the street. "I suppose it is."

Rajiv could see that she was distracted. He thought keeping her in conversation until someone came inside to attend her might be best. "Sleet too."

"I hadn't noticed."

"Looking at the shop windows? Fortnum's has wonderful windows this time of year."

"No, you see, I couldn't remember quite where you were. So I came along here, not sure if the shop were still here. Jermyn Street in my grandmother's day, now, was quite disreputable."

"Really?"

"Yes, I believe there was a famous madam at the Cavendish Hotel."

"I didn't know, Ma'am. It's all men's shirts along here now."

"Yes, I see that. But whenever anyone calls me 'Madam' now, you know, instead of '*Ma'am*-rhymes-with-ham,' I always laugh to myself and think of that madam of the Cavendish Hotel." Rajiv's politeness and his being smoothly unsurprised by her visit to the shop made The Queen forget for the moment that she was absent without leave from the palace.

She might be distracted, thought Rajiv, but she still had a sense of humor. She was good even at telling a little harmlessly wicked story. "I don't think the Cavendish is quite so *louche* now."

"No, I expect it isn't."

"Saudi princes, I imagine."

The Queen heard the slight dismissiveness in Rajiv's voice and thought she'd better stick up for the Saudis and multicultural Britain, of which she was rather proud. "Well, they're wonderful breeders."

"Breeders?"

"Horseflesh, I mean," said The Queen.

"Of course."

"Which brings me to my errand."

"Can I help, Ma'am?"

"Yes. I'm sure you can. Now, there's a very peculiar horse. Born on the same day as me, it turns out. Not the same year, of course. But we share a birthday." The Queen said this as if she expected him to congratulate her.

"What fun."

"Yes, I think so." The Queen looked with a momentary brightening off over Rajiv's shoulder.

"And this particular horse likes cheese?" offered Rajiv.

"*Yes.* How did you know?" The Queen was surprised that this young man should have so quickly divined the purpose of her excursion.

"Well, I have a friend . . . well, not a friend, more of an acquaintance really. She's, well, we've only just had coffee once. This afternoon, but . . ."

The Queen could see the change that had taken place in Rajiv's face. He was speaking of something that caused him both pleasure and embarrassment. Made him hopeful and disappointed at the same time. "I see," she said, raising her eyebrows to him in an encouraging way. "Do go on."

Rajiv thought she was the one who needed help, but now she was helping him, and he was grateful. "Well, she has flame-colored hair. Looks after horses somewhere. She first came in a little while ago, a month or so back, about a horse of hers that liked cheddar, a particular cheddar I think we have here, and maybe, well, I doubt it can be found anywhere else."

"Rebecca," said The Queen.

"God, do you know her?"

"Well, there can't be many flame-haired girls who look after horses in London, can there be? I think I know the one you mean."

"Rebecca is her name right enough," said Rajiv, still amazed.

"Rinaldi. Yes, well she's at the Mews."

"Oh, well, she wouldn't tell me where she worked."

"Good girl."

"Yes, I expect she has to keep it confidential."

"Oh, you can't imagine. If anyone so much as finds Queen Victoria's nail file at a car boot sale, they all run to the papers with it right away. You can't come near the palace these days without signing fourteen legal forms. Fees to lawyers are the biggest claim on the Privy Purse. Costs us much more than Princess Michael of Kent."

Rajiv was uncomfortably aware that he'd twice in recent months submitted his photographs to a newspaper and been paid handsomely for them. So he started in a little defensively, "Well, Ma'am, don't you think that as long as there's curiosity, as long as people still want to know about what goes on inside the palace, that, well, basically the monarchy generates interest. And that must be a good thing. Wouldn't apathy be worse?"

"A little apathy might be welcome now and again," said The Queen quickly. "Would certainly lead to a quieter life," she said, snorting. "But you see that interest, 'curiosity' I think you called it, can easily turn to its opposite. Just as extreme love, in a marriage, for example, can turn to hate. They're the same coin, just different sides."

Rajiv had no direct, firsthand experience of either love or marriage. These were big, unexplored continents for him, though he did hope to go there one day himself, soon if possible. He was aware that the woman for whom he'd felt such sympathy when she walked in the door had experience of all these big countries, not only love and marriage, but the monarchy, popularity, and getting up every day not to write a poem, or come to work on Jermyn Street, but to be sovereign. To embody the state. He took a step backward, and addressed her a touch more deferentially. "I see what you mean."

"Oh, but the papers, now, they're not all bad, are they?"

"No, Ma'am."

"Free speech. It's what a democracy's all about, isn't it?"

"Yes, Ma'am."

"And one of them, I can't remember which one, well, when Queen Beatrix of the Netherlands was here in the autumn, published some pictures, *quite* illegally, of the state banquet." The Queen looked angry for a moment.

Rajiv immediately looked away in embarrassment. It had never occurred to him that The Queen herself would be looking at his photos. Did he now have to confess that he'd been smuggled into the palace by one of the under chefs? For the second time since she'd walked in the shop, he felt badly confused.

The Queen's look of annoyance passed off as she remembered something brighter. "Some of those cheeses at the banquet might have been sent over from here, mightn't they? And the carvings were so clever. Queen Beatrix loved them. All the Dutch tradesmen were so jealous. They're so proud of their cheese export, you know. We quite showed them up. Score one for Britain, eh? Holland, nil," said The Queen, chuckling.

The Queen paused and once again seemed to drift away from the conversation into some reverie that it would have been rude to interrupt. The trouble was that Rajiv didn't really want to tell her how he'd also taken her picture in the rain in the Lake District, even though he thought that too was a very good picture. He'd recognized her, but she hadn't recognized him. She was more smiling then, he noticed. So to prevent her reverting to photography he circled back to why she'd come in the first place. "I expect you'd like some cheese, Ma'am. Particularly cheddar that appeals to horses?"

"Yes, please," said The Queen, returning to earth. "I expect if Rebecca were in here before, you know the one I want."

"I do, Ma'am," and Rajiv then proceeded to show The Queen the orange round and to ask her how much she'd like. That she left to him, so he cut her a generous wedge, wrapped it up, and offered to have it sent over to the Mews for her.

"Oh no, it's not entirely for them," said The Queen quickly. "Some's for me. If Elizabeth pulls a little better with a taste of that cheese, I thought it might work for me too, you see."

Rajiv was a little shocked, but he disguised this as well as he could. "Of course, Ma'am. And shall I have it put on your account?" He wasn't sure if the palace had an account, but he wasn't going to ask her to hand over a banknote or a credit card.

"Yes, please," said The Queen, taking the parcel into her hands. "Now, is there a bus to King's Cross from here?" she asked him.

For the first time Rajiv felt genuine alarm on her behalf. It's true she had come in alone, but he somehow expected that there must be security people, or a car, outside the door. Now it was clear she was entirely on her own and planning to head for one of London's busiest railway stations at the moment the evening rush was about to get under way.

"Well, I think there's the number 38 on Piccadilly that will take you to the Angel, but then you'd have to take another bus from there to King's Cross. Or the Victoria Line from Green Park would probably be faster.

"I see. Number 38. Then change at the Angel. Don't like the Tube," said The Queen, holding her parcel of cheddar in both hands, and looking as if she ought to be accompanied by two or three burly policemen at the very least.

"Look, Ma'am, why don't I shut up the shop and come with you to King's Cross? I could show you the way."

"But you're meant to be open much later, aren't you? You can't just go against the rules," she said with a semi-guilty twinge that she was doing just that herself.

"Well, my colleagues will be back from their breaks shortly. I'll just run you over in a taxi, shall I, and then pop right back here?"

"All right," said The Queen, thinking that's just what she'd do too. Run up to Scotland and pop right back. But then she heard what he'd just said. "A taxi? That would be very extravagant," she protested.

"Well, we don't often have sleet in London, do we? And if you catch cold, you'll have to cancel engagements for days. A taxi will be a savings."

The Queen hated to cancel engagements. It made her feel more ill than flu or a head cold. "Perhaps you have a point there."

"I'll just grab my jacket and be with you in a moment."

Rajiv put on an East German army jacket he'd bought in the Camden Market. He came around the counter and bent over to offer his elbow to The Queen. She reached up to hold the crook of his arm and together they stepped out into the evening.

❧

As soon as Luke dismissed her, Rebecca was on her feet again. She ran out through the iron gates, and ignored the zebra crossing where The Queen had carefully crossed. Instead, Rebecca plunged heedlessly into the traffic and tore off up the Mall toward St James's Palace. If The Queen had disappeared, the only clue she could think of was the cheese. She'd just seen him earlier in the afternoon, and Rajiv would probably still be in the shop. She could maybe warn him that someone in a hoodie might turn up. Or, he could tell her if anyone fitting that description had come in. As it was an emergency, and as she was an impulsive young woman, she thought she'd better see Rajiv rather than telephone him. She ran up the road between St James's Palace and Marlborough House, past the draped female figure, put up as a memorial to Queen Alexandra by Saint-Gaudens. Rebecca didn't know who it was, or its sculptor, but she remembered it because the hard bronze looked like soft melted wax and the woman was very beautiful. She had no idea that she was running in pursuit of Queen Alexandra's great-granddaughter. She ducked into a passageway that went from Pall Mall into King Street, which itself ran down to the right toward Christie's. She didn't care about expensive auctioneers, but she loved London's pedestrian passageways that could take you as a runner right away from the traffic. She then pounded up Duke Street toward the Cavendish Hotel, and at the shop on the corner that sold seventeenth-century tapestries, strange cartoonish geese on perfectly modulated grounds of blue and green, she turned the corner into Jermyn Street. Now she knew Paxton & Whitfield was straight ahead, so she could stop running.

Just as she paused to catch her breath, however, she saw a taxi drawing to a halt in the narrow street. There was Rajiv, wearing the same military jacket she'd seen him wearing only a couple of hours before, helping a small figure in a blue hood into the back of the cab. To her surprise, he not only helped her in, supporting her arm until she was all the way into the back, but then nimbly hopped in the back himself. The taxi then turned off its yellow light, to indicate that it was engaged, and accelerated toward her, standing on the pavement outside the tapestry shop. As it drew even with her, she looked into the back, but the windows were streaming with rain, and fogged up from a previous passenger. It proceeded through the light and down Jermyn Street toward St James's.

She noticed an empty taxi coming down Jermyn Street behind it. She instinctively flagged it down and jumped in the back. "Follow that taxi!"

The driver, a middle-aged man with a smoker's voice, twisted around in his seat and slid open the Plexiglas partition. "What is this? Is it a film we're in, then, young lady?"

"No, we haven't time. Just go. Follow that cab just ahead going toward St James's."

"Who's in it, then?" said the driver as he accelerated away from the tapestry shop.

Rebecca thought to herself "My boyfriend and The Queen of England." However, neither of those were things she wished to disclose. One wasn't true, and it would have been the second time that day she'd lied about having a boyfriend. The other was top secret. She decided the best thing was to say nothing.

"What's a nice young girl like you doing following taxis through the streets on a December afternoon, eh?"

Suddenly Rebecca was aware that she was being looked at in the rearview mirror. The taxi driver was winking at her when she looked up. Rebecca took a closer look at the driver's reflection in the mirror. He was wearing an Arsenal football shirt, also printed with advertising for a Middle Eastern airline, "Fly Emirates." He had the ability to steer the taxi skillfully in and out of heavy traffic while keeping his dancing eyes on his fare in the backseat. "I will pay you for this," said Rebecca.

"Damned right you will," said the driver with a coarse laugh. "But I'm not sure all this cops and robbers is good for you, love. Your cheeks are all red."

"Well, I was running just before I found you."

"You don't have on your trainers. I thought you had on riding boots when I pulled up to the curb. Caught my attention, they did."

There was now no question that the driver was showing an interest in her. It was the last thing she wanted. "Look, it's my boyfriend up there in that other cab we're following now."

"Is it, now? And if things were well and good between you, would you be following him in a taxi? Make more sense to go wherever together, now, I would have thought." He gave another laugh that smelled of smoke.

Rebecca smoked occasionally herself, but she wasn't proud of it, and hated the smell of tobacco on others. She ceased sitting on the edge of the rear banquette and leaned back, to remove herself a bit further from the smoke and insinuations. She thought an angry silence was the best response.

There was a pause as they swerved around two buses, stopped to let a group of women in burqas cross the street, and then drew up at a light, the other taxi still in front of them. At the next light, however, the taxi in front streamed through while they got caught at the signal. Then another taxi pulled in front of them and stopped to let out its fare. The taxi they'd been following disappeared up Kingsway just in front of the London School of Economics.

"Oh God," sighed Rebecca, feeling hopeless.

"Never you fear, my sweet lady, they was going to King's Cross I'll wager."

"How do you know that?"

"Nine out of ten fares is going to the mainline railway stations. The way they took is best for King's Cross. Let's carry on up that way, shall we, then?"

Rebecca sat back against the seat, holding on to one of the leather straps, as the driver sped off up the wet macadam. The equerry had mentioned Scotland. She searched her brain to try and remember which of the stations Scottish trains left from, but it was no use. Trainspotting didn't interest her in the least, and she hadn't any idea. And what was she going to do if she got to King's Cross and found them? What would she say to Rajiv? She'd never seen The Queen outside the Mews. She had no idea what she'd say to her, either, but what the equerry had said had impressed her with the urgency of the situation. She thought The Queen had at any rate better come back with her to the Mews. She felt reasonably confident she could interest her in some sort of news about Elizabeth or one of the other horses. She began thinking of something she might tell The Queen that she didn't already know, something that would necessitate The Queen's returning with her at once to have a look for herself. Before she knew it they were pulling into the lane for dropping off passengers at King's Cross.

"Sorry we lost them, my beautiful young lady," said the driver cheerfully. "But if you nip in there, I have a feeling you might find them."

Rebecca dug into the pocket of her jeans to look for her cash. The jeans were so tight she had to twist and turn on the seat, much to the driver's amusement. She only had a five-pound note, and the fare was £6.50. She remembered that the rest of her cash was in the pocket of her hoodie. "I've only got this," she said angrily handing him her note. She wouldn't apologize to him, and she didn't know what to do.

"Here's my card. You can send the rest to me. You run in there and see if you can find your boyfriend, then. And if you do find him, then you just call me to say all's well," said the driver handing her a card through the Plexiglas divider. "Or, better still, if you don't find him, you just call me too. Promise?" he said with a cackle.

If this was what it was like to enter fully into the world of adult flirtation, Rebecca wanted to walk firmly in the opposite direction. She did manage a brief smile, and "Thank you," but was out the door and bounding onto the station concourse before the taxi driver could say anything more.

The station itself was a chaotic carnival of fried food for sale, crowds of people looking at the departures and arrivals board, as well as queues everywhere, some for trains soon to depart, some for the till at the newsagent's. Rebecca happened to walk in under the station's nineteenth-century roof near a platform where an intercity train stood with a yellow-nosed engine and passenger carriages painted midnight blue.

A guard in uniform was already blowing his whistle and the last doors were slamming to indicate the train's immediate departure. In the carriage nearest the barrier Rebecca glimpsed Rajiv handing The Queen into the last door. He was just pulling the door closed as he stepped in after her. Rebecca took a run at the barrier and with one hand on the metal stand that read electronic tickets, she vaulted over it in a giant leap, thinking of the first horse who had taken her over a hedge when she was eleven years old. What rapture. She ran up to the last carriage just as the electronic signal was sounding from inside the train to indicate that the doors were about to lock. She tugged the handle down and, wondrously, it still opened. She climbed in and slammed the door to find the guard with an angry face outside the window, blowing his whistle at her. The electronic signal stopped. The door lock sounded audibly. Moments later, with the guard still gesticulating at her furiously, the train glided out of the station and delved into a tunnel.

"A word, Major Thomason?" said Lady Anne popping her head into The Queen's sitting room after a knock on the door. She was surprised to find Luke and William together bent over a computer screen. They both shot her looks as if they'd been interrupted in the midst of some private discussion. They were both also preoccupied with what they had before them on the computer screen.

"Ah, William."

"Lady Anne," said William simply. He wordlessly picked up a tray and headed for the other door.

"Where are you going?" said Luke to William's back.

"I know when I'm *de trop*, Major. I'll just make a few inquiries on the backstairs."

"William, I think you'd better stay," said Luke, but William had already disappeared quietly out the door, without even a sound of the latch.

Lady Anne glanced at Luke and raised her eyebrows for a moment, not in disapproval, but as if to say, "What was that?"

"It's not what . . ."

"Come now, Major Thomason, we have other things to discuss."

Luke relapsed into a distressed silence.

"I've just been speaking with Mrs MacDonald."

"Yes?"

"She thinks The Queen may have gone to Leith."

"Why ever Leith? On a Monday afternoon? With no one to take her?"

"*Britannia*. Tied up there. Now a tourist attraction."

"Surely she's seen it before without having to buy a ticket and wait in the queue?"

"Not only seen it. Lived it. Loved it. It was her life. Many golden moments on that boat, Luke."

"But it'll be shut up for the winter, surely. And why go by herself?"

"Well, Mrs MacDonald thinks The Queen has not been quite herself lately. A bit down. The Queen asked her to sing 'My Favorite Things' not so long ago, apparently."

"Mrs MacDonald?"

"Yes."

"The Queen's dresser?"

"Yes."

"'Raindrops on roses'?"

"I'm afraid so."

"Not what Her Majesty usually speaks to me about."

"Nor me. But she and Mrs MacDonald have been together for a very long time."

"And what has that got to do with *Britannia*?"

"Don't be so dim. If The Queen has not been feeling entirely herself, she may have gone to *Britannia* to cheer herself up, as it were."

"She might have told the equerry first." Luke gave Anne a resentful look. "I could have arranged the transport."

"It's not about you, darling. Don't take it personally. Now, look here. Mrs MacDonald is in The Queen's confidence. More than we are. We have to face it. And I believe you found a Scottish railway timetable?"

"Yes, on her computer."

"Well, then, that's enough to suggest where she might have gone. Mrs MacDonald and I are going to Edinburgh as soon as possible. I've spoken to my nephew. He won't give us the company plane. Don't see why not. I suppose an elderly aunt is not important enough." This time it was Anne's turn to shoot Luke a resentful glance. He was, after all, a young man of about her nephew's age, and sometimes she wondered whether all young men weren't in league against all old ladies. Young men hadn't looked at her on the street for a long time and she still minded. "However, he's offered two seats on the last flight to Edinburgh. British Airways, leaving at 2100 from Heathrow. Also a car to the airport. And the use of the flat in Charlotte Square when we get there. So the two of us are off."

With a somewhat guilty flash, Luke saw for the first time that there was sense in sharing the news. Lady Anne had discovered evidence of where precisely in Scotland The Queen might be headed. She had also devised a strategy for finding her and taking care of her once they arrived.

"Well, under the circumstances, that does seem the best plan," admitted Luke. "Perhaps I'd better stay here until we're sure there are no further reports. If there's nothing, we'll follow you later tonight and be there first thing to arrange transport for the return. Assuming that's where she is. And assuming she's willing to return."

"We'll follow?"

"William de Morgan and I."

"The butler?"

"Yes, Lady Anne," said Luke, drawing himself up to his full height. "The butler. Any questions?"

"None whatsoever, Major Thomason. Not a moment for questions, I shouldn't think. Not a time like this," she said, looking at him steadily in the eye.

Just at that moment a double ring from the telephone sitting on The Queen's desk interrupted them. Luke looked at the phone with alarm.

"I think you'd better pick that up," Anne said levelly.

"But it's The Queen's private line."

"Nevertheless . . ." Anne said, raising her eyebrows.

"Her Majesty's Sitting Room," said Luke tentatively.

"Ah, Major Thomason. Arabella Tyringham-Rode here."

Luke prevented himself from taking a sharp breath. He knew the name. Anyone who read the papers would have known it. Arabella Tyringham-Rode had been appointed a month previously as the first woman head of the internal security service, MI5. "Lady Spy Numero Uno!" the headline in one paper had cried. "Spooks Get First Female Chief" said another. Luke was fully accustomed to dealing with The Queen and members of the royal family. Since coming to the palace a few months previously, he'd also met several senior officers in the army, but the head of MI5, perhaps one of the most powerful members of the entire civil service, still intimidated him. He was determined not to show it. He thought saying as little as possible was the ticket. But what to call her? Better to keep it simple. "Um, hello."

"Can you please tell me what's happened to The Queen?" Her voice was Oxbridge and indicated brisk efficiency.

"Well, I believe she has just stepped away."

"Major Thomason. No nonsense, please. We have audiotapes of your asking Sandringham and Windsor and St James's if they know where she is. Also your call to security asking about her."

"You've tapped Her Majesty's phone!" said Luke indignantly. "How dare you?" For a moment his chivalric notions of honor and fair play got the better of him.

"Look here, *Major*," she said, emphasizing his comparatively junior rank, "The Queen is one of the nation's most important assets. We have to use all available means to protect that asset. If she's been taken—I believe 'kidnapped' is the more old-fashioned term—the security service will need to assume command of retrieving her."

Luke heard only the word "kidnapped." He hadn't even conceived of that until now.

"She has not been kidnapped."

"How do you know?"

"Well, we've got a few items here, that, um, suggest otherwise."

"Tell me."

"No."

"Now, Major," Tyringham-Rode said, using a smoother and more propitiating tone of voice. "We have some trying circumstances before us, do we not?" She could tell he was rattled and needed to be calmed down. "MI5 is prepared to take the burden off your shoulders."

"No," repeated Luke.

"Perhaps you don't understand, Major. Losing Her Majesty is a threat to the integrity of the state of serious proportions. We have a Parliament. We have a Prime Minister. We have a judiciary and courts of law. But The Queen represents us. She is our history. She is the emblem of everything we associate with continuity and correctness. In a secular era, she is the last thing that is sacred." She paused a moment as if considering a philosophical question. "Not in a doctrinal sense, of course, but informally, yes, sacred. And that's just for the United Kingdom. She is, of course, a figure of global significance too. If anything were to happen to her, it would be a blow not only to us, but to people everywhere. You do recognize that this may be not unconnected to the war on terror, don't you?"

Luke listened to this lecture with beads of sweat beginning to trickle down his sides under his shirt. Still he said nothing.

"So you see, Major, it's better if you hand off to us, because the search for her has to be made quietly, quickly, and with all the technological facilities we have at our disposal."

"I quite understand what you're saying, Miss, um, Ms . . ." Luke knew that the palace convention of avoiding "Ms" probably didn't apply here, but he was also momentarily confused.

"Roadie. Nickname since school. Everyone calls me that. Tyringham-Rode's such a mouthful. Why don't you call me 'Roadie' too?" She thought this might be one way of reassuring the frightened major, calming him down, putting him at ease.

Luke was not going to call one of the most important officials in the country "Roadie." "Look here, Ms Roadie, um, sir, um, I mean, ma'am." He breathed heavily outward, angry with himself, and looked at the ceiling. He didn't dare look at Lady Anne, a mixture of apprehension and sympathy in her eyes as she watched him on the phone. "Here in the Household, we have a notion where Her Majesty may have gone. We'd like to bring her back on our own without alarming her. She won't be happy to disturb MI5. That would displease her very much. So why don't you let me handle this? I think I may be able to find her and have her back here within twenty-four hours." Luke had no idea whether that was possible or not. The number had just stuck in his head from William's having mentioned it earlier.

"No, Major, twenty-four hours is too long. I can give you thirty minutes."

"Half an hour?" said Luke incredulously.

"Look here, Major, I have your details in front of me. Decorated for bravery in the Middle East. Well done. You better than anyone will understand. I can give you thirty minutes. And if nothing then, you will hand over to us." She hung up the phone without saying goodbye.

Luke quietly put down the telephone.

"Oh, Luke. Was that Arabella Tyringham-Rode?" Anne had heard and guessed that much. "Poor boy. She gave you a rough time. I'm so sorry. But Her Majesty will *not* like it, wherever she is, if MI5 are the ones who turn up to find her."

"No," assented Luke, still dazed by the telephone call. "No, she won't." In agreeing with Anne, and thinking of The Queen's likely reaction to half a dozen men in dark coats with tiny audio phones in their ears turning up out of nowhere, he found some strength he didn't have the moment before. "And if we get there before them, she won't have to know about them. We can protect her from them." Then he turned to Anne, more indignant still, and said, "Do you know she *actually* wanted me to call her 'Roadie.'"

"Unbelievable," said Anne. Then she paused a moment, wrinkled her nose, and said, "What is a roadie, by the way?"

"Road crew. Set up the speakers and things for a rock concert."

"Oh dear, no, we can't have The Queen being interfered with by Roadie and her crew." She gave an involuntary shudder. "Why, she'd rather give Mr Putin a pedicure than go to a rock concert. But look at the time. Mrs MacDonald and I have to get to Heathrow. You and William will . . . ?"

"We'll follow. When we're sure there's nothing more to be learned here. Yes."

"Good," said Lady Anne, walking out the door, "Household versus Roadies. I know which side I'm on."

Luke smiled wanly and then fished his mobile phone out of his pocket to check the time.

~

Rajiv hopped into the taxi after The Queen because he was worried about her. When he flagged down the taxi, and told the driver she was going to King's Cross, he just jumped in beside her without asking. The Queen protested. "Wouldn't a bus be more economical? I'm sure you should be staying to look after the shop. But thank you nevertheless." She noticed for the first time the intoxicating cheesy smell of his jacket, the beautiful contrast of his brown hands on his blue jeans. "What part of India is your family from?" She thought it safer to ask whether his family was from India, as he might have been born in Britain himself, and might be touchy to be called "Indian" rather than "British." She did not make the same mistake as the senior courtier at the dinner in the Castle.

He appreciated the distinction. "Ahmedabad, Ma'am. My great-grandfather was a doctor there. My grandparents came here after the war."

"Ah, just like Queen Victoria's *munshi*."

"Pardon me, Ma'am?"

"Well, Queen Victoria had two Indian servants. She grew rather fond of one of them, Abdul Karim. His father was said to have been a doctor too." She paused to look with interest out the window. How different busy London looked when the police hadn't cleared the road for her car. "I don't blame her. He was quite handsome. She had herself photographed with him working on dispatch boxes. He started as someone who waited at table. Then she asked him to give her lessons in Hindustani. She ended by giving him Frogmore Cottage to live in for his lifetime, and a title that was something like Indian secretary, or *munshi*. The Household loathed him, of course. They were all quite, quite conscious of skin color in those days, weren't they? I suppose we are still, aren't we?"

Rajiv didn't know quite how to speak to the sovereign about race. Many of his friends whose families had begun in India some generations earlier, though well-integrated Londoners in every other respect, still felt that they were looked down upon as "black." "I suppose we are, Ma'am," Rajiv said evenly.

"Have you experienced any unpleasantness?"

"I have, Ma'am."

"Would you like to tell me?"

"No, Ma'am."

"Let's see if we can't start, here and now, to make things better together, shall we?" She slipped her arm, clad in its blue sweatshirt material, through the corner of his arm in its army jacket and held on to the roundness of his bicep.

Inwardly, Rajiv began to radiate with the heat of this honor she'd done him, partly as the sovereign, but even more than that as a strange elderly lady who trusted him and who was grateful for whatever small services he could provide for her. He would have died for her at that moment. He glowed.

"He grew quite fat later on."

"Ma'am?"

"The *munshi*. Mind you don't."

"No, Ma'am." Rajiv felt he'd just been engaged to do something, he wasn't sure what. He was ready to do anything she required of him.

"What do you know about yoga?"

"Nothing, Ma'am."

"Well, then, perhaps you could tell me a little about Swami Vivekananda."

"Swami who?"

"He brought yoga to this country. I thought you would know him. You see, I thought yoga was Hindu in its origins?"

"Well, it may well be, Ma'am, but I was born here. I'm Marmite-on-toast in origins."

"Oh, yes, Marmite. Lovely." The Queen thought a moment and then circled back. "But, you do practice yoga now, don't you? I was under the impression that all the young did. Just as they all have mobile phones."

"Well, I have a mobile phone, Ma'am, but I've never practiced yoga."

"Really?" said The Queen with some incredulity. "But even I practice yoga."

Now it was Rajiv's turn to look at her and express surprise. "Really?"

"Yes. Quite hard work it is too. Not as easy as it looks. But I'm getting better. I was quite stiff at first. I find it relaxes me, stretches me out, helps clear my mind."

"It does?" said Rajiv, still skeptical.

"Well, I know I don't look flexible, but actually I am. Very. I find the *balasana* very relaxing indeed."

Rajiv looked at her curiously. He had no idea what she was talking about.

"Child's pose," said The Queen proudly. "It's one of the basics. I couldn't do it at first. You kneel down and then lean forward over your knees, holding your arms out. Rather hard on the knees to start out with, but lovely for the lower back. Now I can do it," she said, looking him in the eye and smiling.

"Good for you, Ma'am."

"I think so."

They were soon at King's Cross and standing beneath the digital screen listing the impending departures of intercity trains. The Queen pointed up to one that said Edinburgh Waverley departing at 1700. "That one, five o'clock," she said. "Now, we haven't much time, perhaps you could help me find the platform." He found the platform, but they were stopped at the closed ticket barrier. He thought it was beneath her dignity to have a train ticket, so he brought her to where the guard was standing. The guard looked at this young man helping a pensioner in a scarf under her blue hoodie, smiled at them, and then pressed a button releasing the barrier. She gave him her usual percussive "Thank you" as she walked slowly past him on Rajiv's arm. It sounded familiar to him. He looked at her curiously, but he could not place her.

It was already just minutes before the hour as Rajiv helped The Queen into the last carriage and found a seat for her at a table for four where there was one space free. The carriage was crowded, as everyone who was boarding the train at the last minute had been finding their seats in this carriage closest to the barrier. The Queen settled down into her seat and then turned up to him an appealing face. "Now, you've done more than enough. You've got to get back to the shop or they'll give away your post, you know?" There was something slightly hectoring about her concern, as if she were his nanny, but he appreciated the fact that she was thinking of him rather than herself. "You must get off the train before it goes. We'll be in touch," said The Queen, turning to survey the three people sitting at her table. He knew that he'd been dismissed. The other passengers at her table seemed relatively harmless. She'd ordered him to go, so Rajiv turned on his heel to get off the train. Just as he arrived back at the doorway from the carriage to the platform, he heard the electronic signal sounding. The door was flung open. Rebecca jumped onto the train, slammed the door, and looked back out the window at an angry guard who was blowing his whistle at her. Then the signal stopped sounding and the door locked.

Part IV

Pranayama

The Queen came back from her drive in the pony cart with the Prime Minister. She mulled over the loss of the royal train. First it had been the dedicated aeroplanes, then *Britannia*, and now this. She looked back ten or fifteen years earlier and recalled 1992, her *annus horribilis*. It was a bad year for a number of reasons, really the crisis of the modern monarchy in her recollection, and she thought, quite secretly, for she wouldn't admit this even to the Duke of Edinburgh, that it was her fault. Above all she believed she'd been a failure because she couldn't find the right words. Everything that she was now suffering through, not just this proposal to get rid of the royal train, but even the sadness she could see around her eyes when she looked at herself in the mirror in the morning, followed from that year, and from what had happened then.

The marriages of all three of her married children had broken apart. Anne had been divorced from Mark Phillips. Andrew had separated from Sarah Ferguson. Most spectacularly of all, the Morton book about Diana had led to her separation from the Prince of Wales. How had this happened, all in a matter of months? The monarchy seemed to do well when the marriages were rubbing along all right. It was when marriages went foul, when divorce, and *divorcées*, came into the picture, that the throne wobbled, as in 1936, when her Uncle David caused so much trouble by wanting to marry Mrs Simpson. And what was the secret to a happy marriage? She didn't know. Her own marriage was based on putting up with a cantankerous old man who shouted and blustered and bullied, who disappeared for months at a time to Australia or New Zealand just when she wanted him most, who made her laugh during the Braemar Games by muttering *sotto voce* on a windy day, "Keep your kilts down, lads. The Sovereign's watching."

No, the success of her marriage, if you could call it that, was based on having gone through the Second World War, taken tepid baths, sat down to dry teacakes that hadn't enough butter or sugar, interrupted her riding life to try her hand at being a truck mechanic in a regiment for women. She didn't do all these things willingly. She put up with them because it was the war. Her children hadn't that spirit-of-the-war endurance or sense of self-sacrifice or ability to resign themselves to a less-than-ideal daily life. They wanted to be happy. All their generation did. Of course she loved the Duke. Loved him very much in fact. They'd been through so much together. He knew her better than anyone, wasn't afraid of her as so many others were. But it wasn't a sentimental romance. It was more like a battered estate wagon in which they bounced along together, sometimes cheerfully amused by the same joke, other times grimly tolerating one another and determined to get where they were going.

She had a formula when any critical decision was in contemplation. Give it a trial of six months. Don't do anything hasty. Whenever she brought on a new private secretary, she'd say, "Shall we give it six months? Let's have a trial period." Or if any minister complained to her in an audience that he couldn't decide about an important policy, her advice was always, "Can you give it six months? Mull it over and decide then?" So in June of 1992, when the Morton book had come out, and there was pretty authentic information all over the press, the broadsheets as well as the tabloids, that the marriage had come unstuck, she knew what she was going to say. The Prince and Princess of Wales happened to be on the spot, staying in Windsor for the annual house party that accompanied the races at Ascot. It was the Duke of Edinburgh's idea to shanghai them into a surprise audience, confront them with the Morton book, and get them to make up or break up. She wasn't so sure this was a good idea, but in family matters the Duke was King and all she could do was try to be helpful.

All four of them were in the sitting room overlooking the Long Walk. It was before luncheon, and soon they'd have to go down and join the others, for the hour they were to be off to the races was two pm sharp and they mustn't miss that. The Queen checked her wristwatch. Charles stood at one end of the room and hung his head miserably. Diana stood at the other end and hung her head too, not in misery but in disguised defiance. The Duke paced back and forth, giving a naval rant as if to his most junior ratings. "What in the devil's name do you two think you're doing? Everyone in this damnable country just wants you to be happy. Why can't you put on a good show and then go off and have your own things on the side?"

The Queen wasn't sure she liked this. Was that what he'd done with her? Put on a good show? Was that *all*? The Prince and Princess of Wales said nothing.

"If you won't bloody listen to me, then think of The Queen. What are you putting her through? Her father shoved into the job in 1936 when he wasn't ready for it and then came all through the war. Died a young man. It killed him. Now The Queen's been doing it since she was in her twenties. You'd think she'd be entitled to a little rest after, what? Nearly sixty years! Instead of which you bloody fools are going to bring the whole ceiling crashing down on all of us." The Duke then turned to The Queen and roared at her, "Talk to them! They're not having it from me."

For the first time both Charles and Diana looked up. They both wanted to obey her, she could see that. Even for them, at war as they were, she personified something bigger than themselves, something to which they both hoped to remain loyal. They were both willing to listen to her if she could put it eloquently and reasonably, if she could say it the right way.

"What if you were to jog along together for six months? Give it one last try and then decide?" said The Queen weakly. She could see as soon as she said it that it wasn't enough. Charles was tongue-tied in the face of his two parents. Diana looked down again and fiddled with the blue sash of her Ascot frock.

They'd both agreed to try to repair their marriage, but then it emerged that Diana had given her full cooperation to the Morton book, which they hadn't known before. Secret tapes of their conversations with lovers were broadcast and transcripts published. Windsor burned. The Government refused to pay for its repair after a media storm of abuse, which blamed her. Questions about royal payment of income tax had made things worse. The Prime Minister announced the official separation of the Prince and Princess of Wales in Parliament. On the night she'd watched the Castle go up in flames, on the verge of public tears for the first time in her life, The Queen had told her mother that she was so distraught that she feared for her sanity. All that happened that year was the beginning of where she was now, the dull, aching sadness that wouldn't go away.

Then Diana had died in Paris and the little boys had been pulled, against The Queen's will, by public demand, into the midst of a media circus. The orgy of public grief was, in The Queen's eyes, not Britain's finest hour. If she'd only wept then, perhaps everything would have been all right. But The Queen's tears were internal. The great mountains of flowers reminded her of the plastic bouquets and wooden crosses sometimes found on Italian roadsides to mark automobile smashes and in perpetual memory of someone who died. When had Britain become so Mediterranean?

No, Britain had changed, and against her will the monarchy changed too, under the influence of marketing experts at Number 10. She was sent out more rarely to lunch with the Grenadier Guards, and made to go instead to visit a new McDonald's. She wanted to face the cameras less often than before, but now every time she looked at a briefing paper from the private secretary it seemed that a new television crew was inside the palace walls, filming something. She didn't mind the old school of photographers, Tony Snowdon and Cecil Beaton, but now they wanted to invite in the Americans and *Vanity Fair.* Miss Annie Leibovitz had been telephoned for, and she was flying over from the States, bringing eleven people, and her daughter, to do a snapshot, as if it might save the day and repair the soundness of something she'd worked all her life to keep running smoothly. It made The Queen angry, but she felt there was nothing she could do. She'd been taught by her father that she had to accept the advice of Number 10, and nowadays her own private office and Number 10 appeared to be in cahoots to humiliate her in one way or another.

Leibovitz's crew had been in touch in advance of their arrival. They wanted to photograph The Queen in the saddle, mounted on a horse—in the sitting room, of all places! She put her foot down at that. "Absolutely not," she told Shirley, who'd been deputized by the private secretary to tell The Queen, as he was afraid of her reaction if he told her himself. Shirley had dutifully returned to the private secretary and told him The Queen didn't think it was a good idea.

Next they'd heard from the Americans that they thought of recreating a famous Cecil Beaton photo in which she'd stood wearing a naval cloak for him. Cecil was charming. She'd been younger then. No grey in her hair. She remembered the session vividly, "You won't need your crown for this session, Ma'am," he'd said, "but I shall need mine. I've grown so bald that I need something to cover it up." She'd given her laughing assent to his wearing his hat indoors. But why try to imitate what he'd already done so perfectly? Hadn't Miss Leibovitz any ideas of her own? Still, she was conscious of having turned down one request, so she agreed to the naval cloak. She and Shirley were upstairs, arranging the cloak, when they got word from the photographer's crew downstairs. Could she put on the Garter robes first? They'd do the naval cloak later? The Queen was indignant. Putting on the Garter robes was serious work. It meant a different floor-length gown underneath and being strapped by several dozen internal ties into the long velvet cape that went on top. And a tiara too, which meant a special arrangement of hair.

"Really! This is the last straw," said The Queen to Shirley, who thought it better to remain silent as the sovereign vented. As Shirley worked on the ties inside the mantle, The Queen checked the clock on the chimneypiece. "This will make us late!" She was aware that the photography session would now delay her engagements for the rest of the day. The ambassadors would have to wait, and the Chancellor of the Exchequer too. She might not even be free at the dogs' teatime to feed them herself, the one part of the day that always cheered her up.

Shirley and a page gathered up The Queen's Garter robes as she streamed down the corridor toward the elevator, still grumbling. When they arrived in the Bow Room of Buckingham

Palace, where Miss Leibovitz had set up her equipment, The Queen had recovered a modicum of civility. The press secretary knew the sovereign was angry and gave her an especially low curtsey, the young woman's gym-toned left leg shooting out from her short skirt and bending around behind her for support as she bent the right knee deeply. She then introduced The Queen to Annie Leibovitz, who introduced her to members of the camera crew and to her daughter. The little girl gave The Queen a large chrysanthemum. The Queen passed this to Lady Anne, who stood unobtrusively behind her, and sat down on the seat which Miss Leibovitz had indicated in front of the window. Shirley expertly arranged the Garter robes behind her so as not to pull The Queen over. Leibovitz began clicking her camera shutter. After a dozen clicks, she turned around to her assistant and said, "Could we try something a little less dressy? What about taking off the tiara?"

The Queen heard her distinctly. "Too dressy!" she said irritably. "What do you think this is?" If she hadn't been firmly moored in place by the heavy train of the Garter robes, she would have stood up and walked out. The Order of the Garter went back to 1348. It was the oldest and most valuable honor in her gift. It coincided with the birth of the medieval monarchy itself. It was not a costume for charades.

Leibovitz looked at The Queen. She was used to catering to the whims of Hollywood celebrities, but she wasn't quite sure how to handle an angry monarch. Was she being ironic? Was she joking? An instant's examination of The Queen's face, with Shirley speeding in to try and make things better, and Lady

Anne hovering in the background with a worried expression, suggested to her that The Queen was not joking. She began trying to explain what she meant, using the tone of voice she used with her daughter during a tantrum.

The Queen, for her part, boiling hot from the robes to begin with, upset about the timing, feeling as if Miss Annie Leibovitz was just abusing her as everyone else had started to do in the wake of 1992, suddenly remembered something. Her yoga instructor had spent several whole sessions just breathing with her. "The breath, Your Majesty, the breath! *Pranayama*." It was the key to what she called "mindfulness," to calming down. Breathing did help. So, ignoring the pleas of photographer and photographer's assistants and press secretary and dresser and lady-in-waiting, all of whom were buzzing and clucking their tongues encouragingly around her, she began breathing deeply and clearing her mind.

At Eton, teachers were "masters," and for English literature Rajiv had a teacher who was a master. The boys thought of him as ancient and decrepit. They liked to make fun of the dandruff that covered his shoulders like a fall of snow. This English master had no use for impertinent boys. He ignored them. To bright boys, though, he gave all his energy and attention. He beamed upon them, chivvied them, chastised them, encouraged them, and praised them inordinately. Like small seedlings in a pot, they warmed to the glow of his sunshine. Their leaves increased and they grew. As he observed them growing, his own soul, deep in his withering body, also prospered and grew.

Rajiv was one of these boys. The English master had noticed him right away because his eyes were always wide open, while most of the others always looked half asleep. The text which especially stirred Rajiv was Shakespeare's *Henry V.* A young English king takes an English army to France, where, though badly outnumbered, he wins a great victory and takes away a French wife as his prize. Why should a teenaged boy be interested in that? The English master sat at night by himself in his study wondering what he could do with the boys that would appeal to them, shatter the hard carapace of their indifference, persuade them to love what he loved.

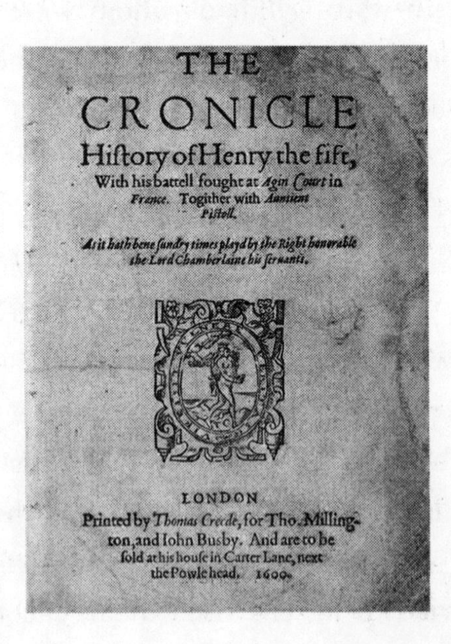
THE
CRONICLE
History of Henry the fift,
With his battell fought at *Agin Court* in *France.* Togither with *Auntient Pistoll.*

As it hath bene sundry times playd by the Right honorable the Lord Chamberlaine his seruants.

LONDON
Printed by *Thomas Creede*, for Tho. Millington, and Iohn Busby. And are to be sold at his house in Carter Lane, next the Powle head. 1600.

The next morning, he showed the boys the cover of the famous "bad quarto" of the play, reconstructed from an early performance and only a fraction of the length of the standard edition. He pointed to "The *Cronicle* History of Henry *fift*" and remarked dryly, "The publisher spelled as well as you lot do." He then turned to video games. As he suspected, their favorites were those that involved killing opponents with instruments of medieval torture. They enjoyed any gothic fantasy that included a frightening beast, a haunted castle, or a zombie returned from the dead. The boys also relished heroic feats required to destroy any of these three. This was his start. One group of boys he assigned to assemble all the ghost stories associated with Windsor Castle they could find. Another group he asked to design a video game involving armies assailing one another with longbows, the instruments Henry V had used at the Battle of Agincourt. A third he asked to find the most gruesome images they could discover online of injuries sustained during medieval warfare. The boys, even the sleepiest ones, all woke up and began to enjoy themselves.

Next the English master brought in a video of Kenneth Branagh's *Henry V*. He asked them to watch the opening scene several times. Derek Jacobi, wearing a naval cloak and standing on an empty soundstage, recited Shakespeare's lines. Jacobi plays "Chorus," a single character, who tells members of the audience that they are going to have to use their imaginations if they are going to succeed in recreating a big battlefield inside a small theatre. The English master took the boys outside and made them look up at the high walls of the Castle dominating Eton and the river.

He asked them to take turns reciting Chorus's lines,

Suppose within the girdle of these walls
Are now confined two mighty monarchies,
Whose high upreared and abutting fronts
The perilous narrow ocean parts asunder.

"What is 'girdle of these walls'?" he asked one boy.

"Um, not sure, sir."

Rajiv's hand went up.

"Laroia?"

"The theatre, sir?"

"Yes, boy," the master said wearily, though he was secretly delighted. "And what are the 'two mighty monarchies'?" he asked another.

"Is one of them The Queen, sir?"

"No!" thundered the English master.

Rajiv's hand was up again.

"Well, isn't it the English monarchy, sir, but in 1415, at the time of Agincourt? Then the other monarchy would be France, wouldn't it?"

The English master nodded his head yes while rolling his eyes in mock exhaustion. Some of the boys understood that he was playing with them, and tittered. "And so, Laroia. You seem to know everything." He had saved his hardest question for last. "Will you tell us, please, what 'high upreared and abutting fronts' are?"

"Well, um, that's poetry, sir."

The English master couldn't help smiling at that. Nothing

better than being surprised by an intelligent boy. The other boys would have hated Rajiv for being a know-all, but he had such a reliable supply of sweets and snacks that they always had fun in his room, so they gave him a pass.

For his part, Rajiv was absolutely bowled over by the play. He got his own copy of Branagh's *Henry V* and played it over and over on his laptop. When he had his housemates in his room late in the evening he would also do burlesque send-ups of the play, modeled on the film, for their amusement. One of his favorite gags was to take the blanket off his bed, drape it over his shoulders as if it were a naval cloak, and pretend to be Derek Jacobi playing the part of Chorus. In the film, Jacobi suddenly raises his voice at the end of the prologue where he asks the patience of the audience, "Gently to hear, kindly to judge, our play." Rajiv had memorized these lines and liked saying them with ascending loudness until he was shouting "OUR PLAY!" with a bullfighting flourish of his blanket. The boys thought this was hilarious. If he put the wicker wastebasket on his head at the same time, they wriggled as if they might wet the bed.

He enjoyed the laughter and took it as his applause. It was a lot better than playing Lord Mountbatten in India, anyway. In fact, the history of Indian independence inspired him a good deal less than what he'd read of princely India, with its elaborate courts, where legend had it that maharajahs made love to beautiful maidens next to splashing fountains and were served sherbet afterwards. This was a great deal more attractive to Rajiv than modern India, with its cowboy capitalism. The counterpart of princely India, in his mind, was medieval England. He loved the legend of St George, who killed a dragon that was about to eat a princess. St George got the princess instead. This appealed to Rajiv's deeply chivalric instincts. He also loved the part of *Henry V* where Henry, leading a charge of his men on the besieged town of Harfleur, cries out to them,

For there is none of you so mean and base,
That hath not noble lustre in your eyes.
I see you stand like greyhounds in the slips,
Straining upon the start. The game's afoot:
Follow your spirit, and upon this charge
Cry 'God for Harry, England, and Saint George!'

He recalled the attitude of the boys in the alley, and of the senior courtier who'd said he wasn't English. He knew that they all thought of him as "mean and base." What he loved about King Henry was that he seemed always to manage to bring his men together despite what the English master had told them about vast social differences that separated different sorts of men in medieval England. Henry brought the men together, not by giving them chocolates, but by using his language, his poetry, his skills as an orator, his words, and it was in this discovery that Rajiv's desire to be a poet was born. The English master had shown Rajiv Shelley's *Defense of Poetry* from 1821 in which he said that poets were "the unacknowledged legislators of the world." This proposition was on the face of it so impossible, so absurd, that Rajiv devoted all his adolescent idealism to wondering how it might be made to come true.

The young man from the demo had started calling Rebecca almost right away after the night they spent together. He was attracted to her, and her being younger than him seemed to make her more pliable than girls his own age. He was not put off by her disappearing in the middle of the night after they slept together, and he wanted to do it again. He had no idea how awful it had been for her. For her part, she was surprised to see a number she didn't recognize popping up on her mobile telephone the next day when she was back in school. When she answered, curiously, there he was, chattering away about going to another antihunt demonstration. Did she want to come along? She managed to put him off without giving an excuse, but then he called again a week later and asked again. This time the demo was not in town but somewhere out in the country. He'd stop by and pick her up. The badger was going, he told her winningly, and wanted to see her again. She did, frankly, want to see the badger. She also thought she could avoid returning with him to the Elephant by asking him to drop her off somewhere near Waterloo, where she could catch the train home without alerting her parents to where she'd been.

So one Saturday in the autumn, she found herself booming along the motorway in his rusty Austin Cooper, the pavement of the roadway racing dangerously near the bottom of the car and each bump they hit feeling as if it might send both of them flying toward the ditch. He told her excitedly about the demo. It was an actual meeting of the hounds, a real foxhunt. A group of protesters was collecting to disrupt it, if they could. He talked about all the groups that were coming, "sending delegations," as he put it. Not only were the antihunt people, the organizers, going to be there, he said there would be a "whole damned Iraq War coalition" of forces. There were also the Greenham Common women, who'd been camped outside the American airbase for years to protest the nuclear weaponry housed there, a crew of anarchists, and some radical vegans, as well as many others. Rebecca only half listened to this narrative as she had the badger, which usually travelled in a wooden cage that sat on the backseat, out of his cage and in her lap before the young man could protest.

When they left the motorway and pulled onto a small two-lane affair, she briefly felt a stab of love for the country. You could be more alone in the country, and although London had many parks and trees, they didn't compare with actually living on her parents' vegetable farm. She longed for independence from her parents, but she also loved the rural landscape of her childhood. They drove through newly harvested fields shaved gold, and not yet plowed under for the winter, next to coppices, the tree leaves having already turned brown. Soon they came to a halt when they came over a rise and found the highway blocked by police cars with flashing blue lights. Along the verges of the road several dozen cars and vans had been parked. A group of protesters were milling about on one side of the police blockade, with uniformed officers holding the people back. They parked the car and approached the group along the barrier. The young man knew many of the people in the crowd and started talking with them, in what Rebecca thought of as a slightly conspiratorial way. She didn't want to be introduced, she was too shy for introductions, so she hung back with the badger.

She noticed that quite a few of the protesters had ski masks, either rolled up on their heads or bulging in their pockets. She wondered why they had them, for although it was chilly, it wasn't cold enough for gloves or skiwear. A lot of the men were wearing military-style flak jackets, as if they were on an armed operation somewhere. It seemed to be the fashion.

As she milled about on the edges of the crowd, observing, she could see in the distance that on the rise of one of the plowed fields, a group of people on horseback were following at a walking pace behind a huntsman who was with a group of dogs. She couldn't make out how many there were, but a good many were wearing red—"pink" was the proper term—and many of the others were in tight-fitting black jackets. She could see ladies who had their hair rolled in buns underneath their black caps.

Rebecca hated the arrogance of foxhunters, posh people who swanned about in their fast cars, raised their voices in country pubs, and watched idly as dogs ripped foxes from end to end, but she did admire the spectacle of foxhunting, and was secretly proud of it as something that English people did. Foxes had killed some of her most cherished hens, and she thought of them as vermin; but, on the other hand, foxes were only acting on instinct. She wanted foxhunting banned. She was sure of that. But she would have preferred to keep the spectacle while somehow preserving the lives of both foxes and hens.

Suddenly, the huntsman, the dogs, and the following riders started moving off the hilltop and downward, clearly intent on crossing the roadway. The police had blocked off both protesters and automobile traffic in both directions and were making way for the hunters to cross onto another neighboring field. Some signal seemed to have been given among the protesters. The ski masks and other dark scarves came out of pockets, and people started pulling them down over their faces. The young man whom she'd driven down with now had on one too, and he had the boot of the Austin Cooper open with half a dozen others gathering round him. She moved closer to see what they were doing. She saw them handing out knives, with the sunshine glinting on steel blades.

"Hey, what the hell are you doing?" she asked, her shyness forgotten in the instant of seeing the knives.

"Stay back, Rebecca," the young man told her. "Steer clear. Get in the car, turn it round, and have it running for when I get back."

"But what are you doing with the knives?"

"We're going to disrupt the hunt."

"How?"

"When the horses cross, we're going after them."

"Going after who?"

"The riders. We're going to get them thrown off."

"And then knife them?" said Rebecca, not believing what she was witnessing, feeling as if she were in the midst of some great, slow-moving, automobile accident she was powerless to stop.

"No, no. We go after the horses and then the horses will throw 'em off into the road."

"You're going to kill the horses!"

"Not kill them. Just surprise them. Give them a little a jab, a little gouge, until they rear up and throw the riders."

"You *cannot* do that."

"Look, if you're not up for this, just stay away. Start walking back up the road. You'll get to the village in about ten minutes. You can get a train back to London from there. But this is too important to let you interfere." With that, he turned his back on her and ran up to join the rest of the ski masks who were making their way to the front of the police barricade.

Rebecca felt sick to her stomach, but also desperate to stop any injury to the horses. She quickly put the badger back in his cage in the car and then ran up to the blockade. It was quite difficult to make it to the front. The number of people kept her back, and no one felt inclined to make way to let her go forward. She ran up to a policewoman standing at the edge of the crowd, away from the barrier, just beside a hedgerow.

"You've got to stop them." Rebecca cursed herself—she gave an involuntary sob and tears started rolling down her left cheek. "Damn, damn, damn," she said to herself. "You useless coward."

"We *are* stopping them," said the policewoman, not happy to be addressed by one of the rabble.

"No, no, no," Rebecca wailed. "You have got to listen to me." But she couldn't speak further as her sense of panic made it impossible for her to communicate what she had to say.

"Go and sit down, miss," said the policewoman impartially, keeping her eyes on her colleagues at the barricades. There seemed to be some forward surge from the crowd. The hunters on horseback were now reaching the roadway and beginning to cross. Rebecca was in full flood, and she couldn't get out more than a few words in between deep wracking breaths. "They have . . . knives." She bent her head over and the tears ran hot down her neck. "They're after the horses."

The policewoman heard her and took two steps forward. "*Oi*, Rod!" she yelled to one of her colleagues. "Watch out! They have knives!"

Just then the first horses and riders began clopping onto the hard surface of the road with the iron-shod hooves of the horses. At the same time, five people in ski masks slipped under the barriers and pushed past the police, who were outnumbered by the protesters. They ran forward with their knife blades exposed and the first horses started screaming, not from being wounded but from the shock of being approached by strangers in ski masks. The police radioed for reinforcements. One of the first riders was thrown from her horse, and confused shouts went up from the crowd. It was a mess, a muddied, muddled, disorderly jumble of police, protesters, riders, and horses, with humans and animals crying out in distress. An Independent Television Network camera and crew had taken up their post on another rise in the ground and were filming it all for the evening news.

Rebecca crumpled up in a ball beside the hedge, her knees in the mud, her head in her hands. She couldn't stop crying. Another young man approached her and got down on his knees next to her. "Becca? Is that you? Becca?"

Who was here? Who could possibly know her? Only the young man she'd driven down with knew her name. She looked up and recognized another boy who was a little older than her. Her parents used to take vegetables to a group of protesters who were trying to stop a road being built, she couldn't remember where. She couldn't be sure, as he used to live with some other protesters up in the trees. She'd never had a very close look at him. "Oh, hi. Um, sorry. I'm useless." She looked up at him with tear-streaked misery. She managed to get out, "I don't remember your name."

"Dickon Bevil." He smiled at her. "I suppose I was always too high up for a proper shake hands. Are your parents here?" he said, looking around over her shoulder. "They used to send us up vegetables in a basket tied at the end of a rope."

"No." She now remembered sending the baskets up. "Did you come here to hurt the horses too?" she asked accusingly.

"Lord no. It was planned as a nonviolent protest. Greenpeace is just here to lend moral support. Swell the numbers. I think a fringe element must have brought the knives. Anyway, the police have now got the upper hand." He added, with disappointment, "Won't be a good story for us on the news." He nodded toward the television crew.

As they spoke, Rebecca still on the ground, and Dickon crouching near her, the police brought several of the ski masks by in handcuffs. One of them was the young man she'd accompanied to the protest, his wrists chained behind his back. "Rebecca!" he said. "Hang on a minute," he said to the policeman leading him to a police van down the road. "Let me give the keys to the car to my girlfriend."

"I'm not your girlfriend," said Rebecca, still angry and shocked about the knives.

"Okay, whatever. Look, can you get the car back to London? Leave it near my flat? I don't know how long they're going to lock us up for. We could be at Her Majesty's pleasure for a while."

Rebecca was torn. Here was the only man who'd ever shown her kindness, who'd wrapped her in a white sheet, who'd never said to her, "You stink!" He was asking her to help him. She was secretly pleased at the same time as she was still upset with him.

"Come on, love, just come and take the keys out of my jeans pocket." He hadn't hands to gesture, so he nodded her toward him and pointed his eyes down toward one of his front pockets.

The policeman seemed inclined to allow this. It would be one less car that they had to tow away during the clean-up operation.

"She is not putting her hand in your pocket, I'm afraid. *Mate*." Dickon suddenly stood up from where he'd been kneeling down next to her. Rebecca could see he was angry. She was surprised at how posh his accent was. His voice had seemed normal when he was talking to her before. Now he seemed to be using 1950s BBC English to take charge of all present.

"Who are you, then?" asked the young man with a sneer.

"Never mind who I am. Do you realize you lot have ruined what might have been a very effective peaceful protest? We will have lost credibility with the public. That won't get the legislation through Parliament." He spoke with authority, as if his family had once owned half a dozen pocket boroughs to which they could nominate their own MPs without need of election, as indeed the Bevil earls had, about two centuries previously.

The policeman pushed the young man along. He wasn't standing by to listen to internal disagreements among the protesters. "Look, there isn't time for this," said the young man. "You take the keys out of my pocket, then. Hand them to her. Go on, have a squeeze of the family jewels if that's what you're after." It was an insult, not an invitation.

"Not my taste. Can't tell what yours might be." Dickon stepped forward, shoved his hand in the young man's pocket more roughly than was necessary, and gave the young man's testicles an intentional jab in the process. Then he fished out the keys.

"Bloody fucking hell," said the young man as he doubled over.

"All right, you lot, that's enough," said the policeman, and he pulled the young man away by the crook of his arm, still groaning.

Rebecca watched all this with disgust. She'd seen rival cocks fight among the bantams. This was the same.

The Queen had driven off to have luncheon with the Airlies on the other side of the hill, so Luke and Anne had the afternoon off. It was unusually warm for late September and they'd decided to go on the footpath below the ruin of Knock Castle. Luke had been doing some research online, ignoring all the pamphlet literature on local walks that was literally stuffed into the equerry's desk at Balmoral. He had discovered something called the "Seven Bridges Walk," which took in a big stone arched bridge over the

Dee, a smaller bridge over the Muick, and, most spectacular of all, a Victorian footbridge called Polhollick. He and Anne had parked the car near the entrance to the road that led to the Queen Mother's fishing lodge and started along the stony footpath through the tall pines.

"Don't know if I'll make it across all seven bridges," said Anne, laughing a little ruefully. "You may end up having to carry me on your back like a sack of potatoes."

At this Luke went charging off into the underbrush, and came back with two tree branches, which he broke into size for sturdy walking sticks. "There you are. A wand for you. A pike for me."

Anne took her stick gratefully. Luke was a courtly young man, the equerries often were. What was different were the dark clouds that sometimes crossed his brow, the awkward silences, his having wept in front of her, a virtual stranger. But she liked him more because of all these things, not less. She was sure he needed professional help. In the middle of a silence between them, she wondered about how to return to the subject. Instead, he surprised her by asking, "Do you have children, Lady Anne?"

"A boy, a son, only one."

"Perhaps wish there were more?" He looked not at her, but up into the pine boughs.

"No, I think not. I have enough trouble with the one. We don't speak."

Luke saw that this was sensitive territory and wondered whether it was better just to be quiet and let her carry on, or to press for more. He said nothing.

"I suppose I interfered too much. Saw what he needed. Told him what he should do. His father died when he was quite young, so I had to be both parents at once, you see?"

"Mmm," said Luke sympathetically.

"Well, he got involved in environmental politics when he was at school. And before I knew it he just upped and left. Went to go live in the trees. To prevent a bypass from being constructed."

"A lot to be said for trees," said Luke, surveying the military ranks of pines along the path. They had been planted as a cash crop for ultimate harvesting. They were now reaching their adult growth.

"Yes, yes, of course. But you need qualifications, training, a university degree."

"Oh well. University of life, and so on, you know."

"Yes, I know," said Anne, unpropitiated. After a pause, she continued, slightly more cheerfully. "I did find a picture of him in the paper the other day."

"Oh?"

"In a pontoon boat, harassing a Japanese whaler. Trying to prevent them catching whales. Greenpeace."

"Good cause. Brave chap."

In her heart, Anne loved Luke more for saying this, as it was near one of her own divided reactions to the picture. She articulated the other reaction, "But he should be working toward a degree now. Greenpeace could wait for later."

"Got to discover that for himself."

"Why risk his life six thousand miles away?"

"Why go to Iraq?"

"That's different surely?"

"Not *that* different. Chaps like showing their stuff in a *Boy's Own Paper* sort of way. Scouting. Going into the wilderness. Living off nuts and berries. Oriental travel. Enduring hardship. Contributing a very little bit to a very big cause."

"Yes," said Anne bitterly, "and getting themselves killed."

Andy's face passed in front of Luke's eyes for a moment and he stopped walking. Anne turned around to look at him behind her, leaning on her stick. His face was blank. "Oh! I *am* sorry. Forgive me." She walked back two paces to collect him. She said, "Come now, help an old woman whose rheumatism is bothering her." She put the walking stick in her right hand and slipped her left through Luke's arm. She knew in her aching bones that now was not the time to bring up the friend Luke had lost. He will have regretted telling her as much as he did.

Helping Anne, who leaned on him more than women usually did when they took your arm, made the Andy moment pass. They took some paces together, saying nothing. Then Luke said, "You might write him."

"Don't have his address. Don't know where he is. Haven't heard from him in more than a year now."

Luke heard her quiet wail underneath what she'd said so calmly. I've been a failure as a mother. "What's his name?"

"Dickon."

"Well, that's it, then. Write him at 'Dickon Bevil, Greenpeace,' and hand it to the Royal Protection. They'll give it to MI5, and MI5 knows where everyone is."

"And what do you propose I should say?" said Anne a little

hopelessly, remembering her earlier faltering attempt to find the right words.

"Oh, that you've seen his picture. That you talked about him to a strange soldier you met in waiting, who thought he must be quite a courageous sort of man. That you're thinking of him." Pause. "Just be with him like you are with me."

Anne squeezed his arm and they walked on. After a hundred yards more, they came out of the pine forest and had a fantastic view of a white suspension bridge over a wide spot in the river, with open fields, and a range of the green Grampian hills in the distance. The sun was making it as warm as summer, and some local teenaged boys were paddling in the water with their jeans rolled up and their shirts off. Anne and Luke walked up onto the bridge and stopped to watch the boys skimming flat stones across the water.

"How pale those boys are." She could sense his interest in them even as he pretended to be bored at her stopping. "They remind me of those pictures of soldiers bathing in France during the First World War. How white they looked. How vulnerable."

Luke said nothing.

"Of course that was the war where they first discovered that the real trauma might come after the war was over. Psychological. Do you know? They tried to treat it with electric shocks?" She breathed for a moment indignantly. "Didn't work. But then that man Rivers had some success treating Siegfried Sassoon with a talking therapy. At a hospital somewhere up here, as a matter of fact. Near Edinburgh, I believe."

Luke sighed and pulled on her arm gently to show that it was time they started moving along. Anne followed Luke's lead, but carried on: "Sassoon would have taken an interest in those boys, of course. He wrote quite a good book about it. The war, the men friends, the uneasiness. Anyone can read it and understand. I did. *Memoirs of a Fox-Hunting Man*, and then the whole Sherston trilogy."

Again, Luke said nothing, but he made a mental note to look for the book, just as she'd intended him to.

Shirley had a secret addiction to cheese. She found that it calmed her down. She had secret stashes in The Queen's clothes closets: wedges of aged Stilton so old that it didn't hurt them to be kept wrapped in clingfilm at room temperature, and foil-wrapped portions of cream cheese with a laughing cow on the label. When the anger that kept her going got to be a little too much for her, she'd steal away to the cupboards and nibble something from her supplies. She'd heard her contemporaries complain about their doctors' orders. "Oh, I've got the cholesterol, darling. 'No more cheese,' he said. High blood pressure too. No more salt. Said I've got to use the hot sauce instead." Shirley solved this problem by not going to the doctors. She received regular notices from the National Health Service in Windsor Castle that she was due for a checkup, but she ignored them. The Castle had a large enough population to have its own NHS medical unit, and the waiting time was much less than outside the Castle walls. Still Shirley refused to go.

The Queen gave her little natural remedies in tiny green bottles. Both The Queen and her mother were great believers in homeopathy. When once Shirley complained of lacking energy, The Queen had said, "I have just the thing for it." She unlatched the powerful snap on her boxy handbag and brought out a little vial of lavender oil. "Wonderful for tiredness. I take it. It works." Shirley accepted the bottle and tried the lavender oil. She wasn't sure, but she thought it helped a little.

She and William one night in Buckingham Palace, when The Queen was out late and they had to stay up to welcome her back and put her to bed, sat in a room with The Queen's shoe cupboards. They watched an old American Western on television. At one point John Wayne had said with contempt of a gun-toting opponent, "Why, he's nuthin but a snake-oil salesman." They'd both laughed out loud, as The Queen's latest enthusiasm was snake oil, and she'd given them both small bottles as a topical remedy for aching joints.

Still, Shirley had her own tonics and cure-alls as well as The Queen's. In addition to the cheese, she kept airline-sized bottles of scotch in the pockets of her apron. She also went and smoked a quick cigarette five or six times a day. She didn't think of this as a serious vice. Her grandmother and mother had both smoked, and though her mother died young, it wasn't from lung cancer. Her grandmother had, after all, lived into her late seventies, which Shirley thought, taking as she did a rather pessimistic view of life, quite long enough.

Shirley and William often found themselves together late in the evening when their devotion to their jobs kept them on call after the rest of the staff had long ago gone home.

Those closest to The Queen mirrored her work habits. As she didn't like giving up duties and was used to standing on her feet for long hours of the day, the senior members of staff all did too. This didn't mean that Shirley and William couldn't fit in a drink and a film while they were waiting for the silver polish to dry or the washing machine to finish its cycle. William had a source for an endless variety of videotapes and DVDs. He'd bring in three at a time and ask for Shirley's help in deciding which one they'd sit down to watch.

That evening he proposed her a film she'd rejected before. He did it with a sense of mischief and malice. He knew it would make her feel uncomfortable, and he thought he might just introduce the showdown he suspected they had to have in their friendship in the guise of a tease. "Look at this, Shirlers," his pet name for her that rhymed with curlers, one of the tools of her trade, as she often dressed The Queen's hair as well. "*Priscilla, Queen of the Desert*! It looks like great fun. It's all about these wonderful Australian queens getting into drag. Doing their hair. Zipping themselves into these amazing dresses. You could get a few clues for Mrs Thing. You know, add in a bit of sparkly eye shadow. Might make a world of difference."

Shirley bridled. She did not like the comparison of Australian transvestites to the sovereign, and was a little shocked at having them mentioned in the same sentence, and by using the same word. "No. I'm not having Danny La Rue now," she said, mentioning a 1960s female impersonator who once had a successful West End revue. "I told you that before. What else have you got?"

He was annoyed and upped the ante a little more aggressively than he was used to doing. It was his way of retaliating. "Oh my, Mrs Prude doesn't approve of drag queens, does she?"

There were more gay men than straight men in royal service, and Shirley early on had got to be completely unshocked by reckless chatter about picking up younger men, wearing women's clothes, and visiting gay saunas. The predominance of gay men on the palace staff also meant that, like the theatre, the ballet, and the art world, the palace had suffered more severely from the AIDS crisis than had other places. Shirley had lost colleagues whom she respected and attended more funerals than she liked to remember. She understood that the peak of the crisis had now passed, and that there were drugs that allowed men who were HIV positive to live with the condition. But because she didn't believe in doctors or conventional medicine, she also didn't really believe the crisis was over. She thought of it as just a lull and expected it to come back with redoubled force. She'd been brought up to believe in the apocalypse, and it informed her thinking on many unrelated topics.

She loved William. He was her most reliable companion. He was as fanatical about his work as she was. She felt protective toward him, almost as if he were the younger brother she never had. He never talked to her about his love life, but she was convinced that in off hours, when she wasn't around, he was off visiting some of London's sinks and cesspools. She couldn't think of them any other way. This was in fact the language that had been used in the Scottish evangelical chapels her grandmother had taken her to as a little girl. Although she was broad-minded about homosexuality in general, and could joke about it with the rest of them, she was still convinced that it was a terrible sin, a sin that could be forgiven, a sin that could be lived with, but a sin nonetheless. She didn't condemn William for his sin. The bottles of scotch in her apron were also sinful, as the chapel condemned all consumption of alcohol. But she did worry about him. She wasn't convinced that even if he looked after his health, he wouldn't be beaten up by skinheads and hooligans as he crawled home late some evening. So for her to watch *Priscilla* would have represented looking the other way, or even looking with approval, at all the danger William considered fun.

"I'm not a prude. You know that."

"But they do song and dance. Come on, it's fun."

Shirley wheeled around in her chair to look at him over her bifocals. "William, I want you to look after yourself."

In a moment he saw that the tease wasn't right. Her main worry was his safety, which overcame her nagging moral disapproval of going out to dives to watch drag divas. "Don't you worry, my darling. I don't do half the things you imagine I do.

Lead a very dull life, in fact. Look at the two of us! Here we are shut up in The Queen's shoe cupboard when just beyond that wall London is heaving and throbbing and singing and dancing and dressing up."

He was right, of course.

"It's a school night. We're not going anywhere."

And she was right too.

In a conciliatory spirit, she swiveled in her armchair so that she could reach into a cupboard. She pulled out some of the wrapped cream cheese and offered him a packet. "*Vache qui rit*?"

"Shirley, you are dreadful. You mustn't eat that stuff. It's applied right to the arteries." Then he bent over and took some of the cheese. "Don't mind if I do."

"William, we still haven't anything to watch. Did you already send back *High Noon*? Haven't we any Clint?"

"Yes, I know you've got a *petit faible* for Mr Eastwood."

"He's no fable, William. He's the real stuff."

"I know your tastes, darling. The secret is safe with me," said William as he slid a copy of *Dirty Harry* into the tape player.

On the very first night that Andy visited the British regiment, they put on a special dress dinner to welcome him in the officers' mess. Among the American units serving in Iraq, formal dinners were rare and dress uniforms almost never worn. Andy found that among the British, any occasion for a dress-up party and the bringing out of regimental silver was seized upon with alacrity. Andy hadn't even brought his dress uniform along, so all he could do was change into some clean camouflage gear, while the British officers had all their polished buttons on. They were disposed to like him, having seen him tackle Luke and wrestle in the sand. For them it was so appallingly the wrong thing to do that it was grand.

When Andy entered the tent they used as a mess, he was surprised not only that he was dressed wrong, but that the table was covered with glasses and silverware. Where had all this stuff come from? Luke's colleagues caught him staring at the table.

"Not used to dining at tables in the States, I expect?" one joshed him.

"Oh yeah, we eat at tables," said Andy, "but we don't steal silverware from the Hilton."

This was considered quick-witted and good-humored. Everyone laughed. Another of the British officers tried a different angle of attack.

"You look so nice in your camouflage fatigues, Captain Brainard." This brought another round of laughter. "The enemy will never find you in here. You blend in so." More guffaws.

"Actually, I'm surprised you guys still wear those red coats. You look kinda like my high school marching band." He pronounced this "hah skewl" even though he hadn't anything remotely like a country accent ordinarily. This produced more hilarity, as the accent was exactly what the British expected all Americans to sound like.

When they sat down, Luke saw with a repressed thrill that his commanding officer had placed him next to Andy. He also saw Andy looking in confusion at his place setting. There were three forks and three knives on either side of his plate, as well as a spoon and a fork placed across the top of the plate. Which to use? They were having smoked cod for the first course, sent out from Britain in vacuum-sealed plastic packs that didn't have to be refrigerated. Luke picked up the outermost fork and a knife that was flatter than the others, elbowed Andy, and made a silly face as he waved his utensils in the air. Andy saw that Luke was trying to help him and was grateful. He did feel a bit ganged up on, as he had to think of replies to all the different jokes that were sent his way. He was relieved to find that Luke was not only by his side, but also on his side.

After the tackle and the first night's dinner, there were many work assignments Luke and Andy had to do together. Andy didn't feel like it was his job to make friends with all the other British officers too. He had enough to do as it was. So he was happy sticking near Luke on his downtime as well. They grew accustomed to one another, and, without putting it into words, their being comfortable with one another was one of their principal pleasures for both young men. When they were sent out into the desert to camp with some of the men for a week and to do some observation of suspicious Bedouin activity, they spent hot afternoons under an open-sided awning secured to the side of a Humvee. They'd lie on air mattresses and compare their favorite foods.

"Blueberry pie with vanilla ice cream," said Andy.

"Sticky toffee pudding," said Luke.

"I bet you've never had steak on a Weber grill," said Andy. "Too foggy to light the charcoal."

"Oh, no, we do have that kind of thing. I believe delivery van drivers dine on it by the side of the road."

"Man, if you weren't such big snobs about truck drivers, you could get rid of The Queen and have a free country."

"Um, could we leave Her Majesty out of this, please? Unless you'd like me to bring up your absurd, flag-waving traditions. I mean flying the stars and stripes you're wearing on your shoulder right now at used-car dealerships . . ."

"Hey! Brits aren't allowed to criticize Old Glory," said Andy, laughing and slugging Luke sharply on the shoulder. Luke returned the blow, but it was too hot really to have a proper fight so they both lay back on their air mattresses and wheezed.

In the desert night it grew very cold. Although they both had good sleeping bags, they instinctively lay close to one another for warmth, curled into similar fetal positions, though zipped into separate sacks. Sometimes, too, during the day, when they were looking at a map together, their elbows and upper arms brushed against each other and neither one would pull away. Neither one would have mentioned this, but the truth was that in a place where death was not far away, and neighboring units lost men on a regular basis, the human contact was as necessary to keep up their courage as food or water.

A more difficult situation to explain away occurred one weekend when the men in the Guards regiment arranged a night of music and skits. They invited the officers to put on one of the acts. Luke was having nothing to do with this, but some of the other British officers persuaded Andy that he should join them doing a lip-synch song-and-dance routine of one of Lady Gaga's more famous dance tracks. Several of their number planned to gyrate and mouth the backup part of the song around him. He would take the lead, because since he'd tackled Luke, he was famous for being fearlessly immune to embarrassment. Andy was pretty confident this would be good for laughs, and the men had roused his competitive spirit. The best skit was to be awarded a prize. He wanted to win.

Luke stayed away from the rehearsals for the weekend performance. He generally tried to protect Andy from the merry-making traps of the other lads, but Andy had agreed to do the show so enthusiastically, and entered right away into the fun of it, that Luke felt a bit left out. So he went to his corner of the tent and sulked. On the Saturday night, after a dinner in which both officers and men had been drinking freely, the performances were fairly predictable until Andy and the other officers came on. They'd actually put together an excellent dance sequence along with the karaoke. The combined audience of British and American soldiers whooped to see the officers making fools of themselves, but then grew quiet when their synchronized movements aligned with the thud of the beat. When it was over a huge cheer went up, and it was clear before the judges announced their decision who'd won. When Luke went backstage afterwards to congratulate him, some barrier between them seemed to be lifted. Luke gave Andy a bear hug while everyone watched and laughed.

"That was amazing. Already more than a hundred hits on YouTube and it's only just been posted!" said Luke.

"Did you send me those roses?" said Andy, gesturing to an imaginary vase on an imaginary dressing table.

After that they became a settled item, "buddies" to the

Americans and "mates" to the British. Luke's fellow officers had, many of them, like him, been to public schools where idealized boy-boy romances were common. The possible erotic element in the mix didn't interest them as much as the potential social awkwardness of Luke bringing Andy home to meet his parents, minor land-owning gentry in Rutland. Social embarrassment was much more amusing to them than homosexuality. "Gosh, what'll you tell them when you want to bring Minnesota home for Christmas—eh, Thomason?" asked one, when Andy wasn't around.

"Make sure he doesn't get up and leave with the ladies when the port is passed," said another.

"Oh, tell him not to douse the flame on the plum pudding with his water glass. Yanks aren't so keen about fires at the dinner table," said the first one, giggling.

As Andy was the only officer among the Americans, he had no equals who could tease him about his friendship with Luke, but the American men observed the friendship and muttered darkly about it. They were more worried about the sexual angle. "I hate fags," began to be scrawled on the plywood walls in the men's latrines.

The week after the musical performance a small detachment made up of both British and American soldiers, commanded by the American sergeant, was going out on a routine patrol in two armored vehicles.

"I think we'd better go too," said Andy to Luke as the day's orders were being reviewed early in the morning.

"No. We have other things to do here. Leave this to the staff sergeant. We'd only be in his way."

"Look, if the men are going out, and might be shot at, we have to go too."

"It's a routine patrol, Andrew," said Luke, using the long version of Andy's name to emphasize the fact that he thought his friend was being childish. "They don't need us."

"If the men have to do it, we have to show we can do it too."

"We've both been out on patrols before. We don't need to go every time."

"If you don't lead from the front, you get left behind. I'm going."

"Show-off."

"What?"

"That performance Saturday has gone to your head. You're showing off."

Andy looked at Luke and glared at him. He was a soldier before he was a friend. He was a can-do young man from the Midwest before he was an international diplomat. To be told that going out to do his job was actually just being cocky, well, that was about as low a blow as he'd ever been dealt. It briefly occurred to him to say, "You fucking take that back," but he knew that would make them both laugh. They'd be friends again. The men would go out without him. That seemed like cowardice, so he looked at Luke and said nothing. Then he strode out of the tent and toward the waiting armored vehicles.

Before he walked out, Luke saw the line cross Andy's mind. He willed him to say it. Say it, please just say it. Standing by himself, watching Andy go, Luke murmured, under his breath, "Goodness me, calm down, my dear."

[illegible]

have to go.

[illegible] that they don't see.

[illegible]

[illegible]

[illegible]

[illegible]

[illegible]

[illegible]

Part V

Plank

The Queen was sitting at a table in the last carriage of the 1700 from London King's Cross to Edinburgh Waverley. It was already occupied by a blind man and his Seeing Eye dog, a German shepherd lying underneath the table, the blind man's companion, who, by the look of her thick spectacles might have been nearly blind herself, and a young man with several piercings through his nose, as well as large disks that stretched out his earlobes. After Rajiv left, the young man took a can of lager from a plastic bag and put it in front of him on the table.

The Queen looked at him with interest. He was unlike anyone she'd met before. She wondered if he were a football hooligan. Before she could think what to say to him, he gave her a friendly wink and said, "Like the skull and crossbones." He could tell she was an old lady with an unusual sense of style, but the scarf under her hood created a shadow that effectively obscured much of her face.

The Queen had no idea what he was talking about and looked confused.

"On the back of your hoodie. Seriously piratical," said he, lifting his can of lager and toasting her.

Though The Queen still did not understand what he was talking about, she smiled back as she understood he was paying her a compliment. "And what are those rings through the nose for?"

she said to him as a way of sustaining the conversation. She'd only seen them before as a way of leading oxen, but she thought it tactful not to say so.

"Not *for* anything, love. Just decoration."

"Ah, rather like me," The Queen instantly replied. Seized as she was by unusual melancholy, his not making a fuss about her lulled her into a sense of complacency about what she was doing. She rather thought that, like the young man from Paxton & Whitfield, he must know who she was, and would appreciate a little self-deprecation on her part. People generally did. It was one of her little tricks to make them more comfortable with her.

"What?"

"Oh, nothing," said The Queen, "only a bit of a joke really."

"Sorry it's so crowded here with my dog," began the blind man.

"Nonsense," said The Queen. "Plenty of room. Isn't there, darling?" she said as she offered her hand to the dog, who licked it.

"The fact is, the dog belongs to both of us," the blind man's companion, a shapeless matron in an old tweed coat, put in. "I'm legally blind myself, though I can catch some light and some shapes through these spectacles."

"How brave you both are," said The Queen. She'd found that it was better to address people's disabilities straightforwardly, rather than to avoid speaking of them, or to make light of them. "And have you both been blind for a long time?" It was a slight variation on her standard "Have you lived here a long time?"

She had no trouble making the adjustment as the circumstances required.

"Well," began the man, assuming the question was addressed to him, "since I was born. So I'm quite used to it."

The lady in the tweed coat was used to the blind man going first in whatever they did. Some sort of male prerogative. After he finished, she added, "My vision's always been poor, but it's been getting worse and worse. Soon I'll be just as bad as him," she said, nodding her head at the man on the other side of the table, and she gave a little laugh.

The Queen looked at her steadily as she said this, even though the words of the couple were addressed only vaguely in her direction. She allowed a small interval in the conversation to let them know she'd heard them, and that they'd told her something solemn. Then she said, "And the name of this very intelligent dog, who helps you both?"

"Hohenzollern," answered the blind man. "But born in England, and eats British beef."

"Of course you do, darling," said The Queen, rubbing the dog's ear. "Like British beef, don't you, Hohenzollern?" Her pronunciation of the dog's name was somewhat different from the blind man's. She took every syllable and said it separately, though quickly. Her diction suggested she'd met a few of them in her lifetime and heard the way they actually said it. "Of course, the Hohenzollerns themselves used to come here often a hundred years ago, didn't they? Queen Victoria was always complaining about the cost of entertaining Kaiser Wilhelm. Said he could come to Windsor for a cup of tea, and that was all!" said The Queen with a gay laugh. "But then he'd go to the Isle of Wight and race his boat with the Prince of Wales. The dinners afterwards cost a good deal, I'm sure of it."

"Sounds as if we're on the way to Scotland with someone who knows history," said the blind man, relishing the prospect of showing her how much he knew on the same subject. "You must have seen that documentary on the Kaiser. BBC 2. Someone pointed it out to me in *Radio Times*, but we missed it."

"Oh, was there a documentary? Just recently?" said The Queen with some disappointment. "I must have missed it too. No, no, I didn't see it. Would have liked to."

"I hated history in school. So boring. Memorizing names and dates. Who cares when Agincourt was?" This was the first the man with the piercings had said to the table.

"1415, wasn't it?" said the blind man to The Queen, attempting to be courtly to this stranger who might allow him to display his knowledge.

"Why, yes, I think it was," said The Queen, who wasn't entirely sure of the date herself. She liked Victorian history and Victorian medievalism, yes, loved all the imitation battlements at Balmoral. The real Middle Ages left her a bit cold, though she seemed to recall some of the grandchildren going through a Dungeons & Dragons phase, and had bought them some games for their computers at Christmastime.

The Queen turned to the young man. "I suppose to like history you must have a good teacher, mustn't you?" As the blind wished to talk about their blindness, she sensed that the young man's disability had something to do with not being noticed by his teachers.

"I had crap teachers."

"Tell me," said The Queen, looking into his eyes.

"Well, they never had much time for me, did they? I suppose I wasn't the brightest in the bunch. But they usually didn't learn my name until the third week. Didn't even notice I was there. They saw my marks and decided, 'Well, what's the use?' so they didn't bother. They were always droning on about Winston bloody Churchill, or the Industrial Revolution, or imperialism. You know, oppressing the nonwhite races?"

He looked over at The Queen for her reaction and saw her dismay. "Oh, sorry, that was a Paki bloke who put you on the train, wasn't it?"

"Yes, a very nice young man. Perhaps about your age. 'Paki' isn't what he'd like to be called. An insult, you know? He's quite English. Born here, and parents born here too. Winston, now, you would have liked him."

The young man with the piercings looked back at her as if she were crazy. She was an old lady. It was true that the lager in front of him was not his first, so he wasn't seeing entirely clearly. But there was no way in the wide world that she had known Winston Churchill. She was barmy. The old often were.

She could see by watching his eyes that he had no interest in Winston Churchill, so she changed tack. "But perhaps you had Dungeons & Dragons when you were a boy?"

"I *loved* Dungeons & Dragons!" he said, warming up with real enthusiasm.

"I thought you might."

"Monsters that would eat you up if you weren't careful. Wizards. Magic. Scary castles. It was a game too, that made it fun."

"I suppose more history teaching should be like that, shouldn't it?" said The Queen smoothly, playing to the passion that the young man had just revealed.

"If we'd played that in school, well, I would've come top."

"I'm sure you would." She then turned to the dog so he wouldn't feel left out of the conversation. "He would, Hohenzollern, wouldn't he? Have come top?"

The dog was already her firm friend and gave a brief yelp as his affirmative.

"Now, Hohenzollern," said the blind man, looking under the table, "we've a long way to go. And no barking, please."

The dog whined as if to protest that he'd been spoken to and it was polite to reply.

Having looked at her carefully now that they'd talked, the young man said to The Queen, "You look familiar."

For the first time, The Queen felt a little alarm. No one had recognized her walking to Paxton & Whitfield. As the shop had a royal warrant, they were nearly family. The young man there had spoken to her so respectfully, and gone out of his way to look after her, that she'd forgotten that she'd boarded something other than the royal train. It suddenly occurred to her that the people on the train might start making trouble, wanting to know what she was going to do in Edinburgh if they knew that she was outside the palace cordon. She'd done it so few times before. How could she possibly tell them about the Prime Minister wanting to abolish the royal train?

"Tell me about your earrings," said The Queen, firmly changing the subject.

He had large skull-and-crossbones insignia in the lobes underneath his ears. "It's not an earring," he said crossly. "It's a plug. You get it pierced first. Then you gradually stretch it out. Then you get a plug fitted. It stretches out the earlobe and then you can wear all sorts of things."

"Sounds painful," said the matron in the thick glasses, turning her head to try and see the young man's ears from the only oblique angle she could see anything at all.

"No, it doesn't hurt."

"You see, mine are stretched out too," said The Queen, fingering her earlobe beneath her scarf. She untied the scarf so the young man could see her ears. Seven decades of heavy jewels had stretched out The Queen's earlobes, though her ears hadn't the same sort of tribal look his had. Still, the deformation was noticeable.

The young man looked at the pearls in her ears and said, "That's it! I've got it. Helen Mirren, that's who you are!"

"Oh, wasn't she lovely in *The Queen*? We liked that one!" said the woman in thick spectacles.

"What would Helen Mirren be doing travelling second class to Scotland?" said the blind man with a dismissive snort.

"Helen Mirren, now, she's a beauty. Much more *svelte* than me," said The Queen, patting her tummy.

"Well, you do look like her," said the young man defensively.

"Tickets, please! Tickets, ladies and gentlemen." Suddenly the guard was upon them. The blind man handed over two tickets for himself and his wife. The young man took a crumpled document from his jeans pocket. The guard inspected them briefly and then wordlessly validated them. Then he turned to The Queen. "And your ticket, young lady?" he said cheerfully.

This caused The Queen some momentary confusion. But she reached into the pocket of her hoodie and came out with a £20 banknote. "There you are," she said, handing the banknote to the guard, and making a mental note that she must reimburse Rebecca from the Mews.

The guard laughed. "That'll cover part of the penalty for paying on board, my love, but it won't cover the fare."

"It won't?" said The Queen, shocked. "Fares have gone up."

"That they have, milady."

"Well, how much, then?

"Where to?"

"Edinburgh Waverley," said The Queen precisely so he'd know she didn't want to get down at any of the suburban stations.

He punched some codes into his electronic machine before he answered briefly, "£276.70."

The Queen gasped. "That much? It's highway robbery. I haven't got it. Is that what you paid?" she asked the blind man, turning to him incredulously.

"Well, no. We have railcards. So should you. And we paid in advance. That saves you some too."

"I see," said The Queen. "Well, what's the first stop?"

"York!" said the guard.

The Queen briefly considered getting off at York. She had made a considerable contribution to the roof's reconstruction at York Minster after the fire there in 1984. Perhaps the Dean would house her for an evening. No doubt he would, but her showing up at his door would worry him. She knew the man. No, it was not possible. She must carry on to Scotland.

"Perhaps I could advance you a small loan, Miss Mirren?" said the blind man *sotto voce*. "Would that help?"

"No, no I couldn't let you pay so vast a sum," said The Queen. "Let me see what I have here." The Queen pulled her black patent handbag up onto the table from the seat, where it had been sitting beside her. As the guard and the man with piercings watched with amazement, item by item she slowly emptied its contents onto the table. A starched handkerchief. A lipstick. A pair of white kid gloves. A fountain pen. A small box of wooden safety matches. A compact mirror. A laminated miniature calendar from the *Racing Post* listing the year's Bank Holidays. A small bottle of perfume. And a rabbit's foot. At length, she unzipped one of the side pockets and counted six crisp £50 notes onto the table. "There you are," she said to the guard triumphantly, though still in a bad humor. The guard took her bills, produced a ticket from his machine, and handed her the change.

"Ah, Miss Mirren has some resources after all. I thought so," said the blind man, a deft hand at flirting with people he couldn't see. Had he been able to see them, he would have been terrified.

"He's quite a tease, isn't he, Hohenzollern?" said The Queen to the dog and she silently fed him a bit of cheese she worked off the lump inside the parcel Rajiv had handed her. The dog took the cheese and lifted his snout in the air as he chomped on it with relish.

The Queen addressed the guard just as he was turning to go. "Would it be possible to have a timetable, please? I would like to check our progress."

The guard disappeared to the end of the carriage for a moment, and returned with a timetable he took off a plastic holder on the wall. "Here you are, love."

"And a pencil, please."

The guard was somewhat taken aback, but he was used to difficult old ladies, and since the railway had been privatized under John Major, they were under strict instructions to cater to all passenger whims. This was called "customer service," and it was difficult to keep a smiling face in the midst of the most unreasonable demands. However, he dipped into his jacket pocket, brought out a stub of a pencil, and handed it to the elderly woman in the hoodie.

The Queen thanked the guard, took the timetable, and consulted it. "I see. York at 1850."

"That's the one," replied the guard.

"That's only one hour and ten minutes from now," said The Queen, pointing at the figures with the pencil stub. "Tell the driver. I shall be attending. Let him know, please."

This was a bit too much, as far as the guard was concerned, but he gave her a nod of his head and relished what he'd tell the driver on the intercom when he got back to his post. "Old lady in the last carriage keeping tabs on you. Gave her a timetable. Try and keep it on time tonight, will you?" The driver answered down the crackling telephone line with a series of spluttering, laughing, four-letter words as the train reached 125 miles per hour within sight of Alexandra Palace.

"Come to Scotland with me?" asked Rajiv as Rebecca turned away from the window of the doorway to the railway carriage.

A sudden gasp was all she gave him. The taxi ride, the vaulting over the barrier, and now jumping headlong onto an intercity train without a ticket, all these were so far beyond her ordinary experience that she couldn't speak, only look at him, as if she were trapped by someone whose intentions she wasn't entirely sure of. They were immediately in the midst of a tunnel and as the vestibule light had burned out, they were in the darkness together. He went up to her instinctively and gave her a hug, not a romantic embrace, but an everything-will-be-all-right wrapping of his arms around her.

She allowed herself to be held in the darkness. The carriage rocked, and the tunnel produced a sucking vacuum of the air as the train accelerated.

They were soon out of the tunnel and the London lights illuminated the vestibule again. "Well, we might as well sit down here. No stops until York. No seats in that way, either. Oh, and your boss is in there, by the way. At a four-top. If that's who you're after."

They slid down with their backs against the vestibule wall, their legs spread out in front of them. There was little enough space so they both had to sit with their knees up.

"She's not my boss."

"That's funny. She told me she was."

Rebecca looked at him incredulously.

"Well, she came in after some cheese for Elizabeth. I put two and two together."

"I thought that must have been where she got off to."

"Does she do that a lot? Go off on her own? Seemed a bit odd to me."

Rebecca didn't answer. She'd met Rajiv twice. They'd never been introduced by mutual friends. She didn't know him, really. Now there was the prospect of a railway journey of several hours with him, and he was asking about The Queen's habits. She said nothing.

A wordless, and not infrequently a defiant, silence appeared to be her default setting. It didn't disturb Rajiv. "What about you, then? You're panting. All out of breath. And your cheeks, they're red," he said, stretching out a knuckle to stroke the cheek nearest him.

"Get off!" she said angrily, stretching away from him.

Rajiv smiled to himself. There was something in her anger that he took as a compliment. It was a lot better than his friends' sisters, who just passively looked the other way when he spoke to them. Why else get so upset at every small meaningless gesture of his? "Had to run for the train, did you?"

She said nothing.

"We just barely got on ourselves. She told me to disembark and go back to the shop."

She heard him using "disembark," a strange word, as if he were imitating The Queen's speech. "You shouldn't have been with her at all."

"You're right. I shouldn't have. And how did that come about?"

Again, Rebecca did not answer.

"Did you know that she was going to Scotland? On her own?"

Rebecca looked out the window. She felt for the first time she might need some sort of help. The equerry had told her it was a crisis. If the papers found out, he'd told her, they'd injure her. Now here she was, alone, with a boy, practically a stranger, and the only person, quite possibly, besides her who knew The Queen was alone, with no security, on a train to Scotland. She knew animals. She didn't know newspapers or how to look after an old lady, whom she only knew how to serve by caring for horses. "I saw you in Jermyn Street, handing her into a cab."

"Came back to see me, did you?" Rajiv said brightly.

"Not you. No. The equerry called me after we had coffee at St James's. When I got there, he told me The Queen had disappeared. Nobody knew where. Asked me if I knew. I didn't. He thought she might get into trouble. And if the newspapers found out, well, they might accuse her of being, well, not quite right." She couldn't go further. She'd said more than she intended.

"I wouldn't say 'irrational,' now. And 'mad' isn't right either," said Rajiv staring up at the ceiling of the rocking carriage.

"*Distrait* was more like it. A touch unhappy perhaps. Looking for something to cheer herself up with, maybe." He laughed to himself. "She knew that cheddar pleased Elizabeth. The cheese she came in to buy wasn't for the horse." His shoulders started shaking. He found this very funny.

Rebecca didn't like it. "Stop it," she said shortly.

"Okay, all right. I didn't mean anything bad, did I?"

"Stop it. Now."

"So she came in," Rajiv continued. "She bought the cheese. Took the parcel and put it into her hoodie. Where'd she get that, by the way? Brilliant disguise. I have to give it to her."

"No, I gave it to her. She came over to the Mews after lunch. Didn't have a coat on. It was sleeting. I said she should put my hoodie on. She did. I guess she's still wearing it."

"That she is. The Pirate Queen."

"She took the cheese, and then what?"

"Well, she wanted to know the best way to King's Cross. She said bus. I said Tube. So we compromised and took a taxi!"

"What else?"

"We talked about the 'dark races,'" he said, imitating a comic Indian accent. "She wants me to be her *munshi*."

"What's *munshi*? Breakfast cereal?"

"No!" He pretended to be offended. "Her Indian secretary. Servant *rajah*. Gentleman *wallah*."

"Best evidence so far that she's not herself."

"She was perfectly sane," said Rajiv reasonably. "Queen Victoria had one. She wants one too. Told me she'd 'be in touch' with me later. She did. Go up there and ask her yourself," he said, cocking his head toward the interior of the carriage where he'd said The Queen was sitting.

"Are you sure she's okay in there? Who's she sitting with?"

"They looked harmless enough. And I didn't hurt her when she came into the shop. Why should they?"

"God! Rajiv, don't you realize? She doesn't do this sort of thing every day."

"What? Don't worry. She knows how. Meets strangers every day. She presses the flesh three hundred days in the year. Probably more."

"But there are policemen with her then. Ladies-in-waiting. Secretaries. Plainclothes officers in the crowd. People are looking out for her."

"Well, she has me, her Indian secretary. And she has Miss Rebecca, of the Royal Mews, her mounted maid of honor, temporarily without her mount," said Rajiv, smiling. "We are going to look after her."

She smiled at him once again, in spite of herself.

Rajiv saw his opportunity and he took it. Putting his hand on her hair, he leaned in and kissed her on the mouth.

Rebecca kissed back for only an instant before she pushed Rajiv away. "Look here, I didn't say you could do that. We barely know each other."

"We know each other well enough," said Rajiv. "And we're going to Scotland together, aren't we?"

She didn't like the way he took liberties with her. He wanted some cold water thrown on him. "You have to realize something."

"Okay," said Rajiv equably.

"I like this man I met."

He understood immediately what she was telling him, but pretended to make light of it, as if he hadn't entirely grasped her meaning. "Well, that's all right. I like you too."

"No, not you. And I don't know what to think about it. And there was a cab driver who brought me to the station. He was leering at me in his mirror. It made me feel awful."

Rebecca was a woman whose emotions and whose confessions rose quickly to the surface, like the color rushing to her face with exercise. She had a way of getting angry quickly, of having a temper as molten as the color of her hair. Rajiv had observed all this. As they were together for some time, it seemed as good a time as any to try and make her talk, even if it let him and his romantic feelings out of the picture. "We may as well be mates, no matter what," he told her then. Her temperature did seem to decrease a bit. "Who is he, then?"

"The taxi driver? He gave me his card."

"No, not the taxi driver," he said, rolling his eyes. "And if you don't want to encourage them, don't take their cards. The other one."

She stopped for a moment to gather some strength. "I went to a demo. Trafalgar Square. Maybe three years ago? I can't remember. Against cruelty to animals. Different groups there. Opposed to hunting. No drug testing on animals. Lots of different speakers. One man had the most amazing passion. Told about how they stopped up badgers' dens. You know, rich people? Just to prevent the badgers interfering with foxes. So there are foxes left to hunt. I'm not sure. Anyway, the badgers suffocate when they stop up the holes to their dens. And he had a little badger with him, held it up for us to see. Tame. It was, well, it was adorable. He came down off the stand, away from the microphones, and I was standing right there. He saw me looking at

him. Asked me if I wanted to hold the badger. Handed him to me. I could feel his heart beating! His claws were quite sharp. His fur almost oily smooth. I could have held him for hours."

"Mmm-hmm," said Rajiv, frankly a little bored with how women had paroxysms of joy over small animals, but he wanted to encourage her to carry on. She wasn't thinking of him now. She was in some sort of trance. Their shoulders occasionally touched one another as the train rocked over points or level crossings.

"Then he said we had to go find him something to eat. He wanted me to come along. So I did. He let me carry the badger. And we got on the Bakerloo Line and went right to the end of it, Elephant and Castle. His flat was nearby. So we fed the badger some vegan cheese."

"Ugh," said Rajiv.

"Do you want to hear this or not?"

"Yes, carry on."

"Well, we had some of the cheese ourselves. And then he had some lentils, and we had that and some wine. After that, it was getting late, so he said to me . . ."

Just at that moment they both heard the guard in the carriage behind them calling out what sounded like "Tickets! Animal fares, please!" but which was probably "Any more fares, please?"

In a moment he was towering over them in the vestibule. "Tickets, please! Sir? Madam?"

Rebecca panicked. She'd given the last of her money to the taxi driver. "I haven't got a ticket," she said simply.

"Second one today. It will be £276.70 including the penalty," replied the guard cheerfully. "And you, young gentleman? Ticket please."

"I haven't got a ticket either," Rajiv answered truthfully.

"That makes three!" said the guard as if he were keeping a private count that might help him win a bet later on.

"Look, I haven't got the money," said Rebecca.

"Then you will have to give me your address and fill out an Unpaid Fare Notice. If you don't pay the railway in ten days, there is an additional fine." He stayed upbeat as he handed down this sentence.

Rebecca hadn't much money of her own, and didn't know how she would tell her parents about this. Nor, in her experience, was this an expense which she could submit to the Mews. She looked bewildered.

Rajiv pulled out his credit card. "Both our fares on there, if you can, please."

"Rajiv, no! I cannot let you do this. I will not." She was not going to become obligated to him in this way. She'd never get rid of him then, and she fully intended to give him the slip when they got to Edinburgh.

"Relax. The bill goes to my parents. I don't pay it. I'll tell them I went to visit someone from school with a chum and we had to jump on the train without our tickets. They won't mind."

"Well, I will repay it when we get back to London. I'll get the money."

"Of course you will. No worries. We're in this together, you and me?"

Rebecca didn't answer. She looked down into her lap.

The guard slid Rajiv's card through his machine, issued their tickets, and observed, "There's more seats up front. Why don't you move up there?"

"Oh, we're fine here, aren't we?" he said, turning to look at Rebecca.

She continued staring into her lap, but the edges of her ears turned a dark shade of plum.

The Marquess, Anne's nephew, had turned down his aunt's request to use the company plane. His priority was preservation of capital, and he regarded his aunt's demand as a waste of money. He did give her the use of the family flat in Charlotte Square, but he didn't much like the peremptory way she had asked for it. She had a way of regarding all the family's possessions as hers, only on loan to him, when, as she well knew, everything had passed to him with the death of his father. All she had now was a courtesy title, "Lady Anne," and he meant to keep it that way. She'd had a generous dowry, a considerable charge on the family fortune in the previous generation, and he didn't see why she should drain the reserves now. He did sit on the board of British Airways, however, and one of the perks was a relatively free allowance of flights. He knew it wouldn't cost the company much to put two old ladies on the last flight on a weeknight from Heathrow to Edinburgh. Practically no one on that flight, ever. He knew this because he often used it to fly up and visit his mistress. So he provided his aunt and Shirley with a car from the palace to Heathrow, two seats on the plane, and sent a text message to the porter in Charlotte Square to open the door for them when they got there. He thought he'd done enough. He didn't ask his Aunt Anne why she had to go to Edinburgh at such short notice. He thought that would only lead to his becoming more deeply involved in her affairs, and he wanted as little to do with her as possible. She could expect an annual invitation to Shropshire at Christmas, but that was about it.

Meanwhile, it was just as the Marquess had expected. The two women had found their seats side by side in an aircraft that was thinly populated. The plane took off shortly after nine in the evening. The stewardesses pushed their trolley with unseemly haste down the aisle as soon as the FASTEN SEAT BELTS light was turned off. Shirley asked for whiskey, Anne for red wine. The stewardess gave them two sandwiches wrapped in see-through packages, as well as half a dozen mini bottles. This was her way of not having to return to give them more if they wanted it. She intended to spend the rest of the flight with her girlfriend in the back with a new *Hello!* magazine.

Faced forward, with only a black night outside the window, the two women, aided by their drinks in plastic cups, felt a little more at ease with one another. Shirley was not in the least put out by not having a private plane. She marveled at the way Anne had produced a car to Heathrow, on top of tickets, and a place to stay once they got to Scotland. This brittle, porcelain cup did have some know-how, it turned out, and Shirley grew to respect her a little more.

Anne, for her part, knew that Shirley was probably on to something in recalling The Queen's odd mentioning of Leith. For all her sometime resentment of The Queen's asking her to do menial tasks, for all her amused contempt that The Queen should be on more intimate and friendlier terms with the dressers than the ladies-in-waiting, Anne thought of herself as mainly a servant of the Crown. It was her position to serve, and she regarded the proximity she enjoyed with The Queen as the job's chief honor and emolument. No, she did not regard The Queen as a remarkable woman. She did regard her, however, as the living embodiment of something else, higher, more meaningful, and more historical than the mere woman herself. She didn't like to put what she represented into words, but it had to do with art and legend and myth. Anne was a servant of that history, told and retold around many campfires on long winters' evenings. Shirley was too. That was the basis on which Anne's respect for both The Queen and Shirley rested.

"Do you think those boys had any leads? You know, any they hadn't mentioned to us?" said Anne, swirling the airline wine in the plastic cup to warm it up and coax a little flavor out of it. She recalled the moment she'd witnessed between Luke and William.

"Boys? What boys?" said Shirley, scoffing.

"Well, I had the impression Luke and William were joining forces."

"Luke? Who is Luke?"

"Oh, you know, the equerry. Major Thomason."

"Oh, him. I don't know if that young man's any use. Is always staring off into space when I've seen him."

"He was in Iraq, you know," said Anne defensively.

"Well, I had two uncles in the last war. The real war. In Germany. They never seemed any the worse for it after they came home."

"That was a long time ago. They're not prepared for it now. So few of them join. They haven't anyone to share it with. And then the people at home don't support the war. It's not like the war with Germany. Everyone was behind that. No one cares about Iraq now, but men are still going and fighting and seeing dreadful things when they're there. Makes it hard for them when they come home. They try to draw a line under it, put it behind them, and they can't."

"I suppose," Shirley allowed. "How do you know all this?"

"Sat next to him once at luncheon. Have talked to him a few times since. He's not like the others. Not so confident. Is a bit of a sparrow with a broken wing, I think, but I'm not sure he's prepared to admit that."

Shirley could see very well that Anne was a little in love with the young major. She thought the possibility that his going to war had caused him some damage that he wouldn't admit to was also real. Her intimacy with the older woman was too new for her to feel comfortable teasing her. Because they were not exactly friends, she couldn't sympathize either. So she kept quiet.

Anne understood Shirley's quietness as a mark of her delicacy and liked her more for it. She also left a pause purposely unfilled before she asked, "Do you think William knows anything?"

Shirley cleared her throat. Her friendship with William was something that had grown up over years between equals. She wasn't about to disclose anything she knew of William to Anne, even though she was beginning to find her just about all right. "He just said she was gone. They were sure of it. And that he and Major Thomason, um, Luke did you say he's called? They were going off to look for her. Leaving for Scotland after us and would try and meet up with us once we were there. Something which the equerry had found on her computer. I don't understand computers. I didn't follow what he said."

"Seems an unlikely alliance."

"William and that equerry? No more than you and me, Lady Anne." Shirley said the "Lady" with an ironic inflection.

"Both unmarried, I believe."

"Is that what you think they're up to?"

"I hope they're up to nothing more than we are, finding Her Majesty, before the papers and the secret services and God knows who else is out there get to her." A pause. Then Anne continued a little more softly, "I see nothing wrong with two young men who like each other joining forces."

"In my experience the upper and lower members of staff don't often take their tea together."

"You sometimes breed strong stock from strange crosses."

"We're not talking about *that*, are we?"

"No, we're not. We are not." Another pause. "I do think Luke needs a little companionship, though, and soon, or his wound will fester."

"They had soldier servants in the last war. 'Batmen.' But William won't be his batman. I doubt that now."

"I'm not talking about having his boots polished. I'm talking about friendship, real genuine friendship between two men who like and respect one another."

"They have to make their own way, Anne, there's nothing we can do for them."

"Well, we can wish them the best and we can tell them so. Acknowledge them. They want our blessing."

Shirley did not immediately reply to this. She saw the truth of what Anne had just said, but she'd grown up in a Scottish household that was austere on the emotional front. Love between men and women was barely mentioned. Between man and man, well, that was off the map.

Shirley cleared her throat and put in a word for her colleague. "William seems a bit flighty, but that boy is tough. The queer ones often are. They have to be to survive. I can't imagine he'll have much to contribute to a talk about life in the army, but if Major Thomason needs some protection, he couldn't have anyone fiercer than William."

"No, what I'm saying, Shirley, is that they might both need for us to recognize them. Give our approval."

"They're grown louts. They don't need anything from us."

"Ah, you don't think your opinion counts with William, then?"

Shirley knew that it did. They were more than coworkers. They were allies, they were co-conspirators, they were friends. Yes, if William were to be having some sort of, what was it, *relationship* (the word sounded like California, Islington, and Sigmund Freud all rolled into one) with the equerry, he would want to know she thought it was okay.

Shirley looked over at Anne, caught her eye, and gave a quick affirmative nod of her head. The two women then sat back into their seats, lightly closed their eyes, and were blanketed by the roar of the engines.

"Are you okay?" Rajiv was worried that Rebecca refused to speak, or even to look at him, after the guard left them alone in the vestibule once more.

"Look. We're here together. I'll put up with that. We may as well try and look out for Her Majesty together, as she's just on the other side of the partition from us. But that doesn't mean you're my boyfriend. I've told you about the man in Trafalgar Square. But I didn't tell you that as a way of saying we should be together, as a pair. I told you, in fact, because he upset me. And

I'm not about to let another man do it again. Probably there's something wrong with me." The flickering darkness, relieved only occasionally by the train's whizzing through small towns, emboldened her to be more truthful than she would have been otherwise. "I don't entirely know who I am or what I want."

"I do."

"You do what?"

"Know what you are."

"What, then?"

"A beautiful woman who once had a tryst with a badger and a man somewhere near the Elephant."

She smiled at him.

"And who frankly liked the badger best of all."

She gave an involuntary snort through her nose.

"Look, let's just enjoy it. We don't have to define what you are or what we are, you and me. We're going on a little trip. That's all." He looked appealingly into her eyes.

She returned his gaze for a split second longer than was normal before looking down to dig in her pocket.

He felt a rush of blood to his face. That was her consent.

"I've got to call the equerry."

"Strange word. Second time you've said it. What's that?"

"Man who works for The Queen."

"What's he do, then?"

"Look, I'm not here to answer all your questions. The equerry needs to know we're with her. If we're going to keep The Queen from being harmed, we've got to stick by her, bring her back.

She might not be totally . . . herself. Why else would she have got into a taxi with someone from behind the till at Paxton & Whitfield."

Rajiv chose to regard this as a playful insult and did not take offense.

Rebecca found a signal on her mobile phone and reached Luke. She told him she was on the 1700 from King's Cross to Edinburgh Waverley and The Queen was also on board. She thought she could keep an eye on Her Majesty and when they got to Edinburgh, well, she'd look after her as best she could. Luke wanted to keep The Queen's journey as secret as possible. He hadn't wanted to raise any alarm by having the police get on the train, or having the train met in Scotland. If he could get up there quickly enough himself, perhaps he and William and Anne and Shirley, and now Rebecca, could persuade her to turn around and come back. The women would all be there before him, and as The Queen was more influenced by the women than by the men of the Household, perhaps it was as well that she should be shepherded on the train by the Mews and met in Edinburgh by the Mistress of the Robes's department.

"What do we do now?" Rajiv asked, the paparazzo in him hoping for some disclosure of the palace's plans. When he was with The Queen, he felt he had to look out for her. When he was with Rebecca, he began to hatch a plan to capture The Queen's unusual excursion with the camera in his mobile phone.

"We keep an eye on her and make sure nothing happens to her."

"What else?"

"Nothing else. Nosy Parker. Now move to the side and let me see if she's still there."

Rebecca got up and cautiously looked through the glass doorway. The Queen was still at the table, facing forward in the direction the train was traveling, talking to a blind man and a woman with thick glasses. A man with some piercings was across from her. The Queen's hood was still up. No one seemed to have recognized her. Nobody was paying her serious attention but the blind.

Rebecca slid back down against the partition wall to sit on the floor next to Rajiv. "Still there."

Rajiv had his phone in his hands. "Um. Perhaps I should just take a picture of her. For record keeping's sake."

"Take her picture?" Rebecca said incredulously. "We're trying to keep this a secret, mate. Not publish it in the papers. That's what we're trying to *avoid*. I thought you brought her to King's Cross in the taxi because you were looking out for her?" Rebecca was really angry with him.

"Look, pictures don't always do harm. Did you see those pictures of her and the Dutch Queen in front of the carved Gouda? People liked those. They didn't do harm."

"Didn't see them, but heard about them. Taken by some undercover chef who wasn't a chef. The papers are trying to smuggle people in all the time. That time, it worked."

"I was the chef," said Rajiv proudly. "I took those pictures."

"I can't believe it. You?"

"Yes, me," he said, beaming.

"Then you are an absolute shit and I don't even know why I'm here with you."

"Okay, okay, okay," he said quickly. "Nothing to worry about. I'll follow your lead. I'll do everything you say." A pause. Then he put in mischievously, "But what about your picture, then?"

As she whipped up her head to look at him in disbelief, he already had his phone positioned to take a close shot of her face. And he captured her, hair flying, and anger around the eyebrows.

One of the silent side effects of Luke's service in the Middle East was his heightened suspicion of everyone outside his immediate circle. Indeed, aside from the men he'd served with, most of whom were not in London, or not free at the limited times he was, his immediate circle sometimes diminished to a circle of one. Himself alone. He had to rely on people in the Household to get things done, but they were not his friends. Evenings and weekends he spent quite a lot of time alone in his Bayswater flat, going to bed early and sleeping late. He slept more since returning from the Middle East, aware that it probably wasn't a sign of good mental health, but aware that sleep was effective in reducing his vague distress. He had few people with whom he could talk over his anxieties and problems, so they were slow to dissolve and disappear. This sometimes impaired his judgment and heightened his misgivings about the people around him. Had he confided what he knew to MI5 following the phone call from Rebecca, the train might have been met at an intermediate stop and The Queen whisked away in a car behind darkened windows. At the very least, Holyrood might have been alerted, so The Queen could have a place to stay in Edinburgh.

After Rebecca's telephone call, he was relieved. The Queen had been found. Yes, she was on a public train to Edinburgh without proper security, but at least she could now be followed. He'd agreed to Shirley and Anne getting on a plane to Edinburgh, the last commercial flight of the evening out of Heathrow, but he hadn't thought to ask for either of their mobile numbers, so he couldn't tell them what he'd learned from Rebecca. The problem was somehow to have The Queen taken care of in Edinburgh, and he didn't quite know how to manage that. The last fast trains had gone. He imagined there would only be buses now, and he silently determined to catch one of these. Victoria Coach Station was not far away. It would take longer than a train or a plane. But the night buses would be there by the first thing in the morning and then he could supervise whatever The Queen needed in Edinburgh himself, ideally persuading her to come back as quickly and quietly as possible. Beyond these vague calculations, he wasn't quite sure what he was going to do, other than run immediately for the bus.

Luke told William, when he returned to the sitting room, that The Queen had been found on the 1700 from King's Cross to Edinburgh Waverley. "You're off the hook, mate." He was going to get on a night bus to Scotland by himself as soon as possible. It would be better if William could "hold the fort," as it were, at BP. "Hang on a minute," William had said, hands on hips. "Who is meeting Her Majesty at Edinburgh Waverley?"

"Well, Mrs MacDonald and Lady Anne are on their way to Edinburgh and will be there shortly after she arrives."

"But not in time to receive her?"

"No. But Rebecca from the Mews is with her."

"Who is Rebecca?" said William with some incredulity.

"Works with the horses. Last to see Her Majesty before she left."

"What you're telling me is that The Queen is by herself on a public train, unattended by anyone other than a girl who forks hay in the stables. No police. No security. And no one to meet her when she gets there. You have *got* to be joking."

It surprised Luke to find William really rather impatient with him, both in terms of the shaky intimacy they'd recently established and of the palace hierarchy, where, technically speaking, William ranked fairly far beneath him.

"I'll arrange The Queen's reception on the bus. I've my mobile with me. But I'm not telling the secret services that The Queen's left." He then remarked, separating the words as he said them, "They cannot be trusted."

William could see that Luke was a little mad. He liked Luke. He thought he was handsome. He respected Luke's experience in the army and his having fought in Iraq. He looked fantastic in his clothes. But he was still a little off. The look in his eye at that moment was of a person who was talking to himself on the street, and to whom you would automatically give a wide berth.

William's own protective instincts now kicked in. "Well, I'm going with you. We'll settle it together. On the bus."

"No." Luke had decided to retreat from his earlier position that they should go together. He now thought he should address only one of his problems at a time.

"Yes."

"No."

"Look, I've been at the palace longer than you. I'll be here long after you're gone. It's my job to look after her too, as I think you went out of your way to remark earlier," added William drily. "You're not all there, and you're going to need some looking after yourself. I'm coming. Quit. I'll just go and tell the page that Her Majesty has retired early with a head cold. He'll have to mind the dogs."

Luke shot William an angry look mixed with something that might have been gratitude or an appeal. Just then the telephone on The Queen's desk rang again.

"Oh God," said Luke glancing at the clock.

"Go on, pick it up. It might be some news."

"No, it's not. It's Arabella Tyringham-Rode."

"MI5? Good. They'll help us."

The phone continued to ring.

"They will *not* help us," Luke said, his eyes blazing. "She told me earlier that if I hadn't found The Queen in thirty minutes I had to hand over to them."

"Nothing here at SW1A 1AA happens as quickly as that," said William. "She knows that." He then went impatiently to the phone, picked it up, and said, "Yes?"

"To whom am I speaking?" asked Arabella Tyringham-Rode coolly.

"William de Morgan, Senior Page of the Chambers," answered William, using his formal palace title.

"Ah, one of Her Majesty's legendary members of staff. Look here, Morgan," she said, guessing instinctively that the "de" was probably fake and that he needed to be put in his place. "This is a crisis. Major Thomason agreed to hand over to MI5 half an hour ago if he hadn't found Her Majesty. Time's up."

"No, you listen." William was incensed at her high-handedness. "Major Thomason is a decorated soldier. Saw action. Fought for us, you and me." He summoned a little bravado for his own performance. "I will not allow you to intimidate a serving member of the armed forces. The Queen is still head of the army and in command of her own Household. Word has not been left me to follow any instructions other than hers. I'm sure we shall be in touch in due course." With that, he hung up the phone.

Luke looked at William in silent horror.

"Come now, bright eyes," said William. "We've a bus to catch. Let's go."

"And did you see *The Queen*?" asked the woman with thick spectacles after her husband's little joke about Helen Mirren. "We loved it."

The Queen wasn't accustomed to being asked such direct

questions, and certainly not on subjects that might prove awkward. She became uncomfortably aware that what had started out as a little impromptu sidestepping of her usual routine and responsibilities, perhaps rather desperate, but from which she hoped for a little relief nevertheless, might be harder work than she expected. Usually, the courtiers protected her from awkwardness. The people they allowed her to meet were generally too afraid of her to ask her anything that couldn't be answered easily and smoothly, as she'd done a thousand times before. "How are the corgis?" "Is your Mother well?" That last one still made a lump come to her throat, as, even though her mother had died several years ago, people did still bring her up, and The Queen hadn't entirely accustomed herself to not being able to telephone her in the morning as had been their usual habit.

She was saved from having to reply immediately by the young man with piercings. "If you'll pardon my asking," he said, clearing his throat, "how do blind people see films?"

"We hear them, don't we? And I can see a little bit if it's on a big screen and I turn my head like this. But him, no, he's never been able to see them."

The blind man nodded his assent. Films were all right, but he wanted to get back to history.

His wife continued, "And perhaps because we only hear them, we catch things that often other people don't. They get distracted by the pictures. That's why we're called 'differently sighted' sometimes, because our other senses are more developed than they would have been if our vision weren't impaired."

Her husband harrumphed at this. "Politically correct. 'Differently sighted.'" He said the words with a sneer. "Blind is what I am. Always have been. Don't need to dress it up with polite words."

"Well," his wife started in again, used to being corrected by her husband but anxious nonetheless to show that she had understood the film at a deeper level, "blindness, that's what the film was about, wasn't it?"

"What?" said the young man with piercings, almost as dismissively as the blind man had spoken the words "differently sighted." "No, it was about Lady Di and her crash, weren't it?"

"Yes, of course, it was," persisted the woman with spectacles, "but it was also about how blind The Queen was to how much we all loved Diana. How the palace abused the poor girl. Wasn't it?"

For the first time that afternoon, The Queen felt stung. She knew she was struggling with some kind of indefinable grief, but she had been only half conscious of what she was doing up to now. She felt so unhappy that a bit of cheese and a visit to *Britannia* had seemed like good ideas. She'd not anticipated being at a table discussing a film that troubled her, no matter how sympathetic its portrayal of her had been. With three members of the public, no less. She now became vaguely aware that she had to tread lightly, that discovery of her little unofficial visit to *Britannia* might have consequences.

The Queen steeled herself to take part in it. She recalled the first time her yoga instructor had shown her how to do the plank position. It was really a sort of press-up that you held in place, and it was very hard to do, especially if you'd lost the strength in

your upper arms, as The Queen seemed to have done. But the yoga instructor had been very patient with her. She'd counseled her to begin by taking the position on her knees, and that was much easier. Over a month or so The Queen had gradually built up to it where, now, for a few moments, she could actually do a proper plank with her knees off the floor. She thought to herself, if I can do that, I can also handle this.

The Queen also felt some sympathy for the woman in thick spectacles. She'd now been spoken to with scant respect by both men at the table. The Queen didn't like being characterized as blind, but she saw that if she were to avoid speaking, she was going to have to draw out the others a bit more.

"How much Diana was loved," repeated The Queen. "Yes, do go on."

"Well," said the woman in spectacles, happy to have been asked to speak a bit more, "the palace didn't understand Diana or how much she meant to people, did they? That's why they wouldn't lower the flag. That's why they wouldn't bring the boys down for the funeral. That's why they couldn't believe all the flowers. But it didn't surprise me one bit."

"The boys had just lost their mother," said the blind man. "Why should they come down to London and listen to Elton bloody John?"

"Right," put in the man with piercings. "Elton *bloody* John! What a wanker."

On some level The Queen agreed with the blind man and the pierced man, but she didn't approve of the swearing. She thought it might be better to get the subject out of this contemptuous vein and into something the two men could speak of admiringly. "And what music would you have had in the Abbey?"

"Guns N' Roses," said the pierced man without hesitating.

"Tchaikovsky's *Pathétique*," said the blind man with equal conviction.

"So difficult to please so many different tastes, isn't it?" The Queen asked the table. No one could possibly disagree with that. She didn't expect to be disagreed with, but again the woman with spectacles joined in: "But you see, Elton John was Diana's friend. That's why it made sense for him to play."

"We have a tradition of choral music in this country that is centuries old, my dear," the blind man said with some condescension. "Choral music at the Abbey stretches back long before the Reformation."

"Who wants your ancient history?" shot back the woman with spectacles, finally provoked into a display of impatience with her husband. "Diana didn't read *History Today* or any of those dull magazines you like. She liked a bit of *Tatler* and *Vanity Fair*. Just like the rest of us. That's why people loved her."

"I didn't love her," said the young man with piercings. "She was just more bread and circuses to keep the proles quiet, weren't she? Smoke and mirrors. Magic tricks so the rich stay rich and the rest of us work for a living."

"I quite agree with you," said the blind man. "She was just one of those images displayed on the wall of the cave for the imprisoned. It keeps the cave dwellers happy so they forget their chains. Plato wrote about it in the fifth century BCE."

The Queen didn't feel she could follow either of the men here. Nor was she entirely pleased with the tack the woman with spectacles had taken, either. The Queen reflected to herself that, in her own way, she had loved Diana as much as she had loved the other people her children had married. Mark Phillips, now, she loved him too. What she objected to in the Diana hysteria, for it was that and she had no doubt of it, was the way all the traditions she valued had been rejected. All the public mourning struck her as positively Neapolitan, certainly not British. Where was the stiff upper lip? Plenty of young men Diana's age whom she'd known personally had died horribly in the war. It was a mark of respect and toughness and grit not to give in, to maintain emotional control in those conditions. It was important *not* to break down. But now, if one didn't break down, one was considered cold.

She recalled sitting in the Abbey and hearing the crowd's roared approval outside. It was when Spencer had referred to the palace treating Diana badly. She herself could remember holding Spencer in her arms when he was a baby with a fouled diaper. She was letting his parents their house on the estate at Sandringham, and at a reduced rental too. Now he'd inherited the earldom and was old enough to stand in the pulpit, he thought he could give *her* a lecture in how to behave. That was gratitude for you. Had she the power, she certainly would have thrown him in the Tower at that moment. But, no, she was quite powerless, she had to do as she was told.

She had to sit there and listen to the impudent boy as the public cheered, rather as if they were at a football match or the Roman Colosseum, instead of a young woman's funeral.

Moments later, after saying good-bye to the clergy at the west door of the Abbey, she stood there with her mother, waiting for the car to come around. The old lady had teased her. "A revolutionary moment, eh, Lilibet? I fancy they'll be rolling out the gallows for you soon, my darling." Very much like her mother, to choose a moment when she was feeling quite miserable and make it worse with a few slyly chosen words. The Duke of Edinburgh

was no help either. He just raged and railed at Spencer's effrontery. She preferred to sit by herself in a room, brooding over what had happened, silently asking what she had done wrong.

The Queen was unaware that she had drifted off into this reverie. The blind man, kindly thinking this elderly woman was embarrassed that she didn't know what he was speaking of and needed a little instruction, put in helpfully, "The allegory of the cave, from Plato's *Republic*, of course."

"Of course," said The Queen vaguely. What did Plato have to do with anything? But she also saw that if she didn't reassert some control, the conversation might go anywhere. "And the stag? Was The Queen supposed to be the stag? In that film they killed the deer, and so they'd killed The Queen? Was that it?" This had been the part of the film to which The Queen objected the most. She hadn't minded that actress, Miss Mirren. The Queen knew that Miss Mirren looked much better on the screen than she did. It was really rather flattering, but she did hate all that animal-rights sentimentality about the stag. It was as if the whole film had been shot by hunt *saboteurs*.

"Oh, well, I don't think it was meant to be a one-to-one correspondence. The stag was a noble animal, captured by the hunters. They shot it. The Queen is noble too, no one doubts it, but the hunters didn't get her. At the end of the film, she lives on. She's still there," added the woman with thick spectacles.

"But you see, this is why it doesn't work. Those deer are pests. They eat all the roses. They eat the kitchen gardens. They'll eat any variety of sapling if you don't protect it with a wire cage. They *have* to be put down or the Highlands would be one bald hillside after another. Creates erosion too. No good for cultivating the pine forests. And a good deal of whatever income you can squeeze out of those granite hillsides comes from the pine, of course. The deer also multiply so quickly that they overpopulate. Not enough heather to go around. Watching deer starve is dreadful. That's why they're culled."

The Queen's three travelling companions were amazed that she knew so much about the economics of Scottish forestry and animal husbandry. It stopped the conversation, as none of them felt they could contribute anything on those subjects. Just then the chief steward made a crackling announcement on the train's public address system. "The buffy car is open for snacks and light refreshments." He added that those wishing to have supper should take a seat in the restaurant adjacent to the buffet. At this the blind man, feeling generous about a table that had been willing to listen to him on the subject of both Tchaikovsky and Plato, offered to stand his companions at the table a round of drinks before dinner, "if everyone would join me in the *carozza ristorante*." This met with universal approval. Led by Hohenzollern the Seeing Eye dog, the blind man, the woman with thick spectacles, the man with piercings, and The Queen got up and paraded single file down the carriage's central aisle. All eyes were fixed upon the dog. So the old woman in the hoodie and headscarf once again escaped recognition.

Rebecca was furious. "I didn't say you could take my picture."

"Well, let's take a look at it first, shall we? And then we can just delete it." Rajiv brought the screen of the phone up and displayed the picture of her he'd just taken. She was livid, it was clear from the photo. But there was something about her red hair in the passing glare of light from outside the train that made the picture surreal, otherworldly. The flush in her cheeks also made it undeniably an attractive image—even Rebecca, angry as she still was, could see that. "Oh, come on. We can't delete that. It's beautiful." Rajiv looked up at her. "You're beautiful."

"That's not me."

"Oh yeah? Who is it, then?"

"Someone in your imagination."

"Do you think I just pressed the 'imagine' button on the phone?"

"No, but you're just making up some fantasy. You don't even know me. 'Girl with red hair.' Or 'Someone I just met.' Or 'I want to sleep with her.' It's all to do with your mixing up the picture with your own dream of what the woman in the photo is going to do for you. How she's going to be a mirror for your great accomplishments. Or, how she's going to do everything you want in bed. That sort of thing."

"Hang on. Just because you walked in the shop and I thought you were hot, that doesn't mean you can make me into some sort of ogre."

"Okay. I'm not saying you're an ogre." She stopped a moment to think. "What is an ogre, anyway? Someone out of some sort of Paki fairy tale?"

"Oooh, darlin'," Rajiv said, putting his arm around her. "You must like me if you're calling me that. Because you know very well you're not allowed to say it to a black man."

"You're not black. Sort of cappuccino colored. Anyway, people say 'Paki' all the time."

"That they do. But it's stupid, isn't it? Why should a short form of 'Pakistan' apply to all the different varieties of South Asian ethnicity? And people don't say 'Paki' to my face usually. Not unless they're about to hit me. Or unless they're my very good friends." He gave her a sudden nudge of his shoulder. "Oh, sorry. The rails are so uneven up here."

She giggled contentedly, having forgotten she was annoyed with him. An announcement on the train's public address system that York was the next station stop and would be coming up shortly dispelled the moment of accord between them.

"Okay, stop it now. There will be people coming through soon, and we've got to make sure no one notices her in there. Or bothers her."

"Nothing we can do to stop that. Anyway, she's got her disguise on. I think you were in on this from the start, weren't you? Helping her make her escape. Loaned her your jacket so no one would ever recognize her with that hood over her head?"

"I told you. I loaned it to her because when she walked in to speak to Elizabeth she hadn't a coat on and it was sleeting outside."

"Hmm. What else?"

"Well, we're proceeding on a 'need to know' basis, aren't we? If you find out too much from me, you'll have some telephoto lens trained on the horse stalls, won't you?"

"No, I like getting my shots spur of the moment. Just as you find them. You know, before people can make up a face to meet the camera."

"And photos of The Queen when she isn't expecting to be photographed, that's your service to humanity, is it?"

"People want to see her. It gives them pleasure."

"And her? What about her pleasure?"

"Well, I think in a long life, she must've got used to being photographed. And it must please her to give pleasure."

"I'm not sure she feels that way about it."

"Okay. How does she feel about it?"

Rebecca actually had no idea. "Well, I don't know for certain, but I guess she prefers being photographed when she can actually anticipate the camera's being there. And doesn't like it when she's taken by surprise. Who likes to be taken by surprise?"

"You didn't mind it. A minute ago. After you saw the picture."

Rebecca did not intend rising to this bait, and in fact, the train was slowing down for the platform at York, so she didn't have to. People were beginning to appear in the vestibule to get ready to step over them on leaving the train, so they both struggled to their feet to make way. The station stop was brief and whatever intimacy they'd managed to establish had evaporated by the time the signal had sounded, the door had been electronically locked, and the train was again rolling out of the station.

They both settled back onto the floor, but an awkward silence descended. Rebecca was uncomfortable with it. "Okay, your turn to check that she's still there."

"Why? She didn't get off at York."

"No, not through this door she didn't. But we've got to make sure she's fine. She has no police with her. We're all there is."

Rajiv struggled to his feet. "Then I will go and do the bidding of the representative of the Master of the Horse."

"God, we're not under him anymore."

"Well, what division of Her Majesty's Household are you, then?"

"Just go and look, okay?"

Rajiv went up to the glass door next to several aluminum racks loaded with oversized cases and bags. He looked cautiously through it into the carriage. The seats were all practically full, with the exception of the table nearest to the partition on the left. There four seats were empty except for some newspapers and coats. What looked like an aluminum dish filled with water sat underneath the table. The small woman in the hoodie, the man with the piercings, and the blind couple were all gone.

"Houston, we have a problem," said Rajiv sliding down the wall next to Rebecca.

"What?"

"Table's empty. Rest of the carriage full. She's not in there."

"Christ! This is my fault. If I hadn't listened to all your nonsense, I'd have kept better track of her. Come. On." She was on her feet with a snap and striding off down the central aisle of the carriage. Rajiv had to run to keep up.

At the next vestibule, he cried out. "Hang on a minute."

"Hurry. Up." She was impatient. She wanted no conversation.

"Look. We've got to have a story. I'm not supposed to be on this train. She told me to get off. I can't just turn up next to her wherever she's sitting now. She was already a little annoyed with me that I left the shop to put her on the train."

"All right. Go find the guard. See if a woman in a hoodie got off at York."

"What would she want there?"

"You fool. There's the Minster. She'll know the Dean and all the canons. It's the first place she'd go. And if she did get off there we're stuck on the train until the next stop, Darlington, which is useless."

"If she wanted to see friends, she'd hardly walk away from the palace by herself, would she?"

"Look, I'm not arguing with you. Go and find the guard." She was off. Rajiv could just see the soles of her riding boots, like the hooves of an antelope, disappearing into the vestibule of the next carriage.

He wasn't sure what to do next. He was pretty certain The Queen hadn't got off the train at York. Old ladies don't walk longer distances than necessary, and it would have made more sense to get off using the door where he and Rebecca had been sitting than for her to walk all the way to the other end of the carriage. Further, he had an intuitive dislike of the lower levels of British officialdom. He was convinced that people with brown faces didn't get the same treatment as others, so he wasn't about to approach the guard with unusual questions. It was true that he'd been born in England to an educated father and rich grandparents, but in his experience, the elderly, some of the provincial working classes, and almost all of the unemployable underclass regarded him as "foreign." He was on the alert for slights and hazards and racial prejudice of all varieties. Instead of seeking out the guard, he decided The Queen must have gone with the other passengers from her table to the carriage with the restaurant and buffet. He took his time walking there and sloped up behind Rebecca, whom he found leaning against the wall of the buffet portion of the carriage with a view down a short corridor into the dining part of the car.

"In there," she hissed to him when she looked around behind her and found him standing there with a crooked smile.

"Thought so," said Rajiv. "What do we do now?"

"We wait here and see where she goes."

"Oh, well then, if she's having her supper, it will be a little while, then. We might have a cup of coffee or something. What do you like? White or black?"

She looked around at him a little anxiously.

"Not me, love. The coffee. What kind of coffee do you like?"

William and Luke arrived at Victoria Coach Station after a fifteen-minute run. Luke had no difficulty whatsoever, but William, who exercised less and was ten years older, had to rely on adrenaline to keep up. They both jumped on a Scottish coach that was just about to leave. Before they knew it they were sitting together, shoulder to shoulder in the darkness, with only the light from the passing lamps on the motorway flashing greenly on their faces.

Luke quickly made it clear, in response to William's repeated appeals, that he was not authorizing telling anyone else about The Queen's movements. The women would care for her in Edinburgh. There was nothing to do until they had a further bulletin either from Rebecca or Mrs MacDonald and Lady Anne. William saw there was no arguing with Luke on this. He was unreasonable about it. William could only stick with him and make sure nothing more foolish was undertaken.

There was some unease between them. They weren't friends exactly. Too much divided them. And yet here, outside the palace, beyond their normal roles, something of the gap between them seemed to be reduced. Although Luke was the younger of the two, his instinct from his palace position was to try and kindle a conversation, to keep it going. He also knew, though he'd insisted on the plan of their telling no one else, that there was a chance he was wrong about this. He was prisoner to what he himself could recognize was the less rational half of his brain. The only thing for it was to seek some forgiveness from this older man who had, after all, expressed an interest in keeping an eye on him. The best way he could think of seeking forgiveness was by getting William to talk a bit about himself. Everyone liked talking about themselves. It was the only thing he had to offer his traveling companion.

"So you think you'll be at the palace long after me, do you?"

"I don't think. I know. The equerries serve for two or three years at the outside."

"Well, um, not if they get appointed to the private office, or the Privy Purse, or um, as racing managers, now?"

William laughed shortly through his nose. "I'd wager you don't know the first thing about racing. And even the private secretaries serve for a limited spell. They tend to have a few more qualifications than you, my darling." This was meant as a truthful tease, and William added the "my darling" as a way of indicating it was a tease, though an affectionate one.

"And why are you content to remain there with so many temporaries about, brilliantly qualified though they may be?"

"Well, I was born in a dreary little place. The people I went to school with, when they left, if they finished, went off to live dull lives, without much color, certainly without any style. I always wanted something better than that. The palace isn't perfection. Plenty of rivalry, politics." William paused for a moment and thought of one of his colleagues, Reginald Brown, a butler who was senior to him at the palace. They called him "Le Brun," or "Brunello," or plain "Bruno" behind his back. As a tease someone told The Queen that he actually liked being called "Bruno," so she started calling him that too. Bruno was furious and blamed William for it. One day last week Bruno had sneered into William's ear, "I hear you're friendly with the new equerry. Watch your step, young William. Careful you don't trip." William had heard the threat distinctly, though he pretended not to understand. If anyone knew how to trip him up, Bruno did.

William quickly decided that he couldn't tell any of this to Luke. So he continued, "The pay's not good. But the standard of service is high. And they appreciate it, as a kind of art, you know. How to appear at the elbow and disappear behind the curtain. It's a bit like being onstage, but the best performance is the one that gets noticed the least."

It had never occurred to Luke before to see a butler in this light. In a dozen luncheons and dinners with The Queen he could never recall having seen what precisely they were doing. Maybe this was their art.

"Everyone thinks of being a waiter, or, worse, a butler, as humiliating. They think of the butler in, what was that film? *The Remains of the Day.* He's pathetic. Gives his whole life to serve a Nazi. The audience loves to think of what we do as sad. They all want to be on the sofa in front of the telly, serving themselves. They think we should all be out making money or a name for ourselves. But, actually, you see, service is something that takes time and effort to do well. It takes self-denial to do it right. It's like knowing the rules of a wedding ceremony. Or how a cab driver memorizes all the backstreets of London. I know what fork goes out for oysters, where it's placed, and which wine goes with it. Coming by that knowledge, doing it properly, all those are worthwhile things."

"And does The Queen appreciate it?"

"She does. She performs the same sort of act, goes through similar rituals every day. If anyone knows the order of a ceremony, she does. And even if she didn't appreciate it, even if, say, whoever's king or queen after her doesn't appreciate what we do, it would still be worth doing, because it's part of life at the palace. It's the gilt on the ceiling, the Gainsborough in the frame, the brocade on the sofa. It's not about putting a tea bag in a mug, mate."

"No, I see that. And what about Emma Thompson? What was she called? Miss Kenton or something? Or is it impossible to serve The Queen and have a life outside too?"

"Not impossible, no. But I haven't put as much effort into finding my own Anthony Hopkins as I have into learning the drill. Surely it's obvious that Emma Thompson is not really my type."

Luke was alarmed. The conversation seemed to have taken a dangerous turn toward declaring sexual preference. Luke himself had never had a proper girlfriend, or a boyfriend either, for that matter. Confessing that lack, that total absence in his life, seemed a more damaging admission just then than saying that he was either straight or gay. Still, it also seemed rather churlish, cowardly even, to clam up at such a moment. "Well, being in the army, it means moving from place to place every few years. There's no time for settling down with anyone. Maybe it's been like that with you too. You're always travelling with Her Majesty. Away from London for what must add up to some months every year, I guess, year in and year out."

"True," said William simply. He was aware of having volunteered quite a lot about his own life already. He wanted to hear what Luke's life was like, but he wanted him to tell it of his own accord.

Luke had been taught to abhor a silence at The Queen's table, or over cocktails in anterooms of the palace. It was his job to make sure that no one felt ill at ease. Mixed with that social instinct, however, was his postwar tendency not to have entire control of his emotions and to sleep too much. He was always restraining himself from blurting out something that was more personal than the rules of palace social conduct generally allowed. So now he rushed forward, just as William hoped he would. "I mean, I've been in the army practically since school. I've never had a girlfriend. Just mates. I guess you must think that sounds pretty bizarre."

"Not necessarily," said William evenly. "You're the one who matters. What do you think about it?"

"Well, I don't really know how it feels to be otherwise. When you're serving abroad, it's nice to have mates you can laugh with, whom you can count on." He looked out the window. "If they don't let you down." He had rushed forward with one confession, now he seemed to be teetering on the edge of another.

William thought about what Luke had said for several minutes before he said, "And did one of them let you down?"

Luke said nothing for a long time. Then he said quietly, "Well, I think I might have let him down."

William knew that what he'd just heard was a tremendous disclosure. He thought it more tactful to pretend as if he'd fallen asleep. It would save Luke embarrassment. He closed his eyes and began breathing regularly. Luke looked over and saw William sleeping. He didn't know whether to be hurt or relieved that the older man had not heard what he said.

The Queen and the blind couple and the man with piercings made their way to the restaurant, which was one half of a carriage. The dining half had a row of tables, draped with white cloths, set for four persons each. They found an empty table, and a waiter dressed in a red waistcoat came to take their orders for drinks as he passed around menus. The blind man was aware that his new train acquaintance had what he regarded as a highbrow accent out of a Nancy Mitford novel, so as he took his seat, he began by apologizing. "It's a bit early for supper, isn't it? Perhaps we should regard it as a meat tea?"

"No, no!" said The Queen. "Hohenzollern is starving, aren't you, darling?" The Queen was pleasant to everyone at the table, but also held them at arm's length with practiced politeness. Her replies were her shield. The dog she addressed with real warmth.

"Now, madam," the blind man said, bowing in what he took to be her general direction, "what shall our railway waiter bring you to drink?"

"A martini, please," said The Queen, smiling to herself.

"A martini?" said the waiter, thinking that she wanted a Manhattan-style cocktail made with a silver shaker. There was no way he could produce this in his minuscule kitchen.

"No, not an American one. An old-fashioned English martini: two parts Dubonnet, two parts gin, and a bit of lemon peel. All mixed up together. On ice."

"I'm sorry, Madam, there is no space for a shaker. We don't have one."

"Well, bring me the bottles and a glass of ice and lemon and I'll put it together. It doesn't have to be shaken in the air to do the trick."

"And you, young man?" said the blind man in his friendliest way to the man with piercings.

"Mine's lager."

"And gin and tonics for myself and the lady wife, please," said the blind man, doing his best Rumpole imitation and hoping it was recognized.

The waiter saw right away this was going to be a difficult table. He skipped off, swaying down the aisle with the motion of the train to fetch the drinks.

"You'll have to help us with the menus," said the woman in spectacles to the young man with piercings. "The nice restaurants always have Braille menus, but . . ."

"But this is the Great North Eastern Railway, darling. We shall be lucky if they warm our baked beans on a ring," put in her husband.

"These prices are out*rage*ous," said The Queen, examining her menu.

"I shall be beginning my talk on the Elizabethan court before long," said the blind man jovially. "Perhaps that will take some of the sting out of the tariff of Great North Eastern Railway."

"Not that," said the young man with piercings.

"Oh, please, darling, no," said the blind man's wife, laughing, but meaning it.

"Hohenzollern and I would be very pleased with a cheese sandwich from the buffet car." The Queen really thought the expense was getting out of hand.

"My dog is descended from the Kaiser and he does not eat in the buffet car."

"And looks a bit like him too. *Don't you*?" said The Queen, grasping the dog's velvet ear.

"Now, tell us, please, what's for supper, and no cheese sandwiches," said the blind man to The Queen.

"Well, there's a steak of Aberdeen Angus. Loch Fine salmon. Lincolnshire roast duckling. Morecambe Bay prawns in a curry sauce. And look here, Welsh rarebit too! All British. A fine menu, don't you think?" The Queen's voice, for the first time that evening, indicated real pride.

"Where's the Irish coffee?" muttered the young man. The blind man's wife heard him and chuckled.

The waiter returned with their drinks and took their orders for supper. He was stacking the menus in his hand and made ready to turn on his heel when The Queen stopped him short. "Just a moment, young man."

"Madam?"

"Hohenzollern will be dining as well," said The Queen, nodding to the dog, who looked up expectantly from underneath the table. "You haven't taken his order."

"Madam, we haven't any way of feeding dogs on the train."

"He'll have some minced beef. Browned quickly. Add to it some plain white rice and a little *bouillon*," said The Queen. "That's beef broth. Put it together in a soup bowl and he'll be happy."

"That's not on the menu, madam. I can't do that. You don't know our chef. He can produce wonders in his kitchen. But it's not big. We haven't the space. We can't do special orders."

Under the table Hohenzollern growled.

"Then I'll have a word with Cook." For an old woman, The Queen was out of her seat very quickly and stalking down the aisle, the waiter following her, protesting. They both disappeared into a small door from which pans clashing against one another could be heard.

Reduced to three, the conversation resumed. The young man with piercings said, "I can't put my finger on it, but she reminds me of someone. And not Helen Mirren, neither."

"Well, she does have an unusual voice, doesn't she?" agreed the woman with spectacles.

"Too old for Helen Mirren, darling."

"No, I know. Not Helen Mirren. But she reminds me of someone else. I think this young man is right," said the woman in spectacles.

"Judi Dench perhaps? Or Prunella Scales? An actress playing a part out of Alan Bennett certainly," said the blind man, once again proud of the fact that he could move so swiftly between history and contemporary fiction.

"I *love* Alan Bennett," put in his wife.

"Yes, we have his entire *oeuvre* in Braille," said the blind man, intending to send up his wife's reading material, though in truth he quite enjoyed Alan Bennett too. "Bennett for the Blind, it is," said he, taking a sip of his gin and chortling.

"Did you read the one about The Queen becoming a reader?" said the woman in spectacles to the young man at her side. "I did enjoy that one. So funny. And of course, being a reader myself, I liked that side of it."

"Thought of yourself as The Queen, did you, darling?" called out the blind man, employing the kind of low blow that long-married couples sometimes give one another.

"No, not The Queen," said the woman in spectacles, feeling some annoyance until the right riposte occurred to her. "No more than you fancy yourself Regius Professor of History."

The Queen reappeared at the table in the midst of this testy exchange.

"We were just discussing Alan Bennett," said the blind man.

"Oh yes," said The Queen reseating herself. "*The Uncommon Reader*."

"That's it!" said the woman in spectacles delightedly. "Did you love it? I did!"

"Didn't read it," said The Queen briefly. She was on such relatively friendly terms with her table companions that she forgot to concentrate on keeping up her disguise. Her focus once again shifted. "The private office prepared some briefing notes for me. I had to meet Mr Alan Bennett with some other writing chaps. A Foyle's literary evening. One of those things. I gave out the prizes. Fancy making *me* out to be a reader. There's imagination for you," said The Queen, taking a sip of her drink, which she'd quickly mixed together after the waiter brought her a glass and bottles. With her other hand she tugged on Hohenzollern's ear under the table.

The conversation ceased abruptly.

The woman in spectacles audibly drew in her breath.

The young man with piercings, who didn't care about Alan Bennett, and was not attending to the conversation, also looked around to examine The Queen more carefully.

Only the blind man was brave enough to speak. "You? Not a reader? You gave out the prizes at Foyle's?" And, most incredulously of all: "You *met* Alan Bennett?"

"Yes, I met him. Charming man. Kept smiling at me all the time. Rather tongue-tied."

"But. Are you, then, The, um? Are you Her . . . ? Are you," the blind man dropped his voice and said in a whisper, "You're not The Queen?"

The Queen saw her error. Everything suddenly snapped back into a clearer focus. She now saw that these people were on the verge of identifying her.

"Oh, yes! Why, yes I am! Queen of all I survey," and she laughed delightedly as if she were a little girl and not an octogenarian.

The blind couple exhaled and began laughing with her. The young man with piercings was not so easily persuaded. "You do look like her."

"People tell me that a lot." The Queen decided to go after him as a way of keeping him quiet. "Now, you, of course. Who do you resemble? It's as if I've seen your picture a thousand times." The Queen had no idea who he looked like, but she knew enough about people's vanity to know that he probably had an idea of some famous figure he thought he looked like.

The young man reddened. The Queen saw this and said triumphantly. "Ah, I see. You do look like him. You've just turned three shades of crimson. Who is it? Tell me who it is."

"Sometimes they say I look like Johnny Depp."

"That's it!" said The Queen. She had no idea who Johnny whatever was. "Mr Jonathan Depth, of course!"

"But what were you doing giving out literary prizes at Foyle's, then?" said the blind man with renewed skepticism.

"Oh, that. They wanted The Queen of course, but couldn't get her. Went to bed early that night, she did." The Queen threw back her head and gave a little rehearsed laugh to show them what a good time she was having. She had to do that sort of thing often enough, to calm people's nervousness about speaking to her. "Then they wanted the Prince of Wales, but he has a thousand things to do, now The Queen is slowing down a tiny bit. Doing all his own things, plus quite a lot of hers. So they went on down the list. And settled on Princess Michael of Kent. But she wanted 'expenses,' you know, and an honorarium. So they couldn't afford her. And, well, I own a few shares in the holding company. So they said, well, she must be interested in books if she has the shares. And they had to take me," said The Queen, holding the table now, and bending over with amusement. Her body spoke a silent invitation to laugh with her. They all did, and the moment passed. The train rocked back and forth. The four of them were reflected in the window against the dark night, moving with the motion of the train, talking and taking sips from their glasses. Hohenzollern had his bowl of minced beef under the table, and The Queen looked down to confirm that all was well with him. She whispered under the table, "*Und dir, Hohenzollern? Wir geht es meinem Kaiserchen? Reden wir lieber nicht vom Krieg, nicht wahr?*"*

It became clear to Rebecca that The Queen was enjoying herself speaking with the other people at her table. She could also see there was a dog under the table whom The Queen addressed occasionally. "She's not going anywhere."

* And you, Hohenzollern? How are you my little Kaiser? Don't mention the war, eh?

"What do you mean?" said Rajiv.

"If the dog's happy, she's happy. The dog's had his dinner. Now he's asleep. Under the table. She won't want him to move."

"God, what a crazy country. Everyone bows to The Queen, and she obeys a sleeping canine."

"What's wrong with keeping animals happy, then? I thought Hindus were vegetarians too. Shows a certain respect for the animal world, if you ask me."

"I'm a long way away from all that. I grew up here. Loved burger bars when I was a kid. Went to school here too. But you want me to quote Gandhi and worship cows. That would make you happy, wouldn't it? She wanted me to tell her about yoga."

"Why do you lot think we're all against you? You wear it as some kind of badge of honor. 'They hate us.' You might as well have it pinned to that jacket you're wearing."

"It's because you think of us, you think of me, as 'you lot' and not as Rajiv. Also, when you're growing up and boys corner you in an alley and call you a bastard, it tends to leave an impression."

Rebecca didn't have anything to say to that. He'd won that round.

Rajiv thought perhaps he was overdoing the race question. He wanted her to know he'd suffered, but he didn't want that to be the keynote of whatever it was that was developing between them. "You were going to tell me about the man from the animal rights demo."

"I don't think there's anything there, really."

"Hang on. A minute ago you told me he was your boyfriend."

"Well, we went out. Okay? It was my first time. None of the

boys liked me in school. Then a bit later he wanted me to go to a hunt with him."

"What? You! Tally-ho?"

"No, you idiot. Not that. Just the opposite. He and a group of his friends were hunt *saboteurs*. They were going to a hunt to stop it. Wearing ski masks."

"Oh, well, I don't think I'm much in favor of galloping across country in order to kill a poor fox myself."

"They had knives. They were going to hurt the horses so they'd throw their riders."

"Oh," said Rajiv flatly.

"I couldn't believe it. He's been calling me since, but usually I don't answer. Hadn't heard from him in almost a year. Then he called me earlier when we were having coffee." Rebecca didn't herself understand why. Was he that attracted to her?

"That's why you left."

"That. But other things too. Here's the truth. I've never cared about boys. They hated me. Said I smelled. Not worth the trouble they cause. Horses, yes. Boys, no."

"Wait a minute. You wanted to sleep with a horse? Isn't that what killed Catherine the Great?"

"Not sleep with them." Why did he always have to make schoolboy jokes when she was trying to tell him something she'd told no one else? "But they've always seemed more real, more interesting than boys. Not interested in you either, not as a," here she wrinkled her nose, "as a penis. Only semi-like you as someone who makes me laugh, seems kind."

"But if I were hung like a horse, it would be different?"

She rolled her eyes. "See?"

Rajiv made a face as if he were T. S. Eliot on "Poetry Night" of an old-fashioned radio programme that usually featured classical music and intoned:

Rebecca has no use for this man.
Elizabeth of course as a horse counts far more.
But Elizabeth's in her stable, and The Queen's at her table
So Rebecca has to put up with this man so far as she's able.

Rebecca laughed delightedly. "You call yourself a poet! What was that? Some sort of limerick?"

"Well, you have to start somewhere. It were spur of the moment, weren't it?"

"Not high art, if you ask me."

"Stick with me, kid," said Rajiv, leaning in to put his arm around her waist, "I'll show you some high art. And did I tell you? You smell gorgeous to me."

For the first time she didn't mind his touching her. He seemed to want it so badly. What would it cost her, she thought, to let him have some physical contact?

Just then The Queen, with the blind man on her left arm and Hohenzollern's harness in her right hand, the dog leading the way, appeared in the buffet car. "Who's this canoodling in the corner? I believe it's the young man from Paxton & Whitfield! Who's looking after the shop?" She sounded a little indignant. Then she looked at Rebecca. "And here is a representative from the Mews. Going to see a friend in Scotland? Hmm? Or, perhaps, taking him with you?" said The Queen, looking at Rajiv. She felt it was a little strange to see these people whom she recognized on a public train, but then she so rarely boarded public conveyances—never, really—that she wasn't quite sure what to expect. Maybe it was common to find people one knew on ordinary buses and trains? Life beyond the palace walls was foreign to her. Nor did she want to interrupt what was clearly a private moment between them. It had nothing to do with her. She confined herself to a nod in Rajiv's direction as she went past and said in a stage whisper to Rebecca, "Very nice young man." She trooped by, followed by the man with piercings, who had the woman with spectacles on his arm. They disappeared down the aisle of the next coach.

"Busted," said Rajiv to Rebecca.

"Oh God," she groaned.

"It's not the end of the world. She didn't mind seeing us. We can go and join her now if we like."

"No, we can't. You don't just go and *join* The Queen. You have to be invited. Who were those people with her, anyway?"

"Oh, her coach was crowded when I put her on at King's Cross. They were the ones who were already at the table when she sat down. I expect they've become chums."

"They are not her chums, whoever they are. And now we've certainly got to mind where she goes with them."

"Well, they can't have gone further than back to their seats."

Just then the man behind the counter of the buffet car called out to them that he was about to close. Edinburgh was in twenty minutes. Did they want anything before he had to shut up shop?

They thanked him, no, they didn't want anything. They started to return to the last carriage where The Queen had been sitting, but the announcement over the train's public address system that the final stop was coming in a matter of minutes brought everyone out into the aisles, pulling their cases and coats down from the overhead racks, throwing away their newspapers, standing in the vestibules in order to be the first off the train when it pulled into the station. This blocked their passage and when the train arrived they were still several carriages behind where The Queen had been sitting. When at length they found her place, the spot was empty. They both rushed off onto the platform, ran backwards and forwards, had a look at the taxi rank and the bus stops, but The Queen, the blind man, the woman with spectacles, and the man with piercings were all gone.

William's simulated slumber turned into the real thing. When he woke up and looked over at Luke, he saw that he was asleep too. He was a little disappointed, but also a little thankful that their conversation hadn't gone any further. William didn't actually know how to proceed with Luke. Being friends with someone younger, rather confused, and without the least gay affect did not offer any immediate clues about how to proceed. Most of William's closest friends, since he was a boy, had been girls and women. It made him laugh to hear gay men called misogynists. He adored women, always had, but it wasn't as simple as people thought. It wasn't that he wanted to be a woman himself, or that they spent all their time talking about girly things. Far from it. He had a highly chivalric attitude toward women. Enjoyed holding the door for them, pulling out chairs for them, deferring to them, not because he had to, or because they were weak, but because they were ladies and it was an ancient code. He liked the politics and economics of modern egalitarian Britain; but the hierarchical rules and regulations of a partly Catholic, semi-medieval kingdom were rituals he believed in passionately as well. He didn't see why women shouldn't have equal pay for equal work. He could also imagine putting his jacket down so a lady friend could cross a puddle in the road.

His most beloved partners, his most fulfilling relationships had always been with straight women. They weren't as emotionally constipated as men. He could recall going somewhere in the car with his father when he was ten or twelve. He thought there was something wrong that there was no conversation. He would occasionally throw out a topic he thought might interest his father, only to have the shortest possible, most ill-tempered reply. He was in his thirties before he discovered that men friends liked being together without talking, that wordlessness was generally considered a desirable attribute of masculinity.

He had no close men friends in the Household. There was certainly camping and carrying on with some of the other staff. You could joke with the other gay chaps, but it never went much further than that, and they kept their distance from one another. They wouldn't be working for the Household if they didn't take their jobs quite seriously and they all knew that having an affair with someone at work would get found out, turn awkward, and lead to someone losing his job. Bruno was perfectly capable of putting the knife in his back.

Luke was also strange to him in having apparently reached his thirties without any long-term romantic or sexual commitments. William had never been in any doubt about his own sexuality. Luke, on the other hand, seemed to be questioning his abilities as a romantic partner well into a decade when most young men were already well and truly married, most of them fathers even.

Luke stirred.

"Awake, Sir Galahad, no more sleeping on duty."

"Oh, sorry," said Luke, squinting at William's shoulder. He couldn't see anything in the dark. "What happened? Where are we? What time is it?"

"Four in the morning. Edinburgh in about half an hour, I imagine. I saw a sign back there about five minutes ago. You fell asleep. What are our orders, Major Thomason? You may as well reveal them to me now. We're nearly there."

"Jesus, oh four hundred. Well, Rebecca from the Mews was on the same train as The Queen from King's Cross. She should have called me to let me know what was happening. They should be there by now. Lady Anne and Mrs MacDonald too. Surprised they haven't called me either."

"Shirley and Lady Anne together. Oh my God."

"What do you mean?"

"Well, Shirley is devoted to The Queen. But she's never been in love with any of the ladies-in-waiting. Thinks they're useless, in fact. Won't have any truck with them. Steers clear of them when she can."

"I suppose The Queen's little, um, jaunt, has created a number of unusual . . . partnerships."

"I'm not your partner, mate. I'm along to look after Her Majesty when we find her. So pull out your mobile and let's see if the women have called."

Luke did as he was told. "Christ!"

"Now what?"

"It's dead. I forgot to charge it."

"Totally useless you are. No wonder Iraq was such a balls-up. You lot couldn't find Colonel Gaddafi or Saddam Hussein or Osama bin Laden himself without it being marked in red on a map."

Luke was again surprised to find William not play-angry with him but truly exasperated.

"Look. I'm sorry. I hadn't been planning on coming to Scotland this evening."

"Well, me either, but here we are, so you better have a bloody quick think about what we're going to do when we get there."

"Lady Anne's nephew?"

"Who's he? Keeper of the Keys of Edinburgh Castle? Fat lot of good he'll do us now, Luke. It's an *honorific* title, doesn't mean he actually has them."

Luke stared down into his lap and fiddled with his nonresponsive mobile phone.

"What is it now?" said William impatiently.

"It's just that, well, that was the first time you called me Luke."

"I'm going to call you a lot worse than that if you don't come up with some more ideas. What's the point of Lady Anne's idle nephew?"

"Well, he got them their tickets to Edinburgh. Last flight out of Heathrow. And Lady Anne said he had a flat in Charlotte Square. Said that if they found The Queen, they'd take her there."

"Okay, good. Now we're getting somewhere. And you put the girl from the stables in touch with Lady Anne?"

"Well, no, I didn't."

"Why in the world not?"

"Because I wasn't thinking of it. Because MI5 was breathing down my neck. Because I was thinking of running to catch the bus. It's not usually part of my job to be exchanging the mobile telephone numbers of the ladies-in-waiting with the Mews."

"Well, I want to know what your job description actually is, then. Because whenever I see you lot, you're just tucking in at Her Majesty's table while I pour the wine."

"Harder than it looks."

"What is?"

"Pretending to have a good time with perfect strangers. Entertaining ministers from Commonwealth countries. What do you talk to them about?"

"Well, you're on for some real work now, darling. Pull out your wallet because we're here now and you're paying for a taxi to Charlotte Square. If we can find one, and you're responsible for that too if we can't."

"Wait a minute. Why don't we split it? Why can't *you* find the taxi?"

The bus pulled into the coach station in Edinburgh. The two men came clambering off the bus, still bickering as if they were blue jays, the noisiest and most cheerful thing about that still Scottish morning.

Part VI

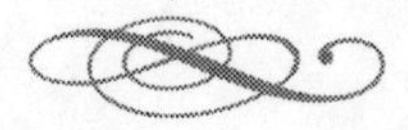

Happy Baby

The Queen had to admit to herself that she was an old woman on a spree and she hadn't the energy she used to have. She'd found her way to *Britannia* from Edinburgh Waverley using the crumpled note from inside Rebecca's hoodie. She'd spent the last of the crisp banknotes from her handbag on her fare and supper on the train. The driver of the bus from the railway station had changed Rebecca's £20 note for her with bad humor and complained that she ought to have brought the exact change. It wasn't how she was often spoken to, but it amused her to find someone as bad-tempered as she'd often begun to feel herself. After she arrived next to the ship, a security man whom she'd managed to call to the edge of the gangplank mistook her for a cleaner. All she'd had to say was "I'd like to go on board, please," and the firmness of her request convinced the man that she knew exactly where she was going. Who else would ask such a thing on a deserted quayside at ten at night? The cleaner often did turn up at this time of night, and though he remembered her as younger and friendlier the last time he'd let her up, he supposed the schedule of cleaners was always changing. He hadn't been on duty that many months himself.

After The Queen climbed on board, she found many of the familiar doors locked, and there was no one to call to have them opened. So she sat down, rather heavily, in one of the chintz-covered chairs in the sitting room to have a rest. "Oh," she thought to herself, "I have been happy here." She recalled a dozen holidays, in cold waters and warm, visiting all seven continents. She could recall going to Florida, when was it? In the early nineties? After the first Gulf War? The tall President Bush was in then. She'd given a party on *Britannia* moored in the harbor at Miami. The private secretary came into her sitting room before the party to ask her to approve the toast he'd written for her. He was wearing a white short-sleeved shirt. With no tie. She'd teased him. He wanted to show off his sunburn, didn't he? Then she'd read the speech while he stood there and found he'd written her a joke about sun cream. How they'd laughed. Then crossed out the joke. They'd had their fun. No one wanted The Queen to be too funny in her speeches. Short, to the point, dull propriety. That was usually her line. Her gloom started to reassert itself.

She struggled to find another memory of the ship. Yes, that night at the party, there'd been fireworks after dinner and they'd all gone aft to watch them on deck in the humid air. The Wales marriage had already grown difficult then, but she'd managed to keep her mind off it while they were on *Britannia*. Her own marriage was not perfect. They'd started out blissfully happy together. She was keenly aware of the sacrifice Philip had made. Without her he might have had a successful career in the navy. Proved that he was more than a penniless Greek. Instead, he married her, stuck by her side. She was grateful. She knew there had been other women, perhaps a good many. She tried to rise above it, not to let it bother her. His philanthropies suddenly required long trips around the world. Long separations with a few happy reunions. They'd rode it out and had real affection for one another. Their having made it through together was a real matter of pride for both of them. They both had the nicks and scars to prove it. She thought that was how most successful marriages were arranged. But the Princess of Wales hadn't been willing to put up with that sort of arrangement, had she? She'd done one desperate thing after another, and The Queen, now feeling and having done something rather desperate herself, had some shafts of sympathy pass through her heart, some flickers of understanding, that she hadn't felt before.

The Queen kept being drawn back to what had been bothering her even though her whole purpose in coming to *Britannia* was to think of happier days. "Let's see, where did we go after Florida?" The Queen thought they went to Mustique to see Princess Margaret for a night or two. Not too long, as her sister had a way of getting on her nerves, but she was curious to see what kind of life she had down there. Margaret had built a house which had been decorated with about thirty varieties of bamboo. Someone had snapped The Queen's picture on the beach. In a straw hat. Wearing trousers! Almost as outlandish as the private secretary in his shirtsleeves. She remembered the photo, and, yes, she had been happy then. The dogs hadn't liked it, though. Sand too fine for their paws, and being at sea often disagreed with them. She was forever cleaning up after their seasickness in a way she rarely had to do elsewhere. But this also made her feel useful.

She'd read antimonarchist articles in the paper that called her "useless," and even constitutional experts tended to agree. She was an ornament and by definition useless. She was there to lend a sense of occasion, and to provide the official seal of approval to all sorts of business that had been negotiated elsewhere. All different words for "useless" really, she thought, pulling off her pearl earrings.

"Is this all there is?" The Queen thought to herself. She'd begun her adventure in such high spirits and now she sat next to a sign directing visitors to the gift shop on her decommissioned yacht where once had stood an ebonized side table. Possibly it had been Uncle David's from Fort Belvedere. She believed his wife went in for that sort of thing. Where it was now, she didn't know.

She realized that despite all the ship's happy memories, she wasn't as confident as she once had been about whether she'd done any good. Or was doing any good. When she was young, all she had to do was smile, and stand through the presentation of troops, and listen to anthems. That seemed to be enough to swell people with pride. Perhaps she was having children and that's what people liked about her. Yes, they'd liked the two late little boys. But it had not recently been the same. She hadn't changed, but she saw that things had changed around her. People were usually polite; but even republicans had ceased to attack her. It distressed her that she'd let this weigh on her mind.

She'd prided herself for so long on keeping her chin up and going right through with the programme assigned to her in all weathers, feeling well or not, that it surprised her to be so powerlessly unable to deal with her feelings of disappointment.

She thought, perhaps a cup of tea. She wandered down to the galley, found a light switch by the door and an electric kettle on one of the counters. She went over to the sink to fill it up and found it full of dirty bowls, tea mugs, spoons, glasses, and smeared plates.

"What's this?" she thought, rather annoyed. What sort of staff had they that they would leave such a mess behind? Instinctively she switched on the hot tap to fill the sink and pulled on some rubber gloves she noticed on the rim of a bucket in the cupboard. In a moment her mood had changed from elderly hopelessness to grim determination. She was happy.

When they arrived at the airport in Edinburgh, Anne took charge. She found a taxi and told the driver they were going to *Britannia* berthed in Leith. She also said they might need him to drive them onwards after that. She admitted right away she didn't know where. She said all this in a tone of voice that brooked no objections, and made it evident she would accept no questions. Shirley had to do nothing but sit back in her seat. Her passion was looking after The Queen, but here, for the first time in a palace career of many decades, she was being looked after herself. There was nothing she had to do. Anne attended to all the details.

"I don't expect any of this looks familiar," said Anne surveying the side of the highway leading away from the airport. It was an acknowledgment that Shirley, though born in Scotland, would regard Edinburgh as foreign.

"No, no, it's not familiar. I'm a country girl, really. Born near Ballater. My grandmother was in service, as you know. So was my mother. When Mum went south, well, she was very young, and she left me with Granny."

"I believe they have some cottages for the retirees round Balmoral somewhere."

"Well, this was before the Jubilee Cottages were built, but yes, there were some places. Not that Granny spent much time at home. She was always up at the Castle, helping with the laundry, keeping things up, you know. Even at home, in the evenings, she mended sheets. Some of them went back to Queen Victoria's time. Proper linen sheets."

"Don't bring it up. Sleeping on that linen is no fun. I have fabric burn on my legs if I don't dress properly for bed there."

This made Shirley angry. She couldn't forget Letitia d'Arlancourt, or forgive her, either. "Oh, how difficult your life is, isn't it, Anne?" she remarked bitterly.

"I'm not saying I haven't been lucky."

"What are you saying, then?"

"Just that sleeping on plain cotton sheets from the British Home Stores is sometimes more comfortable than on Queen Victoria's linens."

With a sniff of disapproval, Shirley said, "There are many who would change places with the likes of you."

"'Likes of me. Likes of me'? I thought we were working together? And might even be friends. Eventually."

"It's not for me to offer the hand of friendship."

"Well, that's just because you and I have lived in or near the palace all our lives. It has warped us. Such as us are seldom friends, no, inside the palace; but outside the palace, women like us have no trouble setting up shop, mucking in together. The world outside the palace has moved on, Shirley. And one day you'll want to retire. Under the new rules from the Privy Purse, they won't automatically give you a cottage anymore, and you're going to have to move in that world."

Anne was right. She was no longer owed a place in retirement as her grandmother and mother had been. The retirement allowances hadn't been overgenerous in previous generations, but at least you had a place to stay. In the current reign, the accountants had taken over The Queen's finances. There was more supervision from the Government, and the older arrangements had been cancelled. She would have a somewhat larger pension than her mother and grandmother when they retired, but she would have no place to stay. She could participate in a lottery to stay in one of the cottages at Balmoral for several weeks in the off-season, when The Queen wasn't there, but she still had to pay for it. This rankled. But there was little she could do. None of the Household ever walked out on strike or set up pickets in front of the palace railing.

"Well, I expect it's fine for the daughter of a lord. Your nephew must have half a dozen houses to give you."

"Pardon me, but if you don't think my nephew runs the estate on exactly the same lines as the Privy Purse you're quite mistaken. I have my London flat and a tiny widow's pension from my husband. It's a place to hang my hat, but I can't afford to pay a cleaner anymore. Why do you think I still do these waitings? For two weeks at a time I save on the food bills. There's a clothing allowance. And there's some travel money, which I'm going to use to pay for this taxi, thank you very much. It's not what I imagined for myself at age seventy. You might be able to retire soon, but I can't. As for my nephew, I'm only invited at Christmas, and that's all. He gave us our aeroplane tickets because he's on the board and he gets a certain number of free flights during the year."

Shirley was used to overhearing rich people complaining about being poor, but there was something about Anne's quiet urgency that made her sense that what she'd just been told was the truth. Her instinct was to change the subject. In the old-fashioned system to which they both still belonged, raw displays of resentment were not allowed.

"Oh, well, as long as you've got that flat, you could do a bit of bed-and-breakfast, couldn't you?"

Both women burst out laughing. The sodium glow of the lights over the motorway cast their unnatural light on the taxi's passengers, who began to feel that the prospects for their journey were not as dismal as they'd once imagined.

Having finished the washing up, The Queen saw no point in hanging about. She was used to doing one thing and then going on to another in rapid succession. She knew she was off her schedule, but not out of her mind. Visiting *Britannia* had certainly reminded her of happier days, but it had also convinced her there was no point in going back.

Returning to London was another question altogether. As it was now late, she doubted there were any more buses. There was nothing for it but to hitch a lift. She knew people had done this all the time in the last war and never got into trouble. She'd also seen people with signs saying where they were going standing by the side of the motorway when she was on her way to engagements. They seemed, generally speaking, cheerful. She thought this was the only way back to Waverley station.

She came down the gangplank, waved at the young man in the security kiosk when he waved at her—it was instinct, really—and then wandered out to the main road where the bus had dropped her off. Not much traffic this time of night. Several cars passed by her at great speed. They didn't seem to pay the least attention, or even to have seen her by the side of the road. She didn't know if they didn't wave back when she waved at them because they hated the monarchy, or because they couldn't see her. At this she reached into her handbag and squeezed the rabbit's foot. "Now hang on, Little Bit. It's nothing to do with the Crown. It's dark and they can't see you, darling." She felt better when she called herself "darling." It meant she was on better terms with her conscience. Eventually she took off the scarf she had on over her head under the hoodie and began waving it at the next motor that came along the road.

Success. It was a young woman who pulled to the side. She opened the passenger side door, and in the flurry of getting in, The Queen dropped her scarf. Its luxurious silk folds carried it off in a cold gust of wind along the gutter. The Queen didn't notice. She was happy to have a ride. The driver immediately began taxing her, though in affectionate tones, for being out so late. "Have you any idea what time it is? Not a time to be wandering the streets, my dear."

The Queen felt safe to be with a young woman who called her "my dear." She cleared her throat. "I expect you're right."

"No buses at this hour, my love."

"Yes, I thought that might be so." The Queen felt the ghost of a maternal pang herself. "And you, young lady . . . aren't you out rather late yourself?"

"Right you are," said the young woman, laughing. "Got me there. Well, I'll tell you my story if you tell me yours."

"All right," said The Queen.

"And where are you headed, then? Home and a warm bed, I expect."

"Well, ultimately, yes. But first Waverley railway station."

"I'm sure the last trains have gone as well."

"Oh, I expect there will be a milk train, or something like that, quite early."

"Milk train? I don't think they have those anymore."

"Well, you mustn't worry on my behalf. You're very generous to have stopped for me in the first place. If you can take me to Waverley, I'm quite sure all will be well."

The young woman driving the car was a social worker who dealt with all kinds of people on behalf of the Edinburgh town council: victims of crime, people leaving prison and attempting to rejoin the community, the homeless, old people abandoned by their children. She knew better than to argue with one of her clients and she immediately regarded the old woman whom she'd just picked up as someone who was in line to become one of her clients. Instead, she said smoothly, "Ah, I see. You live outside of Edinburgh, then?"

"As it happens, I do have a place I can stay here. But I seldom spend the night there."

"Oh, why not?"

"Well, it would be locked now, and when they're not expecting me, well, it would upset them if I were to turn up." The Queen saw that clearly now, more clearly than when her unhappiness had temporarily confused her, impelled her out of Buckingham Palace and into Green Park. Holyrood would be locked and the staff would need to be telephoned in advance if she meant to spend the night there.

"I see," said the young woman. Inwardly she imagined this nice woman's ungrateful children in a council flat, locking her out, and refusing her a bed, even on the sofa, if she hadn't warned them in advance she were coming. She had seen too many similar cases. "Well, I know a nice shelter near here. Why don't I take you there? You could go on from Waverley in the morning."

What The Queen heard was something like a proposal from her private secretary to extend a provincial visit. "If you wouldn't mind, Ma'am, we could add just one more stop at some sheltered housing for the elderly. They'd be so grateful if you'd come and see what they're doing. Acknowledge their hard work. Then we could have you back on the royal train for a cup of tea in no time." She was used to smooth young men from the private office keeping her on her feet for thirty more minutes, adding a dozen more hands for her to shake, and—no fear—there'd be another plaque for her to unveil as well. She was willing to do what she was asked to do on most occasions, but like an old dog scenting a bitter pill in the midst of a proffered biteful of cream cheese, she sometimes set her jaw and refused to accept it. "No, thank you," said The Queen to the young woman driving the car.

The young woman was used to cold negatives from homeless people to whom she offered a lift to the shelter. Some of them liked it on the street, preferred it, in fact, to the loneliness of a single room. Their inner voices were quieter on the street and there was more company. "Very well," she replied. "Waverley, then. And, you know, you're in luck. Because the station is open twenty-four hours, so you'll be out of the weather, won't you? And I believe a church van comes by with cups of tea and sandwiches for whoever's about at this hour. I mean whoever, like you, doesn't really fancy the shelter."

"That will be lovely, thank you." She smoothed down her feathers from having been unexpectedly ruffled. "And you, now? Why driving by Leith at this hour?"

"Oh, well, I work for the council. Care for all sorts. People having a hard time. Need some help to get by from day to day. Need some encouragement if they're not going back to prison. The kind who are usually not free from ten in the morning to six at night, if you know what I mean. Sometimes all they need is a friendly ear, someone to tell their problems to. And there's something about the night that makes them open up. Sometimes all you need to do is listen, and to look interested."

"Yes, I do know," said The Queen. That was mainly her job too. Listen and look interested. She carried on in a more reflective tone, speaking half to herself, "But do they appreciate what you do? Sometimes I wonder if they wouldn't rather just be left alone. Is listening and looking interested enough?"

"Well, I think so. Wouldn't keep doing it if I didn't. People like being looked after. Everybody had a mum once. That feeling of being protected, of being allowed to test your legs and be independent, but to be looked in on every once in a while by your mum. Even your most downcast outcast wants that," she said, laughing. "That's human instinct. It's like those little geese having whoever they see after they break out of the egg imprinted on them. If they see the farmer's wife, they'll follow her around just as if she were mama goose."

Mother Goose, thought The Queen, that's what I am. She descended once again into some self-doubting thoughts about whether or not she'd actually helped anyone in her life of ritual and routine.

The young woman driving the car could sense that her companion was leaving her, drifting away on a wave of unpleasant reflection, so she took a chance. She reached over and with her left hand, which wasn't on the steering wheel, briefly covered The Queen's two bare hands, which were folded together in her lap. "Come now, we're nearly there. The church van will have a cup of tea for you. You might see some of your mates, mightn't you?"

The young woman's hand, touching her skin, sent something like an electric shock through The Queen. People didn't usually reach out to touch her at unchoreographed moments. She knew how to keep her distance when they looked like they might want to grab her hand. This woman had touched her unexpectedly and the human contact suddenly revived her. She remembered how people sometimes glowed when she reached out to shake their hands, usually with gloves on, but sometimes not. They all seemed to adore it. It was a power she had, touching people, the royal touch, a power she'd at that moment just recalled. From the Middle Ages up until Queen Anne's time, people had believed in the royal touch as a cure for illness. The woman had given her a jolt, but not an unpleasant one.

As they pulled into the railway station, The Queen could see a van from the side of which someone was pouring tea into Styrofoam cups. There was a rough group of people of uncertain ages, and in all their bundled clothes it was also unclear whether they were men or women. They were waiting for their white cups. "Here we are," said the young woman. "Now come along, out you go. They'll have a cup for you. And here's my card. You call me if you change your mind about the shelter. I'll come back and get you."

The Queen could feel the young woman's kindness, her willingness to take trouble over strangers. "Thank you, my dear. It's been a pleasure." The Queen reached out with her hand this time, briefly taking the young woman's left hand into both of hers. She looked at her from inside the warmth of her hoodie, caught the glance of her brown eyes, and gave her a military nod, an abbreviated version of what she gave at the Cenotaph on Remembrance Day. Then she gave her hand a farewell squeeze, and swung around to pull herself laboriously out of the car.

The young woman watched the older woman walk deliberately over to the group of homeless. For the first time she noticed the skull and crossbones on the back of her hoodie, the well-cut skirt, and the muddy pumps. "What a voice," the young woman said to herself. And putting the car into gear as she prepared to drive away, she took her left hand and put it up to her nose. Homeless elderly women often smelled as if they hadn't washed as much as they should, but this was entirely different. It was the old woman's perfume, the scent of orange blossom.

The taxi driver drew up next to the *Britannia* at Leith, wondering what two old women could want with a tourist attraction at this time of night. "It's shut," he couldn't help saying when he stopped at the security kiosk, even though Anne's earlier commands had intimidated him.

"Of course it's shut, young man," said Anne impatiently. "It's on the way to midnight. Who do you think we are?"

He didn't like her bullying tone of voice and began to answer her.

"She doesn't mean for you to answer," said Shirley, seeing the idea for a rejoinder cross his brow. "Will you wait for us, please?"

Both women got out of the taxi and walked to where they could see a security guard sitting inside at a desk.

"It's shut," began the guard, as if he'd prearranged his answer with the taxi driver.

"We can see that," said Anne with annoyance in her voice. "We're looking for someone."

"No one here but me."

"Nothing out of the ordinary tonight, then?"

"And why would I tell you if there had been?" In his experience, old women sometimes rose to a bit of impertinence.

She knew they were out of place next to a darkened ship in the middle of the night on an Edinburgh quay, but it still surprised Shirley that a young man could address two women who were both old enough to be his grandmother in this familiar way. She threw him an angry glance in order to give him a visual rap over his knuckles. "Not the way you speak to a lady, young fellow."

"A lady, now. Is that what she is? Is that what you are? I thought you were all just women these days."

Anne interrupted. "This is your demesne. We can see that. But we need your help and we would like to know if you've seen anyone odd here tonight."

Demesne was an unusual word. He wasn't quite sure what it meant. It was the first time he thought these might actually be ladies in front of him. "Odd, like you, you mean?"

Anne had to admit he had a point. "Yes," she conceded reluctantly, "odd, like us."

"No, no one like you. No one at all. Quiet as quiet can be."

"No one's been here the whole evening, then?"

"No one, I've told you that."

Anne sighed. They'd come a very long way to be met with this blunt negative from a night watchman. She had no idea where they'd go next. And she was aware they might have made fools of themselves to have come as far as they had on the basis of one slim recollection of Shirley's.

"Hang on a minute," said Shirley abruptly. She'd been prowling around the guard's room while Anne questioned him, and on a shelf behind his desk she found a scarf. Holding it up bunched in one hand, the heavy silk poured into her other hand as if it were water out of a jug. "What's this, then?"

"It's the cleaner's scarf," said the young man casually. "She dropped it on her way out. I only found it after she left. I'll give it her tomorrow when she comes back on her shift."

"You said no one had been here," said Anne indignantly.

"What would you lot be wanting with the cleaner?"

Shirley held up the scarf with both hands now. It had reins

and horses wearing medieval armor on a red background. It was almost a square yard in size. "Does the cleaner always wear Hermès to work, then?"

"Don't know anything about our May's. Don't know if May's even her name. The cleaners come and go. I'll give it back to her tomorrow night."

"Thank you, young man," said Anne. "We'll give it back to her." Shirley had handed the scarf to her and she examined it, recognizing instantly that it was the same scarf The Queen had sent her back to the Castle for the afternoon she met Luke.

"What if I see her first?" said the guard, feeling as if he had been caught out in a lie, when all he had done was to collect a scarf from the pavement when he was having a smoke, which he honestly intended to return to its owner on the following evening.

The two women looked at one another. What if he did see her first? What if The Queen returned here before they could catch up with her? Anne wrote down her mobile telephone number on a scrap of paper sitting on the young man's desk. "Call me if she turns up again, please."

"Who is she, then? If it's not May, the cleaner, what's her name, then?"

Anne did not mean to answer this and was hustling Shirley out the door when he threatened to report them to his superiors. This,

Shirley realized, might give up the game before they'd found The Queen, and she wanted to make sure he did no such thing. With Anne outside, striding toward the waiting taxi, Shirley stopped back in and said to the young man a little more kindly than either of them had spoken to him before, "Look, it belongs to Mrs Le Roy, a woman we both work for, um, a woman who works with us. We need to find her before she gets into any trouble. Okay? So do please call us if she turns up again." She took a mini whiskey bottle the stewardess had given her and placed it on his desk while looking at him gravely. Then she was out the door.

The Queen got out of the social worker's car. The station was darker than she'd expected. The social worker was right. She went up to check the departures board and found that the first train to London King's Cross was not until after five in the morning. She sighed. A long wait. "Well, no more royal train. That's how it will have to be, Little Bit. Find something to do. Don't just stand there," her internal nanny said to her. She wandered away from the departures board and toward the van the social worker said would have a cup of tea. She was surprised that they were doing such a brisk business in the middle of the night. There was a crowd of perhaps twenty or thirty, both men and women, all ages, dressed in many different layers, some talking to themselves, some talking to each other. Many had weather-roughened voices. Some had more animation than was necessary. Others looked stonily vague. These were the dossers down, the homeless. She knew that. She hadn't had much to do with them. The Prince of Wales, she seemed to recall, had spent several nights with them under Waterloo Bridge. She believed Diana too had been interested and hoped to help. They had never been one of The Queen's specialties, but she looked at them now carefully. Was she so different from them? She had no particular place to go, at least not for a little while. She liked the idea of a cup of tea. So she stood in the queue, waiting for the woman at the fold-down counter to pour her a cup of tea out of an industrial-sized kettle. The Queen was the last to be served. She rather liked that, waiting her turn, going last. It was a new experience. She supposed it was a little like Marie Antoinette pretending she was a shepherd, but she didn't care. It took her out of herself, and that relieved the pain.

"Our last customer!" said the lady at the counter cheerfully when The Queen reached the front. "What'll it be, my love?" She pretended as if she had a large selection of drinks and snacks.

"Well, I'd love a cup of tea, if you can manage," said The Queen.

"You're in luck, my darling. It's all we have left." The tea lady poured out dark tea. "And what about a bacon sarnie?"

"Well," said The Queen doubtfully, "I dined quite well on the train earlier. I don't think so. Thank you."

The tea lady regarded this as an invention. Few of the homeless, in her experience, had actually arrived on trains, and none of them had eaten on board. She wrapped up a sandwich in a serviette and pushed it forward with The Queen's tea. "You just put this in your pocket for later. You might be peckish in a few hours."

The Queen put the sandwich into the pocket of Rebecca's hoodie as she'd been instructed. She then took the cup of tea into both hands and held it, finding it warmed her chilly fingers nicely. "Have you done this long?" asked The Queen. Her instinct began to mingle with a genuine revival of curiosity.

The woman put down the kettle, and, as there was no one else to serve, folded her arms and leaned on the counter. "About fifteen years, I reckon."

"Quite a long time to be staying up so late in the night. In a railway station too. In the cold. And damp."

"Well, it's not me. It's the church, isn't it? I'm retired now. Used to work in an office. And I get more thanks pouring out tea at midnight than I ever did turning up for the old nine-to-five, if you get my meaning."

"Yes. I'm sure that's so," said The Queen. "And what hours do you do?"

"Well, we go to the church hall around nine of an evening to make the sandwiches and put tea things together for the van. Distribute some tea and sandwiches there first. Then come here. Afterwards we go to a few railway underpasses where they're expecting us. Back to the church around two in the morning."

"Quite a long night for you, then."

"Well, it doesn't feel long, because you're helping out, you know? People are happy to see you. Grateful for a kind word along with the cuppa."

The Queen felt it was time for her to be moving on. There must be someone else for her to acknowledge, if not in the van, then roundabout somewhere. So she put her tea down carefully on the counter and said to the woman, "May I just say 'Thank you,' on behalf of all of us, for what you're doing?" She then reached up with her bare hand and took the surprised hand of the tea lady.

The woman was often thanked for the cups of tea she poured out, but seldom in such a formal way, and with such a distinctive, acknowledging handshake. "You're very welcome, I'm sure," she said, laughing. Something about the touch of the old woman's wrinkled hand felt magical. She couldn't say exactly why, but all of a sudden she felt quite giddy and as if she were glowing.

"No, I mean it," said The Queen, who wasn't used to laughter when she thanked someone. "I think you deserve an order." The Queen noted the woman's reaction to the touch of her hand and thought to herself, "The touch. May still be working after all." She then added, because she was honest and needed to point out the difficulties, "Well, you need to be nominated first. It does take a while. I shall mention it in the right quarter."

The tea lady was used to homeless people pretending that they had special access to the Prime Minister. "You do that, my love." She meant to say it skeptically, but she couldn't help smiling beatifically. The older woman nodded to her in a gesture that was in the middle distance between a farewell and a benediction.

Shirley and Anne, having failed to find The Queen at Leith, climbed back in their taxi. At least they knew by her headscarf that she had been there. But where to next? Then Shirley remembered mentioning Waverley railway station in the same conversation in which they'd discussed *Britannia*. They decided to ask the driver to go there. On arrival in the station, they got out of the taxi, wondering what to do, when they heard what sounded like a barroom laugh coming from a group of people gathered around a van. The Queen was on the edge of the group, unrecognizable except for her shoes, and the lined hem of her Hardy Amies skirt. Shirley remembered laying it out for her that morning. Unable to speak, as she felt a kind of wordless horror, Shirley grabbed Anne's bony elbow and pointed.

Anne looked, and she saw the same vision. The two women advanced on tiptoe across the station concourse and stopped short of where The Queen was standing. When The Queen turned away from the van, Shirley and Anne both hurried up to her.

"Ma'am, where on earth did you find that terrible jacket?" said Shirley in a voice that was frightened and angry and relieved all at once.

"But Shirley, what are you doing in Edinburgh in the middle of the night?" said The Queen, with some confusion in the pale pockets around her eyes. She looked at Anne. "And Lady Anne too? Not good for your rheumatism, surely?"

Anne saw The Queen's confusion and said, "We've found a bed for you, Ma'am," as if she'd been a part of The Queen's Scottish planning all along. Shirley immediately understood Anne's plan of not requiring any explanations of The Queen right away. So she went to The Queen's elbow and began making small encouraging noises in her ear. "Now, Ma'am, we're just taking you to a warm bed. Won't that be nice? A soft pillow. What a long day you've had. Where on earth did this awful hood come from?" It was the first time Shirley showed real irritation, as she saw the skull and crossbones on the back of The Queen's hoodie. She felt a proprietary air about The Queen's clothing and was shocked to find her mistress clad in something so unsuitable.

"Rebecca from the Mews lent it me. It's all right, Shirley," said The Queen gently. She didn't like to see Shirley upset.

"Now what, you oaf?" said Rebecca miserably, having surveyed Waverley station and found no one remotely resembling The Queen or her former companions.

"I was an ogre earlier. You seem to specialize in these medieval insults," said Rajiv.

"Look, there's no time for fooling around. We *have* to find her."

"Well, I don't think there's much point in racing off somewhere unless we know where she went. Doesn't she have a palace here, then? Or maybe she's up there," he said, nodding toward Edinburgh Castle, which was above them, alit in the night, outside the station entrance.

"She has a place to stay in London. I don't think she would have come all the way up here just to spend the night at Holyrood. Edinburgh Castle's not hers."

"Well, if you want to go into it, Holyrood isn't hers either. Belongs to us. The people."

"When this is over I'm going to make sure she steers well clear of you. The republicans do well enough on their own. She doesn't have to buy her cheese off one."

"Hang on! I'm pro-Queen, but this is constitutional, not absolute, monarchy. She takes her orders from us."

"Yes, and you're William Shakespeare."

This cut him to the quick. She didn't know how much that hurt. His silence would have given her a small indication if she had been paying attention. What's more, he was afraid she was right. He'd begun calling himself "a poet" too soon, before he was actually sure he could do it. Maybe he was just good at appreciating poetry, rather than writing it.

Rajiv began more formally, addressing her from an injured distance, which he hoped she noticed, "Well, perhaps you'd better telephone *Equus* and tell him where we are. Where we last saw her."

She took out her phone and stepped away from him into a corner of the station's entrance so he couldn't hear her conversation. She telephoned Major Thomason. No answer. She left a message to say that she was at Edinburgh Waverley, that The Queen had arrived on the same train, but disappeared. She didn't know where. She thought it best to say she would stay in the station until she had some further contact or instructions from him. She then turned and went back to rejoin Rajiv.

"Well?" said Rajiv.

"We stay here."

"Is that what he wants us to do?"

"You can do whatever you like. I must stay here until I hear from him again."

It was a rather cold way for a railway journey to end, especially one that had begun with such unexpected promise.

They both slid down onto some plastic seats in the waiting area. Two unhappy young people. Feeling tired, not a little disillusioned, and hopeless. Soon, in spite of their mutual determination to stay alert, they were both asleep.

Rajiv awoke with a start more than an hour later. On the other side of the station, on the edge of a group with white cups, was a small figure with silvery hair under her blue hood. She'd evidently lost her headscarf.

"Wake up. She's back. Wake *up*."

"Leave me alone."

"No, darling, not about you, not this time. The Queen. She's here."

"Where?" said Rebecca, straightening up right away.

"*Là-bas. Avec les homeless.*"

"God!"

"She's all right. No one's bothering her. Must be some charity. Wonder what they'd think if they knew they'd just poured out tea for Mrs Sheba?"

Rebecca took out her telephone. Still no calls from the equerry. Very odd. She tried his number. No answer. Just the voice mail. She rang off without leaving a message. "Damn it."

"Not there? What's the palace good for? They're not even taking your calls, are they, sweetheart?"

"Quit. Fooling. Around. We can't lose her this time. We've got to go after her."

"You said we couldn't go up to her unless we'd been invited."

"Well, it's different if she's surrounded by thugs and bums."

"They're just on the street. They're not thugs or bums. They choose to be that way, most of them. Nothing to fear from them. It doesn't look like she's in trouble."

Rebecca didn't have a better idea. So she sat where she was on the edge of her plastic seat, next to Rajiv, and watched until two strange women approached The Queen directly. One was shorter and a little frail, the other was taller and sturdier. They appeared to have recognized her.

This was enough for Rebecca. She said fiercely to Rajiv, who was also watching the two women, "Okay. Now we move."

"Hang on a sec. Look, they seem to know her."

The Queen talked with them briefly and then the three started off, arm in arm, toward a waiting taxi.

"No, now we go. We can't lose her again. We've got to go after her," said Rebecca.

Rajiv followed behind as Rebecca loped in her riding boots across the station to the three women who were on the verge of climbing into the taxi.

"Um, I'm sorry," said Rebecca as she reached the three women.

"Ah, here you are again," said The Queen, recognizing Rebecca. "And you," she said, nodding at Rajiv. "Glad to see that you're," she said, pausing, and then happening upon a friendly tease, "sticking together."

"And who are *they*, Ma'am?" said Shirley thoroughly annoyed. Having just rescued The Queen from a group of the homeless, she was hardly going to give her up to more strangers.

"Oh, why it's Rebecca from the Mews. And this young man works at Paxton & Whitfield. Or did. He'll probably be given the sack for leaving his post and following his friend to Scotland. Can't remember your name, Cheddar."

Rajiv beamed. The Queen had just given him a nickname.

Rebecca was less pleased and unsure about what to do. It was clear by her "Ma'am" that Shirley knew The Queen, and the frail one seemed to be on equally familiar-formal terms with her. What was her responsibility if The Queen had been recognized and collected by senior members of the Household? Perhaps she was no longer wanted? But she hated to withdraw without first establishing that The Queen no longer needed any protection.

Rajiv saw Rebecca's wordless confusion. So he put in, "Well, Your Majesty, I certainly did follow her to Scotland. You're quite right about that. But, she just wanted to look after you. And to be utterly honest with you, I was also following you. Just wanted to make sure you were okay. That sort of thing."

"Oh dear," said The Queen, returning to a semblance of her former self. She felt a sudden revival of clarity about who she was and what she was doing. What she had done. "You were all looking for me, weren't you? You, Shirley, and you, Anne? And now Rebecca and Cheddar too? What a nuisance."

At the same time Rajiv said, "Not at all," Anne said, "Well," and Shirley said, "That you have been." Rebecca said nothing.

Anne continued, "Perhaps we'd better all have a little sleep.

My nephew has a flat near here. Several bedrooms. Enough for all of us. Why don't we all go there and see if we can't have a few hours' horizontal."

There was enough room for all five of them in the taxi if four squeezed in the back and Rajiv sat up in front with the driver. All four women crowded together and began apologizing for the tight fit. "Nonsense," said The Queen, beginning to enjoy herself. "Isn't this cozy? More adventure," she said, separating the syllables with enthusiasm. The taxi's taillights disappeared in the direction of Charlotte Square as it sped through Edinburgh's empty streets.

Once they'd arrived, William and Luke couldn't find a taxi outside the coach station. They consulted a map they found mounted on the wall inside the station and decided to walk to Charlotte Square. There was no other choice. Walking through the dark streets together, with a destination in mind, they were on somewhat better terms with one another, but they both felt a little disconsolate as well. They had no idea how they'd find Anne's nephew's flat once they got to the square, or if The Queen would be there if they did. While Luke was looking in his pocket for a scrap of paper, to see whether Anne had given him the precise address, and whether he'd written it down, an envelope, with an American stamp, addressed in a woman's sloping script, fell on the pavement.

William looked briefly at it as he picked it up and handed it silently back to Luke. As they'd got on to dangerously intimate territory earlier in the evening, William was determined not to ask about it.

Luke saw and appreciated William's restraint, so explained, "From the mother of a friend of mine, actually. Andrew. Andy." He paused a moment, and then, in a voice drained of emotion, added, "Died in Iraq."

William was afraid of asking and curious at the same time. He forced himself to say, "Go on."

"It arrived earlier today. Funnily enough, I was just going to ask The Queen if I might leave early, go back to my flat, sit down, and reply properly. That's when I found she was missing."

"And Andrew? Who was he?"

"Well, he was from one of the American units near us. Young captain. Sent over to coordinate some maneuvers the Yanks had been ordered to do with us. We had to work together. Became friends."

William sensed some of the large history that must underlay those few words.

"One day he went out without me. Roadside device went off. Killed instantly. Went home in a bag."

They walked some distance in silence.

"And the letter? What did his mother say?" asked William, knowing well that the story wasn't over.

Luke was silent. He walked on without replying, as if he hadn't heard William's questions. William thought it was the wrong time to force the issue, so they continued without talking, coming after a few blocks to Charlotte Square. There was a hotel, and several eighteenth-century townhouses that were now clearly banks or businesses or firms of solicitors. Only one of these houses had lights on in the second-floor windows at this early hour of the morning and they made directly for it. As they'd hoped, they found that one of the buzzers was marked "Thyonville Estate." William was about to reach up and press the buzzer when Luke told him, "Hang on a minute. I'll tell you."

"Tell me now? Shouldn't we see if . . ." William began, nodding with his head to the doorway.

"You want to know, don't you?"

William paused. Luke glared at him. Then Luke sat down on the stone steps that led down to the pavement and began swatting the letter he held in one hand against his other hand.

William said nothing. He had no choice but to follow Luke's lead. He sat down by Luke's side.

"She's written to congratulate me, actually. Someone told her about my being promoted and going to work in the Household. About the decoration." He stopped and stewed in his bitterness a moment. "What good is that when her son is dead?" He turned and looked at William, as if he might have an answer to that, as if the whole awful mess was his fault.

"That bloody medal," continued Luke. "When he died, I couldn't see straight. Couldn't think straight. Just wanted to die too. I got myself put on to several missions. Pretty suicidal, really. We raided a number of positions held by the insurgency. Barking. Mad as hell. Secured them for our side. That's how I got the gong 'for bravery,' but they should have called it 'for revenge.'"

William didn't touch other men easily or naturally or without fear, but now he reached up tentatively and rested his hand between Luke's shoulder blades.

Just then, Anne who was about to pull the curtains across the sitting-room window of the flat before she lay down for a few hours, not of sleep, she wouldn't be able to sleep, but of collecting her thoughts, looked down, and saw the two men sitting on the steps. She went downstairs and opened the door. William and Luke turned around at the noise of the door opening.

"Is she . . . ?" began William.

"She is," said Anne. "Quiet, though. She's asleep now. Come upstairs."

It was a few hours later, still early morning and not yet light out. In that northern latitude in the beginning of winter it wouldn't be fully light until nine in the morning, and it would start to darken again at three in the afternoon. There was a small shaded lamp on the kitchen table in Charlotte Square. Anne intended to switch it on when she came in, wearing a flannel robe she'd found in the loo. She discovered Shirley sitting under the harsher glare of the overhead light. "Could we have this smaller light on instead, Shirley? So unflattering that overhead light."

"I'm no beauty. A change in the light won't help," said Shirley stoutly. She was already fully dressed.

"Yes, I know, darling, but I'm a bit older than you and my wrinkles need to be very carefully lit if I'm not to frighten everyone off."

"Don't exaggerate, Anne. You look fine. Tea?" Shirley gestured to a brown teapot she had on the table.

"Oh, yes, please."

Shirley found a second mug in the cupboard and poured out the tea. Gesturing to the marble countertops and cherry cabinetry, she said, "Your nephew must have spent quite a bit doing this place up."

"He spares no expense on things to do with keeping up property, you're quite right. But he doesn't give me anything from the estate. He knows my husband lost the dowry, but he hasn't advanced me a penny."

"The aristocracy have always had peculiar ways of looking out for family, haven't they?"

"Well," said Anne, raising her chin, "one aims to minimize charges on the estate for daughters and younger sons so that the whole thing is preserved as a going concern to pass on to the next generation." She cleared her throat. "But when the heir so clearly has cash to spare, it does seem he might have a care for the old woman who sometimes changed his nappy when he was a baby."

"You mean his nanny? I can't imagine *you* changing nappies, Anne," Shirley said, laughing.

"But I did, you see. I'm not quite so helpless as I seem." She paused to sip her tea. The two women were now becoming comfortable enough with one another, especially since the undertakings of the previous evening, that they could allow a silence to fall between them without its feeling awkward. "I am getting older, though, and may be more helpless shortly."

"Looking for a nurse, are you? Don't look at me."

Anne was thrown off balance by this. It was harsher than she'd expected. The idea had occurred to her. She had been intending to raise it by degrees with Shirley. This abrupt rejection of her plan left her speechless.

Shirley was aware that Anne was disappointed by what she'd just said. By way of explanation, she began, "I reach retiring age next year. I thought of buying a place in Windsor. Or maybe Scotland. My grandmother retired up here. So did my mother. I won't have an automatic right to a place, but round about Ballater is less expensive than Berkshire. I might be able to find a little place. Fix it up. Balmoral might give me a bit of help."

"Oh, well, that's not bad. A permanent place mightn't be a bad thing. But, frankly, I can't imagine you retiring to the Highlands, Shirley. Your work has always been in London, or traveling with The Queen to all parts of the world. You think it will be enough for you to go have a half pint in Ballater of an evening? Drive an hour into grey Aberdeen for the shopping? Meet the rest of the Household pensioners once a year for some knees-up at the Castle? You think that will be enough for a happy old age?"

Anne had unerringly put her finger on three of the things it had occurred to her might occupy her time after she retired, and the prospect was not appealing. "I'll be fine," said Shirley briefly. "It was good enough for my granny and good enough for my mum. It'll be good enough for me."

"Of course it will. And you won't miss London, will you?"

"I loathe London. It turns a fresh white blouse grubby in

a day. And if you leave the window open on a July afternoon, there's a quarter inch of filth on every window ledge."

"Yes, filthy London. And the theatre in the West End, filthy. The restaurants of all description, filthy. The Proms, the cinema, and Covent Garden, filthy. The cathedral choirs, filthy. The shops, filthy. The parties, filthy. And all the curious people on the Tube and on the bus, well, they're filthy too, aren't they?"

Shirley knew when she was being made fun of and chose not to rise to these sharp-tongued remarks. She decided to go on the offense to protect herself. "Well, Anne, I imagine you'll be all right, won't you? The Queen has allowed you to keep working for her into your seventies. There'll be a pension from the Household when you decide to go. That will buy you a nice carer to look in on you if you need anything."

"There will be a small pension, yes, but it won't pay for a carer. I do have some odds and ends of money from my late husband, but I'll have to sell the flat when I stop doing waitings if I want to survive. Rather sad, as it's in a good location. Sargent, Whistler, and Wilde once lived in Tite Street, did you know? And I've been in it such a long time, well, it will be hard to go. But go I must," she said, pressing her thin lips together.

They both looked out the darkened window and contemplated their futures. They both felt that they deserved better after lives of work and worry.

"Ow," said Anne shortly.

"What's the matter with you, then?"

"Oh, a little bursitis in the shoulder. Acts up when it's damp out. Bit of a headache too."

"Nothing a little neck-and-shoulder rub won't cure, is it?" said Shirley, warming her hands on the teapot. Then she stood up and walked around behind Anne's chair at the kitchen table.

She put her hands gently on Anne's shoulders and began some circular pressing motions on the muscles underneath her bathrobe. Anne was a little surprised. She liked Shirley, but she hadn't been prepared for this kind of physical contact.

It did feel good, though. "Mmmm, thank you," she said lightly, trying to keep the surprise out of her voice. Soon Shirley slipped her hands onto the strained tendons and flesh of Anne's neck. It felt so warm and comforting that Anne quite forgot that she was being touched by a relative stranger. "For God's sake, you're good. How have you kept this talent a secret for so long?"

"I don't do it for many," said Shirley practically, keeping her attention on her hands and Anne's sinewy stiffness. "I was thinking . . ."

"Mmm?"

"Perhaps you could have a lodger in that flat of yours?"

"Well. Perhaps. Only it would have to be a lodger with some talents, now."

"Like a firm pair of hands?"

"Yes, and maybe someone with a little holiday place for going to in Scotland together when one wanted a change from London."

"But who won't wash your grubby shirts, now, she won't, the lodger won't, I mean."

"Of course not. I wouldn't expect that."

"And this lodger would like to come and go as she pleases.

Have the occasional friend in for tea. Or to watch a film." Shirley was thinking of William. "Have her own key, and not be interfered with."

"No. She may, the lodger may do whatever she likes, but . . ."

"But? There's frequently a 'but' to this kind of accommodation."

"But if the landlady breaks down, or falls down, or catches the flu? If she has a stroke or becomes a cripple, what then?"

"Well, the lodger might call the social services then."

"The social services. I see," said Anne. Discouraged.

Shirley continued to massage the neck just below Anne's hairline. "But the lodger might make the landlady a cup of soup every now and again."

Just then The Queen came softly into the room, still wearing her Hardy Amies skirt of the day before, but less Rebecca's hoodie.

Shirley raised her hands off Anne's bent neck with a start.

"As you were, Mrs MacDonald. Carry on," said The Queen, nodding at Anne's neck. Anne turned her face to one side and noticed The Queen had come into the kitchen, but she was too wrapped up in the sensation of Shirley's massage, and the negotiations the two women had begun, to react. The Queen saw this and said, with an ironic inflection, "Don't get up, Lady Anne."

Under normal conditions Lady Anne certainly would have stood up when The Queen entered the room. She was literally doubled over with the combined pain from her shoulder and headache, however, and found it impossible to move.

"Forgive me, Your Majesty. Feeling a little under the weather at the moment. A kind of *migraine*, I fear." She pronounced "migraine" as if it were a French word.

"I expect it's the stress," said The Queen kindly. "Happy Baby would help with that."

"Happy Baby, Ma'am? The stress?" Anne was beginning to fear that The Queen had given in to old ladies' confusion again.

"Happy Baby. Yes. Yoga pose. You roll on the floor, while holding your legs in the air and massage your back. Relaxes you no end. I could show you here, but we'd need some yoga mats. The stress of looking for me, I meant."

Anne shot a cautious glance in Shirley's direction. When they'd discovered The Queen on Waverley station the previous evening, they'd been so relieved to have found her that they hadn't required any explanations of her. They had wondered whether she hadn't had a small stroke, or was showing the first sign of dementia, not uncommon for someone of her age. Now that The Queen had raised the issue herself, Anne thought she might cautiously explore it.

"Well, we were worried."

"Terrified, Ma'am, is more like it," put in Shirley with emphasis.

"I *am* sorry," replied The Queen.

"We were wondering . . ." began Anne, still bent over.

"What in the world you thought you were doing?" Shirley completed Anne's sentence using the tone of an angry parent addressing a child who'd left home.

Not in the least angry at being spoken to in this tone of voice, The Queen began, "I don't think I was quite myself."

"I should say not." Shirley was still annoyed.

"I expect I've given you that headache, haven't I?" said The Queen to Lady Anne.

"Oh no, Ma'am, I'm just a sensitive flower."

"It was me. Don't try to deny it. I might have said where I was going."

"And where were you going, then?" put in Shirley, barely leaving a space for The Queen to explain. "Do you know what lunatics are out there? How much danger you were in? It made our blood run cold. And now Anne's having a breakdown. Doesn't surprise me in the least. Do you realize what might have happened to you? As it was, I'm sure you were bothered, weren't you? And no Household to attend you. They must have given you a dreadful time. We're amazed you're still in one piece. Did you have any supper, even? Did anyone hurt you? Did they *insult* you? Oh, Ma'am. We were so worried. What in the world did you think you were doing?" This was a cascade of language, with Shirley's Scottish accent, usually suppressed, becoming more pronounced as she went along. Starting out rather irritated with The Queen, but feeling in the end rather sorry for herself.

The Queen noted Shirley's use of Lady Anne's Christian

name without her title. As Shirley's distrust of the ladies-in-waiting was legendary, this softening to a first-name basis was remarkable. The Queen filed the fact away for future use.

"Well, as a matter of fact, I wasn't recognized. Rebecca lent me the most effective disguise. It had a cotton hood attached. Quite warm and . . ."

"We saw it, right enough," said Shirley.

"And there was money in the pocket. I used it to pay my fare on the bus last night. It will need to be repaid. Anne, when you're feeling better, if you could help me repay these kind people."

Anne still had her head cantilevered toward her lap. "Of course, Ma'am."

"Oh, and a nice man on the train bought me a drink."

"And who was he, Ma'am? He might have been Jack the Ripper for all we know."

"No, not Jack the Ripper at all. Liked history. And his wife. Interesting couple. If he were with us now he'd be telling us the odds that Jack the Ripper was actually Queen Victoria's grandson."

"That old canard," said Anne.

"Well, I suppose it *is* a legend."

"Just as we're going to have to tell the papers they're making up things again when they telephone to ask us, 'Is it true Her Majesty went to Scotland by herself on a public train from King's Cross last night? And landed in Edinburgh after causing no end of worry among the staff?'" Shirley was still in a bad temper.

"We must tell them the truth," said The Queen simply.

"The truth being . . . ?" asked Shirley, unable to keep the sarcasm out of her voice.

"Well, I expect I was feeling a bit low."

"'Queen on Prozac!' is what *The Sun* will say, Ma'am."

"Well, when we were all growing up depression wasn't much spoken of, was it? A dirty word, wasn't it? Surely if Diana taught us anything, it's that depression is real. We can't just go on thinking about it as we always have. Wrong to stigmatize people who have it."

"And that's what you think it was, or maybe still is, that you're dee-pressed," said Shirley incredulously, stretching out the word to emphasize her disbelief. "You've never been that way in the forty years I've been with you, you haven't."

"Well, perhaps it was Diana's dying, you know. Feeling as though one had worked at this, tried to do one's best for many years, and having people turn on one, all of a sudden. It brings one up short, doesn't it? I've always done as I was told. Done precisely what the Government advised. For all my life, really. Stood through all those investitures. Rode through the streets even when it gave me a headache. It does give me a headache, Anne, when people cheer at me, do you know? They mean well, but it hurts. I thought, 'This is my job, and I'm doing it the way it's always been done.' But suddenly, after Diana, that wasn't good enough. I was to blame for it all going wrong."

"Diana died quite a long time ago," observed Lady Anne into her lap. "What is it? Ten years now surely?"

"Well, yes, it was some time ago," agreed The Queen. "But I may have been having a delayed reaction. And then Mummy and my sister dying together in the same year. Barely a month apart. At first that was liberating in a way. One was old, the other unhappy. They were both ready to go. But recently it has seemed to hit me more forcibly. That sense of being alone. It'll be me next, of course."

"And the winter coming on now," said Anne bending sideways to look at The Queen. "The darkness doesn't help, does it?" she asked sympathetically.

"Oh, I don't know. That may be contributing. But it just struck me. And I was quite sad. I felt quite, well, desperate. And I thought to myself, 'When are the times I've been happy?' *Britannia* of course came to mind. I thought I might run up and have a look at her. I had a wander over to the Mews to look at the horses. Talked to Rebecca about the cheddar that Elizabeth likes. Some painters turned me out into the road. Didn't recognize me. I had on Rebecca's jacket, you see? And I thought, well, now I'm out, maybe I'll catch a train to Scotland. Did you know the Prime Minister told me they want to abolish the royal train? I'll have to learn to live without it. So I thought, 'I'll sample the public train, have a look at *Britannia*, and take a bite of that cheese from Paxton & Whitfield.' And, well," she put her hands on her hips and began chuckling, "I was away. I was *off*."

The "off" struck Anne as funny, despite the pain in her temples, and she smiled wryly.

Suddenly Luke appeared at the doorway to the kitchen barefoot, bare chested, and wearing rumpled boxer shorts. The three women looked up at him in surprise.

Shirley caught her breath and said, "Major Thomason!"

The three women looked at one another. Shirley began

smiling. Anne looked from the other two women to raise her eyebrows at Luke. The Queen kept a straight face.

Luke had been half asleep and unaware that he'd appeared in his shorts before The Queen until now. She could see Luke's reddening face and his increasing distress. She thought to help him by asking, "Major Thomason, you have a report?"

The conversation coming from the kitchen awoke William, who was still asleep in the sitting room. He was aware of its being colder than it was before and wondered why. He was by himself. His first memory was like that of a child who has curled up for an afternoon nap with a parent and is distressed to find that warm presence absent when he wakes up. The difference was, and now he could distinctly recall it, he'd gone to bed with a younger man and been cradled in the middle of the night by someone barely old enough to be his little brother. After Anne had let them in she'd told them The Queen was asleep in the double bedroom. Rebecca from the Mews and a friend of hers who'd been on the same train as The Queen were in one of the twins. Shirley was asleep in the remaining twin-bedded room. The only place for them was on the sofa bed. They were both too tired to protest when Anne told them they had to sleep together if they didn't want to sleep on the floor. They undressed after the light was out, looking away from one another in embarrassment. They got into the bed together. At first they had maintained a rigid distance between them, but it was a terrible mattress that sent them both rolling toward a trench in the center, and there was not enough room for two adult men anyway. So they allowed feet and legs to brush at first. Then, groggily realizing that some barrier was being breached, William awoke from a light doze to find Luke's arm around his middle. He didn't see the point of resisting any longer. He grabbed Luke's hand, pulled it up to his chest, and holding it in his own, fell away into a dark cavern.

Neither man was awake when Shirley and Anne tiptoed past them into the kitchen. Neither man was aware when the sovereign came by their bed, observing the two men sleeping, one with his arm around the other, then moving noiselessly through the room. Nor had William woken when Luke disengaged himself to go and do some reconnaissance in the flat. He realized that his commanding officer was present and the only security in attendance was him.

Now William knew that he was alone and he could hear voices. Sensing that The Queen might already be awake recalled him to his duty as well, not as a burden, as a job he had to do, but instinctively, as a role he could perform better than anyone else. If she were up, she'd want some coffee. She liked a special mixture of muesli. He knew Lady Anne's nephew would not have it in the cupboard. He might have to nip around the corner to find something—mix it together himself—if there were a corner store open. He found his clothing of the evening before. He fished a tie out of his pocket, buttoned his top button, and knotted the tie in the baroque mirror over the chimneypiece. He then appeared in the lighted doorway to the kitchen. What he found there surprised him. The Queen and Shirley were dressed and ready for business. Lady Anne was still in her nightgown, doubled over, apparently in some pain. Luke was standing there in his boxer shorts.

"Luke, for God's sake!" said William.

William stood there in his tie, looking crossly at Luke in his underwear.

They all turned to look again at Luke.

"I think the equerry had better go and put on his uniform," said William.

"Don't have a uniform," said Luke. "Didn't bring it."

"We may all be on an unplanned junket," William glanced at The Queen as he said this, "in a strange flat in Scotland," casting a hostile glance at Anne, "but Major Thomason, may I remind you that you are in attendance?" William would never have addressed the equerry in this way before, especially in front of The Queen, but as the circumstances were unusual and he was feeling a new sense of protectiveness about Luke, he couldn't stop himself from being a little severe.

"Now, gentlemen," said The Queen, thinking it was time to smooth over these hard words. "I think you'd better both have seats at the table. I've brought some of the most marvelous cheese. I gave some of it to Hohenzollern last night of course, but really it's worked a treat with me. Quite cheered me up. Set me on my feet again. I think you'd better all give it a try."

"Hohenzollern, Ma'am?" asked Anne with an inward groan. This sounded distinctly like a return of her odd behavior.

"Seeing Eye dog. Alsatian," said The Queen. "Belonged to

the couple I met on the train last night." She turned to Shirley, "Now, if we could only find some eggs, we could put it with the cheddar, couldn't we? And have a proper breakfast?"

"I'm not cooking for all this lot," said Shirley, annoyed at the suggestion.

"Of course you're not. You'll have a place at the table with the others. I'm Cook this morning." With that, The Queen looked into the cupboard to the side of the oven and said, vaguely, "Now, where does the Marquess keep his pots and pans, do you suppose?" She reached in and brought out a large pot for boiling pasta. "Now, this is the thing."

"Oh no," said Shirley, rolling up her sleeves and looking into the refrigerator. "You may serve, Your Majesty, but I'm cooking. William, you sit down. Major, go look in the medicine cabinet. Find some pain pills for Anne. Her head is killing her." William did as he was told and Luke was on the verge of leaving the kitchen when Rajiv appeared at the door.

"Your Most Gracious and Imperial Majesty, good morning," said Rajiv, giving an absurdly low bow with several rolling hand movements. Luke had never met him and didn't recognize him. So he moved to block Rajiv from approaching The Queen.

"It's all right, Major Thomason," said The Queen. "We know him. Came north on the train with me last night. Even though I told him to get off. Works at Paxton & Whitfield. Sold me the cheddar. Working at the shop in his gap year. Now sit you down right here at the table, young man. Shirley is Cook. She's going to put some of that cheddar into an *omelette*." She pronounced the word as if they were dining at Maxim's in Paris.

"And I'm serving." With this, The Queen took a dish towel she found hanging by the sink, and arranged it carefully over her lower arm.

Rajiv was so surprised by this gesture that he sat down at the table just as she'd told him to do. Luke was about to leave the kitchen again to dress when Rebecca, with tousled hair and her cheeks the color of a bruised apple, appeared in the doorway.

"My, isn't she lovely?" said Anne.

"Oh yes, she's a beauty," said Shirley with approval.

"An exceptional young woman, true enough," agreed The Queen.

"Who's this, then?" said William, amazed at someone else whom The Queen apparently knew but whom he did not recognize from any staff party.

"Rebecca Rinaldi from the Mews. Came north last night with Cheddar. Sit down, Rebecca, there's another chair for you here. And now, Shirley, hadn't we better make another pot of tea?"

"Before everyone gets too comfortable," said Luke, straightening up and beginning to speak once again as if he were on duty as equerry. "I took the liberty of faxing MI5 and Sir Robin on the Marquess's landline last night. Sent them a short note about your whereabouts, Your Majesty. Said you'd been called away. At short notice. Unofficial business. Unforeseeable circumstances. Quite unexpected. And so on. The private secretary has sent me a reply. It says he has rearranged your engagements, Ma'am. Is sending a helicopter of The Queen's Flight for you to return to London this morning."

"The Queen's Flight?" said The Queen impatiently. "They'll charge that to the Privy Purse. It will cost a fortune. Couldn't we just go back on the Great North Eastern Railway? It was more than comfortable coming up."

"Well, apparently, Ma'am, there's something on tonight at the Old Vic that cannot be rearranged. Gala performance. *Henry V.* He'd like to have you back in good time for it."

"Oh, well, then," said The Queen, heaving a sigh that signified she'd remembered her duty. There was no choice. What she had to do, she would do. She'd long ago accustomed herself to thinking about her duty as something over which she had little control, but still, it was sometimes hard work, hence the sigh. "But," said The Queen, brightening, "we must all have our breakfast. No work without breakfast."

"Ma'am," assented Luke with a brief bow from the neck. He then left the room, walking backwards, to go into the sitting room and look for his clothes.

The Queen whispered aside to Shirley and Anne. "It's the first time in sixty years I've had the 'reverence' from a man in his boxer shorts."

They both looked at the ceiling and smiled. Rajiv and Rebecca and William, who were all sitting at the table out of earshot, looked at one another and wondered what she'd said.

Part VII

Savasana

Luke had arranged two unmarked Daimlers to take The Queen and her party from Charlotte Square to the airport in Edinburgh. Shirley, William, Rajiv, and Rebecca went in the first car. Luke, Anne, and The Queen followed in the second car. On arrival at the airport, they drove right onto the tarmac in an area reserved for private planes. There stood the last aircraft of The Queen's Flight, a maroon Sikorsky helicopter.

There had once been a variety of jet aircraft exclusively for The Queen's use. Now she could borrow a smaller aeroplane that was in a pool, also used by the Prime Minister or other senior officials. The helicopter was the only aircraft that remained to her. A steward stood at the bottom of the steps. The pilots were looking out the side windows and ready to fly the Royal Standard when The Queen came on board. Shirley and William went up the steps and

took two seats toward the rear. They both had been on board the helicopter before and knew the drill. Rebecca followed their example and slipped quietly into a rear seat. Rajiv, however, was as excited as a schoolboy and immediately went exploring. He opened the door to the lavatory, leaned over a table that was configured with four seats on the right of the aisle to look out the windows, and even poked his head in the cockpit, where he received a frosty welcome. Anne came on board and motioned with her head toward the rear, indicating his place in the helicopter hierarchy. Rajiv ignored her. He now felt he was on more than friendly terms with The Queen. She came steadily up the steps to find Rajiv in the aisle to welcome her, with the senior pilot behind him, saluting irritably. "Your Majesty! I've never been on a helicopter before!" said Rajiv.

"Enthusiastic boy," thought The Queen to herself, surprised to find anyone other than the pilot to greet her, but under the circumstances, she was prepared to put up with deviations from the established order. "Well, it's very slow, Cheddar, and very noisy. But it will get us to London, I believe." She brushed past him, acknowledged the pilot's salute, and took her usual place at the table for four on the right, facing forward. Ordinarily, the Duke of Edinburgh, if he were along, would have been sitting next to her. The two seats opposite them at the table were left open for private secretaries and others who needed to brief The Queen during the flight and who might join her for small stretches of time. The upper members of the Household, in this case, Anne and Luke, sat in seats forward but on the other side of the aisle from The Queen. The steward came forward as the rotary blades began to hum and placed a wool blanket made of the grey and blue Balmoral tartan over The Queen's knees.

Rajiv jumped into a seat at the table opposite The Queen and looked out the window to observe the preparations for liftoff. Luke began to get up to pull Rajiv to the back of the helicopter, but The Queen looked up at him and said, "It's all right, Major Thomason."

Rajiv turned to The Queen after the excitement of leaving Edinburgh was over and said, "So it's *Henry V* tonight, Ma'am? It's my favorite Shakespeare play."

"Is it?" said The Queen, who wasn't exactly looking forward to the performance, which she expected to be tedious. But then, rather than ask him some *pro forma* questions about when he'd first seen it, or why he liked it, she decided to volunteer some information about herself. Here was a young man, after all, who'd dropped everything to get in a taxi, and then on a train, to follow her. He deserved friendlier treatment than she would ordinarily give him. She was trying very hard to turn the page herself.

"Well, you see, my mother and my sister were the two artistic ones in the family. They understood the theatre. And the Prince of Wales, now, he cares about Shakespeare. Has led an effort to make sure all the schools still teach it."

"Yes, well, that's where the bug bit me."

"Excellent," said The Queen, smiling her approval. "Well, I just go along because they ask me to, but I'm afraid quite a lot of it leaves me cold. Perhaps I didn't have the right teacher." The

Queen hadn't been allowed to go to school at all. Fine nannies and eminent private tutors, she'd had those, yes, but no school, no rough-and-tumble with other children. Something she regretted. Something she'd missed.

"Oh, but Ma'am! *Henry V.* It's one of Shakespeare's most royal plays. It's about your life, surely. It's about the things you know better than anyone," said Rajiv with some disappointment in his voice.

Luke and Anne, who'd both been monitoring this conversation from across the aisle, sprang into action. One thing not allowed in conversation with the sovereign was to refer to her position, to mention that she *is* the sovereign, in such a full-frontal, unambiguous way.

"Look! Out the window. Isn't the Firth of Forth beautiful this morning?" asked Anne brightly.

Luke also stood up and pointed to the rear of the aircraft. "Oh dear, Miss Rinaldi is sitting all by herself!"

For a moment Rajiv looked confused. Then The Queen interrupted Luke, "Do sit down. I've said it's all right." Then she looked back to Rajiv. "Now, Cheddar. 'About your life.' Carry on. What do you mean?"

"Well, right before the Battle of Agincourt, Henry goes disguised among the men, see, in a cloak, you know, sort of anonymously, to find out whether they're ready to fight or not."

She nodded at Rajiv to continue.

"And he comes across several people, one or two of them love him, and are ready to die for him, but there's another who's not. He blames Henry for all the bloodshed that's going to come along with the battle. Henry gets into a fight with him and argues with him."

"I see. And?"

"They go away and Henry's all by himself afterwards, thinking about the life of an ordinary soldier and the life of a king. What has he got that they haven't got? He's just a man, just like they're men, but at least they get to sleep at night. He doesn't. They don't have to worry about battles, and the welfare of armies, and diplomacy, like he does. Private men enjoy 'heart's ease.' 'What infinite heart's ease must kings neglect, that private men enjoy!'"

"Wouldn't it be lovely to have a reliable supply of 'heart's ease.' Sounds like a fine remedy. From dandelion blossom perhaps, or sorrel. I've felt the lack of it myself, sometimes."

"There you are, Ma'am!"

"Go on, what else?"

"Well, then the King, Henry, that is, thinks about what he's got that private soldiers don't. What has he got to compensate him for not having heart's ease?"

"And? What does he have?"

"He's got nuffink, Ma'am," said Rajiv, using a Cockney pronunciation to try and make her laugh. He would have offered her a Mars bar if he had one in his pocket, but he didn't.

"Nothing? Really," said The Queen, smiling.

"No. All he has is 'idle ceremony,' and that's not going to help him when he's down. It only makes people afraid of him."

The Queen did know that feeling of being feared, and her own inability to reach out to the public over the barrier. All she had to offer was small talk and a supply of questions she repeated mechanically over and over. And the ceremonies themselves: the coronation in 1953, the first jubilee in 1977, the next in 2002. Those big parades through the streets with everyone cheering at her. Everyone expected her to be so pleased when they were over. She was content in a way that they went with such military precision, no mishaps, everything according to plan. But they didn't give her heart's ease. Riding by in the carriage and being waved at. It was comforting. All must be well if they're waving flags and not throwing stones, but she wasn't convinced that it wasn't temporary. The mood could easily shift again, just as it had before. No, Henry was right. Ceremony didn't provide heart's ease.

"And . . ." began The Queen tentatively.

"Ma'am?" said Rajiv.

"Does King Henry find anything that helps him feel better? Give him 'heart's ease'?"

While this conversation was going on at the front of the helicopter, William and Shirley were exchanging a few words at the back.

"Hot in here today," said Shirley, shivering.

"No, it's not. It's okay. Why, Shirley, your forehead's all damp." He took out his silk pocket square and began to dab around her temples. "And you're shuddering too, darling. What's wrong with you? Are you all right?"

"I'm fine," said Shirley. "Leave off." She could not conceal that she was suffering from shortness of breath too, and she felt the occasional sharp pang in her upper back. She reached up to rub her shoulder. She was very pale.

"Something's wrong. Hang on a minute."

William was out of his seat in a single leap. He went forward to tell Luke. Anne overheard. They both got out of their seats to come back and look at Shirley. William brought her a paper cup of water from the steward in the galley. Anne surveyed the situation, put her knuckles gently against Shirley's cheek to comfort her and gauge her temperature. She then stood up and brought Luke forward with her. She'd had a small amount of medical training in connection with her work on the army helpline. They both stopped in the aisle next to The Queen. Anne bent over to say, "Ma'am, I think Mrs MacDonald may be having a heart attack."

"My God!" said The Queen, who was, however, not altogether surprised. She knew the genealogy and medical history of all her members of staff. "It's how her grandmother died. Major Thomason, go to the cockpit. Have the pilot radio ahead. Tell them we'll need an ambulance and a cardiac specialist to meet us." The Queen then got up and took her tartan blanket back to Shirley, who sat stricken and immobile in her seat. "Hang on now, Shirley! Only twenty more minutes. You're not leaving us now, you're too young. You've got a lot more work in you yet," she said as she tucked in the blanket around Shirley's waist. "Just have this rug. It'll keep you warm."

Anne sat down in William's empty seat and held Shirley's hand.

~

The Old Vic was a theatre that had first been built in the early 1800s and it was now approaching a major anniversary. During its life it had been a music hall, a school, the base of an ambitious Shakespeare company, and the first home of Britain's National Theatre. There was inadequate funding of the company from ticket sales, and the theatre's director, a Hollywood actor who longed for the artistic respectability—and creative stimulus—that only performing on stage in Britain would bring, had devised a gala to which many American actors and philanthropists had been invited. Because of the theatre's historic importance to the London stage, The Queen's private secretary had advised in favor of her accepting the invitation to the gala that had been sent to her.

Two cars were on their way to the Old Vic from Buckingham Palace, preceded by motorcycle outriders from the Metropolitan Police. The Queen and Lady Anne rode in the palace's newest limousine, with big windows and special interior lighting so The Queen could be seen by onlookers and others who had gathered in a few strategic points along her route. Luke was in a second car, an undistinguished 1980s Rover sedan, with the Royal Protection officer. The drill was that although The Queen would arrive in the first, grander car, she could slip away in the Rover afterwards, for a quicker and more anonymous return to the palace.

Anne asked The Queen, not looking at her, as they were

sitting in the back of the car and both sets of their eyes were forward in case of spotting knots of public who required waving to, "What is the news?"

"She's in the cardiac unit at St Thomas's."

"And?"

"Well, they put one of those balloon thingys in her femoral artery. It cleared the blockage near the heart. Then they put in something to prop open the vessel, so it won't collapse. If she gives up cigarettes, *and* cheese, the prognosis is good. A pity about the cheese. The doctors think she will make a full recovery."

"Thank God."

"Quite."

"A scare, though."

"Yes, well, I couldn't tell which of you was the more frightened when we put her in the ambulance."

Anne let this pass. She wasn't entirely sure what The Queen meant by this. "On the left, Ma'am. Up ahead."

The Queen turned to acknowledge a knot of pedestrians on a paved island in the roadway. They weren't actually waiting to see her. They'd just paused in crossing the street to find out why the motorcycle outriders were stopping the traffic. The Queen raised her hand and waved. The people on the island gawked. Waving at her, let alone cheering "Hooray!" was not their first instinct.

"Well, you see," began Anne, "Mrs MacDonald is thinking of retiring before too long. I thought of letting her have one of my spare bedrooms in Tite Street . . ."

"I know all about it. I think it's an excellent plan."

Anne was surprised. She didn't think even she and Shirley had got down to agreeing upon the details, and already The Queen was ready to write "Approved" in her distinctive rounded hand on the deal. She said nothing.

"You'll both want looking after. Shirley will need to convalesce. And then you and I, we'll both be hobbling around ourselves before too long. I've set aside one of Queen Elizabeth's sticks for you. As a way of saying thank you. Perhaps Shirley can help you when you begin to keel over."

"On the right, Ma'am," said Anne, as they approached a crowd of tourists in Parliament Square.

The Queen leaned forward and smiled at them. They looked back at her as if she were an alien. Only a little girl cried, "The Queen! The Queen!" and waved both arms frantically.

"That's it," said The Queen to Anne as she smiled at the little girl.

"Very kind of you, indeed, Ma'am," said Anne formally, though she was touched, and knew that a gift of anything that had once belonged to her mother was a rare mark of favor from The Queen. "I don't think I've done anything to deserve it."

"Of course you have. You've been many years with me now. And then coming all that way last night."

"It was nothing, Ma'am."

"Nonsense. Wasn't nothing. And I've had a little discovery. Don't need the royal train or *Britannia* to do what I do."

"No, Ma'am. Of course not."

"It's given me a little boost. Done me a world of good. Can't say why."

"I'm so pleased, Ma'am."

"And I've asked the apothecary to prescribe some pills."

"What pills, Ma'am?"

"You know. The ones to cure worrying too much. I want to give them a try. Being unhappy takes up too much time. I've got a lot to do."

Anne was aware how big a step this was for The Queen. Her mother was well known for describing aspirin as "that dangerous drug." For The Queen even to consider taking antidepressants was virtually a revolution in her thinking. Before Anne could come up with the proper remark to acknowledge what The Queen had just said, they were pulling up to the theatre. "Here we are. To work, Lady Anne! To work," said The Queen, grimly and almost gaily.

Luke had requested, and The Queen had approved, a small alteration in the programme that had been decided upon months earlier for her attendance at the Old Vic gala. Ordinarily, only Lady Anne and he would have been in attendance, sitting with her in the royal box, with an officer from the Royal Protection outside the door in the corridor. William had asked Luke to find out whether an extra seat could be found for him in the theatre; and Rajiv had applied for two more on behalf of himself and

Rebecca. Under the circumstances, and as the Old Vic was one of The Queen's charities, to which she subscribed annually out of the Privy Purse, Luke had asked whether the theatre couldn't find three additional seats for "The Queen's guests." The theatre management provided three seats in the center stalls on the ground floor within view of the royal box.

The Queen arrived at the front of the theatre, the big car coming to a slow, infinitesimal halt. As soon as her car door was opened, she got out and then stood for a moment, pretending to admire the front of the building. This was in fact so that the press photographers could get a good shot. She wouldn't pose for them directly, or look at them head-on, but she would hold still while they photographed her doing something else. Afterwards, she went up the red carpeted steps to find the American actor first in the receiving line. "Thank you for all you're doing for the London theatre," she said to him as she took both his hands in both of hers. She would have given him only one hand ordinarily, but she felt she was inaugurating a new regime. The question had struck her as she was going up the steps to meet him. What did a little extra warmth cost her? Very little. It seemed to mean so much to the tea lady on Waverley railway station. So she gave him two hands. Then, swinging his hands deliberately to her left in the direction of Lady Anne, whom he was meant to greet next, she moved on to the next person in the line. It was the most effective way of indicating their conversation was over. Nevertheless, the Hollywood actor was radiant. He turned to Lady Anne and said, "Isn't she cute?"

"Um, yes. Certainly," she said doubtfully. "We're so happy to be here tonight. I can't tell you." He didn't understand that her "Certainly" meant "Stop behaving like an idiot," or that "I can't tell you" actually referred to the last twenty-four hours, when it sometimes looked as if they might never have made it to the Old Vic at all.

For the gala performance, the Old Vic had commissioned a Bollywood version of Shakespeare. The idea was to take his most patriotic play, *Henry V*, and set it to Indian music with a large cast as well as a full orchestra. The theatre had imported two of India's best-known film actors to play the leads. Although the play itself was about a medieval English king warring with France, and reached its climax at the Battle of Agincourt, the costuming, the personnel, and the instruments were all Indian. The cross-pollination of cultures had the effect of universalizing the text, as well as slightly sending up some parts of the play that might otherwise be a little too nationalistic had they not been set to elaborately upbeat song-and-dance routines. The play's memorable words had been preserved, however, and The Queen followed along in her copy of the play's text, which the theatre had helpfully provided for her and all her party. She thought of it as a kind of timetable rather than a work of art. She could see by following along when it would all be over. She walked into the box and without hesitating went to the edge, where she acknowledged the applause of the audience. As she surveyed the crowd, she looked down and saw Rajiv giving her a comically deferential bow from the waist. William's eye sparkled as he gave her a mild nod of the head. Rebecca just smiled shyly and lowered her eyes. She acknowledged them with a flicker of her eyelash, which all of them saw, but which went unnoticed by the rest of the audience.

A handsome young actor who played Chorus came out to ask the audience to conjure up entire mounted armies onstage. "Think when we talk of horses, that you see them printing their proud hoofs i' the receiving earth." At this, Rajiv looked over at Rebecca, and, holding up his two hands as if they were a horse's front hoofs, he made a little cantering motion, smiling broadly. At first she refused to look at him, but when he continued cantering, she looked at him and put her finger on her lips emphatically. He didn't mind. Any attention from her he counted as a kind of victory.

After the introduction from Chorus, the Archbishop of Canterbury came onstage to conspire with another bishop. They needed to distract the king or he would impose a heavy tax on the Church. They hit upon the idea of advising Henry that he had the right to go to war with France to claim territory there. Henry replied skeptically to their advice, "Never two such kingdoms did contend without much fall of blood; whose guiltless drops are every one a woe."

Anne, who was sitting in the front row of the box with The Queen, turned around, looked at Luke, who was sitting behind them, and then reached out her hand to him. He reached forward with his hand and the two of them held hands for an instant.

The Queen, to her surprise, found herself enjoying the performance. Usually Shakespeare was rather heavy going and she would cast covert glances at the number of pages until the end of the act to see how many more minutes until the interval. But something about the music and dancing of the Bollywood *Henry V* made her enjoy the play more than she would have ordinarily. She discovered new resonance in the lines as she read along in her text.

The Queen and everyone in her box had coffee and sandwiches at the interval. "No wine!" she'd said when a waiter brought a tray of drinks to the box. "It will put me to sleep. Don't want to miss anything. Coffee, please." Neither Luke nor Anne felt they could take a glass if The Queen wasn't having any, so they had coffee too. They'd all then retaken their seats to watch the play's conclusion. Just as the play was reaching its climax, with Henry about to speak to his sodden, bedraggled men, vastly outnumbered by the opposing French army, before the battle at Agincourt, a police inspector in uniform came out onto the stage. At the same moment a quiet knock on the door to The Queen's box made Luke step out into the corridor.

"Pardon me. Sorry! Apologize for the interruption! Sorry," said the inspector on the stage.

The Bollywood actors looked at him in shock and fell in disarray from their carefully blocked positions on the stage. The orchestra, which had begun playing music to accompany Henry's Agincourt speech, the most famous lines in the play, grew silent with an unplanned crash of cymbals and a ghostly sitar tailing off in a minor key.

The police inspector then walked out to center stage and turned first to address The Queen's box, saying, "Your Majesty," with a crisp nod of his head, before turning to the main audience in front and saying, "Ladies and gentlemen. I'm sorry for this interruption to the performance. But I have to announce that there has been an incident, close by the theatre, at Waterloo."

At this, murmuring rose from the stalls to the dress circle to the upper balconies.

"May I have quiet, please, ladies and gentlemen?" resumed the police inspector. "A bomb was discovered. It was defused before it could explode, but we have reason to believe that this was a terrorist event, and we are not completely certain that it is over. It may well have been aimed at Her Majesty's presence here in the theatre, no more than a hundred paces from the railway station. The South Bank has been sealed off. We believe that it is unsafe for the public to leave the theatre at this time, so the Metropolitan Police would like to request your remaining here, in your seats, until we can give the all clear. Our duty is to protect the safety of the public, and given the nature of what has just occurred, we do not think it is safe for you to leave the building at this time. As soon as our investigations are complete, I will return and make an announcement to you all. It would assist us if you were to keep your seats until our investigations finish. We anticipate your being free to go before the evening is over, but at this time, we cannot allow you, for your own safety, to leave the premises." The inspector then nodded to the audience, bowed once again to The Queen, and left the stage, walking quickly.

As soon as the inspector finished his speech and walked off the stage, the former quiet murmuring of the audience turned into agitation. The actors broke from their characters and grouped in clusters to discuss what they'd just heard. A woman in the front row fainted. Her husband poured a little water from his Evian bottle on her forehead. Others just faced forward in shock. The sound of a hundred different worried conversations rose into a muffled roar. Many looked up to the royal box for a cue about how to behave, what to do.

The Queen was not in the least surprised or frightened. She'd lived through the blitz of the Second World War. She could recall vividly the Irish Republican Army bombing London railway stations and murdering Lord Mountbatten when he was on his boat with his grandchildren in the 1970s. More recently she'd joined in the memorial service for those who died from the bombs of Islamic terrorists on the Tube and on several buses on the seventh of July 2007, 7/7/07, Britain's own 9/11. During the memorial, she'd stood alone, silent, in front of the palace. She was fully prepared for more trouble. What the police inspector had described at Waterloo was not far different from the sort of terrorist attack that had been anticipated in briefing papers that had been circulated to her by the secret services.

Luke stepped back inside the box. He leaned over to whisper in The Queen's ear. "Your Majesty, the police and secret services would like you to leave the theatre. They think there's a small possibility that you are in danger and they would like to take you to safety."

The Queen looked out into the theatre. She could see that members of the audience were upset and that order needed to be restored. "No, Major Thomason. We're staying right here. We will wait with the others for the all clear signal. We face whatever it is together. If I go, they should all be allowed to go. If they must stay, I must stay too."

"But, Ma'am . . ."

"Tell the police. Thank you." Luke knew he had been dismissed and went back out to the corridor to convey The Queen's decision.

The Queen resumed her survey of the audience and the groups of actors onstage. She picked up her copy of *Henry V* and slowly rose to her feet at the edge of the box.

The audience, through some archaic collective memory of right behavior, seeing The Queen on her feet, struggled to rise to their feet too. Anne quickly followed her example. With all the audience now standing, The Queen looked at them gravely, and then looked at Rajiv. She wanted the play to recommence. It was the only way to calm everyone down, and there was no point in sitting there doing nothing while they waited for the police to come back and let them go. Just as she'd expected, Rajiv had his copy of the play open too, and was following along. She looked at him directly, made eye contact, and then gently nodded her head in the direction of the stage. By a kind of sympathetic telepathy between them, he instantly knew what she wanted.

The audience grew silent, rapt, looking at The Queen looking at Rajiv. Suddenly, in a deep baritone, without consulting his script, as he knew this particular passage in his sleep, Rajiv faced the actors onstage and began with the words of the Earl of Westmorland, who had been about to speak when the police inspector came in and interrupted the action. Standing with King Henry before the English army, Westmorland said he was sorry there were so few English soldiers compared to the French and wished they had more men from England to fight with them. "O that we now had here but one ten thousand of those men in England that do no work today!"

The audience and the actors onstage looked curiously at Rajiv, who might have been a Bollywood cast member himself, planted in the audience, speaking lines from the play, just where the action had left off before the interruption. Was the terrorist event planned or real? Was it part of the play, or was it a true crisis? They were frankly confused. They looked up at The Queen, the stage lights glancing off her large-framed 1980s spectacles. She was now looking not at Rajiv, but at the stage, where the actors were all still in chaotic groups. There was an awkward pause.

Then Rajiv tried again: "O that we now had here but one ten thousand of those men in England that do no work today!"

Suddenly the Bollywood film star recognized this was his cue. He walked to the position onstage he would have taken just after the police inspector had appeared and began Henry's heroic lines in reply to Westmorland.

What's he that wishes so?
My cousin Westmorland? No, my fair cousin:
If we are mark'd to die, we are enough
To do our country loss; and if to live,
The fewer men, the greater share of honour.

The audience and the actors onstage were all transfixed. What was happening? The Bollywood actor continued,

God's will! I pray thee, wish not one man more.
By Jove, I am not covetous for gold,
Nor care I who doth feed upon my cost;
It yearns me not if men my garments wear;
Such outward things dwell not in my desires:
But if it be a sin to covet honour,
I am the most offending soul alive.

The remaining actors now resumed their places. They ceased to look in surprise from Rajiv to the royal box. Everyone now looked at Henry.

No, faith, my coz, wish not a man from England:
God's peace! I would not lose so great an honour
As one man more, methinks, would share from me
For the best hope I have. O, do not wish one more!
Rather proclaim it, Westmorland, through my host,
That he which hath no stomach to this fight
Let him depart; his passport shall be made
And crowns for convoy put into his purse:
We would not die in that man's company
That fears his fellowship to die with us.

There was an emotional current in the air, which everyone felt. When Henry said that he did not wish to die with someone who feared dying with him, many hearts lurched in their chests. They were with The Queen. There was a crisis nearby, wasn't there? She was willing to die. She hadn't left the theatre under heavy police guard. She was staying where she was. Right there in the theatre with them. And they were willing to die with her. It didn't matter whether the crisis were real or imaginary. They would go right through it together.

The Queen, still standing at the edge of the royal box, script in hand, could see that the audience's attention had returned to the action onstage. The police inspector's announcement had electrified the Bollywood actor. He spoke the part with a passion that it was impossible not to notice. She saw that the audience had ceased to look at her. So she sat down. And because she sat down, Anne and Luke in the box as well as William and Rebecca and Rajiv all sat down too. The Queen and everyone else in the royal box having sat down, the audience sat down too. Now all attention went back to the stage, where Henry told the soldiers about to fight with him:

He that shall live this day, and see old age,
Will yearly on the vigil feast his neighbours,
And say 'To-morrow is Saint Crispian:'
Then will he strip his sleeve and show his scars.
And say 'These wounds I had on Crispin's day.'
Old men forget: yet all shall be forgot,
But he'll remember with advantages
What feats he did that day: then shall our names
Familiar in his mouth as household words

Harry the king, Bedford and Exeter,
Warwick and Talbot, Salisbury and Gloucester,
Be in their flowing cups freshly remember'd
This story shall the good man teach his son;
And Crispin Crispian shall ne'er go by,
From this day to the ending of the world,
But we in it shall be remember'd;
We few, we happy few, we band of brothers;
For he today that sheds his blood with me
Shall be my brother.

The orchestra struck up music for the dance number to accompany the choreographed battle between the English and French armies. The audience had forgotten The Queen altogether. At that moment, most of them were no longer thinking of a terrorist scare at Waterloo, either. They were so wrapped up in the action of the play that they were in France in 1415. The play carried on seamlessly to its conclusion, the audience jumping to its feet once again, with a shout, when the curtain fell. The cast came to the front for repeated smiling bows and handholding and acknowledgment of seemingly endless applause. After nine curtain calls, the police inspector appeared sheepishly from the wings.

The audience was not surprised to see him and began to applaud him too. "No, no!" He said, "No. This is just to give you the 'all clear.' No further danger. You're free to go. Your Majesty. Ladies and gentlemen." With two quick nods, he got off the stage as quickly as he could. The house lights came up and the audience stood to go, many still wondering what exactly had happened. Was the crisis real or make-believe? Had the stage Henry brought them together, made them feel as one, or was it The Queen?

The Queen was in no doubt about whether the crisis was real or imagined. She turned to Luke and said, “Now, Major Thomason, I would like to go to Waterloo.”

Luke looked at her with surprise.

The Queen realized that what she was proposing was out of the ordinary, but she was also determined to help. “I must get to Waterloo. The emergency services will still be there and will need some encouragement. The bomb disposal unit too. I would like to thank them.”

“But, Ma’am. We’ll be in their way.”

“Please telephone and let them know we’re coming.”

Luke sprinted down the steps ahead of her to speak to the police at the side of the theatre. The Rover was waiting for her at the side door, where she could make an inconspicuous exit. Anne could do nothing but follow as The Queen made her way laboriously down the red carpet. A group of police officers had circled around Luke, telling him that it was impossible for The Queen to go to Waterloo. Luke took his mobile phone out of his pocket and punched in a redial number for Arabella Tyringham-Rode.

“Hello?” She picked up impatiently after a single ring.

“Ms Rode, Luke Thomason here.”

"No time just now, Major. Doubtless you know what's happened. The Queen herself may have been one of the targets."

"Yes. I understand that."

"Oh, and good show finding her last night. I'm afraid I underestimated you and Mr de Morgan. Took the precaution of removing your security clearances, but they've now been restored. I will also overlook your disobeying the order to remove the Queen from the theatre earlier."

"You what?" Luke had been given no notice of his clearance having been revoked.

"Just a formality. Now completely on the up-and-up. If you don't mind, I do have other matters to attend to. I'm sure you can understand that just now we're rather busy here."

"Yes, um, that's why I'm telephoning, actually." The wailing klaxon of a police vehicle went by and temporarily drowned out the conversation.

"Where are you, Major? You're supposed to be with The Queen at the theatre."

"Yes, well, The Queen feels she could be of more use in the station right now."

"Under no circumstances, Major."

"Her Majesty would like to give moral support to the emergency services. She would like to meet the bomb disposal unit. What I'd like you to do is phone ahead to the police and let them know Her Majesty's coming."

"Are you out of your mind, Major? You cannot take The Queen onto the site of a terrorist attack, even one that has been prevented from happening. It is *out* of the question. The crowd rushed the exits when they were clearing the station. No one trampled, thank God, but there were a few falls and some injuries. They have been taken to St Thomas's Hospital. You take The Queen back to Buckingham Palace right away, do you hear me?"

Luke could understand the logic of her forbidding him to take The Queen to Waterloo, but he also felt that his department needed some defending against the presumption of an arrogant civil servant. He forgot that he had once been afraid of her. "No, I'm perfectly sane, Rode. By the way, in case you've forgotten, Her Majesty was Queen before you were born. Before the Prime Minister was born too. Before the last one that was in too. She knows what's she's doing."

Here a string of vituperation followed from the other end of the line that surprised even Luke. He thought he'd heard it all in Iraq, but Arabella Tyringham-Rode appeared to have the vocabulary of a stevedore.

"Dear me, you're breaking up," said Luke mildly as he waved the phone away from his ear and in the direction of the passing traffic. "Thank you so much," he said, bringing the phone back to his mouth for a moment, and then he pressed the red "END CALL" button.

Just then The Queen appeared at the foot of the stairs at the side entrance of the theatre. "Your Majesty, the secret services are grateful for your offer to help at Waterloo," Luke began. "They feel that the station is still in a state of confusion, however. A number of the public were injured when they cleared the station. They have been taken to St Thomas's. Under the circumstances, they wonder whether it mightn't be better if you were to return to BP."

A look of dismay crossed The Queen's face.

Looking off into the distance, Luke said, "But I see no objection to our stopping at St Thomas's. Visit Mrs MacDonald, who will probably be out of intensive care by now? Perhaps, if we happen to chance on some of the injuries from Waterloo in one of the wards, we might say hello to them too? Some of the emergency services will doubtless still be there," said Luke with raised eyebrows, as if proposing an extra plaque for her to unveil.

"And the secret services have approved that, have they?" asked The Queen with a grim note of irony as she was on the verge of climbing into the unmarked Rover.

"Well, I believe Miss Tyringham-Rode is a very reasonable woman. I'll see to her."

The Queen looked briefly at Luke and guessed exactly the sort of conversation he'd just had with MI5. With a glance into his eyes she conveyed that nothing about her renewed sense of what she might still be able to do as sovereign was simple, and that if he wished to carry on as her equerry, difficult telephone conversations might in future be the least of his worries. "Thank you."

"Not at all, Your Majesty." Luke looked away from The Queen and straight ahead to the open car door in front of them. What he meant was "Count on me."

The Queen set off in the Rover with Anne in the back, the Royal Protection officer in the front alongside the driver. Luke was to have returned to the palace in the Rolls Royce The Queen had arrived in, but he now jumped in the front of the bigger car with another driver and they drove off first to arrive at the hospital before The Queen. The maroon Rolls Royce swept into the forecourt of the accident and emergency entrance and Luke hopped out before the car had come to a complete halt. He walked quickly up to a knot of police officers who were standing at the door. "Good evening, Officers. Her Majesty The Queen will shortly be arriving to make an informal visit. She will be on her way to see a member of staff who is in the cardiac ward, upstairs."

The police officers looked at him with expressions varying between shock, disapproval, and consternation.

"We will not be in your way, gentlemen, I can assure you of that. There is the possibility . . ." Luke here refused to make eye contact and looked at the ceiling of the portico. "The possibility that Her Majesty may, on her way upstairs, wish to thank you for doing your duty tonight on an extraordinary occasion. And to call in on members of the emergency services, medical personnel, and any of those injured during tonight's incident at Waterloo who are in a position to receive her, um, grateful acknowledgment."

The three policemen goggled at him. "Look here. Who are you, then?" began one of them. Just then, The Queen's Rover drove into the forecourt, and she came out of the car with her gleaming handbag hanging over the crook of her arm. They knew it was her from the way she carried the handbag. She came straight up to Luke and the three officers. Anne hung behind at a tactful distance.

"Your Majesty, may I present Police Constable, um," Luke looked at the first officer's badge and nameplate, "Police Constable Mulready."

"Thank you so much, PC Mulready. It's been quite a night for you, I expect."

"Well, not the usual. That's true."

"How many injured?" asked The Queen.

"About twenty."

"Gracious! Badly hurt?"

"Well, a broken leg or two. Quite a few suffering from shock. Several took a tumble coming down the escalator in a hurry. They had to clear the station quickly, you see?"

"Yes, I do see. But nothing too serious?"

"Well, no, Your Majesty. Crisis averted is what I'd say. We go through these training exercises for events such as these quite often. But the public, now, they don't get to practice as often as we do."

"Well, bless the training, then, Police Constable. May I say thank you for the tremendous work you're doing?"

The officer was not sure what the proper reply was and began hemming and hawing, but Luke was already bent over squinting at the next man's nameplate, while The Queen moved forward. The Queen spoke to the next two and then returned to Mulready, who had the greyest hair of all three. She took him to be the most senior officer. "Police Constable, I don't want to hinder anyone's work, but could you please take me to see a little of what's going on inside before I go upstairs to see Mrs MacDonald?"

He knew the answer to that question. This was a command from an officer who outranked him. "Your Majesty," he said, turned gravely, opened the glass door, and waved The Queen through. The accident and emergency unit was on full alert with activity going on at all stations. Although the injuries were not life-threatening, all of them had come in at the same time, so the ward was operating at full stretch. Everyone was so busy that they hardly took notice of The Queen. They were too preoccupied with the medical issues in front of them to be surprised or annoyed. In fact, many of them had seen her on television visiting the cleanup sites of previous historic emergencies, so it struck them as not unusual she was there. She spoke to several ambulance crew members, half a dozen nurses, and a group of the more junior doctors, medical students really, who seemed, for the moment, most available to talk to her. She also stopped by the beds of fourteen of the injured. "Where were you going when they cleared the station?" "And what happened when everyone headed for the exits?" "My word!" "Well, I think you're being very brave." "It's dreadful, isn't it? But you're holding up all right, aren't you?" "Thank you for the splendid effort you're making." "They can hit us, but they can't keep us down, can they?" She had a sentence for everyone. She took off her white kid gloves and held everyone's hand, skin to skin, for at least two shakes, longer if they looked like they needed it. Then she moved on.

After forty-five minutes, she turned to Luke, and said, "Now, Major Thomason, can you help me find Mrs MacDonald, please?"

He had inquired earlier where the room was and led her to the lift that would take her up to the eighth floor. The private secretary had telephoned when Shirley was admitted to ask that arrangements be made to give her a private room, rather than in a crowded ward, where most of the cardiac patients on the National Health Service were placed. When The Queen, Luke, and Anne arrived at the room, they all three looked in with trepidation, slightly fearing what shape they might find the patient in. They were surprised to find that William, Rajiv, and Rebecca had preceded them, all three having walked over from the Old Vic while The Queen was downstairs making her rounds. Rajiv was in the thronelike visitor's chair, singing a Bollywood tune from the play they'd just seen. Rebecca was standing awkwardly behind him, looking embarrassed. William was bending over Shirley and trying to persuade her to have a plastic spoonful of ice shavings.

Rajiv leapt to his feet when he saw The Queen, William straightened up, with the spoon still in his hand, and Rebecca continued to look ill at ease. Shirley was awake, alert, and angry. She had an intravenous tube in her arm. She was still too weak to stand unassisted.

"Ah," said The Queen. "Here before us to attend the patient, I see. Still in one piece, Mrs MacDonald?"

"Semi," said Shirley, unwillingly.

"Well, you look all right. Now, gentlemen, that will be all. This ward is ladies only."

Rajiv protested, "We've been here for the last fifteen minutes and it was all right with them."

"Yes, but you're no longer wanted. Lady Anne and Rebecca

and I shall be taking over. Thank you very much, Cheddar. Thank you, Mr de Morgan. Thank you, Major Thomason." There was nothing for the three men to do but gather their things and depart, two of the three squeezing Shirley's hand and William kissing her cheek on the way out.

When they'd all left, and closed the door, Shirley muttered, "Now we can relax," and all four women chuckled with relief. Anne began to put a little balm on the patient's badly chapped lips. Even before the evening's incident, The Queen had been hoping to circle by St Thomas's after the play. She had packed one or two things for the patient. She took a cotton nightdress out of her handbag and said, "Now, Shirley, let's get you out of that horrible hospital thing and into something a little more civilized. Come now, don't be shy. You've seen me in my underthings often enough."

When they'd managed to change the patient's gown, The Queen then set to brushing Shirley's hair with a wooden brush that also came out of her handbag. She saw Rebecca hanging about awkwardly and addressed her. "Now, Rebecca, sit down in that chair there and tell us about that young man of yours. We all want to know." The Queen's eye sparkled as she stood at Shirley's side, attending her hair.

"Well, I don't know him very well," said Rebecca. "Just met him a little while ago. At Paxton & Whitfield. When I went over to get the cheese."

"I see," said The Queen. "Carry on."

"And then when Major Thomason said he couldn't find you, Ma'am, I followed you in the taxi from Jermyn Street to King's Cross. He ended up on the same train."

"He's quite a willing young man," said The Queen.

"Well, he is that. He sends me e-mail messages or a text every day."

"Lucky girl."

"It doesn't feel that way. You see, I'm not very good at boys. They've never liked me. All through growing up, they didn't want anything to do with me. And now, well, Rajiv's not the only one. There are two more."

"Three boys!" said Anne, brightening. This was going to be a good story. "Who are they?"

"One's a man I met at an animal rights demo in Trafalgar Square. Liked him a lot at first, but it turns out he's mixed up in some pretty rough company. I didn't know about it then. Only discovered it when I went with him to a hunt, and he turned out to be a *saboteur.* Wanted to injure the horses."

"Don't like the sound of him," said The Queen darkly.

"No. Came as a bit of a shock to me too. And that's where the other one came in. He sort of saved me at the hunt, rescued me from a bad situation, Dickon did."

Anne couldn't believe her ears. The name was so old-fashioned that you didn't hear it much nowadays. She couldn't speak.

The Queen glanced at Anne's distress and said calmly, "Not Dickon Bevil?"

Rebecca had never been properly introduced to Lady Anne. She didn't know her surname. "Yes, as a matter of fact, it is," she said with surprise. "Do you know him?"

The Queen knew all about Anne's private tragedy, but never brought it up for fear of offending her, or opening an old wound.

"My son," said Anne simply.

Rebecca wasn't sure how to react. "Well, you see, he knew my parents. He was living in some trees . . ."

"I do know about that," said Anne.

"Well, my parents were against the bypass too. They wanted to help. They used to take food to the people in the trees. Vegetables from our farm."

"I see. Well, I haven't been in touch with him for some time. Don't even know where he's living."

"I have his e-mail address. I could give it to you," offered Rebecca.

"I don't do e-mail," said Anne coldly.

"Oh, come now, Lady Anne, we all have to learn. Even I'm learning. If I can, you can," said The Queen.

"He hasn't been in touch with me for some time," said Anne. "He knows where I am. He could be in touch with me if he wanted to."

Here, to everyone's surprise, Shirley spoke up, though in a low voice, "You've got to get off your high horse, Anne. The young are different. You've got to give him a pass. Forgive him for not writing you. If old age is good for anything it's good for being generous."

Coming from someone whom they'd all seen near death, this seemed like a rare philosophical truth. The oracle had spoken.

Rebecca still remained unsure of herself among these three older women who seemed to know one another, and one another's histories, so well. She searched her brain for some way of contributing, some way of doing something for them that they couldn't do for themselves. She was aware too that she was a young person who sometimes resented her parents, and often steered clear of them when they would have liked to have seen more of her. Perhaps just as Dickon did with Anne. "Well, I've got a laptop in my backpack. I could show you how to e-mail him right here."

"Oh yes!" said The Queen. "Show me too. I've been annoying the young woman from IT, and I can't overdo my requests there. And could you do a refresher on Miss Twitter and Pastebook as well?"

Rebecca understood that The Queen was a little hazy not only on the way to use the principal social media sites but also what they were called. She got out the laptop, plugged it in, propped it on Shirley's bed, and connected to the hospital's Wi-Fi to give the women a little lesson.

After twenty-five minutes, the concentration of all three of the older women was beginning to dissipate. The Queen saw this and said, "Now, Shirley. What about some exercise? You'll never get better just lying there in that bed. Let's take a brief turn down the corridor."

The doctor had warned Shirley that exercise was strictly forbidden, but the generations to which she and The Queen and Anne all belonged believed in exercise as a cure-all. They were not about to obey a young doctor when they'd been brought up on this folk wisdom of the ages. So she allowed Anne and The Queen to pull her out of bed, put slippers on her feet, and bring her to a standing position. They pulled along the IV stand to which Shirley was still connected. They found a hospital-issue bathrobe for her in the cupboard. When all three of the women were standing, The Queen and Anne both wobbled slightly. It had been a long day after a long night the night before and it was now nearing midnight. Here Rebecca saw that she could help again and she got to her feet on the other side of Shirley. The four of them then took small steps away from the bed, The Queen and Anne each with a hand holding on to the rolling IV stand for support, Shirley holding on to Rebecca, the four of them making slow progress into the glare of the corridor's fluorescent lights.

Luke's bedroom had virtually no decorations whatsoever. It had a double bed, with crisp folded corners as a nurse would make of a hospital bed. A desert photograph of his company in Basra was the room's lone picture on the wall. Later that evening Luke and William lay on top of the bed, the sheets and covers still tucked in, their ties loosened, their shoes off, and in their stocking feet. A small distance separated them on the bed. They both were reading from the text of *Henry V* they'd been given at the Old Vic earlier that evening. William was lying on his back, head on two pillows, following along in the text, as Luke, lying on his side and facing William, was reading aloud. They were at the section of the play after Agincourt. Henry was wooing the French Princess Katharine after winning the battle. Henry was trying to persuade Katharine to marry him, even though he would grow old and become less attractive.

"A fair face will wither," read Luke,

> but a good heart, Kate, is the sun and the
> moon; or, rather, the sun, and not the moon; for it
> shines bright and never changes, but keeps his
> course truly. If thou would have such a one, take
> me; and take me, take a soldier; take a soldier,
> take a king. And what sayest thou then to my love?
> Speak, my fair, and fairly, I pray thee.

William put down his copy of the text on his chest and said to the ceiling, "You'd better go and find your fair one somewhere else. Because I'm not fair and never have been."

With an effort, Luke said, "Fair to me."

William looked over for a moment, met Luke's eyes, and then looked back at the ceiling.

"It would finish your career."

"Oh, not necessarily. We have gays in the military now, I believe."

"All right for the lower ranks. But they're not allowing you to shack up with a boyfriend, *and* promoting you to colonel. It just won't happen, Luke."

"You never know till you give it a try."

"And I have to sweep up the bits and pieces when it all comes crumbling apart?"

"Well, you wouldn't want to leave the Household, would you?"

"I don't know. Been thinking of that, actually. What if we were to have a food van? You know, sell Cornish pasties and the like from a window on the side? We could drive it round to Wembley Stadium after the football. Or to the seaside? Bournemouth in season. We wouldn't have to pay rent. And we'd be free to drive wherever we wanted to."

With one stockinged foot Luke reached over to kick and then caress William's stockinged foot close by his on the bed. "We?" he said.

Anne and Shirley were alone in Shirley's hospital room at St Thomas's, reading the same passage from the play. The Queen had left an hour earlier, taking Rebecca with her to drop her off at her flat in the Mews. Shirley was on the hospital bed, still wearing The Queen's nightdress, and her legs were wrapped in a hospital-issue blanket. Anne was sitting in the visitor's chair, her shoes off, her knees bent, and her legs supported by Shirley's bed. The two women both had on, unusually, their reading glasses, and were taking turns reading from the play. Shirley was reading a different part of Henry's speech wooing Katharine.

> Put off your maiden blushes; avouch the
> thoughts of your heart with the looks of an empress;
> take me by the hand, and say 'Harry of England I am
> thine:' which word thou shalt no sooner bless mine
> ear withal, but I will tell thee aloud 'England is
> thine, Ireland is thine, France is thine, and Harry
> Plantagenet is thine;' who though I speak it before

his face, if he be not fellow with the best king,
thou shalt find the best king of good fellows.

Shirley having reached the end of a sentence, it was now Anne's turn. She now took up reading Henry's proposal to Katharine.

Come, your answer in broken music; for thy voice is
music and thy English broken; therefore, queen of
all, Katharine, break thy mind to me in broken
English; wilt thou have me?

Shirley interrupted, "I'll think about it."

The two women looked down across the tops of their reading glasses at one another and laughed gently.

Shirley spoke again. "Do you suppose they could make us a cup of tea in this place? What do the nurses do all night? They haven't looked in for the last hour and a half."

"Shall I go and see?" said Anne, slipping on her shoes and smoothing down her skirt. As she prepared to leave the room, she glanced briefly over at Shirley in her bed to see that she was stretching out her hand, calling her back.

"Anne, thank you."

⁂

In the Royal Mews the main overhead lights had long ago been extinguished. There were only one or two night lights giving faint glimmers along the glazed Victorian tiles. Rebecca and Rajiv were lying in a nest of hay adjacent to Elizabeth's stall. The horse was standing next to them. Rebecca was playing with a tame badger. Rajiv had been reading to her from the same passage of the play that Luke and William and Anne and Shirley had also been reading. But he'd set the play aside in the hay and was trying to get her to kiss him. "Oh, come on. We've done it before."

"Just because I was feeling sorry for you. On the train."

"You weren't feeling sorry for me, baby, I could tell. I could read your lips."

"Well not 'sorry,' then, but just sort of vaguely curious."

"And not curious still?"

"Well, Rajiv, to be honest. I don't think it's a good idea. What would people make of us? I don't think I've decided what I want. Or what we can possibly be. There are a couple of others I haven't entirely said no to yet. Wouldn't be fair to you to lead you on."

Then, from memory, Rajiv recited some of Henry's last lines to Katharine.

> O Kate, nice customs curtsey to great kings. Dear
> Kate, you and I cannot be confined within the weak
> list of a country's fashion: we are the makers of
> manners, Kate.

Rajiv then leaned in and kissed Rebecca, with her shy assent. After a moment, he pulled away, nuzzled her nose, and whispered in her ear, "You have witchcraft in your lips, Kate."

The Queen in her bedroom was feeling as if her nerves had been jangled by all that had happened that Tuesday. Waking up in a strange bed in Edinburgh, Shirley's heart attack, *Henry V*, the defused bomb at Waterloo. It was too much. She wasn't used to being without a programme for such long periods and improvising. But she had got through it. "I went right through it. Yes, I did. I went through it," she said to herself, as if some reassurance were necessary. Her nerves felt overly stimulated and she knew that, though she was exhausted, she would not sleep unless she took some measures to relax and calm down. She suddenly recalled the traditional last pose of her yoga practice, *savasana*, in which, at the end of all the hard work and stretching and holding difficult positions, she lay covered up on the floor, breathing deeply, listening to her breath, but purposely not allowing her mind to wander onto any discordant thoughts. She went and found Rebecca's hoodie, which she had not yet returned to her, put it on, and, stepping out of her shoes, lay wrapped in the hoodie prone upon the floor on top of a yoga mat. She stretched out her arms and legs, closed her eyes, and lay for five minutes, doing nothing, thinking nothing, but breathing deeply.

When she opened her eyes, she felt better. She said a brief word of thanks to her body for supporting her through the practice as she'd been instructed to do by her teacher. Then she pulled herself to her feet by gripping the side of a chair, changed into her nightgown, and walked deliberately over to the small laptop computer that was on her bedside table. She got into bed with the laptop computer on her knees and her copy of *Henry V*. Like the others, she was feeling unusually moved by the conclusion of the play. She found a vaguely remembered passage from Act V, where the French Queen hopes Henry's former hatred of France will come to an end in his marriage to her daughter, Katharine. She notes how angry and poisonous his former view of his French antagonists had been, then adds, "The venom of such looks, we fairly hope, have lost their quality, and that this day shall change all griefs and quarrels into love."

Yes, that was the passage The Queen had remembered. She knew that the terrorist scare would once again arouse ethnic distrust and suspicion. She thought it was her role to help alleviate tensions among the different populations in the realm. She wasn't going to wait for official advice on that. She made a mental note to ask Sir Robin whether he couldn't write a speech for her, using those lines, as a way of asking for mutual understanding. She thought she might just send him an e-mail about it. She'd made an advance in her understanding of e-mail after Rebecca's tutorial that evening. She now felt slightly more confident about how to receive as well as to send her own e-mail messages. Then it occurred to her that something else might substitute for asking the private secretary to write her a speech. She opened her Miss Twitter account, signed in as Little Bit, and clicked on the box where she could post a message. She was still new at all this and was following only one or two other Twitterers, including Number 10, the Household Cavalry and *The Race Horse* magazine. She herself had only a very few followers. Reading her Tweets there were only Edward and Sophie Wessex, Major Thomason, William de Morgan, and Rebecca Rinaldi, as well as a computer robot selling an instant business card service. No matter, she thought to herself. With two fingers she slowly typed in from Shakespeare the three lines of the French Queen's that had pleased her so much. Then she looked at the message box and found she still had ten characters out of her permitted 140 to fill in if she wished. What should she add? She decided to keep it simple. "*Namaste*" she wrote, recalling her yoga instructor's words at the end of the practice. "Let the light within me salute the light that is within you. *Namaste*." She then looked at her message with satisfaction, moved the cursor over the button marked Tweet, and pressed "ENTER."

Photo Credits

Grateful acknowledgement is made to the following for permission to reprint:

page 6	Edward G. Malindine/Hulton Royals Collection/Getty Images
page 19	Tim Graham/Tim Graham Photo Library/Getty Images
page 39	Mary Evans Picture Library/IDA KAR
page 63	© English Heritage Photo Library
page 111	Courtesy of David Gelber
page 151	© Brett Holman via airminded.org
page 161	© Illustrated London News/Mary Evans
page 174	Fred W. McDarrah/Premium Archive/Getty Images
page 188	© Philippe Hays/Rex Features Ltd
page 195	© The Trustees of the National Library of Scotland
page 249	Anwar Hussein/Getty Images Entertainment/Getty Images
page 257	© Stephen McKay
page 285	© SWNS.com
page 287	Courtesy of Oona Räisänen
page 333	Airteamimages.com
page 340	© Steve Fareham